The Girl on the Boat

A Cal Harrison Thriller

Book 1

J D Wood

Published by Kensington Square.

Contents

Prologue

January

Cars began to slow long before the junction. A bell rang in the distance, shrill and insistent, and after a few seconds, barriers lowered beside the track, their lights flashing red in the spring sunshine.

Rob glanced in the rearview mirror. 'Ah, bollocks, just missed it.'

The woman in the back didn't reply. Her eyebrows ticked upward. Not quite anger, more irritation; the kind that said she was already running late and didn't have time for this.

Rob eased the cab to a stop.

'Staying long?' he asked. 'Want me to wait?'

She shook her head. Didn't know how long she'd be.

A middle-aged man on a racing bike, which cost more than Rob made in a week, slipped past on the inside.

Rob chuckled. 'Alright for some.'

Still nothing from the back seat.

Up ahead, the 12.15 from Waterloo started to pull out of Wool station, picking up speed as it trundled across the level crossing on the A352 that linked Dorchester and

Wareham.

Eight carriages, maybe ten. They curved out of sight toward Moreton. The ringing continued, the barriers stayed down.

The woman in the back of the Rob Lord Taxi Company maroon Mercedes, sighed heavily, flicked open a small compact, and began adjusting her makeup. Rob knew what they were waiting for. Three times out of ten, the 12.15 overlapped with the London-bound train from Weymouth, and if it was delayed, it was a right pain. They sometimes sat here for five minutes or more. Better to have the barriers raised in the meantime, in his opinion.

But he decided not to say anything. Let the bitch stew in her bad mood.

Eventually, he heard the train approaching from behind them, coming at quite a pace, beginning to slow only a few hundred yards out. The lights of the barrier continued flashing. There was a high-pitched squeal of brakes. Sparks flared beneath the wheels like someone grinding steel on steel.

From up ahead, he heard a shriek. Three cars away, a man got out, straining to see what was going on. The lead carriage came to a sudden halt just past the level crossing. The bells didn't stop. People gathered around the track, phones in hand.

'Oh my God.'

There was no sign of the cyclist.

Part One

1

Monday 17th October

'*The country's in crisis*,' said the man on the morning show. *'You don't even need to follow the news, you just have to look around you. Hospital waiting lists at all-time highs, the justice system clogged up, prisons overflowing, crime rampant, immigration out of control. Need I go on?'*

'We are all familiar with the issues, Mr Crane,' replied the female anchor, one of two presenting the Start The Day news show on TV that morning. *'But what our viewers would like to know is what you propose to do about them, if you get elected? So far, you're very light on detail.'*

'That's completely untrue…'

'Skimmed milk, love?'

Sofie James snapped back to the woman behind the counter. She was in a north London coffee shop, having jogged here to meet her friend Kate. She was early. The TV was on.

'Semi-skimmed,' she said, offering a tired smile. 'Just a splash.'

Her eyes strayed back to the news channel.

'For example, on the death penalty,' the interviewer was

saying. *'Your views are very clear about that. Can you tell us if you intend to revive it?'*'

God, that politician was ghastly, she thought. They all were. She turned away and began thinking about Kate. Why had she been so insistent they meet? She'd called twice in as many weeks. Would not take no for an answer.

'Here you are, love. Anything else?'

Sofie thanked the woman and went outside to find a pavement table.

Dumping her water bottle on the bench, she shook out her dirty blond hair, flicked it into a ponytail and took a sip of the macchiato. She leaned back and half closed her eyes in the unseasonably warm autumn sunshine, glad to be free of the blaring TV, and went back, for the umpteenth time, to the day of the accident.

There were two theories about what Colin James was doing on the railway tracks when the 12.20 Weymouth to Waterloo smashed into him at forty miles an hour. The first was the simplest - the one Sofie wanted to believe. Her dad had got tired of waiting and figured it was safe to cross. Yes, the barriers were still down and the lights still flashing red, but he was like that, damn him. Impatient to a fault. The bloody idiot had not been paying attention.

But that version unravelled fast. The London-bound train was late. It was a full two minutes after the first had cleared the crossing before it started its approach. Witnesses said he'd been standing there a while. The London-bound wasn't exactly a surprise. He would have seen it coming around the bend. And still, he pushed his bike across.

And then there was the second theory. The one that changed everything. Ten days later, Sofie got a call from her GP. She was in Hove, staying with her uncle, barely holding it together.

'Sofie, I was wondering if you could come in and see me.'

She remembered talking to him through a sea of mist.

'John, please, I'm OK, honestly, I appreciate your concern...'

'Sofie, it's about something else.' There was a chill in his voice that even she, existing in this thick limbo of grief, could detect. 'It's about your father.'

'My Dad?'

'Yes. When can you get back to London?'

She drove up the next day.

'How are you coping?' he'd begun as she'd entered his surgery, concern on his face.

She'd said she was fine. He waited until she sat down.

'Now, Sofie, this may come as a shock. Did you know your father had HIV?'

She still remembered it. The wave of nausea shuddering through her, her mouth suddenly dry.

'HIV? I don't understand.'

The doctor stopped her with a look.

'It's not just homosexuals who contract Aids, Sofie, you know that,' he said, as if reading her thoughts. 'He spent a lot of time in Kenya, is that correct?'

Kenya? What did that have to do with anything? She nodded slowly.

'He seemed so happy recently.'

The doctor got up and walked round to the leather swivel chair behind his desk. Sat down and leaned over to pull something out of a drawer, dropping a fat file with a gentle thud.

'And drinking?'

'No more than usual. He's Irish, for God's sake.'

He scanned the notes.

'It says here that his blood alcohol level was 0.19.'

'At twelve o'clock in the morning?'

He looked up.

'And there's something else you need to know.'

She gulped. 'What?'

'The police are looking into the possibility that your father may have ...' he hesitated '... done what he did deliberately.'

It took a few moments for this to sink in.

'Impossible.' She hesitated, scrambling to make sense of what the doctor was telling her. 'Surely that suggests an accident? His judgement was impaired. No one ignores a rail barrier unless they...'

'Maybe. But you can look at it another way. He got drunk to overcome his nerves. They also found a bottle of unmarked pills in his jacket pocket. We're still trying to ID them.'

~

'Sofie?'

She snapped out of her reverie. Kate stood in front of her, beaming.

'Hi!' Sofie said, jumping up. They hugged, a familiar cloud of Diorella washing over her. Kate pulled out a chair.

'You look amazing,' Kate said, taking her seat. 'Still jogging?'

Sofie smiled faintly, tucking in a strand of hair. Her reflection in the café window didn't agree. She looked drawn. Pale. Eyes a little too hollow.

Kate, as ever, jumped right in. 'So? Where've you been? After the funeral, you just... vanished. Did you go abroad? I mean, I texted you. We all did.'

The last time they'd seen each other was at her father's memorial service in Dorset, in the church next to the small cottage he lived in on the coast at Ringstead Bay.

'I know. I just… needed time. Dad's death... it hit me harder than I expected.'

Kate's face softened, but only slightly. 'You sure did, Doll!' It was a term of endearment that Kate used for all of her girlfriends. 'You went off-grid. We were worried.'

Sofie felt the guilt flicker.

'I spent most of the summer down there,' she said.

'Where? At the cottage? Lucky for some.' A beat. 'Still with that on-off boyfriend of yours? Martin?'

'More off than on.'

'And what happened with your Journalism MA? Did you get it?'

Sofie hesitated, suddenly self-conscious. Why all the questions?

'Not exactly.'

'You didn't drop out, did you?'

'Deferred. I'm going back in January.'

'Good plan.' Kate peered through the window. 'Listen, I'm gasping for caffeine here.' She gestured at Sofie's empty cup. 'Can I get you another?'

'Sure. A double with a splash of milk. Thanks.'

Sofie watched Kate's compact figure, with her wild tangle of auburn hair and taut nervous energy, dart inside. An energy that Sofie had always admired. Kate took up space and didn't apologise for it. She was a real force of nature, a hack through and through. The sort of journalist Sofie aspired to be one day, if only she could get her act together.

She returned with two coffees and dived straight in.

'Tell me,' she said. 'Did they ever find out… *why* your

father went over those railway tracks?'

Sofie's fingers tightened around her cup. 'No one knows. Officially.'

'I mean, he was on some weird drug, wasn't he?'

Sofie blinked. 'Where did you hear that?' How the hell did Kate know? She didn't remember telling anyone. 'Anyway, they never figured out what it was.'

'What did the inquest say?'

'Accidental death.'

'Mmm. Well, listen, Sofe, that's what I wanted to talk to you about.'

Sofie stared at her.

'It's a bit delicate, actually. I'm researching a piece about an illegal drug trial conducted by a big pharma company, Cambridge Bio. And your father's name came up.'

Sofie tensed. 'Sorry?'

'They listed him on some of the documentation I got hold of as a participant in this trial. In the months leading up to his death.'

'Shit, Kate, what are you saying?'

'I thought you should know. And look, I wouldn't bring it up if I didn't think you'd *want* to know.'

Sofie drained her coffee. This wasn't a conversation she felt like having right now. She hadn't even come close to processing the basics, let alone diving into a conspiracy theory. Was Kate here with her friend hat on, or her journalist hat?

'Thanks, well, I appreciate your concern. And for the heads up. But I'm not sure I'm comfortable opening all this up again.'

Her friend held her eyes.

'Listen, I get it. But, these guys…'

'What guys?' she said sharply.

'I've been put in touch with two research chemists who work for Cambridge Bio. They claim to have information about this trial.'

'What, like whistleblowers, you mean?'

'Exactly. One of them says he knew your father.'

'*Seriously?*'

'I've arranged to meet them at the end of next week.'

'Oh my God, Kate.'

'I'm sorry if this is a bit of a shock.'

'That's an understatement! I mean, I don't understand. It was an accident.'

'I'm sure it was. But listen, I do think we should hear what they have to say.'

'*We?*'

'Yeah, because you must come too. As his daughter…'

Sofie shook her head. 'No. I'm sorry. I can't deal with this now.'

Kate regarded her silently for a moment. Then:

'Ok, I hear you. But please, all I ask is sleep on it.' She leaned forward. 'Also, confidentially, I've seen evidence of other people on this trial who lost their lives. Someone needs to be held accountable. Think about it.'

Kate had said her piece. They spoke no more about it. To Sofie's relief, they moved on to other things, but her heart was no longer in it, and she quickly wrapped it up, pretending she had somewhere to be.

They kissed and said their goodbyes. As she jogged back to her flat, her mind was in overdrive, that phrase of Kate's ringing in her head. *Think about it.*

As if she could stop.

2

Wednesday 19th October

FOR THE NEXT TWO DAYS, SOFIE COULDN'T SHAKE IT. Kate's words looped round and round in her mind. What did she mean? That the mystery drug her father was trialling had something to do with his death? That it hadn't been a tragic accident, but something darker?

She was about to phone Kate when her friend beat her to it. The call came while she was in the bath, listening to '*If You Really Love Me (How Will I Know)*' on Heart London and halfway through a chilled bottle of Pinot G. Her happy place. She ignored it, letting it roll to voicemail.

Kate's voice, chirpy and just slightly performative, spilled through the speaker.

'*Sofie, it's Kate. You're probably at Sainsbury's. What exciting lives we lead! It was great to catch up with you on Monday. I mean it. And about our discussion - don't worry, no pressure, I didn't want to freak you out. We should talk. But listen, that's not why I'm calling. I'm having a few people round to dinner next week, and I'd like you to come. You'll know a few of them, they'd love to see you, and there's a music producer I want you to meet. Call me at work and ask for the Features desk. Or leave a message. Love you!*'

Sofie ran the hot tap and submerged her head. Surfacing slowly, the wine glass now warm in her hand, she stepped out and dripped across the tiles to the mirror. What she dreaded most was the *'people you know.'* Not to mention the man she wanted her to meet. It sounded suspiciously like she was being set up.

She wiped a clear patch in the fogged-up glass, studying herself as she towel-dried her hair. She'd developed a hollowed-out look since the accident. She tried to imagine what they would say about her.

Sure, she's still attractive. But did you notice those almond eyes? Once so full of sparkle. Now look at them - a duller brown, tinged with sadness, weary of life.

And if they wouldn't say it, they'd be thinking it.

She flipped open the mirrored cabinet, found her eyeliner, and traced it beneath one eye, then the other, with slow precision. Slowly, they came alive, the weariness morphing into something more ambiguous. Harder perhaps, but, despite it all, still OK looking, no?

She pouted at herself. Sofie James, 26. Single, intelligent, sporty, fun. Plus emotional baggage. Not the least of which was pride.

Let them think what they effing well liked.

She grabbed her phone and, still naked, padded into the bedroom, pulling up a number. Kate had stirred something. Messed with her head. She'd waved it off when the doctor had mentioned it before.

But this was something else. She had to know more.

3

Sunday 23rd October

'Daddy?'

Cal Harrison grunted, wedging the screwdriver into a rusted groove at the base of the washing machine.

'What?'

'Did you shoot anyone when you were in the army?'

Cal paused, hunched down in the cramped galley kitchen. His back ached as he tightened the last screw, then pushed himself upright and wiped his hands down the front of his jeans. Six-foot-one, thirty-seven, and starting to feel every inch of it. He wasn't in such good shape as he had been back then.

'Of course not, sweet pea, I was more like a…'

He hesitated, wondering how to phrase it for an eight-year-old girl.

'… well, a spy, I guess. I watched people. Made sure the bad guys didn't do bad stuff.'

She blinked. 'But Mummy said you killed loads of people.'

His jaw clenched with a stab of irritation.

'Well, she's wrong,' he said. 'She doesn't know what

she's talking about.'

'What about now you're a security guard?'

He laughed. 'Is that what you tell your friends that I do?'

'But isn't that what you are?'

'Not exactly.' He smiled, despite himself. 'I'm a security consultant. It's different.'

Sort of.

God knows what else Lucy had said at school. That he lived in a caravan? That he worked out of a yard like some washed-up handyman? He glanced at his watch.

'Your mum'll be here in an hour. Want to take one last walk? Say hi to the geese?'

She nodded, already skipping toward the door.

Cal followed, grabbing his jacket. Moments like these always left him off-balance. He never imagined he'd be here; nearly forty, no home of his own and raising a daughter part-time. For most of his life, he'd had no family worth naming. Brought up by a glamorous but alcoholic mother who walked out on him at the age of eleven, and a bullying father whom he grew to hate, he'd spent a lonely childhood in a large, cold house in Scotland. In fact, as his friend and former commanding officer Frank Ryan had once pointed out, he'd not so much been brought up as dragged himself up. After years of boarding schools he'd hated, he'd finally dropped out of university with no qualifications, and within a week, had enlisted in the Army, scandalising his father by going into the ranks. For a man who didn't give a shit about him, that was the final straw. They'd hardly spoken since.

But the Army had been the making of him. Finally, something he could be good at. Not so much the fighting elements - he wasn't the toughest or the fastest - but he had a knack for the quiet stuff. It was the street-level reconnaissance skills he excelled at. Blending in, following a target, tracking prey. And sensing when things were about to go wrong.

Unlike his record with women, he thought, watching Lucy bounce down the caravan steps.

Baby steps, Cal. That's what Frank had told him. Lucy had already taught him a lot about love and patience. Her mother? Not so much.

They crossed the gravel yard arm in arm.

'Do you think Uncle Frank's back?'

Cal looked toward the farmhouse of the man Lucy called 'uncle', despite the fact he was nothing of the sort. No sign of his Range Rover.

'Still away.'

It had been eighteen months since his former commanding officer had let him move in. It was meant to be a short-term arrangement; crash in the caravan, get back on your feet, that kind of deal.

But he'd been living on the rambling farm for eighteen months now. It worked. For Cal, at least. He didn't like roots. Ever since he'd left the army, he'd tried to travel light. And Frank liked company. But Frank's wife, Emily - that was a different story. She'd started slipping in snide comments. Passive-aggressive digs. And fair enough, Cal had been between jobs lately. The next gig - some oil conference in Dubai - wasn't for another month. He could see why she got annoyed.

They headed out across the marsh, scanning for the geese that lived near the water's edge.

'Come on,' Cal said, taking Lucy's hand. 'Let's check out the boathouse.'

They set off, Lucy burbling on about a story she'd heard

of a giant eel that lurked in the river, and Cal planning in his head the conversation he would have to have with Frank.

The question was, where would he go? Suffolk was convenient from the point of view of access to Lucy. She lived with her mother thirty minutes away in Framlingham, and he saw her every other weekend unless travelling. Any further, and he doubted Amanda would bother ferrying her over. Besides, how would he ever afford somewhere like this? On the water's edge, quiet and secure, miles from a main road? For ex-Special Forces guys like him, that was a bonus. With the things he'd done and the people he had helped put away, there was a part of him that would be forever looking over his shoulder. Past history had a way of catching up with you.

Father and daughter walked up to the boathouse. The old wooden structure creaked in the wind. Frank's motorboat had been taken to a yard in Woodbridge for repairs, leaving the dock eerily quiet. Water lapped softly under the floorboards. Cal grabbed a fishing rod from its usual spot on the wall. They cast lines and waited. Nothing bit. Two visits ago, they'd caught a fat carp. Not today. When the time came to go, they ambled back to the yard.

'I need a joke, Daddy,' Lucy said suddenly. 'For school assembly. Got any good ones?'

Cal racked his brain. Most of the jokes he knew were army jokes; absolutely not PC. But one surfaced from a train ride, overheard and oddly memorable.

'Mmm… how's this? What's white and black and red all over?'

'What?' she grinned.

'A sunburnt elephant.'

She groaned, laughing anyway, and they went to hose down their rubber boots. Her mother would not be happy with mud in her brand-new Volvo. They heard the gravel crunch as they were putting the hose away.

'Had fun, Lucy?' Amanda asked, climbing out of the car. Lucy hugged her father goodbye and trotted off to climb in the back.

His ex-wife favoured him with a frosty smile. 'Everything go OK?'

'No problems.'

'Gave her lunch?'

He shot her a look. 'What do you think?'

She raised her eyebrows and slid into the driving seat. As she fired up the ignition, she wound down the window.

'By the way, I'm taking her to Wales in two weeks. So I'll bring her over the weekend after, OK?'

It wasn't a question, but a statement.

'Fine,' he said, winking at Lucy.

The car pulled away, and he walked towards his caravan, the air crisp with oncoming dusk. His work phone broke the silence. On a Sunday? He sprinted to beat the voicemail.

'Cal Harrison?' said a voice he didn't recognise.

'Speaking.'

'I'm calling from Cambridge Bio. We've got a last-minute job. Wondering if you're free?'

It was a client he'd worked for before, and they wanted someone to run security for a couple of road shows they had coming up in London and Oslo. The guy they'd contracted had dropped out. Could Cal step in?

'Absolutely,' he said without hesitation.

Anything to get Emily off his back.

4

Tuesday 25th October

The train from Ipswich pulled into Liverpool Street just before eleven. Cal stretched his legs and exhaled, feeling a rare flicker of ease. Ten days of work ahead, straightforward and well-paid, and likely the kind of job he could sleepwalk through. Including a trip to Oslo for the second of the two Cambridge events, flying out next Monday evening. It would be a welcome change of scene.

Still, he was intrigued. He shouldered his backpack, grabbed the duffle from the overhead rack, and crossed the concourse toward the Central Line, his thoughts drifting to the person he was about to meet: Laura Boyd. Chief of staff to Walter Crane, member of parliament and chairman of Cambridge Bio. Which was already unusual. His last two jobs for Cambridge Bio had come through the events team. He'd dealt with faceless logistics people. Never anyone this senior. So what was different this time?

Settled into a seat on the Tube, he pulled out his phone and did a quick search. There wasn't much. No Wikipedia page or anything in the news tab, and no smiling PR shots on the Cambridge Bio website. Did she even work for them?

All there was to go on was LinkedIn. Yale grad; career stops in London, Abu Dhabi, Moscow; follower of a cross-country ski club. Current position: Chief of Staff, Crane campaign team. That was it. Her picture showed a well-groomed woman in a crisp blue blouse, pearl studs, and a smile that was relaxed and controlled. His age.

When he surfaced again at Knightsbridge, the streets were packed. He was thirty minutes early, and for a moment he considered ducking into his old haunt, the Special Forces Club off Hans Place. Instead, he window-shopped to kill time before making his way to Cambridge House, CB's headquarters.

They took his bag at reception and sent him up to the fifth floor.

'Good to meet you.'

Laura came out from behind her desk as he entered her wood-panelled office, hand outstretched. 'I trust you had a pleasant journey?'

'Fine, thanks.'

Cal clocked it all in five seconds. Tailored jacket, neat blonde bob, body language that discouraged small talk. On a table beside her desk sat a silver photo frame with her standing next to a former British Foreign Secretary. Well connected, it seemed.

She gestured toward a seating area.

'So glad you could help us out at such short notice. We appreciate it. Now, have you met Charles?'

Another figure stepped forward. Mid-thirties, designer jeans, just enough bicep to suggest vanity disguised as fitness.

'Charles Gebler,' he said.

They shook hands. He had a solid grip and slightly dead eyes.

Cal wondered where he fitted in. Maybe this was the campaign team? The election to lead Britain's Opposition party was due to take place in six weeks, and Crane was on the ticket. So was this a political function, or a Cambridge Bio event?

They took their seats, coffee arrived, and she outlined the assignment.

'It's an evening donor event,' Laura explained. 'Fundraising for Crane's campaign. But a good chunk of the Cambridge Bio executive team will be there, as it's timed to overlap with their corporate conference.'

She slid a folder across the table - fingernails flawlessly manicured, he noticed - and he tried to look lively, jotting down notes on the papers inside: names, times of arrival.

'Crane arrives Friday. He'll be met at the airport, attend the conference in the afternoon, then give a talk to the guests before the event kicks off.'

Cal fingered the single typed sheet. There was no hotel listed. 'Where's he staying?'

'He's not. He's got constituency business in Hull first thing the next day.'

Cal frowned. 'So he's staying a maximum of, what... ten hours?'

'Correct.'

He looked sceptical. 'Arriving on Friday, and today is Tuesday. I hardly think it'll take me...'

That's when she dropped it.

'There's something else.'

She paused. Cal could feel her watching him.

'Something rather sensitive. Two of our research chemists are flying in from the U.S. on Thursday for the conference, and they are staying on for the party on Friday evening. It's on a Thames riverboat. We've had a tip-off that they may be the target of a kidnap attempt.'

Cal straightened. 'You're serious?'

'Very. These men are... important.'

'They must be. What are they working on?'

'Never mind that,' she said. 'All I can say is Cambridge Bio wouldn't be where it is today without the brains of those two gentlemen.'

She made 'gentlemen' sound ever so subtly like an insult.

'And where did you get this tip-off, if you don't mind my asking?'

'Don't mind you asking at all, Cal, but for obvious reasons, we can't be more specific. We're sure it's nothing, but we don't want to take any chances. That's why I asked for you to cover this. I need the best.'

Cal started to say something, but she waved him down.

'What I'd like you to do is to draw up a strategy to monitor and protect these two men for the duration of their stay. They'll have an official minder - more of a host really - who will be responsible for looking after them, taking them to lunch, showing them the sights, that sort of thing. You are to liaise with him.' She paused to gauge his reaction.

'Are they here with their wives?'

'They're not wifey types.' She let out a sort of half-laugh, but it died on the turn. 'And the two of them are sharing a hotel room, which makes your job easier.'

'I see.' He didn't see at all. 'Have they had any prep, or do I need to brief them?'

'We haven't told them anything, and it's important it remains that way. I don't want them to have the slightest suspicion that they might be in any kind of danger.'

'But I've got to tell them,' he protested, 'otherwise what happens...'

'I'm sorry, Cal, that's how it's got to be.'

Cal was silent for a long moment.

'So you want me to run security for two high-value targets who don't know they're targets. Without alerting them or drawing attention.'

'Exactly.'

He ran a hand through his hair and wondered whether he should refuse the gig. Security for Crane was one thing. This appeared to be something else entirely. What was his political team doing organising security for two CB executives? Granted, they shared an office building, and granted, Crane was the Chairman of CB. But still, it felt highly unorthodox.

'Look, Miss…er…Boyd,' he began.

'Laura, please.'

'Laura. I'm not sure there's enough time for me to prep for this.'

She leant forward.

'I understand that this is not your usual way of operating, but on this occasion, there's a bit of context that I can't divulge.' A beat. 'My team tells me you had a lot of experience in surveillance when you were in the army?'

'Some.'

'So. That's all this is. Surveillance.'

He hesitated. 'How long did you say they were here?'

'24 hours.'

'I suppose…'

'Good. Charles here will brief you right away, and set you up with a desk.'

'I'll need floor plans. Staff lists. Guest list for the boat.'

'Of course. Charles will get you everything.'

He looked at Charles, who nodded imperceptibly. Still icy. He switched back to Laura, but spotted only a faint pursing of the lips. Dismissed.

'That all?'

She regarded him for a few moments longer, then swivelled her chair and rose.

'For now, yes.' She smiled and held out a hand. 'And once again, thank you so much for helping us out.'

5

THE DINNER AT KATE'S WAS NOT AS BAD AS SOFIE HAD feared. In a pair of skinny black velvet jeans and a battered denim jacket, judging by the attention she'd got, she'd more than held her own.

It was now after eleven, and she was slouched on Kate's sofa with a shot of grappa in one hand and a headache growing steadily behind her eyes.

Kate was telling her about a press trip she was going on to Ukraine in a couple of weeks. Ian, the music producer Kate had wanted her to meet, had already left. He had another party to go to. Of course he did. Sofie couldn't say she was sorry. He wasn't her type. He'd flirted most of the evening with Alice, a dark-haired, twinkly-eyed girl to his right. She was one of those left, playing a game of *'Which celebrity am I?'* with a guy called Jack.

'I should go,' Sofie said, when Kate had finished. The moment to ask her about her father had slipped away. Her head buzzed, and not in a good way.

'Why don't you stay?' Kate said, touching her arm. 'Plenty of room. Spare key's under the brick by the bins.'

'*Cara Delevingne!*' Alice shouted, squealing with laughter. '*No, Gwyneth what's-her-name.*'

Sofie shook her head, rising. 'It's late.'

'Wait. Before you go, what about my proposal?'

'What proposal?'

'You remember I told you I was meeting those two research chemists?'

Sofie hesitated. 'The ones who knew my dad?'

'Exactly. I've arranged to speak to them at a reception this Friday. It's on a Thames riverboat. I've wangled an invitation.' She grinned. 'Two, actually.'

Sofie bit her lip, nerves bubbling up. She drained the last of her shot glass, the liquid burning down her throat. She felt a sharp stab of indigestion.

'*This* Friday? You sure that's a good idea?'

'Hear me out. They want to meet you.'

Sofie's eyes shot up. '*They know about me?*'

'I told them I knew you. Will you come?'

Alice was howling with laughter again, something sticky now taped to her forehead.

'*Kim Kardashian!*' she bellowed.

'Jesus, Kate!'

'It could be nothing,' she continued, 'but we ought to hear what they have to say, no? Trust me, you'd make all the difference.'

'Why?'

'Because you're his daughter. They will trust you. Let me tell you, these guys are being very cagey.'

Sofie could feel the stress building up inside her.

'I don't know.'

Kate touched her arm.

'Listen, Doll, it's your call. No pressure. But I could do with your help.'

An explosion of laughter erupted. Alice was squealing, pouring herself another grappa as her companion finished scribbling something on a post-it note, which he then stuck to her sweaty forehead.

For a second, Sofie almost said no. What was she getting into? It made her extremely nervous. But then she heard herself asking:

'You'll come pick me up?'

'Of course,' Kate said. 'I'll be with you the whole time.'

She closed her eyes. The question was, what would *he* want her to do? Framed like that, it was no choice at all.

'Okay,' she said finally. 'I'm in.'

6

Friday 28th October

IT WAS ALREADY SIX WHEN KATE ARRIVED TO PICK HER UP.

'I'll be right down,' Sofie shouted into the intercom. She added a last spritz of musk, picked a T-shirt off the floor and slammed her wardrobe shut with one foot. Snatching a sideways glance in the hall mirror, she downed the end of the PG, grabbed her coat, and double locked the door.

As she turned to go, she heard the faint whine of a tap in the bathroom. She hesitated, wondering whether to block it off. But Kate buzzed again, more insistently this time. No time. She bolted down the stairs.

Kate stood by the cab, vaping and bouncing on her heels to stay warm. The weather had turned, winter on its way.

'Sorry I'm late, Doll, traffic's insane.'

Sofie climbed in.

'You look amazing,' Kate said, giving her the once-over.

Smart casual had been the instruction. Sofie had gone long on casual, in a navy blue wool jacket, silk shirt and designer jeans. Kate, meanwhile, was pure head-turner in a tight green velvet dress.

'Chelsea Harbour,' Kate told the driver.

They sat back.

'So,' Kate said casually, 'I should probably fill you in on a few things.'

'You better had.'

'Our cover at this party. We're hostesses.'

Sofie blinked. 'Wait. What?'

'We've been employed by an agency, A to Z.'

'Are you joking?'

'No, no, you don't understand,' Kate added hastily. 'No funny business. We're there to mix with the delegates, chat, add some sparkle. That's all.'

Sofie let her head fall back against the seat. 'Bloody hell, Kate!'

Kate pulled out a compact and began reapplying her lipstick.

'Honestly, it's purely social.'

'You don't sound too sure.'

'Listen, it's our way in.'

Sofie said nothing. Why on earth hadn't Kate told her before? She was nervous enough as it was.

By the time they arrived, the guests were already streaming in. The boat was docked beside a striped green-and-white awning. It looked like a paddle steamer, minus the paddles. Festive. And freezing.

'Who the hell throws a party on the river in mid-October?' Sofie muttered, hugging her coat tighter. Their breath billowed into the night. Kate handed her a laminated pass.

'Here. Your guest pass. My number's on the back, in case we get split up.'

Sofie flipped it over.

'I already have your number.'

'A different one. Just for tonight.'

Odd, thought Sofie. She looked again. There were two numbers written on it.

'And the second one?'

'Alice's.'

'Alice?'

'Ignore it.' Kate smiled, a bit too brightly. 'Come on.'

They crossed the pontoon. A huge welcome banner hung above the entrance: *'Welcome from Cambridge Bio.'* A photograph of the chairman of Cambridge, Walter Crane, stood beside it.

Sofie did a double-take.

'Kate…' she whispered. 'You never said *he* was behind this.'

Before Kate could answer, a staffer appeared.

'You'll want to speak to Maureen,' he said, after inspecting their passes. 'She's in the stern saloon.'

Inside, the boat was warm and buzzing. Waiters in starched shirts hovered around with flutes of fizz, and in a corner, a jazz trio was tuning up. Small tables with vases of flowers were dotted about, while behind them, Sofie glimpsed a food station. No expense spared, apparently.

Maureen glared at them icily. 'You were supposed to be here at six.'

Kate favoured her with her trademark smile. 'We're so sorry. Traffic.'

'Yes, well, you should have thought of that.' The woman paused, sizing them up. 'New with the agency, I assume?'

'First job.'

She sighed. 'Right. Follow me.'

They were led past the bar into a cramped dressing cabin where girls with long legs and short skirts flitted about like perfume-scented hummingbirds. They pressed back deferentially to let the older woman pass.

'Monika?' she barked. 'Liberty?'

'Here I am!' chirruped someone.

'Have you all finished?'

'Coming, Mrs Fisher.'

Two girls, one dark and the other blonde, appeared before her.

'Take these two. Pair off how you like. Ten minutes. Then I want you at the bar.'

Kate was swept away by Monika. Sofie found herself staring up at a heavily made-up brunette with dagger-sharp cheekbones and an unreadable expression.

'OK, this is how it works,' said Liberty, pulling her to one side. She had a regional accent that Sofie couldn't quite place.

'Stay off the champers, stick to Appletizer, water, whatever. And strictly by the book while you're onboard.' She peered at Sofie more closely. 'You done this before, right?'

'Do I look like I've done this before? And what do you mean, 'by the book'?'

Liberty leaned into her. '*By - the - book*,' she mouthed, her heavily glossed lips formed grotesque shapes in the pale frame of her face.'But,' she added under her breath, 'what extras ya do after is yer own business.' She tapped her nose knowingly. 'Just don't get caught leaving with a guy, is all.'

Sofie stared at her. 'Wait. Extras? Is that what this is?'

Liberty's face suddenly clouded over. 'You're not the Old Bill, are you?'

Sofie laughed. What the hell?

'Police? Of course not! It's just that my friend over there said we were here for conversation only. Social, she told me.'

Liberty looked relieved. 'Totally up to you. No one's

forcing yer to do anything. Sorry, love, must have read you wrong.' A beat. 'You really are green, aren't yer? What did ya say ya name was?'

'Sofie.'

'For real?'

'Why? You don't like it?'

Liberty looked at her pityingly. Then, half closing her eyes, as if the effort of summoning up her imagination took all her concentration, she said: 'What about... Tara?'

Sofie smirked. 'Tara?'

Liberty opened her eyes wide. 'Yeah, that's it, Tara, that's perfick.' She slid off her bar stool like a crocodile who'd spotted dinner. 'You look just like a Tara. OK then, Tara, let's go. And make sure ya stick with moi.'

Sofie tried to steady herself. In two minds. This was ridiculous. There was still time to back out. But, she told herself, focus on the prize. She was here for her father. All it required was to play a part.

Besides, what's the worst that could happen? If any of these men tried it on, they'd get her knee in their balls.

They passed the gangway. Ropes were being gathered, and the last guests were drifting in, singly and in small groups, laughing and chatting. As they were whisked away to the bar area by Maureen or one of the younger girls, Sofie caught snatches of their conversation. *May I introduce Melanie, who's in fashion? And Liz, who's in PR?*

They made for the main reception area. Just outside the door was a waiter with a plate of blinis. Liberty popped one in her mouth, wiping a small black egg off her bottom lip, and they entered the saloon. A man appeared at her elbow.

'You disappeared on me,' he said.

'Mr. Gebler,' she cooed. 'You know I can't resist caviar.'

'Charles,' he corrected. He had a mass of closely

cropped black, curly hair. He turned to Sofie. 'And who's this?'

'A friend of mine,' Liberty said. 'Tara.'

Gebler's handshake lingered a little too long. 'Pleasure to meet you. And what do you do?'

Good question. There had been no time to invent a cover. Liberty came to the rescue.

'She's an actress.'

A second man joined them. Taller, with a slightly loping gait.

'Ah, Cal,' said Gebler, turning to the newcomer. 'Just the man I wanted to see. How are you getting along?'

'Thank you, Charles, no problems,' said the newcomer. His eyes flicked to Sofie, then away.

'And our friends? Are they having a good time?'

He glanced at his watch. Sofie recognised the make - a gold vintage Omega, just like the one her father had worn.

'Like I said, Charles,' he said, with a hint of impatience, 'no problems at all. Laura needn't worry.' His accent was educated and very slightly posh.

Another couple appeared. Liberty and Gebler moved away. Suddenly, Sofie and Cal were alone. He held out his hand.

'Hi, I'm Cal. Cal Harrison.'

'Tara,' she lied.

A waiter approached them with paper wraps of miniature fish and chips.

'Mmm, those smell good,' she said, awkwardly. She took one. Then: 'You with Cambridge Bio?'

'Yes and no,' he said. 'Shall we sit?'

She followed him to a corner table. He had short, dark brown hair, a square jaw, and was dressed in navy chinos and a loose linen jacket. Not corporate like the other men.

He settled on the bulkhead side, and she poured them two glasses of fizz from a bottle on the table. Hers bubbled over, so she fished out her guest pass and rested the glass on top.

'Cheers,' she said.

She scanned the room for Kate, but there was no sign of her. She wondered if she'd met her contact yet.

'Looking for someone?'

'A friend I came with.'

'Girlfriend?'

'Yeah. Wearing a short green dress. Have you seen her?

That got his attention.

'What's her name?'

'Kate.' She regretted it the moment she said it, but had no idea what name she had given herself.

He nodded. 'Up front, I think.'

'That's observant of you.'

She wondered why he'd noticed her. There were dozens of girls here. She took a sip of the champagne. She needed something to settle her nerves.

'So, Cal, tell me what it is you do exactly. For Cambridge Bio.' If conversation was what they wanted, conversation was what they would get. 'I mean, are you management, or what?'

It turned out he wasn't. In fact, he didn't want to tell her much at all. Outside, they were approaching the dark mass of a bridge, and as the boat passed underneath, his face was briefly illuminated. His eyes were blue-grey. Good looking. He appeared preoccupied, constantly looking at a group of tables at the far side of the saloon.

She babbled on about her 'acting ambitions', trying to play the game. But it was odd, he wasn't at all interested in her. Wasn't that the whole point? He asked her, in a distracted sort of way, how long she had been doing this kind of work. She confessed it was her first time. Couldn't do any harm, she thought to herself. He kept refilling her glass. Didn't touch his own, she noticed.

'Steady on,' she laughed. 'I'm not meant to get pissed.'

He sat back. 'You know, something tells me you don't fit in here. Am I right?'

She met his gaze. It was the first time he'd properly focused on her since they'd sat down.

'Doing a favour for a friend.'

He cocked an eyebrow. She could tell he didn't buy it. There was movement behind, and for a brief moment, his eyes flickered away again. But only for an instant.

'Come on, Tara,' he said, returning to her. 'I know the type of girls they bring in. The only way most of these tired old guys' - he gestured around the saloon - 'get any pleasure out of these events is when the hosts have arranged some local talent from an agency to come and chat them up.' His eyes twinkled, amused. 'Not you?'

She looked at him evenly then drained her glass, the sharply fizzing bubbles stinging the back of her throat.

'You're a perceptive guy,' she said eventually.

'Listen, I've been to dozens of these functions. My God, they're dull. But I've enjoyed talking to you, *Tara*.'

So he knew her name was made up. He stood.

'It's been a pleasure.'

Sofie followed him up and stumbled. She could feel the alcohol starting to kick in. If she wasn't careful, she realised, she could easily get wasted.

He looked solicitous. 'You OK?'

'I'm fine. It's been nice to meet you too.'

She gave him a tight smile and turned on her heel, sensing his gaze follow her as she walked away. Somewhere in the distance, jazz was playing. The decibels had ratcheted up a notch.

She wondered how Kate was getting on. She was impatient to meet these so-called whistleblowers. Find out what they knew about her father. The last thing Kate had said before she'd disappeared was that she'd 'play it by ear' and 'come and find her when she needed her.'

By now the boat had picked up speed. In the darkness, a string of lights along the Embankment swayed up and down as they glided past the Tate Modern towards the bridges of the City. She caught a sudden whiff of diesel oil.

Arriving at a gap in the throng, she scanned the room. There was no sign of her. Then she caught a glimpse of someone she recognised: Monika, the woman who Kate had paired up with, sandwiched between two older men. She was laughing loudly.

'That is so funny! The most hilarious story I have ever heard!' she was saying.

'Well, I certainly thought so,' said the man to her left.

Sofie tried to catch her eye.

'Monika?' The face hardened. 'I'm looking for Kate. Have you seen her?'

She looked at her blankly, annoyed at being interrupted. Sofie moved on. The swaying motion was beginning to make her feel nauseous. Two men approached, and it started all over again, and she was drawn into a conversation about Walter Crane's prospects in the forthcoming leadership campaign. But she couldn't focus. Their faces began to blur into each other. Then more people joined, and they wandered over to a table. Grateful to be off her feet, she stayed with them, and somehow the combination of sitting down and the bubbles of the champagne eased her nausea. Time passed.

Finally, she got up unsteadily, excused herself, and

wandered off in search of the cabin that Maureen had taken them to earlier, holding on to the bulkhead to keep steady. It was at the stern, behind the bar. The door was closed. Sofie knocked, pressing her ear against the wood. Nothing. Relieved, she opened it and slipped in.

The room was in half darkness. They must have been above the engine, because a dull thrumming vibration came from under her feet. As soon as she lay down, the room started to spin. She concentrated on breathing, counting the rhythms, in and out, to steady herself. Her eyes drooped shut.

She must have drifted off because when she next opened them, the engines had stopped, and the spinning in her head had given way to a thumping headache. Aware of whispering and fevered breaths, she peered through the porthole above her head. Outside, it was pitch black.

She sat up and immediately became aware of two figures on the opposite side of the room. A girl had her arms draped around the shoulders of a man, who was leaning over her. They were giggling and whispering together, faces illuminated in mottled greens and pinks in the reflection of the deck's fairy lights.

Unaware of her presence, they disentangled from each other and slipped out furtively, the man before the girl, the girl waiting a short while to light a cigarette, which she did next to the window vent, and to rearrange herself. Then she stubbed it out under the tabletop and left, and Sofie was alone again in the darkness. She sank back heavily. Someone else entered.

'Ah, this is where you're hiding,' said Kate. 'I've been texting you. We've got to go.' There was an urgency in her voice.

'I feel awful,' Sofie mumbled, pushing herself upright.

'You can't stay here. That bitch will find you. Come on.'

Sofie ran a hand through her crumpled hair.

'Where are we going?'

'Here, take this,' Kate said, shoving a small brush at her, along with her coat. 'But be quick, will you? We haven't got much time.'

'Why?'

'The guys I met want to go ashore. They're nervous. I think they're worried they're being watched.'

'But I thought we weren't allowed off?' Sofie croaked, fumbling for her shoes. 'Won't someone notice us?'

Kate gave her a look. 'It's a party, Sofe. Couples slip away all the time. That's the point. Ready?'

Her friend turned at the door. 'Oh, and by the way, these guys - they're called Jeff and Mike. You're with Mike. Make out you're having a good time together.'

'Okay, but… '

Kate cut her short. It was a different Kate than the one she thought she knew. A more ruthless Kate.

'It's just till we get off this fucking boat.'

7

After the girl had gone, Cal picked up the small plastic security pass she'd left on the table. It was still damp from the spilt champagne, the printed word *Guest* blazoned across the top and, below in smaller type, *A-Z Agency*.

Huh. She hadn't even made it to 'B'.

He knew the drill. They were hired to take the edge off, flirt, keep the delegates entertained. So, OK, it was sometimes about sex. More often, it wasn't. This one hadn't fit the mould. Maybe she really was doing a favour for a friend.

But one thing he knew for certain: her name wasn't Tara.

It was a simple trick. When she sat down, he'd scanned the local wifi networks, and 'SJ's iPhone' had popped up. There was no one else nearby, the signal was hers. Sarah-Jane?

On the back of the pass were two phone numbers scrawled in pen. He slipped it into his pocket.

Time to focus.

The VIPs he was tailing were on the move, heading

toward the outer deck. He got up and followed. At the reception desk, they paused, greeted by two women, one of whom was laughing. She was the shorter of the two, a coat around her shoulders, the girl he'd spotted them with earlier. The one not-Tara had pointed out earlier as her friend. The other woman was partially obscured, but Cal glimpsed jeans and a silk blouse.

No way. Couldn't be.

He stayed in the shadows, watching. The men looked uneasy, as if they weren't totally sure about what was happening. But a moment later, they linked arms with the women and headed for the gangway.

As they stepped onto the pontoon, the second girl turned her head. Just for a second. But it was enough.

It was her.

He swore under his breath. If these guys really were potential kidnap targets, walking off the boat with two strangers was not just reckless; it was plain stupid. Unless, of course, this was the play. He was ninety-nine per cent certain the girl was not any sort of pro. But her friend?

He tapped the comms button clipped to his belt. Nothing. He cursed again, gave it another try. This time it clicked.

'It's Harrison,' he said in a low voice. 'Mind telling me what's going on? People are coming and going all over the place. Gebler promised me this wouldn't happen. I thought the boat was meant to be locked down?'

A crackle came in reply.

'OK,' Cal replied. 'Alert him that they're leaving the boat. With two of the agency girls. I'm going after them.'

They left the pontoon, and he followed them. As soon as they were on dry land, they delinked arms and picked up pace. Something didn't feel right.

He watched them turn left and veer onto a narrow riverside towpath that led along the side of a shuttered warehouse. He hung back, melting into the darkness. The lights of the landing dock receded, and for a moment, he lost sight of them. Shadows swallowed everything. His eyes adjusted. A window was open fifty metres ahead to the left, and there was a brief flash of headlights from a car as it turned at the far end of an alley, revealing the dark shape of the last in line as they walked in single file. As they passed the end of the building, he saw it was the girl, the glint of a bottle in her hand. He waited until they had crossed a patch of open ground, then silently sprinted after them until he reached a brick wall. He flattened his body up against it to listen, the surface slick with damp. No voices, only their soft footfall growing fainter in the distance, oblivious of pursuit.

He pressed on, scanning to left and right. Old habits: close observation, reading his quarry, watching for tails; hidden in doorways, crouching in hedgerows, flat in the mud in ditches. God, how he missed it!

Up ahead, a faint light - a bracket lamp illuminating a small jetty. He halted. The four figures had stopped. Talking, from the looks of it. Thirty seconds passed. Then the men descended some steps, the women close behind, and, after a moment's hesitation, boarded a small cabin cruiser moored to the dock.

Shit. This he had not prepared for. It looked like they were leading the men into a trap.

He hit his comms again.

'They're boarding a cruiser, about a hundred meters downriver. I'm moving in.'

This time, the voice that answered was Gebler's.

'I've got it, Harrison. Don't move. I'm right behind you.'

Cal turned, scanning the path. It was still and silent.

Then, the soft crunch of gravel. Someone was coming.

8

Sofie trudged after the others in silence. Dry land and the biting cold were helping sober her up - sort of.

Up ahead, the vague outline of a cabin cruiser emerged, an indistinct mass against the night sky, and, beyond that, Tower Bridge, brightly lit up like a postcard. She lagged a few paces behind, coat cinched tight, as they veered onto a narrow jetty.

Someone in shadow was waiting by the boat. She couldn't distinguish a face, just caught a scrap of words: *Make yourselves comfortable. I'll be outside if you need me.* By the time she reached the gangway, the figure was gone.

Onboard was only marginally warmer. The cabin held a table and two worn seats, like old tube benches salvaged from another life. Kate flipped on the bulkhead light, and the sudden glare made Sofie flinch, a hand instinctively rising to block it. Her head throbbed. She was tempted to lie down again, and God, she wanted to. But instead, she focused, for the first time, on the two men, Mike and Jeff. They stood awkwardly, shifting weight, jackets pulled tight like armour. Mike looked twitchy: opening cabinets, tapping on the bulkhead, the way people do when they're assessing a purchase. Except he wasn't: he appeared to be reassuring himself. Finally, they slid along the banquette, one shuffling before the other, drawing their jackets close around them to fend off the chill. Or was it nerves?

'OK,' Jeff said, voice low and flat. 'Let's get on with it, shall we?'

Kate rummaged for cups to drink from and pointed to the bottle.

'Doll, will you do the honours?'

Sofie unwound the wire and gently prised off the cork. It popped with a sharp crack, rebounding off the cabin roof. Both men flinched. Sofie shakily poured the bubbling froth into four plastic beakers, trying not to spill. There was an atmosphere, alright.

'Good to meet you,' said Mike, looking at her. 'Finally.'

Sofie peered at him. 'Are you the guy who knew my father?'

'I knew him well. I was at his memorial. I'm only sorry that I didn't get a chance to say hello.'

'You were there?' she said, surprised. 'How come I didn't see you?'

'I left right after. Couldn't hang about.'

Kate cut in. 'OK, guys, we don't have much time. This evidence you have. What is it? Scientific studies? Clinical trials?'

Sofie raised a hand. 'Wait, I'm sorry, before we start. I need to know. How does my Dad fit into all this?'

Mike glanced at Jeff, then back at her. 'He was part of the Cambridge Bio trial. The one we worked on.'

'Yes, I realise that. But how did you get to know each other?'

'I was the scientist in charge of his case. He'd come up

to London every two weeks, and we became friends.'

Sofie wondered, not for the first time, why her father had never spoken of it.

'Sure, OK. But why would he volunteer in the first place?'

'Because he had HIV, Sofie, and those were the patients we were mandated to test. Though to be honest, your father's involvement struck us as unusual. We mostly worked with full-blown AIDS patients in East Africa. I believe it was your Dad's doctor who put him up for the trial.'

'What you have to understand,' Jeff added, 'was that those doctors were making a ton of money out of this.'

Sofie took a breath to try to steady herself. 'So what you're saying is - it went wrong?'

Mike nodded slowly. 'Let's just say it was very poorly administered. There was not much in the way of risk management. Before long, it had started to generate some very unpredictable side effects. Few of us knew this at the time, because none of the feedback was joined up. There was also immense pressure from the top to keep going, because the higher-ups feared it would be shut down. There were a significant number of suicides. There was a culture in the organisation that considered AIDS patients to be expendable.'

Sofie looked away to hide the tear welling in one eye. She suddenly felt faint.

'And my father?' she said softly.

Kate touched her arm. 'I'm sorry, Sofe.'

'Yes, I'm afraid that he was one of the victims. If you buy the theory of suicide. Which, given the parallels with what happened to some of the others, seems to be the most logical conclusion.'

Sofie blinked hard. The air had thickened.

Jeff shifted forward. 'But listen, Sofie, that's why we're here. We want to get justice for your father. For him and all the others. But it comes with a lot of risk. What we're about to share is highly sensitive. Career-ending. Even if they can't pin it on us, we'd be out of a job.'

'There's also another reason.'

They turned to Mike.

'Which is?' said Kate.

'Crane needs to be stopped.'

None of them touched their drinks. The only noise in the cabin came from the fizz of the champagne dissipating into the cabin. Then a seagull screeched somewhere outside, wheeling off across the river.

'You realise there's a high likelihood that this will be traced back to you,' Kate said.

Jeff nodded. 'We'll take our chances.' He handed her a sheaf of papers in an A4 plastic folder. 'This is a list of names. Doctors and patients, along with outcomes for each of them.'

Kate flipped through the pages. Her breath caught. 'Jesus.'

'It'll help you understand the scale of this thing. It's the biggest medical scandal in decades. And Crane - he may not have signed anything himself, but he was well aware of what was going on.'

'Do you have proof of that?' said Sofie.

Kate turned to her. 'Let me handle this, okay?' she whispered, though not so softly that the others didn't catch it.

A frisson of awkwardness passed between them. Mike pointed at the file.

'The issue is, most of those doctors won't talk, and without them, it might be hard to trace the patients who are still alive.'

'How many of them died?' asked Sofie again.

'We can't be sure. But a significant number.'

'So how do we prove it?'

'With the bloods,' Jeff said.

Kate raised an eyebrow. 'Bloods?'

'Blood samples,' Mike clarified. 'That's what will prove how this developed. How quickly it grew. It shows their state of mind just before they died. Because what they chart is a dramatic change in the chemical levels in the brain over the course of the trial. It's that which we think caused these patients to act so irrationally, and in some cases, fatally. Under the confidentiality agreements that were signed, only the doctors can access them. As you might imagine, they are not too keen to release them, given what has happened. Many of them may already have been destroyed.'

He paused, like there was more.

'Go on,' Kate prompted. Sofie caught the suppressed excitement in her voice.

'But there is one doctor who is prepared to talk.'

They waited for him to elaborate. Mike looked at Jeff. His eyes flickered their assent. Mike turned to Sofie. 'But only to you.'

Sofie started in surprise. 'To me? Why me?'

'Because they were your father's doctor.'

He delved into his jacket pocket and retrieved a small rectangular card. He handed it over. The foreign-sounding name inscribed on it meant nothing to her.

'It's a Gibraltar law firm. All communications must go through them. Understandably, this doctor is nervous. There have been intimidating noises from Cambridge.'

The law practice printed on the business card was three words strung together, typical of partner firms, with a

Gibraltar P.O. Box number: 758001. By weird coincidence, Sofie realised that it was her father's date of birth, written backwards. She used it as a bank security number. Perhaps it was an omen. But the effort of reading suddenly made her feel sick again.

She put it down on the table. 'I'm sorry,' she muttered. 'D'you mind? I need to use the bathroom.'

Jeff pointed towards a sliding door that led up towards the bows.

She got up and weaved her way forward, holding on to the roof for support. Easing the door open, she found herself in a two-berth cabin. A perspex hatch above her head reflected the urban glow of the city, and, through a further door, there was a cramped sink and a pump-action toilet. She slid both doors shut behind her and went in. Silence descended. A sudden wave of nausea washed over her. The whole thing felt so unreal. Was this really happening? She leaned over the bowl, head down.

She stood there for a while, the only sound reaching her the lapping of water against the hull. She inhaled and exhaled slowly, taking deep breaths to regain her composure. It was as she was straightening up to return that she heard it: a loud, muffled splash from the stern of the boat. Then what sounded like a scream, and raised voices.

Her whole body went rigid. She strained to listen. Three smacks came in quick succession, *phut, phut, phut*, followed by a crash, as if a heavy book had fallen off a shelf. The voices ceased.

What the hell was going on? Pulse quickening, she opened the door and came out of the toilet. There was a creak, and then a click. She froze. Silence again.

Trying to quell a rising panic, she tiptoed towards the door that led back to the main cabin. Gingerly, she slid it open. It was as if she'd opened a camera shutter.

Mike was sliding, almost in slow motion, beneath the seat. His head was a mess, half of it ripped apart along one cheek in a bloody gash, eyes staring. His friend Jeff was motionless beside him. Sofie's attention switched to a third figure. She gasped. Kate was slumped forward, her face obscured, softly moaning, her coat rucked up under one arm, and her hair - that beautiful auburn hair - floating in a widening pool of blood on the glossy veneer of the table.

For a second, Sofie was paralysed, too shocked to react. Before she could stop herself, she let out a cry. At the far end of the cabin, in the doorway that led out onto the deck and silhouetted against the night sky, was the back of a figure in a motorcycle helmet. The helmet turned. It was black and full-visor. Sofie screamed and bolted back into the forward cabin.

She didn't hear the shot, only saw the wood splinter into a thousand fragments in front of her. Aghast, all her senses in overdrive, she jammed the door shut again behind her. Whoever was on the far side swore as they caught their arm against the sharp steel runners of the frame. It bounced, and Sofie screamed again, slamming it back and securing the latch.

She stumbled forward.

Behind her, the shooter was shaking the door, but by some miracle, it didn't give way. There followed a few seconds of silence, then a sharp crack as the lock splintered.

Sofie desperately searched around for a means of escape. Above was the hatch with a metal flip-catch. She tugged at it, straining every muscle, and it opened a crack. She gave it a wrench, and it fell back on her hand. With a howl of pain, she scrambled onto a bunk and flung all her body weight upwards.

She heard a bullet smash through wood, splitting the doorframe. A boot crashed against it and the attacker was in.

All Sofie registered as she hauled herself up into the night and onto the deck was a burning sensation as another round sawed past her neck. Instinctively, she closed her eyes, scared to look down.

Then it was up and out in one swift movement, rolling into the icy, ink-black Thames.

Part Two

9

Saturday 29th October

It took almost an hour for Cal to reach the K West hotel across town in Shepherd's Bush. The traffic was heavier than expected for that time of night; clubbers spilling out of bars, their laughter echoing through the streets as the cab navigated the maze from Elephant and Castle to Westminster. He barely noticed. His mind was stuck back on the towpath, running in circles.

What had just happened? He was fuming with frustration. He'd almost had a row with Gebler right there on the towpath after the man ordered him to stand down and return to the hotel. Why? It didn't make any sense. Having tracked the girls and the two VIPs to the jetty and onto the cabin cruiser, it looked like they were about to cast off. Or else the women had lured them there on the promise of sex. Unlikely, all things considered.

Either way, he was about to follow them aboard when Gebler caught up with him. He claimed he wanted Cal back at the hotel to check everything was secure for their return. He, Gebler, would ensure that they got back safely. Cal had strongly objected. Surely that was his job, the job they had hired him to do? But the man was adamant. In the end, he was forced to back off. What choice did he have? Gebler was the client.

Now, as his cab sped across Lambeth Bridge towards the Embankment, he wrestled with motive. Perhaps Gebler was trying to hide the fact that the men were being shadowed? As Laura explained, they 'didn't want them ruffled.' But it was a reckless gamble. Cal knew it. His instincts were screaming. The situation demanded an intervention, not a stand-off.

Twenty minutes later, they drew up in the forecourt of the K West. Cal had already framed what he would say to Laura about it in the morning.

Inside, the lobby was dead quiet. After checking the bar to see if any of the delegates had returned, he exited onto the street to run a quick sweep of the area, as he had done multiple times over the past few days. Same result. A couple of homeless figures curled up in the doorways at the rear of the West 12 shopping centre, and a drunk crashed out amongst a pile of boxes outside Pizza Express on the corner. The petrol station across the road was still open, one person stocking up with food items from the M+S convenience store. But that was about it.

He circled back towards the hotel, past the dossed down figures in doorways. In another place and another world, they could have been watchers, as he himself had been on so many occasions. A classic play to watch the street without being observed. However, not this lot. Wrapped head to toe in blankets, ratty duvets and sleeping bags, they were out for the count. He left a few coins in a plastic cup beside one of the hulks, scanning the parked cars as he passed. The night was bitter, and to keep warm, they would need to have their engines running. But they were all dark, locked and silent.

Satisfied, Cal slipped inside and took up position in the lobby to await the delegates' return. Eventually, soon after one a.m., they started to trickle in. First, two taxis, then an executive Mercedes Vito Tourer with darkened windows. A couple nodded at him, recognising him from the boat.

'Good party?' Cal asked one. He was swaying, having difficulty working the elevator buttons. Cal helped him into the lift, and he slurred his thanks.

He counted heads as they came in. Two were missing.

By 2.30 a.m., the chemists still hadn't shown. Concerned now, he called Gebler's number. No answer. Waited five minutes. Tried again. Straight to voicemail. He went over to the reception desk.

'Could you call a guest for me, please?'

The girl behind gave him a tired smile and dialled their extension. As expected, no one answered.

Room 501 was at the far end of the 5th-floor corridor. Letting himself in with the spare keycard, the first thing that struck him was the smell. Fragrant, with a waft of detergent, as if the place had been cleaned only a short time before. As the door clunked softly behind him, he switched on the bathroom light. Spotless. Towels neatly folded. The little card perched on top of the pile asked guests to leave towels in the bath if they wanted them laundered. But there were no toiletries. No toothbrushes, no signs of life.

With a sense of foreboding, he walked through to the bedroom.

Same thing there. Bed made, crisp and untouched. No suitcases. No chocolate on the pillow. Not even a coat hanger disturbed. The room wasn't just empty; it was sterile. It hadn't been used at all. The chemists had cleared out - or been cleared out - and were never coming back.

He sat down hard on the edge of the bed to think. They

weren't scheduled to fly out until later that afternoon.

Where the hell had they gone?

10

In her brutal fight for survival, Sofie lost all track of time. Amid the inky darkness, struggling against the relentless current, her arms grew increasingly numb.

Somewhere in the chaos, in the pitch-black tangle of water and fear, her hand caught an object. Rough and fibrous - a frayed rope drifting in the water. She grabbed it. Somehow, it held.

Her muscles screamed, but she blocked it out and began hauling herself in, hand over hand, until her fingers met the slimy rung of a ladder. She dragged herself up and collapsed, gasping for breath, onto a hard surface.

Exhausted, she lay motionless on the deck, barely registering the sound of her ragged breathing and the slap of water below. Eventually, her chest stopped heaving. Her heartbeat slowed. She opened her eyes.

She'd climbed onto a houseboat. Beside her loomed the wheelhouse, dark and silent, and beyond, a road. She turned her head slowly, scanning the river, trying to get her bearings. Nothing looked familiar, except for a jagged outline in the distance. Tower Bridge. She hadn't come far.

But the riverboat was gone. The cabin cruiser, too.

And there was no sign of Kate.

Rolling over, she fumbled for her phone. She stared at the black screen, dead and waterlogged. She would have to find help. But at that time of the morning, there was no one about. Grabbing at a guardrail for support, she scanned the road on the far side of the towpath. But the city was asleep. No cars. No footsteps. Just that eerie sodium glow casting long, empty shadows on the riverbank.

She had been so focused on survival that she had buried the memory of her helmeted attacker. Now it resurfaced, making her heart race, as a new fear gripped her. What if he was still lurking, tracking her movements?

Bruised and shoeless, jacket sodden and the silk of her shirt icy on her skin, she limped cautiously along the deck, careful to stay out of sight of the cabin. To her surprise, the door to the wheelhouse was unlocked. She paused, listened. Nothing. Gingerly, she tiptoed into the warm darkness below. The place looked lived-in: a stove, kitchen cabinets, a small dining table. There was another door at the back, probably a bedroom. She collapsed onto a bench.

For a moment, she just sat there, eyes open, mind blank. But then everything rushed back at once. Kate. The river. The masked attacker.

What had she done to deserve any of it?

Tears crept up, silent and hot, even as the rest of her stayed frozen. It was too much to process, too surreal, and she didn't have answers. Only more questions, and the growing certainty that whoever had started this... wasn't done yet.

When she finally stirred, the brass clock on the wall was pointing to three. She pushed herself up and peered through a porthole.

Nothing but the deserted road. Still no movement. Still no sign of life.

What now?

Daylight. She'd wait for daylight. Blend into the morning traffic, find a payphone, call the police. Try, somehow, to pull herself out of this nightmare.

11

By quarter to four, Cal was getting twitchy. The two chemists hadn't shown, and he was now seriously concerned. He grabbed his backpack and asked the receptionist to call him a black cab.

It didn't take long to reach SE1, where the party boat had docked a few hours before. The journey was quicker this time, the clubbers finally in bed. He gave the driver cash and told him to wait.

Shouldering his pack, Cal approached cautiously. The place was deserted. Up ahead was the gangway, illuminated by the riverside lights. The party boat had gone. He peered along the towpath where he'd followed the girls. The small jetty was empty.

No sign of the cabin cruiser.

But there was still a glow in the guardhouse window. Inside, the security guard looked half-asleep. Feet up, TV on mute. He started in surprise.

'Yeah?' he said. 'Can I help you?'

'Morning mate. Sorry to disturb you. We spoke a few hours ago. I was the guy coordinating security for the event last night.'

The guard opened the door and stared at him. He scratched the side of his head, annoyed at being woken.

'Spoke to a lot of people last night.'

'I expect you've had a busy night.' Cal unzipped his backpack and pulled out two photographs. 'I just need to know - what time did the party boat leave?'

The man shrugged. 'Dunno. One, one-thirty? Why?'

Cal held out the pictures. 'You see either of these two guys wandering about after it left? They never returned, and we think they may have got drunk and passed out somewhere.'

The guard inspected the images, then shook his head. 'Can't say I have. Been as quiet as a mouse down here. Everyone cleared out.'

Cal pulled out another. 'What about him?'

The guard squinted at Gebler's photo. 'Yeah. Spoke to him a couple of hours ago.'

'Did you see him leave?'

'Think so. Can't recall.'

'On foot? Or in a taxi?'

'Like I say, can't remember exactly. Lots of people were heading out, all around the same time.'

Cal paused. 'Anything unusual? Anyone acting off?'

The man hesitated.

'Well, there was one thing.'

Cal's attention sharpened. 'Go on.'

'Yeah, after they all left, I noticed a bloody great Kwaka parked up and looking like it had been abandoned.' He pointed. 'Over there.'

'Kwaka?'

'Kawasaki motorcycle. One of those Ninja jobs. Don't often see those around these parts. They make a hell of a racket. Two hundred horsepower at least, I reckon. Odd thing was, I don't remember it arriving. I would normally have clocked that.'

Cal frowned. 'Perhaps it arrived when you were called away.'

'Could have.'

'Where is it now?'

'Well, that's just it. Never saw it leave either. I went to the toilet and when I got back, it had vamoosed.'

'Vamoosed?'

'Vanished.'

'And what time was that?'

'Just after two.'

Cal nodded slowly. 'Ok, thanks. That's useful.' He slipped the photos back into his bag and handed over a card. 'If you see them, or hear anything, can you give me a ring? Name's Cal.'

He fished a £50 note out of his wallet. 'And take this for your trouble.'

The guard looked at it like it was radioactive. Hesitated, then took it.

'Oh. That's very decent of you, thanks. I'll be certain to keep an eye out.'

Cal gave his arm a pat. As he turned, he glanced up at a camera bolted to a pole. 'You've got access to CCTV down here?'

'In emergencies, yeah.' The guard gestured to a small monitor in the corner of the cabin. 'It normally feeds through to that.' He hesitated. 'But I'm afraid…'

'Don't tell me,' Cal said, with a sense of foreboding. 'It's broken.'

The man chuckled.

'Spot on, mate. Like everything else in this bloody

country.'

12

Sofie had been waiting in Interview Room Three of Lewisham Police Station for over two hours. The room was cold, fluorescent, and smelled faintly of floor polish and old coffee. She'd called the police with the help of someone at a service station just after seven, and a patrol car had picked her up and brought her in. They'd given her a dry coat to cover the ripped jacket, but her jeans were still damp, and her face was streaked with dried mud. But she didn't want comfort. She wanted answers.

The door opened, and a man and a woman entered. Both were in plain clothes.

'Apologies for keeping you waiting so long, Miss James,' said the woman, the shorter of the two. 'I'm DC Khan. This is DS Bates. How are you feeling?'

'How am I feeling?' Sofie echoed. 'How do you think?'

'Perhaps you'd like to repeat what you told the Duty Sergeant when you came in earlier, and we'll draw up a formal statement,' said the Detective Sergeant, Bates, pulling out a chair opposite Sofie. His tone was clipped. Professional. Not exactly warm. He put a folder down on the table in front of them and slid a document across to his female colleague.

'Have you found them?' Sofie asked.

Bates didn't look up. 'We'll get to that.'

Khan stepped in. 'Can I get you something? Coffee? Tea?'

Sofie hesitated, then nodded. Khan slipped out of the room. Bates tapped the table once, like he didn't like the pause. The silence sat awkwardly between them.

When Khan returned, she set a steaming cup in front of Sofie. 'Hope you like sugar,' she said gently.

Bates glanced at his watch and flipped a small switch on the recorder. 'Lewisham Police Station. Saturday, 29th October, 09.51. Detective Sergeant Bates, with…'

'Detective Constable Khan.'

'Interviewing Miss Sofie James. Miss James, for the record, please state your name.'

'Sofie James.'

'Thank you. OK, in your own words, tell us what happened.'

Sofie spoke while Khan took notes. Her voice steadied as the story took over. She told them everything, except the parts she couldn't be sure of; whether Kate or the whistleblowers had still been conscious when she ran; whether the gunman had seen her. They didn't interrupt her, their faces impassive. When she'd finished, Bates sat back wearily.

'You met these two men at the event on the riverboat, you say?'

'That's right.'

'And your friend…' he leant across to the notes beside him, 'Kate Winter, invited you, correct?'

Sofie nodded.

'As part of an investigation into the pharmaceutical company, Cambridge Bio. To get information from them regarding your father's death.'

'Exactly!'

'Why did you leave the meeting to go to the toilet?'

'I felt sick.'

'So would it be fair to say that you consumed a considerable amount of alcohol last night?'

'It was a party. I had a few drinks, sure.'

'Anything else?'

'What do you mean?'

'MDMA? Ketamine? Any kind of recreational drug?'

'No. Listen, I know what you're driving at...'

'What am I driving at, Miss James?'

Sofie stared at the detective. Why the hostile attitude?

'So you didn't get a good look at this man?' Khan said. 'The man you said had a gun?'

'No. It all happened so fast. Like I say, he wore a motorcycle helmet.'

'How tall was he?'

'Medium height, I think. Looked foreign.'

'*Looked* foreign?' echoed Bates. 'Because if he didn't say anything, and wore a helmet, how would you be able to tell?'

She sighed heavily. 'Something about his posture. I could be wrong.'

'So foreign people have a different posture?'

Bates glanced sideways at his colleague, but she was busy scribbling notes.

'Now, you said you don't remember any shots before the scream. Sure about that?'

'Yes. Just a crash.'

'Can you describe it?'

'Look, does it matter?' snapped Sofie. 'For God's sake…'

'So what made you go back?'

'Not really sure. I guess I felt guilty. It was me that they had come to see. That was when I heard the scream.'

'How many shots were fired? At you, I mean?'

'I told you. It's all in my statement.'

'Tell us again,' Bates said.

FFS, she thought, what were they trying to do? Trip her up?

'Three.'

'Did they make a noise, or were they silenced?'

'Silenced, I suppose. I don't remember a loud noise. Oh God!' She became suddenly agitated. 'It went so quickly, and then Kate...' She put her head in her hands. 'Is...' she spoke to the floor, drained. 'Is she dead?'

The detectives glanced at each other. Sofie looked up, her eyes misty, her voice quivering with emotion.

'I mean...is it possible...to see her?'

Bates raised his eyebrows in mock surprise.

'Dead, Miss James? We've not found anyone yet. Dead *or* alive.'

It landed like a gut punch.

'What?'

'Nor any sign of the boat you say you boarded. Just your word, Miss James.'

'*What are you talking about?*' she cried. 'I don't understand...' She stared at them both with incredulity. 'I saw her, there was blood everywhere...' Tears started to well up inside her again. 'Surely you must have found her?'

Khan leaned in, softer now. 'We dispatched a unit to the scene right after we picked you up. They didn't find anything.'

A beat.

'No boat, no bodies, no sign of any disturbance,' Bates said, leaning back. 'We also checked the guest list for the Cambridge event. No one by the name of Sofie James appeared to be listed. Nor a Kate Winter.'

'Well, that's because I wasn't a guest!' Sofie cried, desperation in her voice. 'I was working!'

'Working?' Bates leaned forward. 'Doing what, exactly?'

'I was a sort of… hostess.'

He seized on the word. 'A hostess, right. What kind of work is that, then?'

13

It took Bates exactly one hour and a single telephone call to confirm what he'd suspected all along.

He hung up the receiver with a satisfied click. 'Well, that just about wraps it up. She's in Lviv.'

'Who is?' said Khan.

'The Winter girl. Kate. I just spoke to someone at the Sunday Times. They know nothing about a drug investigation. She's a freelancer. She was accredited to them several days ago to do a story on Ukraine. She flew out this morning.'

Khan frowned. 'Really?'

He stood, brushing imaginary fluff off his sleeves, already mentally closing the file.

'Really. Find out who James's GP is. I want her checked out. Medical history, substance abuse, mental issues, anything that might explain this. Shouldn't take long.'

'She's still here,' Khan said. 'She's cleaning herself up. I said I'd drive her home.'

Bates scoffed. 'We've wasted enough time. Call her a cab.'

Khan hesitated, watching him. 'And what about Europol? Or the airlines? Don't you think we should… just to be thorough… get eyes on Kate Winter? Confirm she's actually there?'

Bates shot her a look. 'Cab,' he repeated, glowering.

Nisha Khan knew better than to challenge him right now. But as she walked down the corridor towards where Sofie was waiting, her footsteps echoing on the tile, something gnawed at her.

She had an instinct about this girl. Fragile, yes. Unstable, maybe. But lying? Fabricating the whole thing?

Khan didn't buy it.

14

Cal left identical messages on Laura's office voicemail and Gebler's mobile, but it was not until ten that Gebler finally got back to him.

'Need you to come in,' Gebler said. 'Now.'

That was it. No details. Except one.

Yes, they knew the two chemists hadn't made it back to the hotel. No, Gebler wouldn't say more over the phone.

It was as Cal's cab was crawling up Sloane Street that his mobile lit up with a call from a number he didn't recognise. He answered it warily.

'Yes?'

'Mr Harrison? It's Johnny, from security at Danvers dock.'

Cal sat up straighter. 'Hi.'

'Just a heads-up that the police were down here earlier. Said there were reports of a disturbance.'

Cal caught his breath. 'What kind of disturbance?'

'Wouldn't say. Asked me if I had heard anything unusual.'

'Did they find anything?'

'Not that I could see. They didn't stay long. Two uniformed coppers.'

The cab pulled up. Cal reached for his wallet. 'Alright, Johnny. Mind if I call you back on this number?'

'No problem.'

Click.

Upstairs, they were waiting for him. Gebler looked rough, as if he'd been up all night.

'Good morning, Cal, sit down,' Laura said. Her voice was clipped. No smile this time. Her hair didn't look as immaculate as usual, as if she too had had a disturbed evening.

She cut straight to it. 'Charles tells me that at the party last night, you had some contact with a girl named Tara. Is that correct?'

Tara?

Cal blinked.

'Crome and Latimer never made it back, you know that, I assume?'

Laura nodded. 'We're aware.'

He turned to Gebler. 'I left them with you. So what the hell happened, Charles?'

Gebler shifted uncomfortably.

'Cal,' Laura cut in, calm but firm, 'just answer the question? What do you know about the girl?'

He leaned back, arms folded. 'I talked to her. Briefly. Then I tailed her and the other woman to that cabin cruiser, right before Gebler here pulled me off. Which, by the way, was completely out of line.'

Laura flicked a glance at Gebler.

'She was blonde, right?' he said. 'Five-seven? Maybe five-eight?'

Cal gave a dry snort. 'You think she has something to do

with their disappearance?'

'Sounds like she played you,' Gebler said.

Cal stared at him.

Laura waited. 'Well?'

Cal exhaled slowly. He had to stay calm. 'She was bordering on drunk. Claimed she was an actor. Beyond that? I got nothing. I didn't catch a name. No idea who she was or where she came from.'

Laura watched him carefully, twirling a pen between her slender fingers. 'But surely you got some impression?'

'Oh yeah. She didn't strike me as a hooker, if that's what you're hinting at.' He was on the point of telling them about the business of doing a favour for a friend, but something held him back. 'So what are you saying? That they've disappeared?'

'They have,' Gebler said. 'And we think those two women might've had something to do with it.'

Cal threw up his hands. 'Well, if you mean were they with them when they went ashore and then boarded that cabin cruiser, then yes,' he said angrily. 'But what happened then, you tell me.' He paused, looking from one to the other. 'Whatever it was, the girl was unlikely to be more than a bystander.'

A beat.

'In my *humble* opinion,' he added sarcastically.

They seemed rattled. There was a story here somewhere, and they weren't giving it to him.

He leaned forward. 'Why the hell did you stop me? I mean, why am I here? You ask me to watch over these two guys on the basis that they're prime kidnap targets, and you've got wind of a plot. Then, when I suggest a strategy to minimise the risk, you veto it. In fact, I can't even talk to them, I am to treat them with kid gloves. How can you protect anyone without their cooperation?'

'Cal...'

'Wait, I haven't finished. I then see them leaving with two complete unknowns, I follow. I make a call. And what do you do, Charles? You send me off chasing hotel staff.'

He swivelled back to Laura.

'Now there are two things I'm asking myself. One, what were these men doing with those two women in the first place, given what we know of their sexual orientation? And second, how the hell did you lose them?'

Laura's expression frosted over. 'With respect, Cal, I ask the questions.'

'I'm sorry, Laura, if I seem pissed off, but I would be failing in my job if...'

'Listen, Cal.' She said it in a low hiss, leaning forward. Things seemed to be shifting up a gear. 'There are factors which you are not aware of, so, for the last time, can you please just answer our questions?' A beat. 'You with me?'

He met her eyes.

'So there's nothing more you can tell me about this Tara woman? Her real name? Where she lives?'

'As I said, in my opinion, she was not, as you seem to suggest, the type to pull off a kidnapping. If, in fact, they have been kidnapped. Standing here guessing is wasting time. We have to find out what happened, and I need to get started right away. The longer we delay, the more difficult it will be.'

'You're done here,' Laura said. 'You're booked to fly out to Oslo for the roadshow on Monday evening, right? That's moved up. You're flying this afternoon.'

He blinked. 'Today? Why?'

She got up and came around the desk and, unexpectedly, put a hand on his arm.

'Your assignment here is finished. Let it go. We'll take it from here.'

'That it?'

She nodded. 'You've given us a description of the girl. That's fortuitous. Beyond that, all we need is your report.' She gave him a thin smile. 'And thanks for stepping in at such short notice.'

So that was what Yale did for you, he thought to himself: *fortuitous*. He shook his head.

He played his last card.

'What about the police?'

Laura stiffened. 'What about them?'

'I forgot to mention. When they didn't return to the hotel, I went back to the dock.'

She emitted a soft, almost imperceptible breath, pin-sharp.

'Why did you do that?'

'Because it's what I do. There were two uniforms down there,' he lied smoothly. 'Told me someone reported a disturbance. And the cabin cruiser? Gone. With the chemists, presumably.'

Silence. You could've heard a fly fart. It wasn't the whole truth. Laura looked genuinely shocked. She and Gebler exchanged looks. He guessed they hadn't told the police about the disappearance, and had no intention of doing so.

'We had that report too,' Gebler said eventually. 'They contacted us early this morning.'

Cal snorted before he could stop himself. 'Well, thanks for the memo. You know, I've no idea what sort of ship it is that you're running here, but it would have made all our jobs a lot easier if everyone were in the loop. Then perhaps you wouldn't be in this mess.'

He stood.

'It'll all be in my report.'

'Thanks, Cal,' Laura said coolly. 'We'll be in touch. Do you have everything you need for Oslo? We've booked you into the Hotel Bristol. I think you'll like it. My PA will see to your flight arrangements.'

Why were they so eager to get him out of the way? He nodded curtly and turned to leave. In the outer office, her PA sprang to her feet.

'Ah, Mr. Harrison. This is for you.' She handed him an envelope. 'Your updated flight and accommodation details.'

He looked at it, and at her. Then walked out.

15

A LIGHT DRIZZLE WAS FALLING BY THE TIME SOFIE RETURNED to her flat in Brooke Road, the clouds hanging heavy like slate. The newsagent was pulling an awning over his racks of vegetables on the glistening pavement.

'Ali, I need my spare keys.'

He looked up. 'Good party?'

She blinked. 'Party? Yeah... I mean... I lost my keys.'

He regarded her curiously. 'Sure, no problem.'

A few moments later, he returned with the extra set he kept for her. A pink rubber elephant dangled from a keyring.

'Thanks, Ali.'

Walking slowly up the steps to the front door of her building, she could sense his eyes following her. She opened it and stood stock still on the threshold, blinded for a moment, a tightness in the pit of her stomach. Another morning after another night. Yet this time, so different.

The door closed with a thud behind her, and she began to climb the stairs. Her brain felt fogged, every thought sliding away before it could form. Just six hours ago, she was sipping champagne with Kate. Now she was home again in a ripped jacket, torn and bedraggled. Was Kate really dead? Dear God, please let me wake up.

She stumbled on the landing. Reaching her flat, she fumbled with the lock. She half expected everything to have changed. But all was the same, just as she'd left it. Her eyes welled.

The tap was still whining in the bathroom. Automatically, she shut it off. A puddle of water had pooled in the sink, the plug still in, like some cruel hourglass that hadn't quite run out yet.

Peeling off her still-damp jeans, she walked towards the kitchen. But she never made it, her legs suddenly weak. She collapsed onto the sofa and sat crumpled and sobbing; deep, body-wracking sobs. After a minute, they eased. She picked up the house phone and dialled a number.

The American ringtone droned for what seemed forever.

Then finally: 'Hello?' A voice like sandpaper. Bill. Her mother's second husband.

'Bill, it's Sofie.'

Silence.

'Who?'

'Sofie. I need to talk to my mother.'

The transatlantic line echoed. *...to my mother...*

There was a weary pause. 'It's six a.m. for chrissakes.'

'Bill, it's urgent. Can I talk to her, please?' ... *please...*

'What's so urgent it can't wait till she's up? She's asleep. And so am I.'

Useless then. Useless now. He was an arsehole. Another angry silence followed. She heard the clatter of a receiver. She waited for what seemed like an age. The silence stretched, fathoms beneath the sea. Eventually, her mother's nervy voice came on.

'Really, Sofie, do you realise what time it is?'

'I know, Mum, I just needed to talk to you.'

'About what? Can't it wait? Bill's got to be up in a few hours.'

'I've just been to see the police. You remember Kate, my friend the journalist?'

The echo worked its way back.

'What are you talking about?'

'She's been shot, mum. I think she's dead.'

The line hummed with callous disregard.

'*Shot?*'

'On a boat, a few hours ago, I was there. I saw the whole thing.'

More silence. In the background, she thought she heard Bill say something.

'That's awful, darling.' A beat. 'Are you sure?'

'I just needed to talk to someone.'

'Darling, of course you do ... *alright Bill, give me a minute...* ring me in the morning, will you? We'll talk about it then. Get some sleep. Have you spoken to Dr Evans?'

Sofie felt the tears forming again. That was her mother all over. Call the doctor, don't bother me.

'I'm just upset, that's all. I'm sorry.'

'Don't worry, darling.' She sounded awkward. '*Alright, Bill, I'm coming!* Sofie, now, I must get back to bed, we've got a big day tomorrow, Bill and I have to go to one of his business functions...' she whispered conspiratorially 'terrible bore!... But call me... let me see now... how about six? What?... Oh, he says we're not back till seven, then we're out again... darling, try me just after seven. And... er... look after yourself, OK? The main thing in these situations, I always say, is to keep smiling. OK? Keep smiling. Bye, darling.'

'Bye.'

The line went dead. Sofie stood still, frozen, phone in her hand. Keep smiling? Is that the best she could do? A tear ran slowly down her cheek and dropped, with a soft plop, onto her hand.

Like a parachute that had failed to open.

16

THE EMAIL THAT LAURA WAS WAITING FOR ARRIVED IN HER inbox just after midday. It came from a particular online store, and the headline read '*Unbeatable offers on the latest doll. Or make a splash with a new set of wheels.*' All nonsense, of course, and anyone who stopped to think about it would put it down to an editorial malfunction, given that the store in question sold homewares. But Laura Boyd was not anyone.

The code didn't take long to decipher. It had been sent on a Saturday, the sixth day of the week, so Laura picked out the sixth word: *DOLL*. Next, she went to the tenth, as per the agreed protocol: *SPLASH*. Last, she added ten and six together to find the sixteenth word: *WHEELS*.

Then she opened up her *What3Words* app and typed in *DOLL.SPLASH.WHEELS*. It turned out to be a nine-square-metre patch of grass in Richmond Park. She noted the time of the email: 12.11. That meant the meeting was set for 15.11.

An hour later, she changed into her Lycra, donned her helmet, and wheeled her very ordinary and rather battered road bike out of the back entrance of the office. After cycling to Earl's Court, she carried it onto the District Line train to Richmond, arriving just after 14.20. It was unlikely anyone would be on her tail. However, she knew better than to drop her guard. It was a routine that had been drilled into her.

The ride from the station didn't take long. As she neared the rendezvous point, she began to feel apprehensive. How would the man she was about to meet, codename APOLLO, explain the last twenty-four hours? They had been led to believe that there were only three of them on that boat. How would they have known that a fourth had been hiding in the forward cabin? APOLLO's man, Gebler, was supposed to have handled surveillance, but the intel that there were four of them - two men and two women - wasn't passed on. Or so Tasha, the operative and her colleague, had told Laura in a furious Telegram message early that morning, claiming the whole thing was compromised. She'd warned her that inter-agency operations rarely went well. She had been proved right. Laura had tried calling her ever since. Radio silence.

As she entered through Richmond Gate, the park seemed unusually busy for late autumn. Despite the chill in the air, groups of teenagers were kicking balls about, and there were plenty of couples still out walking their dogs.

She braked to let a stream of cyclists overtake her on Sawyers Hill. When they'd passed, she changed gear to ride the last stretch to the White Lodge turning, where she came off the road and dismounted, wheeling her bike along one of the pedestrian paths that led down the hill. When she caught sight of the lake, she stopped to consult the app. *DOLL.SPLASH.WHEELS.* The map showed a location two hundred feet to the left.

She crossed the grass and reached a canopy of trees. A

man stood waiting for her next to a dead oak with a chocolate coloured Labrador on a leash.

'This is most inconvenient,' she said by way of greeting, removing her helmet and smoothing her hair. 'Did we really need to meet like this?'

APOLLO was a large man with a pale, alabaster-smooth face and a long, aristocratic nose. His knee-length, black cashmere overcoat looked expensive, and he sported a red silk scarf around his bull neck. Who he worked for, she didn't know for sure, though she had her suspicions. Her instructions were simply to cooperate with him.

'Shall we walk?'

He stooped to unleash the dog, and they set off down a gentle incline towards the lake, the animal trotting ahead. A steady line of walkers streamed onto the main pathway, but under the canopy of ancient oaks, there was not a breath of wind, the only sound the squeak of his brogues as they crunched on the wood chip path.

'Tell me what happened,' he said at last, eyes on the trail.

'You know very well what happened,' Laura said. 'One of them got away.'

'That wasn't supposed to be possible.'

'No. But your man, Gebler, missed someone. A woman. Hidden below deck.'

'That's not what I'm hearing.' A beat. 'Gebler tells me that your security guy messed up. Failed to pass on the intel.'

She kept her face even, but her jaw was tight. Unfortunately, she knew that was entirely possible.

They walked on in silence. He picked up a stick to throw for the dog, who hared after it, tail wagging.

'I also understand that she reported it to the police.

You're lucky that they wouldn't have found anything.'

'Are you sure about that?'

'Completely. We took care of the boat.'

'And the journalist?'

'Don't worry about her.'

'But…'

He cut her off. 'Not your business.' He halted to face her. 'In fact, you need to stand down. Effective immediately.'

'What d'you mean? Our operative will want to find this woman. I'm told she had sight of her. We can't allow…'

'No! We really can't afford the risk of anything being traced back to us, do you understand? Your part in this operation is over. We can't have any more amateur fuck-ups.'

Laura sensed the heat rising in her cheeks as she struggled to maintain self-control. The dog saw something and bolted off towards the lake.

'*Poppy!*' he yelled after it angrily. The Labrador bounded back, and he fixed a leash, yanking at her. They resumed walking.

'I hope we are not going to discover that she is another hack,' she said.

'So do I, for your sake. Nothing must be allowed to derail Crane, do you understand?'

'So let us help you fix it,' Laura said again, trying to regain her equilibrium.

He stopped in his tracks and turned his pale grey eyes directly at her.

'Perhaps I did not make myself clear. We will handle this from here on in. Please pass this on to whoever needs to hear it. If and when we need help, Gebler will be in touch again.'

'You're pulling him from the campaign?'

'I didn't say that. It's important we keep all options on the table. He will still need access. However, from now on he'll be less in evidence.'

'So what do I tell the team?'

'You'll think of something. *Poppy!*' he yelled. And then: 'I think we're done here.'

Before she could reply, he turned on his heel with a sharp squeak and stalked off with his dog in the direction of the road. Inside, she felt humiliated. She was being sidelined. Who the hell did APOLLO think he was dealing with?

They might be both working towards the same goal. For now.

But after that…

17

'We just need a card to guarantee the room.'

The girl behind the reception desk of the Hammersmith Novotel smiled at Cal expectantly.

He handed over a debit card in the name of Jonathan Grant. It was linked to a corporate account for an outfit called Grant Industries. If anyone looked into it, GI was a company registered in the British Virgin Islands, its true ownership hidden behind a wall of nominee accounts. That, together with a mobile phone running on a pay-as-you-go SIM, ensured a digital footprint Cal felt comfortable with. That's to say, a very faint one. The phone was topped up monthly with cash, and used a VoIP account from a company which recycled blocks of mobile numbers that couldn't be traced. The less data he left in his wake, the better. Cal Harrison was a hard man to find when he wanted to disappear.

After checking in, he went up to his room, his mind still churning over the night before. What they told him just didn't add up. How could the girl - Tara, or Sarah-Jane, or whoever she was - be tangled up in a kidnapping? He also had a creeping suspicion they planned to pin it on him, and he didn't have long to get on top of it before he was due in Oslo for the next Cambridge job. *If* he went to Oslo.

He shaved, rinsed his face, then sat at the desk. From his pocket, he pulled out the plastic security pass she'd left behind on the boat. Two numbers were written on the back. One was labelled Alice. The other had no name.

Using his pay-as-you-go burner phone, he dialled the unnamed number first. It tripped to voicemail. A woman's voice. Could it be her friend, Kate? He tried the second.

'Knight Frank. How can I help you?'

He cut the call and tapped the name into the browser of the smartphone Cambridge had issued him with, using incognito mode. Scanning the page, he read: *'Knight Frank. UK's leading independent estate agency. Speak to an expert today. Free Property Valuations And Expert Advice.'*

It turned out they were open on a Saturday. With luck, she worked the weekend shift. He rang the number again.

'Hi. Can I speak to Alice, please?'

'Certainly. Who's calling?'

'Jonathan Grant.'

Pause.

'One moment.'

Two clicks. Then silence.

He was about to hang up when a new voice came on.

'Alice Wickman.'

Young, slightly chirpy, professional. He explained he was on the lookout for a flat, somewhere in a good area, in the eight-hundred-thousand range. For a client. But he was in something of a hurry to see what was on the market. Would it be possible to squeeze him in later that afternoon?

She laughed.

'Eight hundred? I'm afraid you've chosen the wrong

postcode.'

He winced. Sloppy.

'Sorry,' he improvised. 'I meant eighteen hundred.'

That piqued her interest, and despite being 'unusually busy', she said she was sure she could 'fit him in.' She sounded pleased to hear that someone had recommended her, but she'd never heard of 'Sarah-Jane.'

Cal wondered whether he'd made a mistake, played his cards too early. He tried 'Kate'.

'You mean Kate Winter?'

'That's the one.' He jotted the name on a hotel pad, and, after some further contact preliminaries - email, mobile number - they arranged to meet at 5.30. But not in her office. It was her last appointment of the day. She'd be driving a pink Fiat Cinquecento, and she would be parked across from a pub called the *Bunch of Grapes* on Brompton Road. The flat she had in mind was a two-bed and just around the corner. It was gorgeous, she said, just what he was looking for.

Cal thanked her and hung up.

18

It wasn't until mid-afternoon that Sofie returned to her flat.

She'd needed air. To clear her head. So she'd gone to grab lunch in a café, then wandered aimlessly until she couldn't avoid it any longer. Returning home, she felt the weight of the shock bear down on her for the second time. It felt like stepping off the train onto an empty platform, with no one to meet her. Now what? She needed to speak to someone, to see friends. But with her phone out of commission until she could pick up a new one, she felt bereft. All her numbers were in it, none of them were backed up. As for the police, all she'd been able to give them was her landline number. But the answerphone attached to it remained solid green. No messages.

She had to do something.

She fired up her laptop and navigated to Kate's Facebook page.

'Please tell me you got away? PLEASE. Where are you? CALL ME. xxxx.'

Next, she found Anna, their old friend from uni.

'Something terrible's happened. Kate's been shot. I was with her. In shock.'

She left the browser open to wait for a reply. For a moment, she considered messaging her on-off boyfriend, Martin. But what was the point? The last thing she needed was his pity.

At four, a reply flashed up from Anna.

'Whaaaaat???? WTF??? Tried calling you, went to vm. What's happening? I'm at a meeting all afternoon, but we must speak tonight. Xxxxx.'

Sofie fired back:

'Sorry, no phone right now. Waiting for the police. I'll message you when I find out more. X.'

Why hadn't they called? It was the police who'd insisted that she should be on hand for their 'enquiries'. What enquiries? They'd found no boat. The A-Z Agency, which had provided the hostesses for the evening, claimed to have no record of her or Kate. She'd left all that to Kate, didn't even know the name of the agency until Kate had told her.

Still, there were facts. Hard ones. Kate was missing. So were the two men. That couldn't stay hidden for long. And then there was Kate's investigation into Cambridge Bio. Someone out there had to know what she was digging into.

At 4:30, the tension got too much. She made herself an omelette - she had to eat something - then pulled out the card DC Khan had given her and dialled Lewisham police station. They patched her through.

'DS Bates.'

'It's Sofie James.'

'Yes?'

'Any news about Kate?'

She heard him sigh. 'Miss James, your friend wasn't even on the boat, was she? She's alive and well.'

Sofie's heart skipped a beat.

'Wait! What?'

'According to her employer, the Sunday Times, Miss Winter is on an assignment to Ukraine. She flew out to Poland on Wednesday. They don't know anything about this 'investigation' you mentioned. So please, Miss James, I strongly advise you to get some rest.'

She staggered back, gripping the edge of the kitchen table, his voice at the end of a long tunnel. Ukraine? No. That couldn't be. Kate had mentioned it over dinner that night, but the trip wasn't for another two weeks. She was sure of it.

She dropped the phone, grabbed her laptop, and started hunting for the number to the Sunday Times. It took ten minutes of bouncing between departments, but she finally reached someone in News.

No one knew anything.

She pressed harder and got transferred to a man who gave her short shrift.

'We don't comment on the whereabouts of staff or freelancers. I'm sorry.'

Click.

Panicked now, she fetched her coat and hurried out into the wet streets to look for a cab.

'Shoreditch, please.'

Twenty minutes later, they drew up outside Kate's flat. She hesitated on the curb. What was she even doing? Hoping for a miracle? That Kate had made it out and was sitting in bed, bandaged up, unable to speak or to contact her?

The windows were dark.

Heart beating furiously, she buzzed. Nothing. Tried again. Still nothing. Then she remembered.

The brick by the bins. Her fingers found the spare key exactly where Kate once told her it'd be.

She let herself in.

The heat hit her like a punch. The place was a sauna, the radiator on full blast. Kate must have switched the heating to constant the night they'd left, warm for her return. A coat lay crumpled near the rack. Sofie picked it up, smoothing it gently, recognising the familiar scent that clung to the collar.

Looking around, she noticed a fat blue desk diary lying next to an empty Styrofoam burger box. Kate loved junk food. She riffled the pages. Mid-November was blocked off in pencil: *"Ukraine."* But there it was: Wednesday the 5th, 7 p.m., Chelsea Harbour. The boat party. Kate wasn't supposed to leave for days.

She flipped back. And stared in shock.

Saturday: *'SJ, The Hair Studio, 3.30 pm.'*

Thursday, the week before: *'SJ, dentist, 27 Great Portland Street, 10 am.'*

Sofie froze. Yes, she had been to the dentist that day. The hair appointment at The Hair Studio on Church Street in Stoke Newington had been cancelled. That same day, she'd finally picked up Kate's call and they'd arranged to meet at the cafe on Monday.

But why was Kate writing down her schedule?

Was Kate… following her?

What the hell was going on?

19

'LADIES AND GENTLEMEN, MR WALTER CRANE!'

The applause hit like a wave. Clapping, whooping, a few overcooked cheers from the party faithful. The candidate for the leadership of the Opposition party stepped onto the podium, blinking in the hot television lights. He wore an American-style gas-station cap, jauntily angled on his head as if he'd been caught short mid-nap by the only truck of the day. Beneath the peak was a lined face, weather-beaten, and below that a plain white shirt, open at the collar. Man of the people. The common touch.

'Crane,' blared the publicity on a backdrop behind him. *'Stop the rot.'*

The noise started to subside. An expectant hush descended.

'We're here tonight,' Crane began, 'because something's wrong. You know it. I know it.'

He paused. Worked the silence.

'Yes, ladies and gentlemen, we're angry. About what our great country has become. About where this country is going. It's not just the mortgage rates that no one can afford, or the creaking NHS, or the sky-high borrowing. It's also the lack of responsibility, the bloated welfare state, and the woke cancel culture.'

He pointed to the backdrop.

'Ladies and gentlemen, we need change! That's why I'm here. To fix it. To lead. To win. And to stop. The damn. Rot.'

'Stop the rot! Stop the rot!' the crowd chanted like it was gospel.

Cal flicked the TV off with a snap. Grabbed his leather jacket from the back of the chair and headed for the lift. At the concierge desk, the girl looked up.

'Mr Grant?'

He paused. 'Yeah?'

'You're in room 101?'

'That's me.'

'There's a note for you.'

He frowned. 'A note?'

'A woman, Alice Wickman, called. Said she got your message, and five o'clock is fine.'

'What message?' Cal glanced at his battered Omega. It was now 17.03. He hadn't left any message about changing the time. As far as he was aware, they were not supposed to meet for another twenty-seven minutes.

'What else did she say?'

'Nothing else. Just that she'd see you at five.' She gave him a sheepish look. 'Sorry, we tried your room but you weren't answering.'

Puzzled, he hurried out into the street and hailed a cab.

20

At the exact moment Cal was leaving the hotel, Alice was watching through the plate glass partition as a guy asked for her at Reception. He was preppily dressed, in a crisp Barbour jacket with all the pockets intact, and pressed jeans. It looked promising.

'Grant,' she heard him say. 'Jonathan Grant.'

She stood, smoothing her skirt, and walked out to meet him.

'Mr. Grant?'

They shook hands. Warm grip. Cool eyes.

'Sorry to mess you about like this,' he said, flashing an easy smile. 'But as I explained to your assistant, something came up.'

Alice smiled back. He was cute-looking. That's what she liked about this particular branch of Knight Frank. South Kensington attracted the right kind of clientele. No one walked in here with much under two mill to spend.

'It's fine,' she said. 'I had a cancellation. Worked out well. It's easier to meet in the office. Still looking for a three-bed? Your budget might need to stretch a bit, though.'

He nodded, and she sensed him watching her as she turned to grab a set of keys from a row of hooks on the wall. She tucked her dark hair behind her ears and caught her reflection in the mirror.

'After you,' he said, holding the door. She stepped out, heels tapping crisply on the stone.

'So Kate recommended me, did she?' Alice said as they walked.

He paused. 'Sorry?'

'You mentioned on the phone that Kate Winter put you in touch.'

'Ah, yes. She did.'

She raised an eyebrow, amused. 'That's a first.'

She stopped on the curb alongside a pink jeep. 'This is me. Do you have wheels?'

'I'll meet you there. Is it far?'

She gave him the address - *just around the corner,* she reassured him - and sped off. A few minutes later, they met again on the doorstep of a large, red brick mansion block. She led the way up the stairs to the first floor and ushered him into the flat. The rooms were empty and echoey, the faint scent of vacuum cleaner and cheap freshener hanging in the air.

She rattled through her routine. Touch button dimmable lighting, retractable blinds, views over the communal garden - a plus, she reminded him. When they reached the kitchen, she motioned to the appliances.

'All brand new. Fridge, washer-dryer. Included in the price.'

He studied her. 'Haven't we met somewhere before?'

She turned. Damn, he was fit. She felt herself flushing.

'Don't think so,' she said lightly, reaching for a cupboard. 'And up here's the boiler.'

She stretched to open it, conscious of a wet patch beneath her armpits.

'Gas central heating. Also heats the water.' She tapped it. 'Volkera. Good make, actually, no problem with spares.'

'Tara. That was it. With Tara something… hell, what was her surname?'

She frowned. 'Never met a Tara. You sure you've got the right woman?'

'Tall. Blonde. An actor friend of Kate's.'

She shrugged. 'Sounds like Sofie. Sofie James. But I don't think she acts.' A beat. 'How do you know Kate, anyway?'

'We worked on a story together. On a drug called Imagine. She ever tell you about it?'

'Nope...don't think so. Mind you, I've got a terrible memory.'

Which was true. Nothing stuck. Kate could have told her she had won the Pulitzer Prize, and she would have forgotten the next day.

'So what's Sofie up to these days?' he went on. 'It would be good to catch up with her again.'

'Coincidentally, I saw her at Kate's place the other day. Lives in Stoke Newington, I think. I can probably dig out her email address. If I *have* to,' she added, flirting.

He chuckled. 'You're right. What are we talking about her for? Why don't I buy you dinner tonight?'

She stopped and stared at him. And giggled.

'That's hardly professional, Mr Grant.'

'Sod professional. Please, call me Jonathan.'

She hesitated.

'I won't bite,' he pressed. 'I'm only in town for a couple of days. I like meeting new people.'

She made a face. 'What kind of a line is that?'

They watched each other. She, awkward, he with a smile playing around his lips.

'Well,' he said finally. 'What do you say?'

His neat black curls *were* rather cute. Why not? Nothing ventured, nothing gained, etc. After all, if she could snare his business, her cut would be enough for a ski trip and a new coat.

~

SHE COULD SMELL THE ALCOHOL AS HE REACHED DOWN to her.

'Jonathan.... this is very naughty...' she murmured, half laughing.

He shut her front door with his foot, swung her against the wall, and kissed her hard.

'You taste good,' he whispered.

Her hands dangled. He laced his fingers through hers, kissed her again.

'When do you think she'll call you back?' he asked. 'Perhaps she's left a message on your answerphone?'

She pulled away from him.

'You've got a thing for her, haven't you?'

He didn't answer. It was, now Alice stopped to think about it, a bit odd. He'd made her call Sofie from the restaurant. Had said he wanted to surprise her. Alice had been reluctant at first, but eventually she'd been persuaded, tipsy as she was. Being almost out of battery, she'd left her landline number on Sofie's voicemail, with a message about a mystery friend - *no names, insisted Jonathan, let's surprise her* - who wanted to get in touch. She had also, surreptitiously, texted Sofie when he'd gone to the toilet:

'Sry for WEIRD vm. Call me for a debrief.'

She'd also seen something else, but she was, by that time, too drunk to think too much about it.

Now, back in her flat 'for coffee', she wasn't so sure about any of it. She slipped from his arms and walked unsteadily towards the kitchen.

'Jonathan, I'm not sure this is such a good idea.'

Her high heels echoed on the bare floorboards as she went to check her landline.

'Nope,' she called out. 'No messages. How do you like your coffee?'

She watched warily out of the corner of her eye as he took off his coat and pulled a bottle out of the pocket. As she rummaged for a capsule, he came up behind her. Placed the bottle on the counter and put his arms around her neck, nuzzling her. She turned.

'Where did you get that?'

'Never you mind.'

She laughed. 'You do realise how drunk I am?'

He nipped her neck seductively. 'Uh-huh.'

Without letting go of her, he twisted the wire off the top of the bottle. The cork started to move, slowly at first, then with a sudden rush. It shot up to the ceiling with a pop, and the champagne frothed over the rim. He brought it up to her mouth. She wriggled in his arms, trying to avoid it, but he had her pinned from behind. Finally, she twisted away, giggling.

'Get the fuck off!'

'I thought you liked bubbles?'

'I love bubbles, but… Jonathan? What are you doing?'

She felt him behind her, pressing into her again. She tried to turn, but the weight of him on her was too great.

'Stop it.' She gulped. 'Please...'

She twisted around more forcefully this time and pushed

him away from her, scattering a packet of sugar and a pile of teabags onto the floor. On impulse, she picked up a cheap disposable camera that someone had given her at a party.

'Smile,' she said, squinting through the viewfinder, and before he could stop her, it flashed.

He lunged, snatching it away. She backed up, startled.

He slipped it into his pocket. 'Sorry, I don't like photos.'

Across the room, they stared at each other. Neither spoke. Like two animals facing off in an arena.

Finally, she tilted her head. 'Why did your card say Charles Gebler?'

He didn't move, his face unreadable.

'Your credit card. In the restaurant.'

His eyes narrowed. 'What were you doing looking in my wallet?'

'I'm sorry... I was being nosy, that's all. It was in your coat. When you went to the bathroom. I don't know anything about you except that you know Kate and Sofie.' She caught her breath, suddenly sensing danger. 'You *do* know them, right?'

'You shouldn't have.'

She gave him a weak smile.

'Curiosity killed the cat?'

His expression had gone cold. Pushing himself off the wall, he came slowly over to her. She flinched.

'Charles... Jonathan...' she said uneasily, 'whatever your name is...'

She tensed as he ran his hand along the inside of her thigh. She needed to end this. Get him out of her flat. It had been a mistake.

'What part of no do you not understand?'

He broke off, seemed to deflate. She grabbed the

champagne and took a shaky sip.

'Lucky for you, those weren't my holiday snaps. You'd be dead otherwise. Listen, I think it's time you went.' She glanced at the kitchen clock. 'I've got an early start tomorrow, got a guy coming who…'

She trailed off as the landline started to ring. They didn't move, both listening. One ring, two rings, three. The machine whirred and clicked into action. The voice was male.

'This is a message for Alice. I left one at your office earlier.'

For a second, she wondered why on earth a client would be calling her so late. She hated to be bothered on her mobile in the evenings, but on the other hand, she never wanted to miss a deal, so her extension was forwarded to her home landline out of office hours. But they rarely called this late.

'It's Jonathan Grant.'

Her blood ran cold.

'You didn't show. What happened? I waited until seven. Call me first thing in the morning. Room 101. It's quite urgent.'

He left a number and the message ended. Neither spoke.

He stepped forward. She backed away, then brought her hands down to his shoulders to fend him off.

'Let go! *Who are you*?'

There was something new in her tone now. Frightened.

'Please... get off... *get off!*'

She tried to push him away, but he brought his hands up to her mouth, viciously slamming her head back against the cupboards. The suddenness of it caught her unawares, but then she began to scream, her eyes wide in terror. The bottle crashed to the floor, smashing into pieces. He struggled to muffle her, while his other hand scrabbled for one of the linen tea towels that were hanging on a rack above him. Finally, he had it and, swiftly, he took his hand off her mouth, grabbed the other end of the cloth, and before she had a chance to react, lunged with it up towards her neck. He jammed it hard against her windpipe, forcing her chin up. She squirmed and struggled, choking, the blood rising in her face, her body pinned beneath his. Her arms flailed against him frantically. Eyes bulging. He didn't let up, pressing against her like a vice, teeth gritted.

Slowly, she lost her strength. It ebbed from her, all sound cut off, helpless. He didn't ease up, remaining there for a full minute, the line of the cloth etched into her skin. Finally, he let go, pulling away from her gently. Her body fell forward and slumped to the floor.

To join the sugar, the teabags and a dying fizz of champagne.

21

Sunday 30th October

It was three o'clock in the morning when Sofie gave up pretending sleep was even an option. As soon as she'd returned from Kate's flat, she had mixed herself a large vodka and tonic, followed by another, until her nerves felt thoroughly anaesthetised.

Something else was keeping her up, though. The voicemail. Alice Wickman, barely more than an acquaintance, had left a cryptic message. Some guy was in town, said he hadn't seen Sofie in years, wanted to reconnect. Alice had been showing him a property and asked if Sofie could call her landline.

Then came the text: *'Sry for WEIRD vm. Call me for debrief.'*

Weird didn't begin to cover it.

She turned the whole thing over and over in her head until eventually she drifted into a shallow, uneasy sleep. It lasted about thirty minutes before a ringing dragged her back. Half asleep, she grabbed her phone. Alice again? The police?

'Hello?'

Nothing. It was dead.

Somewhere outside, the ringing continued. Then, abruptly, it stopped.

She went back to bed, perplexed. Just as she began to fade again, another ring.

And that's when it clicked.

The fax machine.

Of course! Her father's ancient contraption was still somewhere in the flat, a dusty relic he could never bear to part with. There was a switch, she remembered, that activated the receiving end if it.

Stumbling out of bed, she groped around and finally found it. Too late. The ringing stopped. She swore to herself. Who uses faxes anymore, anyway? What a dinosaur her dad had been, clinging on to all this old tech.

Wide awake now, she held her breath in case whoever it was tried a third time, and sure enough, it began once more. This time, she was ready. It cut off at three rings, and there was a soft click. She strained to listen. A municipal truck clanked and groaned in the street outside. When it had moved on, she caught the faint ticker-ticker-ticker of transmission.

She rushed over. A page slid out. Then another. WTF? At three in the morning?

The first page was a grainy photocopy from a newspaper called the Daily Nation. Someone had scribbled a date across the top: *3rd October.*

'The inquest was held yesterday into the deaths of Jimmy Nzugu and Joseph Malindi, killed when their car ran out of control near Willowbrook Mall and ploughed into a wall on October 10th. Witnesses say the occupants were drunk and made no attempt to brake the vehicle, but police found no traces of alcohol in their blood at the time of the accident. Nzugu, the driver, was president of the Naivasha

AIDS Support Committee. An open verdict was recorded.'

Underneath, someone had written in all caps: *'BOTH PATIENTS OF DR WILLIAM MWANGI, NAIVASHA, KENYA.'*

She gulped.

The second page was from The Kenyan Standard, dated October 4th.

'A boy of ten was killed and two women injured Saturday night when a man in his early thirties burst into a store in Westlands and sprayed staff and customers with semi-automatic gunfire. The man, believed to come from Mombasa, was overpowered by staff and arrested by an off-duty detective. He is due to appear in court today. There was no apparent motive. However, unconfirmed reports suggest that the man may have been suffering from terminal cancer. If so, this would be the third cancer-related murder in the city in recent months.'

The words *'The man, believed to come from Mombasa'* had been ringed by a thick black marker pen, and a line led to a handwritten name: *Peter Kisorio.* After it was scrawled *'patient of Dr M, Nairobi'*, with the sentence *'Your father would have been proud of you.'*

She dropped onto the sofa, heart now pounding for an entirely different reason.

She thought back to that conversation on the boat. The drug trial. The list of patients the chemists had mentioned. And now these faxes. Erratic deaths, violent behaviour. Something no clinical trial report would ever admit to.

The question wasn't just what to do next.

It was who had sent this.

And why now?

22

DC Khan was on the weekend shift. As she drove to work through the empty Sunday morning streets, caffeine coursing through her veins, her mind wouldn't stop circling back to the girl.

Twenty-four hours had elapsed since she was brought in. The case, on the surface, was done and dusted. But several things bothered her.

First, the lab report that had come in late the night before. Alcohol, sure. Sofie had been drinking, no surprise there. But what stood out was the adrenaline. Sky-high epinephrine. No matching stimulant, no drugs to explain it. Just one conclusion from the lab tech: a sudden, sharp shock. Somewhere in the last four hours before she was brought in, something had jolted her system hard.

Second, her GP. Khan had contacted him purely for notification, standard welfare protocol. The doctor confirmed a history of mild depression, nothing alarming. It started after her father's death. But this? This wasn't part of the pattern. She wasn't a liar, he'd said, not someone prone to drama or delusions. In his words, she was "resilient."

She'd fought her way out on her own.

So why lie now? What would possess someone to invent a story like that?

Khan had been taught from day one that motive is everything.

She turned onto Trafalgar Road, eyes flicking over the usual blur of signs. And then paused. Hoskins Street. She'd seen it on the map in the interview room, Bates pointing it out to Sofie. At the time, she'd barely registered it. But now it pulled at her.

Impulsively, cutting the indicator, she drove towards the river. There was time enough. She was curious to see for herself.

She parked the Ford Fiesta next to Lovell's Wharf and walked along the towpath, towards where Sofie James said the shooting took place. It was high tide, and the muddy, debris-laden waters of the river lapped against a scummy beach. No one was about. The former riverside wharf was half derelict. It certainly matched Sofie's description. A man in a pair of rust-red trousers and an old sweater was clambering about on a river craft moored alongside a small jetty. As soon as he saw her, he stopped, straightening up.

'Hey there!' he called. 'Over here!'

Was he shouting at her?

'Hey!' he yelled again.

She picked her way between an oil drum and an upturned supermarket trolley, descending cautiously onto the pontoon.

'Things are improving,' he boomed gruffly as she approached. 'I didn't expect them to send anyone. You are a copper, right?'

Khan looked up at him, puzzled. Was it that obvious?

'I'm a detective,' she said.

He nodded like that confirmed something.

'That's good then, because there's a crime wave on. Fat lot of good filing a report. Me, I'm just a statistic.'

'Sorry, I don't follow. I'm not here to meet anyone.'

'You're not?'

'No, I'm just taking a look around.'

'Really? Got time for that sort of thing, have you? Well, I'm glad you're here, love, because I want to report a break-in. On my boat. I've already phoned. Very offhand, they were.'

'This yours?' Khan asked.

She couldn't be sure without going over the statement, but the cabin cruiser seemed to fit Sofie's description. When the patrol car had been down two nights previously, they'd reported finding nothing even remotely like it.

'Yeah. Someone took it out, by the looks of it, left it in a hell of a mess. Kids no doubt.'

Khan climbed up beside him into the cockpit.

'Anything missing?'

'Dunno yet. But I don't keep much on her, you know, nothing valuable. I've had trouble like this before. But see this? They've smashed the doors.'

She followed him. Inside, it looked tidy. There was little evidence that teenagers had been in there. No empty beer cans, no cigarette butts, no wrappers. But the catch on the door that led towards the bows had been wrenched away from the wood.

'Have you contacted your insurance company?'

The man turned, bristling.

'Listen, just because I'm insured doesn't mean these little hooligans shouldn't be given a good hiding.' He sniffed. 'But no, nothing seems to be missing. It's weird. Look at this.'

He led her through to the forward cabin and pointed to a sliding door. It was split right down the middle, as if someone had put a boot through it. A chunk of wood had broken away from the frame.

'Somebody's gone and smashed it, for no reason at all.'

He was about to throw the little brass catch across, but Khan stopped him.

'Wait. Don't touch it. We might be able to lift prints.'

He looked at her blankly. 'Oh dear, I...er...I've touched it already.'

'That's OK, but best not do it again. Now...' she said, turning back. 'When do you think this happened?'

He followed her, scratching his armpit vigorously.

'Well, look, I don't get down here much, could have been anytime in the last week. But I checked the engine to see if it was taken out, and it looks like it has been, and recently. There's a small pool of oil in the bilge, still wet. Plus, these covers here,' he smacked the tartan fabric on the seats, 'feel that? They're damp. Some fucker's,' he stumbled, 'scuse my French, love, some bloke's obviously poured something on it. I'd say within the last forty-eight hours at the outside.'

'There doesn't seem to be a stain,' Khan said, examining the fabric. 'It's not like kids to clean up after them, is it?'

'Tell me about it,' he muttered. 'World's gone mad.'

DC Khan shook her head professionally.

'You find anything that doesn't belong? Anything odd?'

'Like what?'

'Bullet casings.'

He blinked. 'Bloody hell. Not that I've seen. But I'll have a…'

'No,' she cut in. 'Please don't. We may need forensics to

sweep the place.' She took out her notebook. 'Now, how do we get in touch with you?'

She jotted down his name and contact details and left. As she walked back toward the car, she allowed herself the smallest flicker of satisfaction.

Perhaps her hunch had proved correct.

23

Cal dialled the Knight Frank number and eased the hotel phone between his shoulder and jaw as he doodled on a notepad. It was 9.30 am, and he was not expecting anyone to be there on a Sunday, but he had decided to leave another message on Alice's voicemail.

To his surprise, someone picked up.

'Knight Frank.'

He straightened. 'Hi. Can you put me through to Alice Wickman's extension?'

A pause.

'Hold on.'

The line went dead. After a few moments, a male voice came on.

'Hello, can I help you?'

'Yes, my name's Grant. Jonathan Grant. I had an appointment with Alice Wickman yesterday afternoon for a viewing. We were supposed to meet at the property, but missed each other. I'd like to reschedule.'

A beat.

'Hello?' Cal prompted.

'Just a moment, Mr Grant.' The line dropped again.

Then: 'I understand you wish to speak to Miss Wickman?'

The voice was different now. Clipped, more authoritative.

'Well, I wasn't expecting her to be in,' he said. He was beginning to feel mildly irritated. 'I simply wanted to leave a message.'

'You were due to see her yesterday evening at... let me see now… five, is that right?'

'No, five-thirty.'

'Five thirty?' queried the voice.

'Correct.'

'Did you meet up with her, Mr Grant?'

Cal hesitated. 'Did I meet Alice? No, she didn't show. Look, can you put me through or not? What's going on?'

'And how long did you wait for her, Mr Grant? What did you do when she didn't appear?'

'And you are?'

'Detective Inspector Burroughs, Kensington CID. We're investigating her murder.'

He caught his breath. *'Murder?'*

'That's right, Mr Grant, last night, and it may be that you were the last person to have seen her alive. Would you be able to come down to the station to answer a few questions?'

His mind froze. Murdered? He wasn't ready for this. He needed time to think.

'Mr. Grant, are you there?'

He made a snap decision. He hung up and dialled a number on his burner phone.

'Hello?' said a familiar voice.

'Frank, it's Cal.'

'Oh, hi. What's happening? Not seen you around for a while. Emily says you've gone to Oslo.'

'I need to see you. Are you home?'

'Today? Well…'

'It's important. Something's happened. I need your help. Wait for me. I'll be back in a couple of hours.'

And before Frank could say anything more, Cal ended the call.

He was already on his feet.

24

A LINE HAD FORMED AT THE ATM. SOFIE WAITED PATIENTLY behind a lanky kid in a threadbare hoodie, smoking a roll-up and nodding in time to his headphones. When it was her turn, she punched in her PIN code and withdrew a small bundle of cash.

Next stop was an electronics shop, where she used half of it to buy a secondhand phone.

Outside, a light wind was gusting. She ducked into a cafe for breakfast. Picking up a discarded copy of the Evening Standard, she sipped at a coffee. She had to be patient. It was only a matter of time before they traced Kate. A missing journalist? They'd be all over Cambridge Bio like a rash. *Then* they'd take her seriously. Surely.

But she still harboured a niggling doubt. Ukraine. What was that all about? And why, if Kate had been investigating Cambridge Bio, did the Sunday Times claim they knew nothing about it? Either someone was lying, or…

Or what?

It was past eleven by the time she left. To the north, the sky had a face of iron. The forecast was rain. As she climbed the stairs to her flat, she heard her landline ringing.

She got the door open, fumbled with the keys, breathless. 'Hello?'

'Miss James? DC Khan speaking.'

Sofie paused to get her breath back. 'Oh, hi.'

'Where have you been? We asked you to stay available for questioning. I've been calling you.'

Sofie dropped her bag to the floor. 'Yeah, I know. I had to step out. Got a new mobile. You'll get me quicker on that from now on.'

A pause. Then: 'Are you able to come down to the station in about an hour?'

Sofie's heart leapt. 'Why? Did you find something?'

Khan's voice was unreadable. 'Purely routine. Miss James. I'd appreciate it if you'd come in right away.'

'Of course. On my way. But what about your colleague? He doesn't believe me, does he? Thinks I'm wasting your time. Is he still insisting Kate's in Ukraine? Because that's impossible, I was with her.'

'Miss James, all I can tell you is that some new information may have come to light.'

Sofie did a swift turnaround and was back at the police station by one-thirty. The light was duller now, the sun shut out behind a menacing battalion of clouds. Against the solid black of the sky, the pillar-box red of London's buses created surreal images. In another world, at another time, she would have whipped her camera out. But not today. Today, she barely noticed. DC Khan was waiting outside the station.

'Glad you're finally taking me seriously,' Sofie huffed.

'My car's round the back. Mind riding with me?'

'Where are we going?'

'The river. I want you to show me where it happened.'

The detective led her to a maroon Vauxhall Astra parked behind the building.

On the way there, Khan said little, occasionally making a small-talk remark that Sofie barely acknowledged. She was pretty, in her late 20s, Sofie guessed, her jet-black hair scraped back behind her ears and held in place with a brown tortoiseshell clip. She tried to imagine what it was that attracted an Asian woman to join the Met. All things considered.

Ten minutes later, they turned into Hoskins Street and pulled up at Lovell's Wharf.

'This shouldn't take long,' DC Khan said, slipping the keys from the ignition. 'If it's the cabin cruiser you remember, we'll get forensics down here and organise for you to do a Photofit.'

Sofie felt a surge of adrenaline. 'You mean you've found it?'

'Let's not get ahead of ourselves,' Khan replied. 'Now, try to think back to what happened that night. Where was the party boat moored, and which way did you go when you disembarked?'

'God, I hope I can,' Sofie said. 'Recognise it, I mean. It was dark. I'd had a few drinks. But I'll try.'

They walked towards the river's edge. Before them, the old pontoon rocked gently on the water, stanchions empty. Sofie shuddered involuntarily. The surface was getting choppy, little white horses whipped off the waves by the gathering storm.

'There,' Sofie said, pointing. 'That's where we docked.'

Khan scanned the space. 'OK. So you got off the boat with your friend and the two men, and you walked...' she looked about in the fading light '...in which direction?'

'Like I say, it was nighttime. I'm not one hundred per

cent sure.'

'Take your time.'

Sofie squinted. By the light of day, everything felt unfamiliar. Next to the pontoon, she noticed a litter of broken glass strewn against a brick wall. A mass of weeds pushed up between the roughly hewn stones that made up the embankment. Apart from the road, there was only one other way out: the towpath, leading downriver.

She pointed. 'I guess that's where we went.'

They moved off single-file, gravel crunching under Khan's white trainers. The breeze had teeth now, and it bit harder the closer they got to the water, pregnant with the promise of rain.

After a hundred yards, the jetty came into view. And with it, the smell, an overpowering reek of diesel. Sofie's stomach churned. The tide was higher than she remembered, the pontoon closer, but the steps were familiar. Details came rushing back - how cold it had been, how weird she'd felt, clutching that bottle of champagne in an evening dress by the derelict wharf as she waited, shivering, while the men nervously scanned their surroundings.

'This is it,' she said suddenly. 'Down here.'

~

DC KHAN HAD DELIBERATELY OVERSHOT, AS A TEST TO SEE whether Sofie would recognise the place. Now she walked back to where Sofie was standing. Below, a couple of boats bobbed against their moorings.

'That's the one,' Sofie said again, pointing. 'The one with the blue awning. We came down these steps here.'

A peal of thunder rumbled somewhere to the east.

'You're sure about that?'

'Yes. The sign. For Hire. That's it.'

They started down the steps. The cruiser bumped lightly against a line of tyres, rhythmic and insistent, like a sulky child demanding attention. But halfway down, Khan stopped short.

'You mean this one?' she asked.

Sofie looked again. Hesitated. 'I think so.'

But she no longer sounded so certain.

Khan's heart sank. It wasn't the boat she'd seen just hours before. The boat she'd boarded.

Of that, there was no sign. It had disappeared.

25

The train to Ipswich was late. By the time Cal arrived, it was nearly 2 pm, and he'd missed the connection to Woodbridge. He jumped in a cab, and forty minutes later they pulled into the gravel sweep outside Frank's farmhouse. A lazy wisp of smoke was curling up from the chimney, the ground thick with autumn leaves like a rust-coloured quilt. He paid the driver, grabbed his duffel from the backseat, and crossed the yard to his caravan. The place was freezing. He took a quick shower, changed into a new set of clothes, and got a fire going in the little wood stove while texting Frank.

'You free? Good to come over?'

No reply. He poked the fire into life, tightened the vents, and headed out into the wind. The air was sharp, salty, and biting: classic Suffolk on the coast.

He didn't bother to knock.

'Hello?' he called, stepping into the house. He could smell roasting meat.

Emily emerged from a room to the left wearing yellow rubber gloves. She was a small woman in her mid-thirties, slim with delicate hands, elegant and restrained. She looked like she belonged in a magazine ad for very expensive soap. Her fine chestnut hair was worn short and immaculately styled, and around her neck, over a roll-neck cream cashmere sweater, she wore a single string of pearls.

She gave him a polite smile and a perfunctory peck on the cheek.

'I thought you were in Oslo?' she said.

Neither pleased nor displeased to see him. She simply tolerated him, Cal mused, as she did all Frank's old army buddies. Though even that was running thin. It would be so much easier if he could flirt with her. He'd tried it once. Did not go well.

'Next week. That's the plan, anyway. How's Aga life?'

She smiled thinly. 'All good here, thanks. Have you eaten?'

Which meant: Please tell me you've eaten so I don't have to feed you.

'Yeah. Grabbed something on the train.'

'OK, well, if you'll forgive me, must get back to it.' She glanced at her Cartier watch. 'If you're looking for Francis, he's up in the back field.'

Always Francis for his family and civvy friends, only his army mates called him Frank. Cal grabbed a coat from the cloakroom and let himself out through the garden door. Fine skeins of moisture glistened on the hedgerows, and the clods of mud in the fields had flecks of white like petrified seahorses. However, Cal was in no state to appreciate this finest of English scenes. He pushed up the field towards a small hill, scanning the horizon for any sign of his friend.

He reached a fence and halted. The view was breathtaking, stretching for mile after patchwork mile of greens and rusts and browns, the River Deben meandering towards the sea in the distance.

He called Frank's name. Still nothing. He peered along the crest of the hill. Emily had said he was birdwatching, but the nearest clump of trees was three hundred yards away.

He trudged on, muttering to himself, his feet getting heavier with the damp earth building up on them like concrete. When he reached the edge of the copse, he let out a wolf whistle.

'Frank? You there?'

'Be quiet, can't you?' hissed a voice, followed by a clatter of wings as something large and brown shot out of the undergrowth and soared away along the ridge. 'Bugger!'

Frank's wiry figure emerged from the trees. His usual reserve was rattled.

'You bloody flushed it, you dickhead!'

'Sorry.'

'That was a blue bill, a once-a-year Suffolk tick.'

'Look, sod the birds,' Cal snapped, exasperated. 'I need to talk. It's serious.'

'Must be,' growled Frank, straightening up. 'Shall we go in? Go on ahead of me, will you? I need to close the gates.'

~

THEY REGROUPED IN WHAT FRANK PRETENTIOUSLY REFERRED to as his 'library'. It boasted four small shelves of books, mostly trashy novels and bird manuals. The rest of the room was taken up with piles of cardboard boxes.

'More junk, I see,' Cal remarked. 'Had a new delivery?'

'Samples,' Frank said, pouring himself a drink. 'I'm brokering a deal.'

Cal peered into an open box and pulled out a sleek

black plug. He turned it over. On the underside was a USB socket.

'Phone chargers?'

'Officially, yes.' He pointed to a small hole in the flat surface. 'But see that? That's a wide-angle lens. It records audio and video. If you position it in the right place, you get a view of an entire room.' Frank put it back in the box and picked up a tiny widget from the table beside it. A short aerial was sticking out of it. 'Got a bunch of these, too. The world's smallest Bluetooth earpiece.'

'Clearly, I'm out of the loop these days. In my line of work, they're still using walkie-talkies.'

Frank smiled. 'Never too late to come aboard, you know.'

Frank had been asking Cal to join his business - trading military-grade comms gear - ever since they'd left the army together. It had been a tempting proposition at the time. But Cal had a phobia about being tied down.

He didn't take the bait. Instead, he picked up a framed photograph from a side table. Five guys and two girls, posing around a jeep in battle fatigues.

'I heard from Rob the other day,' he said.

'Oh yeah? How's the cab business?'

'So-so. Wants to visit. About time we got the Deniables back together again. It's been too long.'

There had been seven of them in their old squad in the SRR, the Special Reconnaissance Regiment. Frank as a captain, Cal as his corporal-turned-sergeant. The last time they'd had a reunion, Emily hadn't talked to her husband for three days. They had all got blind drunk, rampaging around the Suffolk countryside and writing off Emily's little Mini in the process. As for the name they'd given themselves, the Deniables, it came from 'off-grid' operations they were sometimes called up to do as members of the army's reserve list.

Frank chuckled. 'Not sure Redtop would dare show her face again.'

Sam Le Roux, a Glaswegian cyber specialist now living in Amsterdam with her Brazilian girlfriend, had been the driver of the Mini. They called her Redtop Le Rouge on account of her flame red hair.

Frank's grin faded as he caught the tension in Cal's face.

'So what did you want to discuss so urgently?'

Cal put back the frame. 'Bottom line is, I'm in a shit load of merde. I need your help.'

Frank raised an eyebrow. 'You do know that 'merde' is redundant with 'shit'? It's called a tautology.'

Normally, Cal would've made a smartass comment back. Not today.

'I told you I'd started working for Cambridge Bio, right?'

He explained about the VIPs he was supposed to be protecting; the party on the boat and meeting the girl; and how Gebler had pulled him away when he'd followed them ashore and sent him back to the hotel to await their return.

'Don't tell me,' Frank said, lighting up a small cigar and puffing vigorously to get it going. 'They didn't show up.'

'No. And there was a report of a shooting.'

Frank regarded him impassively from behind a screen of smoke.

'Was it confirmed?'

'Not to my knowledge. The police came down, apparently, and found nothing. The boat had gone, there were no witnesses, no one knew diddlysquat.'

'So what did your man, Gebler, do?'

'That's just it. Not a lot. As far as I know, they didn't

even report the men's disappearance. Now they seem very keen to fast-track me to Oslo for the next gig.'

Frank frowned. 'Anything to do with Crane's leadership race, do you suppose?'

'Almost certainly. But why pull me away? It's like they knew something was coming. Like they didn't want me to see it.'

Frank nodded slowly. 'What do they know about you?'

'About me?'

'Cambridge Bio. Presumably, they are aware of your background?'

'The army, sure. Why do you think I got hired?'

Frank walked to the window, hands behind his back. Outside, the light was beginning to fade. 'That girl you met. Could she have been involved?'

'Doubt it. Said she was an actor.'

'So there you are, an actor. What about the other one?'

'No idea, never talked to her.'

Frank turned, eyes sharp now. 'It's got to be more than simply the leadership election, Cal. Think about it. The risk of a cover-up getting out and damaging Crane is far greater than if they'd been straight.'

'That's the conclusion I came to,' Cal said. 'And it gets worse.'

He told Frank about his own investigation; about the estate agent; the missed meeting; and his conversation with the police.

'Fuck Cal, *murdered*?'

'That's what they said. Before I hung up in them.'

Frank shot him a look.

'What? What else could I do? It's obvious. Someone knew I was meeting her and got to her first, posing as me.'

Frank sat, silent for a beat. Then: 'We need to talk to

Vauxhall.'

'MI6?'

'I've got a contact. Any other electronics?'

Cal blinked. 'What do you mean?'

'Smart speaker, back-up smartphone, Fitbit?'

It was then that it hit him.

'Shit! Gebler gave me a work phone. What if it had a listening device?'

Frank looked alarmed. 'Where is it now?'

'In the caravan. But don't worry, it's switched off.'

'No guarantee, mate. Could have enhanced tracking software, so that even when it's powered down, they can track its position.' He shook his head. 'And what if they've manufactured evidence tying you to that murder?'

'Such as?'

'Does it matter? It'll be stuff you're not even aware of.' He swivelled his chair and stood up. 'Come on, first we need to get rid of it. Then I'll make some calls.'

26

As DC Khan stepped back into the station, a scent of stale coffee greeted her. She'd just dropped Sofie at the bus stop-or rather, watched her storm off into the rain-and her head was still buzzing.

It didn't make sense.

Just hours before, she'd been aboard a boat that almost exactly fitted Sofie's description. Yet it was a different boat, and a different guy, that had greeted them both just now, and this one had a solid alibi: he had arrived from Henley an hour ago, where the boat had been docked for three months straight. Sofie had desperately wanted it to be the one, but they quickly discovered it had no forward cabin.

Meanwhile, the other man, the one she'd talked to earlier, had disappeared. His phone disconnected.

They had a long way to go, Khan told Sofie as she pulled over. Sofie didn't take it well. Slammed the door and walked off. Could Khan blame her? Not really.

'Ah, there you are,' the duty-sergeant called out as he passed her in the corridor, munching on a Twix. 'Batesy's on the warpath. You'd better go see him sharpish. He sounds right peeved.'

Khan knew exactly what was coming. Bates would want answers. The name of the boat, the name of the owner. But all she had was 'Jim' and a mobile number that had gone dead sometime in the last hour. Had she taken it down wrong? It didn't look good. She could hear him now, fuming: *You call yourself a detective?*

She slid into her chair and dialled his extension with a knot tightening in her chest. Outside, peals of thunder broke overhead, the rain hammering on the window with ever-increasing frequency. Absent-mindedly, she glanced up at the TV flickering on the wall. It was tuned to the ITV news, and was showing a scene from eastern Ukraine.

She did a double-take.

'Bates here,' came a gravelly voice in her ear.

But Khan didn't answer.

Her eyes remained glued to the screen.

27

Sofie was getting drenched. The rain was driving sideways, stinging her face, her coat soaked through. But she hardly noticed. She was fuming with frustration. How could they do this to her? There had been solid evidence. The policewoman said so, had seen it with her own eyes. Or so she said. But when it came to the crunch, she'd backed off.

She stopped to shelter under an awning, fifty yards short of a bus stop, wiping water from her eyes with a soggy sleeve. The thunder rumbled, and an answering flash of anger erupted within her. It wasn't just that they didn't want to believe her. It was more than that. They were utterly clueless. The policewoman was sympathetic enough, but what good was sympathy if no one was listening? They thought Kate was in Ukraine. It was delusional.

'Need a cab, love? You alright?'

A taxi had crept up beside her, its roof light off. The driver was leaning out, peering through the downpour, a thicket of raindrops beating on his roof like the pounding of a million tiny fists.

She forced a smile. 'Not sure I can afford it, where I'm

going.'

'Try me. It's the end of my shift. Might be your lucky night.'

'Stoke Newington.'

His mouth twisted. 'Ah. Sorry, love, wrong direction.'

He pulled away, tires hissing on wet asphalt.

A moment later, a 47 bus drew up at the shelter in a spray of water. She ran for it, her coat drenched, and collapsed onto the top deck.

An hour later, she was back in her flat. As soon as she'd peeled off her wet clothes, she grabbed her laptop to search for her godfather Gerald's number. She needed to act. The police weren't going to do anything. She had to find out what had happened to Kate.

The last time she had spoken to him was at her father's funeral. He had told her that if she ever needed anything, she should reach out. He worked in a bank in the City. If anyone knew anything about Cambridge Bio, it would be him.

Her email was short and casual: could he forward her some information about the pharma sector? And one company in particular. She was researching a story on them and needed it ASAP.

Next, she opened up her travel app to check train times to Dorset. She had to get out, hide away in her father's cottage for a while, until she figured out what to do. She grabbed some clothes and a couple of pairs of trainers and stuffed them in an overnight bag, along with two laptops - her father's and her own - and a charger.

She had thirty minutes to kill before she had to leave, so

she made a cup of tea and flicked on the radio.

On the news was some stuff about the situation on the eastern front in Ukraine, with a Ukrainian spokesperson followed by a military commentator. Then they moved on to something else. She was only half listening, wondering instead about her ex, Martin. It had already been two days, but it felt like a week. She knew she ought to contact him. He'd want to know.

She reached for her tea.

'Twenty-seven-year-old estate agent Alice Wickman had gone out to view a property with a client earlier in the evening and was later found dead in her West London flat. The police urgently need to trace a man called Jonathan Grant...'

Her hand jerked. The cup hit the floor and shattered. The news report merged smoothly and seamlessly into an ad break.

She didn't move. Then she felt her mobile vibrating. She stared at the wall in shock, her eyes unfocused, the commentary still singing in her ears: *'was later found dead in her West London flat.'* Her mind went racing back over the message she'd received from Alice. The *'mystery friend...'*

The phone went silent. Then started again. She flinched.

'Hello?'

'Oh, Sofie, thank God!' The man at the other end sounded breathless. 'I'm glad I've reached you. It's Ian. Listen...'

A beat. Nervousness.

'Ian? Ian, who?'

'Ian Jackson. Kate's dinner, remember?'

Her voice was flat. 'Oh.'

'Have you heard the news?'

'I just did. I'm sorry, I'm in shock. Did you call a second

ago?'

'It's unbelievable.'

He sounded shaken. But something was off. Why was he calling her? A guy she barely knew. A dinner companion of Kate's. And he was ringing minutes after the report hit the air?

'I didn't even know she was there,' he said. 'Did you?'

Sofie paused. It took a while for Ian's words to sink in.

'Where?'

'In Ukraine.'

She blinked. 'What?'

'I remember she told us she was going, but I did not know it was so soon.'

Sofie froze with a fierce sense of foreboding, her mind suddenly crystal clear. A small pool of tea had gathered at her feet.

'Ian ... who are you talking about?'

Silence. Then: 'Oh shit, you haven't heard. I thought you... Look, Sofie, this will come as a bit of a shock. Kate's dead.'

Sofie felt like the floor was tilting. '*Dead*? How do you know? Who told you?'

'No one told me. It's all over the news.'

Her voice dropped to a whisper. 'My God! It must mean they've found the body.'

Another pause.

'I don't think so. I mean, at least she wouldn't have known much. It was a mortar round, apparently.'

Sofie returned her attention to him, trying desperately to marshal her thoughts. Nothing made sense.

'Ian,' she said, voice cracking. '*What the fuck are you talking about?*'

'The Donbas, Sofie. Ukraine. They're saying it was a

direct hit.'

She involuntarily grabbed the edge of the table to steady herself, suddenly unable to breathe.

28

Cal and Frank worked fast.

While Cal dug out the Cambridge work phone from his backpack, Frank set about testing that the various CCTV cameras and movement sensors he'd set up around the farm were working properly. Although his wife hated him fussing, if he was going to leave Emily home alone, he didn't want to take any chances.

The neighbours joked he ran a spy shop out of his garage. Cal didn't joke. He got it. Anyone who'd spent time in the world they had - black ops and special forces - understood.

Satisfied, Frank headed into his workshop and grabbed a Faraday bag. A rectangular, foil-lined pouch, it turned a smartphone into a brick, useful for hiding from prying electronic eyes. He knew that it wouldn't buy them much time, but if the phone *was* being tracked, it would give them a head start.

He tossed it into a duffel bag, along with duct tape, a multi-tool, and a flashlight. Then threw the lot into the back of his Range Rover. Emily was furious.

'What d'you mean you're going away?' she said accusingly. 'When are you coming back? We've invited people over for dinner tomorrow night. Or have you forgotten already?'

Frank leaned down and planted a kiss on the top of her head. 'Darling, I'm sorry. It's an emergency.'

'Of course it's an emergency,' she shot back acidly. 'It always is with you lot.'

'I'll be back by Sunday. Monday at the latest.'

She glared at Cal.

'Is this something to do with you?'

He shifted uncomfortably.

'Unbelievable.' She spun on her heel and vanished inside.

They looked at each other. Frank shrugged.

'She'll get over it.'

But Cal feared that his days in the caravan were numbered.

They hit the road, heading north. Technically, their destination lay only seven miles southwest, but with the rivers Deben and Orwell cutting through the landscape, it was a forty-mile loop to get there. East Anglia was like that. Deceptively inconvenient.

Frank flicked on the radio. The news was on. The lead item was about a speech by Walter Crane and his vow to bring back military service. The second was about Ukraine.

'A British journalist, working on her first overseas assignment as a war correspondent, was killed by a mortar round Friday on a road in the Kramatorsk region. The Ukrainian commander for the area said that initial reports appeared to show she had strayed into an area under attack by a Russian unit. The woman, Kate Winter, 27, was working with the Sunday Times and had been in Ukraine for only two days.'

Cal sat bolt upright. 'Bloody hell! Kate Winter? That's

her!'

Frank looked over. 'That's who?'

'One of the girls from the boat.'

'But you were only with her on Friday night.'

'Precisely. That's my point. Unless there are two Kate Winters out there.'

'Can you find a photo of her?'

Cal scrolled through the online news channels on his phone. Then froze.

'Shit, Frank. It's definitely her. Says she arrived in Ukraine on Wednesday. That's impossible.'

'So she was a journalist.'

'What if she was onto something? What if the chemists I was protecting weren't being kidnapped, but silenced? And Kate was working a story?'

Frank didn't answer right away. The Orwell bridge loomed ahead, its steel girders vanishing into the dark. The road was slick from earlier rain.

'It's starting to make sense now,' Cal went on. 'Maybe she was killed that night? It ties up with the reports of a gunshot.'

'But what's the deal with Ukraine? You think it's faked?'

'It has to be.'

Frank rubbed his chin. 'If you're right, it points to some massive forces at play here. It's not easy to make up a report like that.' He paused. 'Besides, why kill her?'

'Because she must have found out something about Cambridge Bio that would damage Crane.'

'That's a big leap.'

'Is it?'

They rode in silence for a few beats.

'And the other girl? What was her name - Tara?'

'Perhaps she survived? Why else is Gebler so keen to

trace her?'

Frank flicked his indicator to overtake a truck. It was beginning to rain again, and he activated the windscreen wipers.

'So you think Cambridge Bio is behind this?'

'Well, if not Cambridge directly, then Boyd and Gebler. One thing's for sure. If she did survive, then Tara's the key.'

Half an hour later, they pulled into a truck stop a few miles short of Harwich. Sodium lights buzzed overhead. The lot was packed with lorries from all over Europe, headlights dimmed, drivers grabbing a meal or catching sleep before the night ferries.

Frank killed the engine.

'Alright,' he said. 'You're up. Good luck.'

Cal slid out of the car. Three trucks stood out: two Bulgarian, one Greek. He walked towards them.

The first was empty, the driver likely having a meal in the diner. The man in the second had his feet up on the dash, reading a magazine under an overhead light. Cal climbed the step and knocked. The window wound down a few inches.

'Evening, mate, sorry to bother you,' said Cal. 'Speak English?'

The driver squinted. 'Hello?'

'English?'

'A little.'

'I heard that there were delays on the boats. Which one are you booked on?'

The man glanced at some papers on the seat beside him.

'Twenty-three hundred tonight.'

'And no delays that you know of?'

'I don't think so.'

'OK, thanks, mate.'

Cal stepped down and rejoined Frank, out of sight in the parked Range Rover on the other side of the lorry park.

'Second on the left. Greek plates, booked on the eleven o'clock ferry.'

Frank nodded. 'Got it.'

He reached into the back seat and pulled out the Faraday bag. He took out the smartphone, powered it up and switched it to economy mode. 90% charge. That would do. Even if it wasn't host to any funky tech, the GPS would keep active for quite a while.

He grabbed the duct tape and a pair of scissors and disappeared into the darkness. Cal leaned against the side of the Rover, scanning the lot. One minute passed.

Then he caught movement: a crouched figure slipping beneath the rear wheel of the Greek truck.

Frank, doing what Frank did best.

29

Sofie stared out of the train window, motionless, her thoughts a mess. Cosy lights of country cottages flashed by in the dark. She was anything but cosy inside. She was scared.

Everything she'd learned in the past few hours had stripped away the last of her illusions. This wasn't just about convincing the police. It wasn't even about Alice anymore. It was bigger. Way bigger. Someone out there could erase evidence like it was nothing. A boat? Gone. A body? Disappeared under cover of a fake news story. If they could do all that, she realised with sickening clarity, how hard would it be to erase her?

The police were useless, minnows in a sea of sharks. And her? Collateral damage.

Alice's death hadn't been an accident. Sofie knew it now. The weird message, the surprise call, that hadn't been Alice reaching out. It had been bait. And then there was the name from the report: Jonathan Grant. She'd never heard of him. But apparently, he'd wanted to meet Alice right before she died.

Sofie shuddered. What if she'd answered that call?

Something still didn't fit, though. Why come at her through Alice? The question gnawed at her the entire ride, until somewhere past Southampton it clicked.

The pass.

Kate had written Alice's number on the back of her security pass, the one Sofie had taken to the boat party. She remembered leaving it on the table. The man she'd been talking to, Cal, must've picked it up.

So that's how they found her.

It was late when the train finally pulled into Weymouth. She normally stopped at Wool, the closest station to Ringstead, but she didn't want to face the memory. She sat very still, eyes closed and breathing evenly, as they trundled across the fateful level crossing.

Coming into Weymouth, the houses looked shuttered up. Grabbing her bag, she exited the station in search of a taxi. The seafront was quiet, just a few fast food joints doing any business they could get this late on a Sunday night. Overhead, seagulls wheeled in the wind, scavenging for stray scraps of fish and chips.

Rob Lord Taxi Company, said the sign, underneath a small top hat illuminated on the roof.

She knocked on the window. 'Can you take me to Ringstead?'

'No worries, love. Jump in.'

The driver was talkative, cheerful in that small-town, late-night kind of way, asking what brought her down, was she on holiday, etc. But her non-committal replies soon smothered his friendly attempts at conversation, and they completed the rest of the journey in silence.

When they reached the crest of the hill above the bay, he asked her where she wanted to be dropped.

'It's a cottage up the track past the caravans,' she said, giving directions. Most cabbies bailed at the village car park. Didn't want to rattle their suspension down that track. But this guy didn't blink.

'You staying up there?' he asked.

'Yeah, coming down for a few days.'

He paused. 'Shame about the gentleman who lived there. Terrible what happened.'

She caught her breath. 'You knew him?'

'Not well. Used to drive him sometimes. Hell of a nice guy.'

She took a breath.

'He was my father.'

The driver turned to look at her, face softening. 'Ah. I'm really sorry, love. Didn't know.'

They descended into the small bay, past the car park and holiday shop, and turned left onto a gravel track that ran parallel to the sea. All but a handful of houses, mostly holiday lets, were boarded up. The cottage was a few hundred metres on, set apart.

They slowed to a halt outside a rickety wooden gate. He helped her out. She reached for her bag.

'How much?'

He shook his head. 'This one's on me.'

The gesture caught her off-balance. Her eyes welled up. She hurried through the gate and let herself in.

As soon as she'd dumped her stuff, she flipped on the heating and stepped back out into the night. The garden path was overgrown, but she knew the way so well, even in the dark. Pushing on through a tangle of brambles, she emerged onto the beach.

The waves were racing up and down the shingle, hissing and sighing. She sat down on the rocks, her eyes straying to the landmarks she was so familiar with; places she'd known since childhood. To the left, the chalk cliff of White Nothe, a dark mass jutting out into the moonlit bay; to the right, across the sea, the twinkling lights of Portland Bill. Like two arms folding her in their embrace.

For the first time in days, she let herself breathe.

Nothing bad could ever happen down here. Could it?

She brushed the hair out of her eyes and glanced towards the skyline, where she knew the little chapel to be, the place they'd scattered his ashes. It was hidden from view in the darkness.

'We're going to beat this, Dad,' she murmured into the wind. 'Get justice for you. Just watch me.'

30

Monday 31st October

The next morning, an email was waiting for her.

'Sofie, nice to hear from you, glad that you're doing OK. Hope this is some help, Gerald.'

At the bottom was a long disclaimer about intended recipients under the heading 'Credit Suisse'.

She opened the attachment.

'Cambridge Bio is one of the largest drug manufacturers in the world,' it read. *'Headquartered in London, the multinational has substantial interests in the US, Europe, the Far East and Australasia, including a rapidly expanding presence in the emerging markets of southern and eastern Africa.*

Two factors have helped boost the attractiveness of Cambridge Bio as an equity investment over the past few years. The first is its research in the AIDS field, and the successful testing and marketing of Oxone-211, a maintenance drug that has since become one of only two currently available.'

Sofie looked up. She was on the deck outside the cottage, wrapped up in an old sweater of her father's. In the distance, two small children and their mother were bracing themselves against the wind, struggling along the beach with a pumpkin. For a moment, Sofie puzzled about what they would be doing on a beach with a pumpkin on a blowy day like this until she remembered it was Halloween. White seahorses blew spume in the breeze, and on the horizon, a ship was battling its way towards Portland harbour. She returned to Gerald's email.

'Second, more recently, CB launched the much publicised Beta-Complex 7, a new breed of personality drug. More commonly known as Imagine, it is used on prescription in the treatment of depression. It is also widely prescribed to those who are HIV positive in conjunction with 0-211. The launch of this medication has been so successful that there are plans to release it onto the over-the-counter market in the near future, subject to FDA approval, and there are currently secret trials being conducted into a successor drug which, it is claimed, will have much wider application.'

So was this the drug that Kate had been investigating? The one her father had been taking? The profile went on to talk about historic P/E ratios, corporate liabilities, debt repayments, *blah-di-blah-di-blah*.

Her thoughts drifted back to the fax. Why didn't the sender want to be identified? Was it her father's doctor? All she remembered was the PO Box number in Gibraltar. A quick Google search brought up nothing. She went back into the cottage and, settling down on the sofa, flipped open her father's old laptop.

It was something she'd been putting off ever since he died, fearing for her reaction. A couple of times she'd been tempted to log in, but she'd never been able to summon up the courage. Now, she realised, it could be a lifeline. All his emails were on it, and all of his contacts. Surely his doctor's details would be listed here somewhere?

The screen was dirty and smudged. She couldn't help smiling to herself. That was one of his trademarks. Along with jeans one size too big, stray white hairs in his eyebrows, and holes in his jumpers. *Oh God*, she thought, *how I miss you. Every bloody day.*

She typed in the familiar password, 'Sofie12' (*good security, Dad, and you thought I didn't know*) and skimmed over the folders and files and various half-completed accounts. He was crap at figures. But she could find no trace of a contacts file. She had no idea what had happened to his phone. Probably smashed alongside him on that railway track. She remembered that he used to have an old-fashioned address book. She kicked herself now for not having looked for it in one of the boxes of his stuff she kept in her flat in London.

Then she saw it.

A folder. Buried deep in the file directory. Labelled Cambridge.

It stared back at her like an unexploded mine. She double-tapped the keyboard, and it opened with a soft ping.

Inside were a series of documents, the most recent dated just weeks before he died.

13th January. Feeling more bullish about this experiment. Alex mailed me a new batch of the drug, hot out of the test tube. Really, I am grateful and privileged to be able to get hold of this stuff. Harry will be jealous. And guilty too. There are so many more people who could use this, who are further down the line than me.

It seems they're pleased with my reports. They've promised some $$$, too, which will come in useful. Signed a disclaimer. A small price to pay. They're trying to save lives.

It hit her like a punch in the stomach.

Further down the line than me? Was he talking about AIDS? And who the hell was Alex? Was *that* his doctor?

It had been his last entry.

She closed her eyes and took a breath, trying to control

the thumping in her chest. Slowly, it subsided. She returned to the laptop and re-read the entry again.

Which was when she registered the other name. Harry. He was a university professor and one of her father's oldest friends. She'd also had a brief fling with him when she was at Oxford. It had caused all sorts of complications.

She flipped back to the earliest file in the folder. Dated July, the previous year.

Naivasha: tried the new Cambridge drug for the first time today. Great hopes. So lucky to have Alex, with the kind of access few can get. Strange side effects, though. Feelings of euphoria and immense confidence. As if life is a game. Reminds me of the rare times when I am dreaming, and know I am dreaming, so the possibilities are extraordinary! For example, sexual. Without inhibitions or fear of retribution, you can do anything. An immense feeling of power.

She gulped. Was this really her father talking?

October 4th: My feelings toward Alex are evolving - a curious thing. I feel more in control, I am beginning to understand the kind of power I have in these situations. Also, what an illusion love is. It's a con-trick nature plays to get us together. Men are not meant to be monogamous. This is an eye-opener.

She stared at the screen, her mind numb.

November 20th: Taking the drug regularly now, A's got me a supply. They are still experimenting, which is why side effects are so weirdly different. Looser regulation over there. It has to be worth it - I'm feeling great on it, if nothing else. Sometimes it's almost like tripping, except you're completely in control and there's no sense of unreality - rather the opposite, a heightened, sharpened sense of reality, stripping away the inconsequential, getting to the essence of life. An example: I was angry for some reason with Sofie the other day. Normally, I would have trouble not showing it, keeping control, so as not to hurt her. Now I just feel detached from it, master of it, a destructive emotion which no longer bothers me. No feelings of resentment.

Sofie remembered his anger. It could be scary. In the early days, when her mother was still with them and when he was drinking heavily, his temper would lead to a binge. He knew that her mother hated him when he was like that, and Sofie guessed he did it to taunt her. Later, when she had run off with her American second husband and he was drying out and going to AA, he lost control less often. But when he did, it led to a simmering resentment that she remembered being almost worse than his bingeing.

Her throat tightened. Was he trialling this drug to manage it?

1st January. I'm having doubts about it, and I'm not sure if I should tell Alex. It's getting almost addictive. Not physically, but mentally. It will be a ground-breaking drug if it works, but right now my emotions are all over the place, especially if I miss a dose, as I did yesterday.

It was followed by his final entry. Her father. Her brilliant, complicated, emotionally scorched father, caught in something far bigger than she'd imagined. A secret drug trial. At last, here was the proof.

A few weeks later, he was dead under the wheels of that train.

31

THEY WERE SITTING IN A PUB IN HAMMERSMITH. THE MAN that Frank had arranged for them to meet came via a back channel in the Security Service.

He certainly didn't look like a spook. His face was grey and flaccid, and he was wearing a dirty, branded t-shirt and jeans, like a computer engineer who had not seen the light of day for weeks. A fleece had already been discarded on the back of his chair, which he had overrun by some margin.

They had skipped pleasantries, and Cal had ordered the three of them pints of the local brew with a Coke for himself. He began to lay out the story. The man listened, unimpressed, his breathing coming in short, sharp intakes and exhalations, like he was trying to inflate a flat tyre with his nose.

When Cal finished, the man finally spoke. His voice was damp gravel.

'Seems to me, mate, you're working on empty.'

He uttered the word 'mate' in a way that suggested it was not his normal lingua franca.

Cal raised an eyebrow. 'How so?'

A large hand drained a third of the pint, leaving a frothy line above his top lip like a band of spume washed up on a beach after a storm. He wiped it away with the back of his other hand.

'You only know this girl's name 'cause of a phone call, right?' he wheezed. 'This estate agent told you she knew someone called Kate Winslow?'

'Winter.'

'Right.' He sniffed, sucking the air back in. 'But why do you suppose that she was the one on the boat?'

'I've got a photo.'

'Yeah,' he exhaled, 'but you said the photo wasn't clear. So you're relying on the name.'

'But the name matched. Tara said the girl was called Kate.'

'And you think a journalist undercover would use her real name?'

Another wet exhale.

Cal ignored him. 'There's a pattern here. The estate agent knew Kate. Tara knew Kate. They've got to be the same person.'

The man waved a fleshy hand. 'Hold it. I thought you said that this Alice whatshername didn't know anyone called Tara?'

'She didn't. But...'

'Well, then.' He drained the rest of his pint and slammed the empty glass down like a gavel. 'Bit thin, don't you think?'

It was hard work. Cal thought he'd got it straight in his head, but now he was beginning to doubt himself. Perhaps these were, after all, merely a series of clues, hints, and suspicions. He realised he needed more. But this guy wasn't helping. He simply picked holes.

After an hour and three pints threatening to turn into four for their guest, they were getting nowhere.

He stood up. 'Thanks for your time. Sorry that I didn't manage to convince you.'

'No worries.' The man offered up a hand slick with sweat, but wasted no effort getting up.

'For Christ's sake,' Cal said, when he and Frank were out of earshot. 'Where the hell did you find that guy? He's an arsehole.'

Frank shrugged. 'Arsehole or not, that was exactly what you needed. Classic spook playbook, testing your story to see where it leaks. And if you go to the police, you'll get the same approach.'

Cal stared at the traffic swirling around Hammersmith Broadway.

'Perhaps I've got this all wrong.'

Frank put his hand on his shoulder. 'You said it yourself. Without the girl, you're flying on empty. Meanwhile, I'll try my mate in the Met. See if they have anything on her.'

'I hope to God they have. I'm running out of options here.'

Frank nodded. 'And good luck at Heathrow.'

They said their goodbyes. Cal turned toward the tube.

He was two steps from the barrier when he felt a tap on his shoulder.

It was the spook from the pub.

'Hey, if you do find anything,' - the pants were louder this time - 'give me a call, OK?'

A quivering hand held out a card. Bob, it said, next to a phone number. Cal grunted his thanks and watched 'Bob' lumber off into the shopping mall.

It wasn't until he was on the platform waiting for the

Heathrow train that he examined it more closely. Oddly, it wasn't a mobile number, as he would expect, but a landline number with an extension.

HEATHROW WAS CROWDED FOR A MONDAY EVENING.

Cal pushed his way through the crush of trolleys and sets of matching luggage until he found the Oslo business class check-in desk.

He put his duffle bag down and joined the short queue. Two armed policemen in bullet-proof vests with Uzi sub-machine guns wandered slowly up and down.

The line inched forward. Three people. Two tourists were arguing over luggage limits. The policemen disappeared from view. His eyes roamed the hall, but it was impossible to know whether anyone was trailing him. This was the flight Cambridge Bio had originally booked him on, and since he'd refused to go on the earlier, Saturday flight, the chances were that Boyd and Gebler would assume he'd be on this one. If they were watching him, he'd like them to think that he was. But the question was, would the police? His plan was a risky one, and he hoped that if they did, the place they would stop him would be at the gate.

He edged forward. He only had one item of luggage. The woman in front of him was wearing a bulky fur coat. She turned round and caught his eye.

'Going for long?'

Cal blinked. 'Sorry?'

'Are you going to Oslo for a holiday? Or business?'

She was smartly dressed and middle-aged, with a set of expensive luggage.

He kept on scanning the crowd. 'Business.'

'Oh? What is it you do?'

He didn't answer. The line moved again. Just her and one other now. The armed police reappeared. Cal's chest tightened. Were they circling? Had they spotted him?

She leaned in. 'Are you in oil and gas?'

That did it.

'For God's sake,' he snapped. 'Do you mind?'

He swung his bag over his shoulder just as a voice behind him said, 'Excuse me, sir.'

He stopped. The policemen stood tensed before him, one with his gun trained discreetly but purposefully at the ground to his right. The other moved sideways.

'That yours?'

Cal followed his gaze. He was pointing at a large suitcase sitting in the middle of the concourse, a few yards behind him. He relaxed.

'No.'

'I'm so sorry!' The woman turned, all fluttering hands. 'It's mine!'

One of the cops turned to her. 'Are you travelling together?'

'No, we are not!' she snapped.

Cal raised an eyebrow at him - *what can you do?* The officer backed off.

'Sorry to bother you, sir.'

A second check-in desk became free. The girl behind the counter beckoned him over, and he handed her his passport.

'I'm booked to go to Oslo this evening,' he said, smiling. She was pretty, with chestnut hair pulled back in a bun and a fresh air of efficiency. 'I've just been to the sales desk, but it was unmanned. Can you change this for a flight to Stockholm?'

She scrutinised the document and tapped some numbers into her terminal.

'That'll be no problem, sir. I'll print out a boarding pass. You need to be at the gate in forty minutes. Aisle or window?'

'Window.'

'Any luggage to check in?'

He shook his head, and she handed him the printout.

Cal glanced at his watch and went to browse the airport shops. If anyone had been watching, he'd made a convincing show of checking in. And if they probed further, they'd see he'd switched to Stockholm.

He bought a magazine, a new novel and a bar of dark chocolate. After fifteen minutes, he walked casually towards immigration control. The line was not long. Slowly, he edged forward. Three spaces short, as if on impulse, he suddenly turned and walked quickly towards a sign marked 'Toilets'.

Inside, he locked the cubicle and got to work. Unzipping his bag on the sink, he pulled out a hand mirror and a small bottle, and, careful not to spill it, began to comb a palmful of thick black liquid through his hair, slicking it back and tying the ends into a ponytail with a rubber band. Then he rinsed his hands in the bowl and drew out a large black overcoat. Finally, he slipped on a yellow silk scarf, a pair of round wire-framed John Lennon glasses, and trainers. He dropped the dye, the comb, and the mirror into his pocket. The shoes he wedged into his waistband, the bag - a lightweight blue nylon affair - he rolled up into a ball and stuffed into his overcoat. He was set. He flushed the toilet, opened the door, and stepped back out into the main concourse.

He made straight for Pret where he could stand with his

back to the rear wall, obscured by the line of people queuing for sandwiches, and dialled Frank's number on his PAYG burner phone.

'All good?'

'I think so. I've not spotted anyone watching me.'

Only three people had gone after him into the gents, an old man and a young boy with his father. Still, you could never be too careful. It might not have fooled a pro, but as countermeasures went, it was probably good enough to deal with whatever Gebler could send after him.

'Listen, I've got news,' said Frank.

Cal's eyes flickered along the queue.

'You were right, a shooting *was* reported to the police on Friday night. My friend in the Met tells me, however, that they found no evidence, so it went no further. The woman who said she witnessed it was not considered a reliable witness. A bit of a crank, in fact.'

Cal caught his breath. 'Who was she?'

'Ah, well, I'm afraid he was unable to help me there. I tried everything, but he wouldn't budge. Looks like we're on our own on that one.'

'Shit.'

'However, I have managed to track down the agency.'

'You have? What did they say?'

'Not spoken to them yet. Let's go see them, shall we?'

32

Tuesday 1st November

Walter Crane could work a room like a magician worked a deck of cards. He spoke in rhythms that made sense even when the logic didn't quite hold, and somehow, by the end, people believed him. His trick was to latch onto people's everyday concerns and mould them into something darker. Laura Boyd had watched it a hundred times.

Today, he was rehearsing for the leadership debate in a hot, overlit hall on the South Bank, pacing a makeshift stage with the kind of restless energy that always made her nervous. Four actors stood in for the real opposition.

Laura stood to one side, arms folded, chewing her lip. No one said it would be easy, but the recent fuck-up on the boat had suddenly taken this to a whole new level.

To keep calm, she reminded herself why she was here. Two years ago, she'd been working in climate advocacy when she'd been told to apply for a role on Crane's team as Chief of Staff. She hadn't asked why, but within weeks, she'd understood. The role gave her access - access to him, his calendar, his messaging, and most importantly, to who was in the room when policy was discussed. While it wasn't her place to influence his agenda directly, she was in a position to decide what was put before him. As an asset, that was priceless. How it was exploited was for others to decide.

But now, suddenly, the whole project was at risk.

She checked her phone again. Nothing. No word from Tasha. Since the op on the boat, she'd gone dark. Laura had tried every number, left every message. Because she needed her. Desperately. She'd just got word - and not via Gebler - that a Sofie James had rented a car in Weymouth, in Dorset.

As she shot off another text, she noticed the moderator wander off for a break. She took her chance, grabbed a cold bottle, and hastened over to her boss.

'How are you feeling about it, Walter?' she said, holding out the mineral water with a tight smile.

Crane looked tired. A tall man in his sixties in a Savile Row suit, his hair was beginning to grey around the temples. He cracked the seal.

'OK, I guess,' he said, mopping his brow. He took a deep swig and wiped his lips with the back of his hand. 'I didn't come off too slick, did I?'

'No. You hit the mark,' she said smoothly. 'Struck exactly the right note. The audience will love you.'

They glanced toward the focus group. Carefully selected, every last one. They'd be split after lunch and their feedback dissected. It was all data and science these days.

'Still feels like a circus,' he muttered. 'I just hope I don't step on a landmine.'

'I'll be in your ear the whole way,' she promised. Then, more quietly: 'But there's something else we need to talk about. D'you have a moment?'

He glanced at his watch. 'Can it wait until our catch-up tomorrow morning? I'm due on again in fifteen.'

'It's about Charles Gebler.'

'What about him? How's he working out?'

'Frankly? He's not. I've not seen him in days. I want his access revoked.'

Walter blinked, surprised but not especially bothered. He waved a hand. 'You don't need my blessing for that.'

'I know. But Gebler came through the donor committee. Someone might kick off. I need to know you'll have my back if they do.'

Walter gave her a tired smile. 'You've always had mine. Consider it mutual.'

She smiled back, tight-lipped. He had no idea who was really behind his back, nor to what lengths they would go to get him elected. If he knew, would he really go through with it?

But one thing was for sure. Once he was prime minister, IF he became prime minister, there were going to be a lot of people who would claim a piece of him.

As he walked away, her phone rang.

'Tasha?

'What can I do for you, Laura?'

'Thank God I found you! Didn't you get my messages?'

'Sorry, needed to go off-grid for a few days.'

'We need a debrief.'

'What's the point?' Tasha said. 'I did the job. It was unfortunate about the girl. That's what happens when you have incomplete intel.'

'That's why I'm calling. I think we've located her.'

She heard Tasha pause at the other end of the line.

'Well. That's something,' she said finally.

'I need you to ID her. You and Gebler were the only ones who saw her face-to-face that night. I'm sending over a couple of images.'

Laura scrabbled with her phone to bring up the photographs. They had been sent to her that morning. They'd been taken with a long lens and showed a girl entering and leaving a Hertz rental office and, more close-up, climbing into the driver's seat of a hatchback.

She pinged them over.

'Where were these taken?' said Tasha when she'd opened them.

'In Weymouth. Is it her?'

'Might be. Can't be certain.'

'OK, can you get down to Dorset this morning? We've traced the car to a hire company down there. We're looking for CCTV sightings, but meanwhile we have a name, address and mobile number for her from the hire agreement. The address is in London. I'm sending someone over there now. But her phone was last active near Dorchester. At eight this morning.'

Laura glanced at her watch. 11:03. If Tasha floored it, she could be there in under two hours.

'On it,' said Tasha.

33

The A-Z Agency sat quietly on a residential street in Bayswater, north of Hyde Park. It wasn't your average escort service. This was the upscale version. Clean website, tasteful branding, and staff who came with "event credentials" and, if you knew what to ask for, a little extra.

They stepped out of the cab, Cal paid the driver in cash, and they set off walking the last few blocks.

'OK,' said Cal. 'Let's go over the drill one final time. The important thing is not to alert them that we're looking for the girl. All this is about is scouting for business.'

'What happens if they don't come up with her?' asked Frank.

'Then you get her out of the room. Give me time to pull the files. Simple as that.'

'Let's hope it's not a single-room setup. Then we're screwed.'

'If that's the case, I'll have to take her to the khazi.' Cal grinned, wolfish and tense. 'Listen, worst case, if it all goes tits-up, she's unlikely to report it. The success of the next few days depends on our invisibility. Whoever's making the running on this must think they've got me where they want me - scared and in hiding. By the time they find out I've not arrived in Oslo, they'll see that I booked a flight to Stockholm.'

'And that your phone's halfway to Greece.'

'Precisely. They won't know where to look. The last thing they'll expect is me back on the scene of the crime.'

Number 45 was one half of a large, red-brick mansion block. According to the brass plate next to the entry phone, the agency was on the third floor. While Cal remained out of sight, Frank rang the bell. A camera lit up on the console.

'Yes?' came a disembodied voice.

'Sorry to disturb you,' Frank said. 'I've got a package for Flat 11, no one's answering. Could you buzz me in? I'll leave it in the hallway.'

A short pause. Then a click. The door unlocked.

Inside, the place smelled of expensive carpets, and gilt-framed prints of old Dutch sailing ships lined the stairwell. They bypassed the lift and took the stairs, stopping to listen at each landing. Everything seemed quiet.

When they reached the top, Frank peeled away. Cal knocked on the door of Flat 12. Solid wood with brass fittings, but no signage whatever. An elegant woman with back-combed red hair, early 40s, opened it.

'Yes?' Her accent was faintly Australian. She looked surprised.

'This is the A to Z Agency?'

She hesitated a fraction. 'We don't normally accept personal visits. Wait there a moment.' She closed the door. He could hear her walking about the flat. A moment later, she returned with a business card.

'Please email your requirements or call this number.'

Cal flipped it in his fingers. 'Mmm. The problem is that

my client needs girls tomorrow night. I've been tasked to sort it.'

Her eyes narrowed slightly, defences shifting.

'Ok, well… I'm sure we can arrange something. Just email your…'

'Not really an option,' he interrupted, apologetic but firm. 'We need to select twenty-five girls today. And he's picky.'

'Well…'

Cal kept smiling. Reluctantly, she opened the door and he walked through.

'We really prefer to do all this by phone, you know,' she said as she ushered him into a reception room. At the far end was a large white cyclorama, behind a purple velvet one-armed sofa, with a lighting rig on a stand. 'This is purely for administration. How did you find our address?'

'One of your girls gave it to me,' he lied.

'Who was that? I'll bloody murder her.'

'Tara, I think she was called.'

Nothing in her face gave away whether she recognised the name. Beyond, through open double doors, he glimpsed a well-furnished office. There were two tall filing cabinets against one wall, and a large white monitor on the desk. She motioned to a sofa and sat down opposite, eying him through thin steel-rimmed glasses.

'So, let me take some details. Venue?'

He gave her the lowdown, sticking to the story he'd cooked up with Frank. At the end of it, he said, 'Do you have images I can view?'

'You've been on the website, I presume?'

'Yes, but we need a bit more than that, I'm afraid. I'm after some background. My client wants girls with conversation.'

She got up and came back with a sheaf of thin document wallets, which she started sifting on the sofa.

'Have a peruse of these.' Every two or three, she would pass one across to Cal to review. 'Erika, she's smart. Lara - she can hold a conversation, does a lot of holiday work.'

Cal flipped through, feigning concentration, as a succession of scantily clad women smiled suggestively at him from beneath the plastic sheets.

Bethany, he read, *22, Polish, 5'7, 54 kilos, red/brown hair, blue eyes, likes speedboats, vintage champagne, humour and naughty fun. Emma, 26...*

She hesitated.

'Any requirements on nationality?'

'Not particularly.'

...5.6, Italian, dark brown hair, green eyes, likes evenings in, cuddling up on the sofa with a good bottle of Chianti.

He looked up.

'Do you have Tara's file?'

She paused. 'I don't think we have anyone called Tara.'

'My client says he met a Tara at the function you catered the other night on the Thames boat. Said she'd be perfect.'

'Ah, you mean the Crane event.' She thought hard for a moment. 'Tara? No. Definitely no Tara working on our books. You sure that was her name?'

'She may have used the name Sarah-Jane.'

Recognition sparked. 'Ah, Sarah-Jane!' She shuffled through the folders again and handed one over.

The girl in the photograph was smiling impishly and had short, chocolate-brown hair. She looked at least three or four years younger than the girl on the boat.

Cal shook his head.

'Nah, the one I am looking for was blond. Never mind.'

Time to activate Plan B.

'Actually, you know what, maybe I should check your website after all. Got a computer I can use?'

She looked at him like he was an idiot. 'You can do it on your phone. It's A hyphen Z hyphen agency dot…'

He pointed at the large screen through the double doors. 'Sorry, I hate looking at stuff on a small screen. My eyesight's terrible. Do you mind if I use your Mac over there?'

'Well. I suppose so,' she said reluctantly. 'But you'll have to be quick.' She glanced at her watch. 'I have to leave shortly.'

Almost certainly a lie, he thought. All she wants to do is get rid of me. Still, the lure of a last-minute booking for twenty-five girls was a strong motivator. It was time for what his psychology professor used to call a 'reinforcement play'.

He got up.

'Listen, if it's too much trouble,' he said with a hint of impatience, 'I can take my booking elsewhere. As I say, my client is very particular, and...' he tapped his Omega '...you're not the only one on a schedule here.'

'No, no,' she said hastily. 'It's not a problem. Take as much time as you need.' She walked behind the desk and wiggled the mouse, and the screen came to life. Good, thought Cal - permanently logged on. She pulled out a chair for him and another for her beside him. The agency website was open by default.

They scrolled through the girls together, she describing each of them in turn and jotting down names as he gave his approval. After a minute, he pulled out his phone and made as if to check his messages, and pressed 'send'.

Thirty seconds later, there was a knock at the door. The woman looked up, startled.

'Don't worry,' Cal said smoothly. 'That'll be my colleague. I arranged to meet him here.'

They had planned it like this for one very simple reason - if they had both appeared at her door, it would have been far less likely that she would have admitted them. Alone, he was less of a threat, and he'd spent the last fifteen minutes gaining her trust. She now had little option but to let Frank in.

She stood up and frowned. 'I'm sorry, this is really most unorthodox. We do expect people to make appointments, you know.'

So she does make appointments, thought Cal. Probably only with her regulars. But he let it go.

'Do you mind if I....' He gestured at her now vacated chair in front of the computer. She looked at him dubiously, then left to get the door.

As soon as she had gone, Cal slipped the USB stick from his jacket and slid it into the port. Frank had promised it would work its magic without any need to find or drag files, so long as the computer was logged on. It started a soft whirr. He could hear Frank introducing himself.

It was then that he noticed the yellow-lined notepad to the right of the screen. Three names were written on it - 'Kate Winter', and underneath it, 'DC Khan', with a number alongside, and 'Sofie James'. Could that be the SJ he was looking for? He snapped it with his phone, one ear out for the conversation next door.

There was the sound of footsteps. The USB stick was still whirring, flashing a soft red. He stood abruptly to block her off at the doorway.

'I think we can work with what you've got,' he said breezily, returning to the sitting room and slumping on the sofa. He nodded at Frank. 'Found it OK?'

'Sorry, lost my way,' Frank replied, playing the clueless assistant.

She hovered between them, looking stressed, giving him the kind of look she might give to an old boyfriend who'd turned up unannounced, minutes before her current one was due to arrive.

'I'm sorry, gentlemen, I really have to get on.'

'Sure,' Cal said, straightening up, business-like, straining to listen to the now faint whirr of the computer next door. He'd positioned himself where he could see the stick, but blocking her view. It was still flashing.

'Like I say, this shouldn't take long. I just need an idea of cost.'

It took less than ten minutes to go through the commercials, by which time the flashing had stopped. He got up and patted his pockets.

'Damn. Where did I put my phone?'

He made a play of glancing around the room before walking back into the office to find where he'd left it, deliberately, next to the mouse. He disguised the movement of retrieving the USB stick by leaning over the desk from behind the screen to reach for it. But he needn't have worried. Frank was asking her about a framed print of a girl on a yacht on one of the walls. She seemed relieved that they were finally going.

They wrapped it up and left. Neither of them said a word until they reached the street. Where Cal finally exhaled.

'Got it?' said Frank.

Cal nodded. 'All of it. And something extra.'

34

The house where Professor Harry Erskine lived was an old wisteria-clad cottage a mile outside Woodstock, some way from the dingy bedsit where she'd known him at Oxford. Although it had taken Sofie over two hours to drive from Weymouth, where she had hired a car for the day, she was not only thinking geographically. He was married now, for a start, and his new lodgings reflected his new status - from the pair of smart, upholstered sofas that faced one another either side of a glass and steel fireplace, to the battalion of silver framed photos that marched across the vast expanse of polished rosewood of a Bechstein grand - his wife's, Sofie assumed.

He closed the back door behind her, ambled into the hall, and scooped up a fat pile of mail.

'My God!' he exclaimed. 'I've only been gone two days, and look at all the junk that's arrived!'

He was a stooping man in his early fifties, with a thick unruly thatch of jet-black hair. His dress sense was as random as ever: in a faded soft check shirt with a collar beginning to fray, and soiled suede loafers under a pair of blue cords that had seen better days.

She looked about admiringly. 'What a beautiful house. A bit different from the shoebox I remember.'

'Well. You know. About time and all that.' They looked at each other in silence. 'Now, what can I get you? Can I fix you a sandwich?'

'I've eaten, thanks.'

'What about tea? Or something stronger?'

'I'd love one.'

'Milk?'

'Black'.

If it stung that he didn't remember how she took it, she didn't let it show.

She followed him into the kitchen as he set about making tea in a pot, depositing his mail on a sideboard. There was the low burble of cricket commentary in the background.

'I haven't seen you since... what? Dorset?' he called over his shoulder, referring to her father's funeral. 'This is a surprise, I must say. How are you faring?'

'Things are complicated. Something's happened. Like I mentioned on the phone, I need your help.'

'Absolutely,' he said. 'Whatever I can do. Let's sit down and you can tell me all about it.'

She'd phoned him the previous day from the top of the hill behind the cottage, as the signal was patchy in the bay. She'd decided not to broach the whole story. All she'd said by way of explanation was that she was researching a magazine article about new drug developments, in particular a drug called 'Imagine'. He'd needed no persuasion to meet up with her. So they'd agreed to rendezvous in a pub in Woodstock at lunchtime the next day. She'd asked him whether he'd rather not meet in his college, but he'd said no, he'd been away and had to get home, and besides, it was quieter. Even so, he'd been over an hour late, and she was about to give up on him when he hurried in, very apologetic, something about some unexpected work, and since the pub kitchen had closed, he had insisted they go back to his house. As it was a short distance across the field, she left her car in the pub car park and they walked, entering his house via the back garden gate.

'Is Sarah here?' she asked.

'Gone to London.'

'Did you tell her I was coming?'

Harry looked sheepish. 'You know how she is. She gets so difficult. Especially about you.'

'What, even after seven years?'

He grimaced. 'Afraid so. I think it was more to do with the fact that you were my best friend's daughter. She disapproves of that sort of thing.'

So there it was. Her hunch seemed to be correct. He'd agreed to meet her in the pub because of Sarah, but without telling her. But at the last minute, she'd driven to London, so now he was alone, and they could relax in comfort.

They sat. He placed a hand on hers. 'I'm sorry. About your dad. The service was beautiful. It must have been very hard for you.'

'It was.'

They were silent for a moment.

'So,' he said finally, 'what on earth gives you an interest in cutting-edge drug development all of a sudden? Imagine, did you say?'

'Like I told you, I'm doing some freelance work for a magazine.' She grinned. 'So I thought - I know just the guy!'

'So where do you want me to start?'

'How about the beginning?'

He laughed. 'Easier said than done. Where was the beginning?'

His gaze shifted to the garden, where two birds were pecking at a plastic feeder.

'They've been searching for Imagine for a very long time. It's been over seventy years since that Australian bloke stumbled on lithium.'

She placed her phone on the table between them. 'Harry, you'll have to forgive me, but I'm an idiot when it comes to all this. You'll need to explain everything, and slowly.'

'Of course,' he added, eyeing her as she searched for the recording app. 'But I'd like to make one thing clear before we start, if you don't mind.'

She looked up.

'I... er... I'd rather you didn't record this.'

Sofie hesitated. 'Oh?'

'Yes, if it's not too much trouble. That also goes for quoting me.'

'Any particular reason?'

'Let's just call it… professional integrity.'

She put the phone away. 'Sure, if that's the way you want it.'

'One has to be very careful when one's dependent on industry money for so much of one's research these days.' He stopped for a moment to brush something off his sleeve. 'Right. Where were we? Lithium.'

He cleared his throat.

'Now, Lithium's a chemical that's used to treat manic depression, and it was discovered in rather an amazing way.

An Australian scientist was experimenting on the urine of manic patients and found it was virulently toxic to guinea pigs. Had them staggering about all over the place. So what does he do?'

'Give them a cold bath?'

'He looks for substances in the urine that might be responsible. One of these was uric acid, the most soluble salt of which is lithium urate. He was amazed to discover that far from poisoning the guinea pigs, the lithium salt, when extracted and tested on them in higher doses, actually protected them from the urine. It also sedated them, suggesting an absence of lithium in the urine. It was pure coincidence, of course - he was looking at lithium only because of its relationship to uric acid, not for any intrinsic qualities of its own.' He stooped to sip his tea. 'That's the most exciting thing about science, Sofie - accidents. And from there it was a short step to testing lithium on his patients, all of whom miraculously recovered.'

Sofie tried to look suitably impressed. Once started, she remembered, Harry could go on for hours. It had initially attracted, and finally exasperated her. But she listened patiently as he ran her through a potted history of psychiatric medicine, trying to maintain concentration. After twenty minutes, he finally got to the part she wanted to know about.

'To cut a long story short… ' he was saying.

Please do, she was thinking.

' …it was discovered that the brain goes through more or less permanent chemical changes in response to major stress - i.e. if you suffered trauma in your early, more formative years, you would thereafter be more prone to depression or mental disturbance. It was as if your nerve endings became permanently sensitised. More and more, it looked like the chemical that kept you on the straight and narrow was serotonin. It was precisely this amine that they were unable to isolate.'

He paused for dramatic effect.

'Until Imagine. You see, serotonin has been described as being rather like a mental police force. These amazing little amines are running around your brain, making you feel safe, especially if you are pre-programmed by earlier trauma to be particularly sensitive to stress. They smooth the wrinkles, give you self-confidence, help you shrug off the little disappointments. If they're not around, it doesn't mean there'll always be a riot. Only that if you do have trouble, however small, however insignificant the upset, there is no regulatory authority to prevent it from spreading and getting worse. Neat, eh?'

'Mmm. I could do with some of this serotonin stuff,' she said.

'You probably have high levels of it already. I mean politicians, entrepreneurs, high achievers - these people have tremendous amounts of energy. They need little sleep, they are naturally optimistic, they take risks. Above all, by brushing off failure, they succeed. So no prizes for guessing what Imagine does. It recruits police. It's more than a mere antidepressant. It's a personality changer.'

She blinked. 'I see. So what now? Are they developing it further?'

He stopped pacing and turned to face her.

'Absolutely. That's where the whole thing starts to get complicated. What they're looking for is a refinement of Imagine that will target different amines to order. A cosmetic medication - the ultimate designer drug. It will rectify, if you will, our deficiencies, and be tailored to each individual patient. Like a kind of neurological MSG, making life taste better.' He sniffed. 'That's the theory, anyway. But there are ethical problems. It's bloody dangerous if you ask me.'

'Oh? Why? Sounds like heaven.'

'For one thing, they will make the same claim as with Imagine - no side effects. It's all part of the same trend. But we don't know, do we? I mean, it's going to take a very long time to discover whether what still lies buried under there will come out one day in a vast explosion. Let's take the analogy one step further.' He tapped his temple. 'Imagine you've got a police state up there. All the malcontents will be kept under control for a while. But eventually, there's likely to be a revolution. Moreover, is it desirable for everyone to be socially successful, thrusting, self-confident? I'm not so sure. It's going to be another thing we'll need to rely on, a quick fix, without working stuff out for ourselves. Because there's already evidence, with Imagine, that at the same time it enables you to be more socially adept, it tends to make you more self-centred. No time for your ageing mother any more, or your handicapped neighbour, no more guilt-driven good Samaritan stuff.'

She hesitated. 'I know it's not your field, Harry. But...is there any crossover between these mind drugs and AIDS drugs?'

For a second, something flickered across his face. Gone as quickly as it came.

'Crossover? How d'you mean?'

'Cambridge Bio develops both, don't they?'

'Indeed. In fact, Imagine is often prescribed alongside the regular AIDS drugs and cancer drugs as an antidepressant. That is something you might like to... investigate for your article.'

He began to gather up the tea things.

'I will. Thanks. By the way,' she called out casually, as he disappeared into the kitchen. 'Were you aware that my father had a… '

For a moment, she couldn't say it. It felt strange. She was scared of what Harry might tell her.

He reappeared at the kitchen door. 'Had a what?'

She cleared her throat. 'A girlfriend.'

He paused. Just slightly.

'A girlfriend?'

'Her name was Alex. A doctor. Ring any bells?'

His expression relaxed.

'I did hear of an Alex, yes. I seem to remember that they spent half the year in Africa.'

'I'm surprised you never met her. Given the field you're in.' She paused. 'Any idea how I get hold of her?'

He shook his head. 'Your father kept this…' here he hesitated '… friend of his rather under wraps.'

'Odd, though. You were close.'

'I think he just… liked his privacy. Now, what about a proper drink?

She wasn't sure she bought that. He sounded a little too quick to change the subject.

'Oh, alright then,' she laughed, despite herself. She suddenly felt fragile. 'I'd love a G and T. My amines feel shot to pieces.'

It was closer to the truth than he could have guessed, she thought to herself ruefully.

He disappeared into the kitchen. She stared after him, mind spinning. So it was true. Well, of course it was true, it was in his diary, but still, somehow, she'd thought... what? That it had all been a fantasy of his?

'Can you believe it?' she heard him cry. 'They're still batting. They're only on two runs an over and they haven't hit a single six. There's going to be no time left to bowl out the West Indies!'

She rolled her eyes. 'Harry, do me a favour, will you?'

He reentered, holding two glasses heavy with ice.

'Stick to neurotransmitters, OK?'

~

It was nearly seven by the time Sofie returned to Weymouth. It had been a busy day. She was hungry. After dropping the hire car keys in an out-of-hours box outside the rental company's office, she wandered about the seafront looking for a decent place to eat, but everywhere was either closed or deserted. Dejected, she gazed across the sea towards Ringstead on the opposite side of the bay. There was nothing in the fridge in the cottage. The village shop would be closed. And then she remembered. The pub in Osmington Mills. She could grab a bite to eat there, then walk back to the cottage along the clifftop. It would be lovely in the moonlight. Just like old times.

She hastened over to the cab stand outside the station. A different taxi this time. She jumped in the back.

'Osmington Mills, please,' she said to the driver. 'The Smuggler's Inn.'

35

It took nearly an hour to get to Stoke Newington through the evening rush hour. As before, they got the cab to drop them a few blocks short of their destination and paid the cabbie in cash. But this time, they were more careful. It was quite possible that Gebler would also have Sofie's Brooke Road address by now.

They split. Frank crossed to the far side of the street and vanished behind a deserted bottle bank. Cal kept to the near side, ducking along the pavement past a parade of shops. The street was thankfully busy with people milling about the Hummingbird pub across the road. Easy to melt into.

As he walked, he pulled a burner phone from his pack and thumbed in her number. It hadn't taken them long to locate it, using straightforward OSINT: LinkedIn, Facebook, Instagram. Sofie James's page hadn't been updated in two years, and there was no trace of a mobile number, but they'd found a landline linked to a charity Sofie had once volunteered with. As for her home address, it was listed on a public directory website.

Voicemail clicked in. It was unmistakably her. He redialled Frank.

'She's not answering.'

'Maybe she's just not picking up.'

'Only one way to find out.'

He crossed the street, eyes scanning the darkness ahead. The house looked normal. Four floors and a basement, the same Victorian terrace design repeated a thousand times all over London. James, flat four, the buzzer said. No lights showing. Frank lurked behind a parked Range Rover, phone to his ear.

'Anything?'

'Looks clean,' Cal said. 'Let's do another lap.'

He continued around the block, checking the cars. Nothing seemed out of place. No open windows or fit young men in new trainers, or anyone whose profile seemed at odds with their environment.

The only possible that he clocked was a girl in a doorway, doing her best to look homeless, begging for money for a bed for the night. He gave her a fiver and chatted to her for a minute, at the end of which he was as sure as he could be that she was nothing more than she seemed to be.

They regrouped across from the flat.

'Top or bottom?' Frank said.

'Ground floor starts the numbering. Which makes hers the one with the curtains closed.'

'Perhaps she went to bed early.'

'At seven? Hardly likely. Maybe she's already fled.'

The house was an end-of-terrace, next to a small newsagent. Frank walked over to the pub, while Cal sauntered into the shop.

'Evening.'

The man behind the counter looked tired and uninterested.

'I'm looking for someone who lives next door. A woman named Sofie James. She said she was renting her flat out. Do you know her, by any chance?'

That got his attention. 'Miss James, renting her flat? I don't think so.'

'I just rang her doorbell, but there's no answer and, well, I thought I was expected. Any idea when she gets back from work?'

'I think you must have made a mistake.' Someone called him from the back of the shop. '*Hold it, Asha*,' he shouted. '*I'm serving a customer. I'll be with you shortly*.' He returned to Cal. 'She went away a couple of days ago. Told me she'd be gone for a while. But she didn't mention anything about renting.'

Cal thanked him and headed across to The Hummingbird.

'Not good, I'm afraid,' he said, dropping into a chair across from Frank. 'He says she's left. No forwarding address.'

'How would he know?'

'She told him herself.'

'Damn. What we need is her mobile number. Then at least we could track it.' He paused. 'But take a look at this.' He slid a folded Evening Standard across the table. 'Second page, inside right.'

The headline read *'Hunt for Murder Suspect'*. It went on to identify Cal by his real name, wanted in connection with the death of an estate agent, Alice Wickman.

Cal blanched. 'Fuck's sake.'

'What's interesting is what's not in there. No mention of you working for Cambridge Bio. They're keeping that part quiet.'

Cal scanned the story again, then sat back and stared out of the window.

'The problem is... the longer I leave it, the more incriminating this whole thing becomes. I've got to go to them sometime.'

'You mean the police? Too early.'

'Then what? Your MI6 friend was a dead end. If I wait any longer, I'll appear so fucking guilty I won't have a leg to stand on.'

'Listen, stick your head above the parapet, and you're toast. You know as well as I do that if somebody wants to nail you, they'll nail you. No, we need to prove there's someone out there trying to frame you. Be patient.' He glanced out into the street. 'Besides, who knows what we'll discover up there?'

Cal laughed grimly. 'Sure. Gagged and bound and drowned in her bath.'

'That would probably count as a good outcome. Means you'll have a case, no?'

'Means I'll have another bloody murder to account for.'

Frank stood. 'Come on. Let's find out, shall we?'

He went ahead. As they had anticipated, there was no response from her buzzer. Carefully, Frank slid a length of wire into the lock, and it snapped open with a click. He briefly turned to signal Cal and disappeared into the house, leaving the door on the latch. With one last scan of the road, Cal crossed and slipped in behind him.

They climbed two flights of stairs. The common parts looked unloved, with textured wallpaper on the walls and paint flaking off the ceiling. Rented, clearly.

Number four was on the third floor. Here, everything was different. A heavy-duty high-security night latch had been fitted, and at a glance, Cal could tell that the noise and mess that Frank would have to make to get in would likely alert the neighbours.

'We're not kicking this in,' he whispered. 'Too noisy. Let's try the roof.'

Frank nodded and followed Cal up to the top floor, where a door opened out onto a flat terrace.

The view was impressive. Row upon row of blackened chimneys stretched away toward a low rise to the north, and to the east was a large expanse of dark where no lights were showing. To the south, the orange glow of the Canary Wharf lit up the sky.

Cal surveyed the junk. It was an odd assortment: a few old bottles, a defunct washing machine, and several coils of blue plastic piping. It looked like someone had had a party up here at one time. A low brick parapet ran around the edge, and leaning over, he noticed a cast iron fire escape running down the back of the building.

'If I'm not mistaken, I'd say that goes right past the back of her flat.'

A minute later, Cal broke the glass with a muffled jab. He unlatched the window and eased his hand out, careful not to drag any of it back out onto the metal stairway. It was her bathroom. They both stood silently for a moment, waiting for a reaction. But the flat was dark and empty. Donning green latex gloves, they climbed in.

'Remember,' Cal whispered, flicking on a torch. 'We're looking for addresses. Places she might have gone. Plus anything that links her with this Winter woman. Or Cambridge Bio, come to that.'

Clothes lay scattered about on top of a laundry basket. Washing had been draped over the radiator, and a dirty espresso cup rested on the edge of the sink. On its black and white chequered floor, unswept, were the shattered remains of a glass. Frank bent down to examine it, sniffing.

'Looks like she left in a bit of a hurry,' he said. They went on through to the hallway, where an answerphone was flashing a message.

'Jesus, who still has these?'

Cal pressed play.

It was Alice's message about a *'surprise friend'* who was *'in town for a few days and was keen to meet up with her again.'*

He looked at Frank. 'So that's what they were after. Sofie. I bloody knew it. OK. We need to be quick. I'll search the kitchen and bedroom. Where are you going to fit your little gizmo?'

Frank unshouldered his pack and pulled out one of his Wi-Fi recording devices.

'Somewhere she's unlikely to notice.'

'That'll be behind a sofa, then.'

'Oh, very funny.'

'I'm serious, mate. That's the one flaw with that thing. If you put it where it'll get the best view, it'll also be the most noticeable by someone not expecting it.'

While Frank got to work, Cal started in the small galley kitchen. He opened the fridge. Almost empty, just a couple of cartons of oat milk - out of date - a coconut yoghurt, and a half-full jar of rose harissa. On the door, she'd pinned a card with a pink elephant fridge magnet. He flashed his torch. '*Happy 26th*', it said, and inside, a message - '*To the most beautiful daughter a father could have - love Dad x x*.' Next to it was a flyer for a talk on the Iranian Women's Rights Movement in Hackney three weeks ago.

He scanned the cupboards. Nothing of interest, other than she liked noodles and sugar-free cereal. He found her driving licence in the drawer of the small pine kitchen table, as well as a day diary shoved at the back. The photograph on the license showed an unsmiling young woman with hair brushed back, pouting, no make-up, her expression saying, *'Do you have to take this picture?'* The diary was blank. An unused present? Plates and a mug were waiting to be washed in the sink. He moved on to her bedroom.

On a bedside cabinet was a photo frame with a picture of an older man. He was looking away, slightly diffident, seemingly unconscious of the camera. A boyfriend? Her father? Tall, with tousled hair, wearing jeans and a red bandana around his neck.

Rummaging through the discarded pens, earrings and coins in her bedside drawer - the usual detritus - he felt a strange intimacy with this woman. Unlike many people's houses he walked into, it didn't feel alien. Was it the smell, he wondered? So often, this scent of femininity felt suffocating, but not here. Maybe it was the sense of semi-chaos that he recognised: mugs left unwashed, blonde hairs on a hairbrush, packets of cereal hurriedly put away.

He opened a built-in closet. It was the wardrobe of a girl who gets by. Vintage, lots of cheap colourful tops, a mess of scarves, the odd flamboyant dress with bits falling off. Nothing looked expensive or designer, though she obviously liked dressing up. But the flat, its location, its contents: they were all clues that she didn't earn much money doing whatever it was that she did. There was nothing here, in fact, to suggest that she was anything other than she claimed to be: an out-of-work actor doing odd jobs on the side.

And yet, other than the license, he could find no photographs of her. Which was odd for an actor.

He yanked out the drawers of a large wooden chest, tipping the contents onto the floor. The broken window meant they needed to cover their tracks. However amateur, they had to make it look like a regular burglary.

He returned to the bathroom. A range of mascaras were lined up in a small mirrored cabinet, alongside two kohl eyeliner pencils and three expensive lipsticks, all shades of red. A henna hair dye appeared unused.

He rejoined Frank in the living room and ran his finger along the spines of her books, which were ranged on five short wooden shelves spanning the gap between an open Victorian fireplace and the far wall. A row of hardback biographies, including ones on Mao, Nelson Mandela, and Michelle Obama, vied for space with a series of green Virago Modern Classics in paperback - Vita Sackville-West, Molly Keane - and some schoolgirl classics: *Persuasion*, *Catcher in the Rye*, a Chekhov play, and Albert Camus. A copy of Dolly Alderton's *Everything I Know About Love* rested on its side.

On the bottom shelf was a fax machine. Cal stooped down and picked up a sheet of paper that looked like it had recently been spat out, resting undisturbed on the plastic tray. He swung his light onto it. It was a list of names, under columns marked patients and doctors, with some ID references beside each.

'Frank,' he whispered urgently. 'Take a look at this. Top of the page.'

Frank joined him and stared at the document.

Cambridge Bio trials: 1 of 3, someone had written in the right-hand corner.

'Just an out-of-work actor, huh?'

36

Tasha's Kawasaki Ninja sputtered noisily as she decelerated into the bend, the roar of its 900cc engine smacking against the dry stone wall like a machine gun. Half a mile further on was the turning to Osmington Mills, the location of the most recent phone ping. Tasha eased off the accelerator, slowing to a crawl as she fell into the dip of the lane that turned off the A353. She glided downhill cautiously, the engine purring beneath her, pitch black beyond the arc of her beam. Halfway down, the headlights of an approaching car made her pull into a narrow cutting. She peered in and caught a brief glimpse of the driver. A farmer, by the looks of him. He raised a hand in thanks as he passed, and she eased back out into the lane and started climbing the hill on the opposite side of the valley.

Cresting the ridge at the top, she pulled into a gravel lay-by, flicked open her visor, and sucked in a lungful of air. Salty mixed with cow shit. Charming. Below her, the sea shimmered, catching the moon, and a string of lights twinkled across the bay. She could make out the shapes of farm buildings and a smattering of cottages leading down to the water and, to the left, the bright glow of a pub in a hollow.

The girl had to be down there somewhere.

She pulled out her phone.

'I've arrived.'

'Have you found her?' Laura asked quickly.

Tasha ran a hand over her buzz cut, wiped the sweat from her neck. Beads of it cooled on her forehead. She strained to see into the night.

'Not yet. The last ping was in the vicinity of the pub. I'm heading there now. Any updates?'

'Nothing. She's gone dark.'

'And her flat?'

'We've got someone in position, in case she returns.'

'Want me to intercept her when I find her?'

'No. For now, I simply need eyes on.'

Tasha slowed her breathing and narrowed her eyes. The girl was a loose end, and she hated loose ends. She had always prided herself on her forensic attention to detail, on her economy of action. What had taken place on that boat was a complete blindside. It's what came from relying on others.

A pickup started climbing the hill, headlights sweeping toward her.

'Tasha, you got that?' Laura said again. 'Do not approach her.'

'Yeah. Got it. Visual only.'

Tasha slid her helmet back on and began to coast silently towards The Smuggler's Inn, thinking that she'd be the judge of that.

37

The pub was barely half full when Sofie arrived. It was out of season. The only customers were locals, and few of them were eating dinner.

She settled down on a banquette and ordered a Chicken Caesar salad and a glass of white wine. The food took an age to arrive, so when it did, she was ravenous and wolfed it down. By this time, a few more people had drifted in, including a tall blonde with short hair in motorbike leathers. Something about her seemed out of place. Sofie watched her order a drink at the bar. Soft, she noticed.

She finished her salad, drained her glass, paid the bill and left. Outside, the moon had risen further in the sky. It was almost full, there was not a breath of wind, and the fields ahead were still, silent and eerie. As she started the climb towards the coast path, the sea slowly revealed itself, its surface like liquid silver.

At the top of the hill, she paused for breath. It was a magnificent night. How many times had she walked this path as a teenager, she wondered, when she'd come down to stay with her Dad? Her mother had never liked the place.

Too remote. There was an old gun emplacement here somewhere, now overgrown with brambles, where tramps would sometimes come down to squat over the summer and startle them on their way home from the pub.

She started along the clifftop. In the far distance, the glowing chalk of Whitenose towered over the bay like a sleeping giant.

Suddenly, she heard a rustle behind her. She stopped and turned. Surely there was no one else on the coast path at this time of night? She stood very still for a minute. But all was deathly quiet. Putting it down to a rabbit or a fox, she went on her way, and before long, a cluster of holiday cottages came into view. Just as she reached the point where the path became a track, she dropped down to the beach to walk the last stretch on the sand. Ten minutes later, she arrived at the rickety wooden steps that led up to the cottage.

Once inside, she poured herself a vodka from a dusty half-bottle she'd found at the back of a cupboard and went back out to sit on the deck under the stars.

She had gleaned a lot of information from Harry. She couldn't pretend to have a particularly scientific mind, but what he had told her was fascinating. A drug that could be tailored to order, to alter our personalities, in the same way as plastic surgery could alter our looks? It was both awesome and terrifying.

As for her father, it seemed increasingly likely that he'd been prescribed Imagine along with the trial drug, as Harry had hinted. Thinking back, she remembered little things about his behaviour in his last days, that she'd brushed over at the time. How unpredictable he'd become: one minute uncharacteristically loving towards her - he'd never been very good at showing his feelings - the next dark and irritable. He had admitted as much in his diaries. Was it a side effect of the medication? Could it have played a part in what happened?

She didn't want to say the word suicide. It didn't fit. The man she knew wouldn't have done that. But then again, how well had she *really* known him? That's what stung. And it had happened to others, according to the faxed news reports.

She needed answers. Everything seemed to point to one person - Alex. The doctor, his girlfriend. However, the idea of confronting the woman made her stomach twist. Because of what she might find.

She'd thought they'd told each other everything. She had, at least, telling him all about the guys she liked, the dramas she was having, the struggles she was going through. And him? He was always deflecting. *This* woman was too neurotic, *that* one had no sense of humour. Yes, granted, he was her father, so she wasn't expecting him to tell her everything. But a full-on girlfriend - why had he kept that a secret?

Sofie shivered and looked out to sea. A freighter she'd spotted earlier had rounded the headland and vanished. She finished the vodka and headed inside.

Rummaging in a kitchen drawer, she pulled out an A4 notepad, a marker pen and a small roll of Sellotape. Tearing out three pages, she sat down at the table and laid them out side by side, carefully taping them together to make one large sheet. Then she began to draw two circles, one above the other. It was a technique she had learned on the Goldsmiths journalism course. Nothing beats paper when you want to get your thoughts in order, her tutor had told them, to visualise connections, when someone questioned why you wouldn't use an app.

In the first circle, she scribbled the words *Cambridge Bio*; in the second, *Investigation*. Above *Cambridge Bio*, she wrote *Walter Crane*, and *drug trial*, and under *Investigation*, she added *Exposure of - proof?*

Next, radiating from each, she drew a series of lines. The three from the Cambridge bubble at the top of the page, she labelled *Chemists*, *Bad Guys* and *Alex*. Beside *Chemists*, in brackets, she wrote *Lawyer*, and beside *Alex*, she scribbled *Dad*.

The single line from the *Investigation* bubble at the bottom of the page, she marked *Kate* with a dash and *SJ* in brackets. Then she joined them up: a line from *Chemists* connected a line from *Kate*, broken by an arrow from a question mark where they met in the middle. A second, unbroken line ran from *SJ*, by-passed the question mark, and went... where? Not to the chemists, because they were likely dead. Her pen veered to the left, where she scribbled another question mark.

It seemed to leap from the page: Who was sending the faxes? They made sense now. *"Your father would be proud of you."* That was personal. It proved there had to be a connection between the question mark and her father, and by implication between the question mark and Alex. Either the question mark knew Alex, and through her, of her father's fate, or Alex *was* the question mark.

She leaned back. It felt close. Like she was circling something important. But there were still too many blanks.

In the margin, she scrawled a heading: *Background* - and the words *Harry*, *Kate* and *Alex*. She ticked off *Harry* and stared at the page.

Could there be something in Kate's apartment that she missed the first time? A note? A document?

She raised her glass.

'Dad,' she said aloud into the wind, *'what the hell were you mixed up in?'*

38

Wednesday 2nd November

Tasha woke with a grunt, body aching. The spot had been dry enough, but the floor of the World War Two shelter she had bunked down in was hard concrete. Sleeping on her leathers had given her some relief, but it was a while since she'd dossed down in the open. She was getting too old for this, she thought to herself ruefully.

She sat up slowly, muscles protesting, and pulled on her jeans. Slinging on her jacket, she stepped outside. It was a few minutes past sunrise, and already light. The fallen branch she'd wedged across the gate to the girl's cottage fifty metres away had not been moved. Which meant she must still be in there.

She ducked back inside to finish dressing. She was travelling light, with only her Glock 19 for company. It was one of her favourites. Not just for its compactness, but also because it came with a handy conversion kit to accommodate a lightweight carbon fibre suppressor.

She slid the breech back, checking the action. Then hauled the panniers up the rise to where she'd stashed the Kawasaki in a hedgerow. Everything prepped, she returned to the coast path.

She glanced at her phone. 07.17. Still no word from Laura. She had been tempted to finish it last night, under the cover of darkness, but decided to give Laura the benefit of the doubt.

<*Eyes on*>, she'd messaged after she'd followed the girl back from the pub. <*I'm moving in this first thing in the morning unless I hear back.*>

She crossed the path and slipped over a sagging barbed wire fence. The lawn, slick with dew, sloped down toward a squat, two-storey building with mismatched windows. Moving low, Tasha flattened herself against the whitewashed wall, listening for noises. All seemed quiet inside. She peered through a window. It was the sitting room, and didn't look lived in. A sofa and two armchairs had dust covers draped over them, and everything had been cleared off the surfaces.

She circled to the back. French windows led out onto a terrace from the kitchen. Locked. Inside, a coffee cup and a half-empty bottle of vodka had been left on the table, but other than that, like the sitting room, the place looked tidy and unused, the units wiped clean. She took a step back. Upstairs, all the curtains were drawn back in the bedrooms. The place appeared abandoned.

Which didn't make sense. She'd seen the girl come up the path from the beach at nine the previous evening.

She walked the perimeter. It was easier to get her bearings now it was daylight. The nearest house was three hundred metres away. No one would hear a thing.

She went back to the front and tried the door. Also locked. Either the girl was paranoid about security, or she had left. There was only one way to find out. She knocked. Loudly.

Nothing. She tried again. Still no movement. She went around the side and rapped on a window.

Nothing. She had gone.

Tasha moved toward the garden gate and shoved through the overgrown path to the beach, thorns grabbing at her sleeves, until she emerged onto the shingle. In the far distance, beyond the caravan park, she spied a figure moving. A girl. Backpack slung over one shoulder, heading for the slipway.

Tasha followed her line of sight. Up above the beach, a red Mercedes idled with the door hanging open. Waiting for her.

Shit.

She turned and sprinted back up the hill to the cottage and across the path to the field where she'd left her bike.

She wheeled it around, dropped it onto the path, and bumped down the rutted track as fast as she dared, towards the village.

39

It was as he was passing the famous White Horse carving on the Ridgeway east of Weymouth that Rob first noticed the powerful motorbike weaving in and out of view two cars behind. He glanced in the mirror, then back to the road as it snaked down the hill towards the bay.

'Returning to London, love?' he said to his passenger. 'Nice stay?'

Sofie mumbled a reply, distracted.

As they approached the causeway, Rob checked his mirror again, waiting for the bike to overtake on the straight stretch so he could get a proper look. But oddly, it appeared to be maintaining speed and distance to match him.

Rob eased off the gas a little more. The last thing he needed was another ticket. He was already skating close to a suspension after two in as many months.

Entering the town, he remarked on how all the scruffy B&Bs along the promenade, hidden behind scaffolding, were finally getting a facelift.

'We'll soon be the new Margate,' he chuckled.

No response.

Three minutes later, he pulled into the forecourt of the railway station. He hopped out, opened the boot, and handed her her bag. She gave him a faint smile, paid him and mumbled a thank-you, then disappeared into the building without a backwards glance.

Rob climbed back in his cab. And there it was. Pulling in behind him.

It coasted to a stop. The rider dismounted, helmet still on, and walked into the ticket office.

Curiosity got the better of him. Rob got out again, pulled his phone from his jacket, and casually walked over.

The bike was a beast, a black and silver_Kawasaki Ninja. Sleek and immaculate. You didn't see many of those in these parts.

Rob circled it once, snapping a couple of quick shots. No harm in that.

Then he fired up the engine and headed off to the petrol station, thinking how much more driving he would need under his belt before he could retire with one of those.

40

SOMEWHERE IN HIS CONSCIOUSNESS, THERE WAS A LOUD bang. Cal sat up with a jolt, heart racing. For one panicked second, he didn't know where he was.

For the last hour - or minutes, for who knew how long dreams lasted - he had been back on a rooftop in south-west Afghanistan, fifteen years earlier. It was the team's last operation. They'd been tasked with bringing in a notorious warlord nicknamed The Red Fox. In the event, the op had gone wrong, and they had killed not just him, but the entire family.

All but one.

A ten-year-old boy. Cal had been the one to find him cowering on the roof. His hate-filled eyes had fuelled his nightmares ever since.

'Wakey-wakey!' Frank's voice cut through the fog like a razor. He flung open the curtains. 'Looks like we've got their attention at last.'

Cal was sweating.

'Christ, Frank, don't wake me up like that!'

'Sorry, but you've got to get cracking. That list from the

girl's flat that we sent to Bob? MI5 are interested. It appears that Crane may already be under investigation. They want to see you. ASAP.'

Cal wiped his forehead and swung his legs to the floor with a thud. He looked at himself in the hotel bathroom mirror, at his drawn, weary face and tousled hair.

It was good news of sorts. Perhaps they really were getting somewhere at last. He might still be having nightmares about Afghanistan, but could this one soon be over?

He'd learned a long time ago, though, that when the spooks called, it was never that simple.

~

Two hours later, Cal exited the tube at Southwark and walked the short distance to The Canteen, a no-frills coffee shop on Union Street. There was no Bob for him this time. Instead, a young guy in a bomber jacket was waiting for him at a pavement table. He seemed to know exactly who Cal was. He was friendly and non-committal as he led him to a parked Range Rover. They drove south, eventually coming to a halt outside a six-storey office block in Croydon.

The ground floor space felt like any ordinary corporate waiting area, with a semi-circular reception desk and a flatscreen TV showing *Sky News* on silent. A board behind it listed all the tenants in the building. Cal scanned them, trying to find clues that would hint at a government agency, but they all sounded like PR or marketing firms.

After a short wait, he was escorted up to the fourth floor via a keycard elevator. The doors opened onto a minimalist lobby with sweeping views toward Crystal Palace. A woman at the desk waved him to a seat without pausing her phone call.

He thumbed through an old issue of 'The Week' and wondered about who he was about to meet. He didn't have to wonder long.

'Mr. Harrison?' the woman said, finally off the phone.

He stood.

'Sorry to keep you waiting. He'll see you now. But first, I'll need your phone.'

She held out a plastic tray.

'Any smartwatches, tablets, electronic devices?'

'That's it.'

'Thank you. Now, please remove your shoes and step through the scanner.' She pointed to a row of assorted footwear. 'You will find a pair of slippers over there.'

He raised an eyebrow but did as he was told and picked out some brown leather slip-ons. The woman pressed the intercom on her desk. A muffled voice replied.

'You can go straight in,' she said, gesturing to a door at the end of the room. As he approached, it clicked softly open.

The office was large and surprisingly plush. Square and dimly lit, with discreet uplighters bracketed on the walls, the outside world was kept at bay by drawn Venetian blinds. Under a window, on a small antique table, stood a bust of some Greek archer holding a bow.

A man stood behind a desk. No slippers for him, Cal noticed. At least not on his feet, because a burgundy velvet pair monogrammed JH were lined up nearby. With his aristocratic nose, slightly rumpled suit and hair a distinguished grey, he could easily have passed for the chairman of a FTSE 100 company.

'Cal,' he said warmly. 'James Hart. Thanks for coming

at such short notice.'

They shook hands.

'Now, before we start,' said Hart, holding out a stapled two-sheet, 'I need you to sign one of these. Just a formality. I'm sure you're familiar with the procedure.'

Cal glanced at it. It was a simple memorandum confirming that the signatory understands that they are bound by the Official Secrets Acts 1911-1989, and that they have read and understood Section 1 (1) of the Official Secrets Act 1989.

He'd seen it more times than he cared to remember.

'Can I get you a coffee? Tea? Something stronger?'

It was not yet midday. Was this some kind of test? If they'd done their homework, they would know he didn't drink. Or perhaps it was a sign that they hadn't.

'Water will be fine, thanks.'

Hart fetched an Evian, poured it into a spotless glass, and set it beside him, then picked up the signed sheet of paper and slid it onto a tray.

'Sorry about the housekeeping. Bit of a pain, I'm afraid, but there you are.'

'Sure, no worries at all.'

Hart was silent for a moment as he flicked through a manila file, his index finger tapping lightly on the desktop. There was an odd, intermittent squeaking sound, which Cal couldn't quite place. The air-conditioning?

'You've had quite a career, I see. Why did you leave?'

'You mean the army? A few reasons.'

'But you're still on the reserve list?'

'Yes.'

'And Francis Ryan?'

'What about him?'

'You two go back a long way. SRR, am I right?'

'Yeah. He was my section commander.'

Hart looked up.

'But you didn't follow him into his civilian business.' It was a statement, not a question.

Cal smiled faintly. 'I'm not really a techie guy.'

'Pity. He's done well.'

Hart looked like he was going to push further, then seemed to think better of it. He closed the file with a snap and leaned forward.

'So. Tell me everything you know about Sofie James.'

The debrief lasted nearly an hour. Cal ran through the whole story, starting with his involvement with Cambridge Bio twelve months previously to run security for one of their Middle East conferences, to the last-minute call to help out with a Crane fundraising event in London.

Every so often, Hart asked a question to clarify a point, using a fountain pen to jot down notes on a lined yellow legal pad in front of him.

Cal explained about the kidnap threat, and how he had been tasked with looking out for the two research chemists; about the party on the boat; their going ashore with the two girls; and how he had been pulled away by Gebler at the last minute.

He finished with the meeting at the Cambridge offices the following morning, and his subsequent efforts to try to find out what happened.

At the end of it, Hart steepled his fingers and sat back.

'Sounds like a very hectic few days.'

'You could say that.'

He nodded in sympathy.

'We appreciate you coming forward. Cambridge has been under scrutiny for some time. What you found in her flat was very interesting.' He paused. 'Do you have any idea where Sofie is now?'

Cal shook his head. 'I wish I knew.'

'Because we believe she's in danger. That's where you can help.'

Cal raised an eyebrow. 'You want me to bring her in?'

'Yes.'

He paused to consider for a moment.

'Do you have a plan?' he said eventually.

'We're working on that. We've got her flat under surveillance, and we've picked up chatter that she may be on her way back. If she does turn up there, we need to be ready for her. But we don't have much time.'

'Meaning?'

'Forty-eight hours at the outside.'

Cal fell silent again.

'Well,' said Hart, eyes steady. 'Are you up for it? You've spent time with the girl, after all. She might trust you.'

Cal frowned. 'Not sure I would go that far. But potentially yes. It depends.'

'Good. Have a think about it. But don't take too long. We'll need your answer in the next few hours. In the meantime, before you go, I want you to meet someone.'

He picked up his desk phone. 'Send her in,' he said softly.

He turned to Cal.

'She's the person running point on this. A colleague from Thames House.'

Ten seconds later, there was a knock.

'Come,' he said.

The door opened, and a shape blocked the doorway.

Cal turned. And froze.

41

Sofie's train drew into Waterloo just after eleven. By then, her unease had curdled into full-blown dread. She didn't want to go back to Kate's flat. Nor to hers. But if she were to get answers, she saw no other way.

The station was busy. Crowds of travellers were milling about under the departure boards, waiting for their train to be called. She waded through them and made for a snack bar to grab a sandwich and a bottle of water. She was famished. Unwrapping it on the go, she headed down to the Northern Line.

It didn't take long to reach Kate's street. As before, she climbed down to the basement and rummaged under the brick.

But the key had gone. Now her pulse really started to race.

Shakily, she retraced her steps and pressed the buzzer to the ground-floor flat, marked Fitzgerald.

The door opened. More than a crack, though not fully. Guarded. 'Yes?'

'Hi, it's Sofie. Sofie James.'

The woman looked her up and down, her face like granite.

'I'm a friend of Kate's,' Sofie explained.

Recognition flickered. 'Oh yes, hello,' the woman said, her face breaking into worry. 'What terrible news, isn't it? We're all shocked.'

'Can I come in?'

'Oh yes. Of course.'

She was a large, florid woman with a mass of unruly white hair, wearing a plastic apron over a floral pattern dress in clashing colours and a pair of fluffy slippers. The ankles that stood out of them were swollen and lumpy beneath their red stockinged sheaths, like country salamis. Sofie followed her into a lounge thick with heat from a bar fire. Next to it, a smoky blue Burmese lounged on a sofa. Its eyes followed Sofie suspiciously.

'Can I get you a cup of tea?'

She swatted the cat off the couch with a practised flick. It shot onto the floor and stalked off into the hall. Shifting a tangle of knitting, she beckoned for Sofie to sit.

'That's kind of you, but no thanks, I can't stay long. I just wondered whether…'

She hesitated, not quite sure how to broach the subject.

'…whether anyone has been round asking about Kate? The police, for example?'

Mrs. Fitzgerald's mauve eye shadow creased as she raised an eyebrow.

'Haven't they half!' she said. 'Been twice in three days. First time, they said she was missing. Next thing I know, she's been killed in Ukraine. Dreadful.'

Sofie smoothed her hair nervously. 'D'you mind my asking when they were here?'

'Let me see now... the first lot, Sunday I think it was. In

the morning. I told them she was away, if she wasn't answering, like.'

'Did they want to check? Go up there, I mean? Did you give them a key?'

'No. Didn't ask. But the second time... yes, two of them, in plain clothes, said they had a search warrant. I let them in.' She shook her head. 'Turned the place over, they did, made a frightful mess.'

'When was this?'

'Last night. Around ten. Funny thing was, they knew nothing about the earlier visit. The man was very polite, very charming.' She scratched her head. 'Now what did they call them, the uniformed fellas? Hopscotch merchants.'

Sofie frowned. 'But they were police officers, you're sure of that?'

Mrs Fitzgerald looked alarmed. 'Well, who else would they be?' She chewed the side of her finger. 'Terrible,' she repeated. 'Just awful.'

'Has anyone else been by? Her parents, for example?'

'They were over yesterday morning. It was odd, though.'

'What was odd?'

'Well, I'd met them a few times before since Kate moved in. They're normally very friendly. But yesterday…' She gazed at the ceiling. 'They didn't want to talk at all. Just took a bag of her stuff away. In and out in twenty minutes.'

'Maybe they were in shock.'

The woman shrugged helplessly. Sofie was anxious to move things on.

'Would you mind taking me up there? Kate normally leaves the key under a brick, but for some reason it's gone.'

Mrs. Fitzgerald heaved a sigh and shuffled off to fetch a spare. Sofie walked to the window, pulled back the lace curtain, and looked out. The street was quiet.

A minute later, they climbed the stairs in silence, the woman puffing heavily. As they entered the flat, Sofie gasped.

It was a tip. Drawers had been emptied, rugs taken up, books pulled from shelves.

'See what I mean?' said Mrs. Fitzgerald. She began to make a start at tidying up.

This was not the work of the police. If there had been any clues as to what had happened to Kate, they were certainly not here now. Sofie cursed herself for not having looked before. She had a sudden urge to get out.

'I'm sorry,' she whispered, voice cracking. 'I can't do this.'

Without stopping to explain, she bolted out of the door and down the stairs. Behind her, she heard Mrs Fitzgerald call out.

'Sofie? Are you alright, love?'

Her heart was beating furiously. If they had found Kate, how long before they found her too?

42

Thursday 3rd November

Sofie now knew one thing for certain. She couldn't go home. She made a snap decision: she'd stay the night in a hotel while she figured out what to do.

The Rose and Crown in Stoke Newington High Street was close to Brooke Road and a place she knew well. She'd spent many evenings drinking in the pub with friends. But it was still early, so she spent the afternoon wandering around Clissold Park before checking in at six.

Once in, she went straight to her room and locked the door. She didn't want to be seen, nor to bump into anyone she knew in the bar. Plus, she was exhausted, emotionally as well as physically. By the time she'd soaked in a too-hot bath and had an hour of mindless channel hopping - anything to distract her - she was feeling drowsy. She kept trying to think of how she was going to get back to her flat, to find her father's stuff, without being seen. But her brain wouldn't function, and by nine, she was asleep, the TV still on low in the background.

The next morning, she woke with a sense of impending doom, the gravity of her situation weighing her down. Until an idea came to her.

A brilliant idea: a way both to protect herself, find her father's address book and, perhaps, get evidence that would convince the police. Because if the state of Kate's flat was anything to go by, what were the chances that they'd done the same to hers?

She grabbed her phone and scrolled through her contacts until she found DC Khan's number. The detective seemed surprised to hear from her. At first, she told Sofie that if she had new evidence, she needed to come in. But when Sofie outlined what she and Mrs Fitzgerald had witnessed the day before in Kate's flat, and how she feared that her own flat might have been broken into, Khan softened.

As it happened, the detective said, she was due to be in the area on another matter later that afternoon. She could meet her at five.

Sofie rang off with a feeling of triumph. Now they would see! Now they would take her seriously!

At four, she was back at the newsagent.

'Hey Ali, have you got my key?'

He looked up at her in surprise.

'I didn't recognise you, Miss James, in that scarf. By the way,' he said, reaching into a drawer and handing her a rubber elephant ring, 'You didn't tell me you were renting out your flat.'

She paused. 'I'm not. Who told you I was?'

'A man came in a few days ago looking for you. Said he wanted to rent it. Asked when you'd be back.'

'And what did you tell him?' she said sharply.

'Said I didn't know.'

Her eyes darted around the shop, but apart from an old lady browsing the card rack, they were alone.

'Thanks, Ali. If anyone comes back, that's what you tell them. I'm only stopping for a few hours.'

She hastened across the road to the café. She would watch for the detective's arrival, and they would go up together. The young girl behind the counter recognised her and smiled.

'How's it going?'

'Fine, thanks,' said Sofie, collecting a coffee.

So it was true. They had found her. She prayed that her flat was trashed. Then they'd see. Together.

She had an hour to wait. She nursed the coffee, sipping it slowly, examining every car and passer-by for any sign that they might be looking for her. She forced herself to stay calm. DC Khan would be here soon.

At five to five, her phone rang. Her ex, Martin.

She knew she should pick up. He'd probably found out by now, wanted to check that she was OK. But what if her phone had been bugged? She swiped 'decline'.

Thirty seconds later, a maroon Vauxhall Astra pulled up. She should have remembered that the detective wouldn't arrive in a patrol car, and only realised it was DC Khan when she saw the woman climbing her steps and ringing her bell.

She paid up and sprinted across the road.

'Officer?'

Khan turned, startled. 'Miss James.'

'I'll explain everything,' Sofie said, breathless, already fumbling with the key. Her fingers felt thick and uncooperative.

'All OK?'

She stepped in hurriedly, ushering the DC after her.

'I'm fine. Please. Say nothing until we're upstairs.'

They climbed the narrow staircase in silence. Sofie

paused at the top, staring at the lock. It looked untouched.

Her stomach dropped.

She turned the key. The first thing she saw was the books: half a dozen were stacked on the floor. She hadn't left them like that. And the answerphone was blinking. Not the normal slow pulse, but fast. Reset wrong. Tampered with.

Khan stepped in behind her. 'Miss James, do you mind telling me what this is all about?'

Sofie walked toward the kitchen. The cupboard was open. Not huge, but… she always closed that cupboard. Always. It hung right at head level, and she'd clocked herself on it too many times not to be careful.

But it was when she got to the bedroom that it hit her for sure.

The place had been torn apart. The drawers had been pulled out, and clothes were scattered all over the floor.

She felt a mixture of terror and elation, fear and relief.

She turned to Khan, heart hammering. 'There!' she said triumphantly. '*Now* do you believe me?'

Khan surveyed the mess. 'When did this happen?'

'While I was gone.'

'And when did you discover it?'

'*What d'you mean?* Right now! I haven't been back since I left!'

Khan frowned. 'So how did you know?'

'I didn't, but I suspected. Because of what we found in Kate's flat.'

Khan didn't reply. Sofie turned away and started checking on the rest of her flat. Broken glass was scattered on the bathroom floor from a jagged hole in the window.

'Here!' she called.

Khan came over.

'Anything missing?'

'Nothing will be.'

'Why do you say that?'

'Because they were after something I don't have.'

DC Khan's eyes narrowed. '*They*? Who are *they*, Miss James? Do you know who did this?'

'It's to do with the boat, don't you get it? I witnessed the shooting. They want to find out what else I know. They think I'm a journalist like Kate. And they know where I live. For all we know, they're watching my flat right now.'

'Mmm.'

She stared hard at the detective. 'That's why I brought you. So you could see it for yourself. So you'd understand that I'm not paranoid. I'm a witness. I need protection!'

The policewoman didn't look as impressed as Sofie expected.

'OK, let's rewind a minute,' Khan said, sitting on the edge of the bed. 'You're jumping to conclusions. First of all, your friend Kate was killed in Ukraine. I get it, her death hit you hard… '

'*She was not killed in Ukraine!*' Sofie screamed. 'She was shot on that boat, I saw it!'

Khan laid a hand on her arm, but she brushed it away.

'So the BBC made it up?'

'I've no fucking idea! They must have been misled. All I know is what I saw. I mean, don't you think it's weird that I should report a killing two days before it's supposed to have taken place?'

Khan followed her gaze. 'I'm not paid to conjecture on weird, Sofie. I'm paid to ascertain facts. Until we have some evidence…'

'But what about *this*?' she cried. 'Doesn't this qualify as evidence to you?' Her voice dropped to a hoarse whisper, and she slumped to the bed. 'Help me. Please.'

Khan sighed, stood, and checked her watch.

'I can see you're upset. And I'm going to get you some help, I promise you.'

She laid her hand on Sofie's shoulder. This time, she didn't shake it off.

'But I'm afraid I have an appointment in half an hour. I'll follow up in the morning, and we'll work something out. You have my word.' She rose to go. 'How's that sound? Meanwhile, try to get some rest.'

Sofie shook her head slowly. She felt stunned.

'That's it? I just snuggle up under my duvet and pretend this never happened?"

'Sofie…'

She got up. 'Thanks for your time, Detective.'

She let her out with a cold nod, locked the door, and leaned against it as it clicked shut.

She couldn't believe this was happening.

43

The techno beat started up around nine. Sofie had hardly stirred since the detective left. What a fail. Khan clearly didn't believe that there was any connection. Nothing could get her past the fact - their fact, not Sofie's - that Kate had been killed in Ukraine. Where before the woman had seemed sympathetic, it was now clear that she had begun to look at Sofie in a completely different light.

Her neighbours upstairs were having a party. A new girl called Vicky had moved in. She was a friend of Martin's, and Sofie had found an invitation shoved under her door. Maybe that was what he had been calling about? There was laughter and crashing around in the stairwell as people began to arrive. Several times her buzzer went, but after the first time - *'Hello, Kat here. Am I early? Oh, soz, got the wrong bell!'* - she ignored it. Instead, she lay on her sofa, staring blindly at the ceiling. The music thumped louder. She felt vulnerable. Exposed.

But then, slowly, a plan began to form. The party. It provided the perfect cover to slip away. Guests would be coming and going all night. Moreover, she could lay a false trail and leave word that she was off to see her mother in America. She smiled to herself grimly at the shock her mother's husband would get if he found people snooping around for her. It wouldn't fool anyone for long, but it would buy her some time.

But first, she needed to do what she came for, which was to find her father's address book. It didn't take long. It was tucked inside one of his storage boxes. A quick flick through the pages yielded nothing right away, and she stuffed it into her backpack. Rummaging around for anything else she might need over the next few weeks, she added some warmer clothes, a couple of scarves and a fresh pair of trainers. And her passport. Last, she taped up the hole in the bathroom window. By ten, she was ready.

Before leaving, she rang for a cab to pick her up in thirty minutes. She didn't plan to stay long. Just long enough to speak to Vicky. Then exit via the fire escape on the roof.

She switched off the TV, tidied up, and made to leave. On her way out, she caught sight of herself in the mirror.

She looked terrible. Hair everywhere, eyes hollow and pale. Hurrying into the bathroom, she scraped on some makeup and dragged a brush through, tying it into a ponytail.

As she was closing the door, her pocket started to vibrate. It triggered a thought: shouldn't she get rid of it? Isn't that what they did in all those spy movies, snapping the phones, dumping them in bins? It was Martin again. She swiped left, sprang open the SIM card and tossed it into her key basket, along with the phone. Finally, she locked up and climbed the two flights of stairs to the top flat, backpack looped around one shoulder.

The door was ajar, the noise deafening. She stepped in.

The party was packed. A thumping bass thudded out of

speakers on stands against the wall, and in the far corner, a trestle table held rows of bottles and glasses. She pushed her way through the press of bodies until she spied her new neighbour at the end of the room. She had been very friendly when she'd moved in three weeks earlier. Sofie had even helped carry some of her potted plants. Now she looked out of it, despite the early hour. Someone beside her was rolling a spliff.

Sofie hesitated. Would Vicky even remember if she told her that she was going abroad? She glanced at her watch - twenty minutes before the cab would be downstairs.

Vicky smiled vaguely when Sofie reached her. 'Oh, hey.'

'Great party,' Sofie said, raising her voice over the din.

She nodded at the drinks table. 'Grab yourself a cocktail.'

'Thanks, I will.'

The girl turned and whispered something in the ear of the man next to her. Sofie was on the point of interrupting, but stopped herself. The timing wasn't right. Too loud. Too chaotic. She'd message her later. She turned away.

She remembered from a time she'd been to a dinner with the previous tenants that the door to the roof was through the kitchen. She battled her way towards it. People were laughing and drinking, helping themselves to ice from the freezer. Half-drunk bottles of Prosecco dotted the worktop.

On the way through, she could have sworn that someone called her name. But without pausing, she made her way towards the end of the room and climbed the steps. At the top was another door, opening outwards on a latch.

The roof smelled damp, like it had just rained, and pools of water lay dotted around the uneven asphalt. A couple of smokers were huddled in conversation, leaning against a parapet that ran around the edge. In the distance, a string of neighbouring chimneys was silhouetted against the dark mass of Hackney Marsh to the east. The moon was up, waning now but still bright. A battery of arc lights beyond marked the marshalling yards of Stratford.

She hurried towards the far end and gingerly stepped onto the slippery metal platform that led to the fire escape.

The first level she came to was directly opposite Vicky's bathroom. The light was on, and a girl was leaning over the sink. She glanced up at Sofie in surprise, but she ignored her and plunged on into the darkness. Next, she passed her own bathroom. She stopped to check that the flap of cardboard she'd taped over the smashed window was secure. Small slivers of glass were scattered on the metal steps, shards she had not had time to tidy up. She wondered when she would be back.

She carried on down.

The last two levels were illuminated by reflected light from the street, and below her, she glimpsed the foot of the fire escape in the basement well. But as she reached the first floor, someone else came into view, climbing onto the bottom step.

She tensed. A guest? A gatecrasher?

She pressed back to allow whoever it was to pass, her heart thumping. The figure climbed towards her, oblivious to her presence.

At five metres, by the light of a street lamp, she made out the shape of a woman, now stopped two steps below and looked directly up at her. There seemed to be a flash of recognition in her eyes.

'Sofie?'

Sofie stared, startled, and backed up.

The stranger bounded up towards her, arm

outstretched.

Sofie screamed, fear gripping her, and fled back up.

But the woman was too fast for her. In two bounds, she was on her. They grappled, but with the advantage of height, Sofie was able to kick out and break free. Terrified, she flew back up past her flat, momentarily wondering whether she could make it through the broken window and lock the bathroom door behind her to slow the woman's progress. But, in an instant, she realised she would never reach it in time. She shot past, focused on reaching the roof. Two steps at a time. But the woman was gaining again.

Suddenly, she stumbled, her knee crashing against metal. She screamed again, clawing her way up. A hand grabbed her foot.

'Who the fuck are you!' she cried. 'Let go!'

Sofie lashed out with all her force, wrenching herself away. Then bolted, breathless, past the window of Vicky's bathroom - empty now - and onto the roof, backpack swinging wildly. A figure emerged from the stairwell at the far end, music pulsing from below through the open door.

Martin!

She shrieked.

'Sofie?' He stopped, a look of confusion on his face.

'*Martin!*' she cried, stumbling towards him. 'Thank God!'

He stared at her. 'What the hell's going on?'

He stood with his legs slightly apart, defensive.

She twisted her head towards the fire escape, a look of terror on her face. But her pursuer was nowhere to be seen.

'*There's someone after me!*'

He looked past her. 'After you? Where?'

'On the fire escape!'

He hesitated.

'Are you on something?'

'*Of course I'm not fucking on something!*' She had a wild look in her eyes.

'So what were you doing on the roof?'

She put her arm in his and tried to propel him backwards.

'*Come on, please!* Help me out of here!'

He stiffened.

'Seriously? Where the hell have you been?' She was urging him towards the door. 'I heard that you were in some kind of trouble.'

They stumbled through, and she yanked it shut behind her. The latch clicked shut. Safe. For now.

'I've been calling you,' he said as she hustled him down the stairs. 'I was worried. You weren't answering your phone.'

'I'll explain,' she said, breathless.

As they re-entered the kitchen, she stopped dead. Shit! Where was her backpack? She remembered she had it with her as she stumbled off the fire escape.

Without a word, she turned and ran back up the stairs. Heart pounding, she eased the door open and scanned the roof. The woman had disappeared. Had she gone back down to the street to wait for her there? She realised that she would have to mingle with people leaving, and dive into the cab before her pursuer could get to her. She'd need Martin's help.

Five metres away, halfway across the roof, she spied it.

Cautiously, she stepped out. The door swung behind her with a click. She spun round. Too late. It had latched shut.

She grabbed her backpack and raced back, hammering on the door. But through the music, no one could hear her.

Then another noise. Behind her.

For a second, she stood there, stunned, but before she could react, a hand was around her mouth. She tried to scream, but nothing came out, as the woman began to drag her towards the edge of the roof. Sofie twisted against her, jabbing her knee sideways, but the force of their backwards movement was too strong. She yanked Sofie's head back, her hand in a fistful of hair. Sofie felt a sharp stab of pain.

It was all over fast. Before she knew it, her body was arched over the parapet, the hard metal rail digging into her spine. For a second, the woman released her hand from Sofie's mouth, and she screamed, but instantly, a fist smashed into her jaw. There was a flash of steel, and she began to choke, tasting blood.

She felt her strength ebbing.

The woman went about her work with almost clinical precision. She began with Sofie's shirt, ripping at it under her jacket, and she felt the buttons pop in rapid succession, the noise of the shredding material, the violence of it, filling her head. Hands fumbled for her bra, fingernails digging into her flesh as they yanked at it, snapping the clasp at her back. Her breasts tumbled out, marble white in the darkness. Oh God, please God, she thought, waiting for what was coming in powerless terror.

Was she going to rape her? Or kill her?

Sofie's hand flailed out into thin air. Far below, there was the sound of laughter, and a car door slammed. Music was blaring out across the street. Even if she screamed, they probably wouldn't hear her. But she dared not. There was a knife at her throat.

'Please,' she whispered desperately. '*What have I done?* I don't understand!'

She felt her keys tumble out of her pocket. Everything began to slow down. With a sense of detachment, almost divorced from what was happening to her, Sofie no longer registered the pain. There was something dangerously cold about this woman.

She was tall, her blonde hair cropped short, her skin smooth and flawless. A tattoo covered the back of her neck. And now she was close-up, oddly familiar. Where had she seen her before?

How could one woman do this to another? No hurry, no frenzy, just methodical and deliberate. And then, with horrifying clarity, she understood. This wasn't a sexual assault.

She was just making it look that way.

Sofie snapped out of her shock, a burning fury welling up inside her. She scrabbled blindly for a loose brick, a stone, a shard of glass; anything to use as a weapon. The brickwork was old, and small lumps of mortar crumbled in her hands. Two feet down, barely within reach, was a narrow ledge, and her hand strayed against something thin and hard. It almost rolled off into space before she was able to grab hold of it.

Her father's flag pole!

He'd fashioned it for a party she'd had out of a steel rod, not long before he died, and fixed it in a bracket on the outside wall to hang the Irish tricolour. Redundant, forgotten and untouched since he'd abandoned it.

And now a lifesaver.

Straining with the effort, barely able to hold the weight and the muscles of her arm screaming in pain, she swung it above her and brought it crashing down on the woman's head. The knife scraped against her neck as she staggered backwards. Sofie arched up, pushing against her, concentrating all her weight as she swung her fist. Her attacker fell, off balance, and Sofie was up and away from the edge and racing towards the fire escape.

'What's going on?'

It was a man's voice.

Dimly, she registered the woman swinging around to face the new threat. It was Martin. There was a violent struggle followed by a piercing yell. In the distraction, she stumbled down the steps, taking four at a time.

One level down, she realised she wasn't going to make it. The woman had reappeared above her and would surely catch her before she reached the ground. As she reached Vicky's bathroom, she crashed through the open window and skidded to the floor. A man was bent over the bath. A girl was with him. She shrieked.

'Be careful, fuck it!' the man yelled. His mouth dropped open as he saw the state of her: 'Hey, what's going on?'

Without a word, Sofie ran past them, shirt ripped, blood smeared across her mouth. Someone appeared in the passageway.

'Where's Vicky?' Sofie cried. 'I need a phone!'

The man stared at her in shock. 'I think she's through there.'

Sofie lurched on. Beside the front door was a retro black landline phone on a cord. Without checking for a tone, she dialled 999, each nine crawling around the face of the old-fashioned dialer agonisingly slowly.

The line was dead.

The bathroom door to her right opened, and the end of the corridor was suddenly bathed in light. Someone came out, and everything plunged into gloom again. Could it be her? Sofie didn't wait to find out. She dropped the phone with a clatter and rejoined the throng.

The noise was more startling this time around. Drinks were flying, people were chatting animatedly, laughing, gesturing, swaying to the rhythm. The lights were dimmed, and nobody noticed her.

'Has anyone seen Vicky?' she shouted 'Help me! Please… *someone…*'

A girl laughed, her teeth flashing white. Sofie searched the faces for someone she recognised. The woman would not try anything amongst all these people. Surely?

And then she saw her. An indistinct figure standing tall in the doorway, scanning the room over the heads of the dancers. Ducking out of view, Sofie ran at waist height along the wall to the door. A couple coming in almost fell over her.

'Hey, careful where you're going!' she heard one of them say.

Shoving past them, she leapt down the stairs.

Downstairs, a Toyota was idling in the street, its telltale triangular cab licence visible in the rear window. She didn't stop to check whether it was hers. She shot into the back.

'Go!'

The driver glanced in the mirror in surprise. He folded his newspaper.

'Are you Sofie James?'

'Yes! Please hurry! There's someone after me!'

He slid his window down and peered out into the street.

'*Go!*' she screamed.

The driver checked his rearview mirror and pulled away smoothly. Ten metres back, she saw the woman explode from the front door. She disappeared from view behind a line of cars. Sofie held her breath.

'Are you hurt?'

Sofie didn't answer. All her senses were focused on what was going on behind them. A motorbike drew away from the curb. It began to accelerate after them, rapidly reaching a crescendo.

Sofie froze in her seat and closed her eyes. So this was it. In moments, it would be over. She crashed forward as the car skidded to a halt, and she dimly registered a door opening. Then there was a bang, followed by a metallic clatter as something swerved across the road. She huddled in the footwell. Someone grabbed her by the neck, and a damp cloth was jammed over her mouth.

It was the last thing she remembered.

44

Friday 4th November

WHEN SOFIE CAME TO, THE FIRST THING SHE REGISTERED was the silence. The second was the pain. Everything ached. Her head pounded like she'd been drugged, her arm throbbed, and her mouth tasted like gun metal. She blinked hard. Light was bleeding in around the edges of drawn curtains, but it took a while, longer than it should have, for her to focus.

She was in a bed. And it wasn't hers.

She sat up. A thick tartan throw covered a white duvet. Opposite was a sash window, and beside her, a bedside table with a glass of water. She leant over and took a sip. Slowly, her eyes became accustomed to the light. On the walls were paintings of sailing boats, and on the back of the door was a fluffy blue dressing gown. She strained to listen for noises, but everything was quiet, not even the sound of traffic.

Where the hell was she?

Easing her legs off the bed, she stood up unsteadily. She was fully dressed, minus her jacket, which was laid neatly in a corner, along with her shoes. Her backpack was leaning against a chair.

She limped to the window, the floorboards creaking beneath the carpet, and pulled back the curtain. And started in shock. Below was a gravelled yard, and beyond that, outbuildings. To the right, across a small river, green fields stretched into the distance.

What the hell? This felt all wrong. How had she got here?

Turning back to the bed, she noticed the door to the bathroom. She fled inside, bolted it, and slumped down on the toilet, head in her hands. Think, Sofie. What was the last thing you remember? It had been nighttime. The party. A woman had attacked her. She remembered Martin and fleeing down the stairs.

After that, nothing. A blank.

She remained motionless, listening to the silence of the house, waiting for something to make sense. Finally, she stood, approached the mirror, and flinched. Her reflection was ghostly. A bruise blossomed across her jaw like a purple brand. She began to wash furiously, splashing water into her eyes. As she unbolted the door and stepped back into the room, she heard another door open.

A woman appeared.

'Ah, good. You're awake. How are you feeling?'

Sofie stared at her, open-mouthed. This person looked fresh-faced and efficient, pretty with short dark hair and wearing a navy blue cashmere sweater.

'Cup of tea?'

'Why…' stuttered Sofie. 'How…'

The woman smiled thinly.

'Ha. You'll have to ask my husband. He's got a habit of bringing strange women home for the weekend, but you take the biscuit.' She placed the tea on the bedside table, then drew the curtains open with one brisk movement. 'I'll send him up.'

Without waiting for a reaction, the woman strode out, leaving the door ajar behind her.

Sofie sank into an armchair, stunned. She wrapped her hands around the mug like it might anchor her to reality, her mind thick with confusion.

She didn't have long to wait. Shortly, there was the creak of stairs and footsteps approaching. A man poked his head around the door.

'You decent?'

She started in alarm. 'Who the hell are you?'

He stepped in, a second man behind him. Sofie almost spilt her tea. His companion had blue-grey eyes and a light dusting of stubble. It was the man from the boat. Cal.

She stood up so fast that the tea sloshed.

'*You!*' she cried. 'What the hell are you doing here? What is this?'

They sat down on the edge of the bed.

'Sofie, I can understand how you feel. How this looks…'

She backed away towards the window. Suddenly fearful.

'Where are we?'

'You're in Suffolk,' Frank said. 'This is my house, and you're our guest. You are free to go, any time you like. We won't stop you, I promise.'

'That's right,' Cal added. His voice was softer, familiar. 'It was we who saved you back there at your flat. We've been trying to track you down all week.'

'*You what?!*'

'We picked you up. Someone was trying to kill you.'

'They want you dead, it seems,' added Frank.

A beat. Sofie stared at them.

'Yes, I know that.' She narrowed her eyes. 'But why you?'

Somewhere outside, a flock of geese flew low over the water, screeching.

'We'll get to that,' Cal said. 'But first, rest. Eat. Then we'll talk.'

Sofie held his gaze. Defensive.

'How can I trust you?'

He hesitated. Then reached into his pocket and handed her a scrap of paper and a beat-up Nokia.

'Dial that number,' he said. 'Ask your questions there. If you still want to leave after that, we'll drive you to the station. No pressure.' He raised an eyebrow. 'How's that for a deal?'

She squinted at it. Frank smiled at her reassuringly.

'Nice to meet the girl from the boat finally. Cal's told me a lot about you.'

'What can he possibly know about me?' she muttered.

'And if you're still here in an hour, come down for lunch. Emily's making shepherd's pie.'

The two men left, and the door clicked shut.

Sofie stared after them. She sat down on the edge of the bed and peered at the note. Police? It was a mobile number, so it couldn't be Lewisham police station.

Was it DC Khan's personal number?

After a moment's hesitation, she punched it into the phone. It rang twice.

'Sofie?' said a female voice.

Her breath caught.

'Sofie, is that you?'

'Who is this?'

A beat.

'Doll, it's Kate.'

Part Three

45

Rewind to two days previously

'Hello, Cal.'

The words stopped him cold.

The woman sitting in the wheelchair blocking the doorway was copper-haired and bandaged. She gripped the wheels tightly, watching him.

It couldn't be.

Cal rose to his feet slowly. 'Do I know you?'

She gave a crooked smile. 'Well, we know *of* each other, let's put it that way.'

Hart got up to help her spin the chair around to face them. She moved stiffly, like every motion hurt.

'Cal,' he said. 'This is Kate Winter. She was on board the boat that night with Sofie James.'

So it was her.

'My God. I thought you were dead. The BBC reported that you were killed in Ukraine.'

She grinned.

'Yeah, I'll admit, it came as a bit of a surprise to me too, when I finally regained consciousness.'

'So what happened?' he said quickly. 'How did you get

off that boat?'

Kate glanced at Hart, who gave a small nod. She took a breath and began to talk.

She retold her story from the day she'd had coffee with Sofie in the cafe in Islington a fortnight before, to the evening they'd boarded the riverboat ten days later for the Cambridge Bio event on the Thames. She explained how they had met up with two whistleblowers who had information on a secret drug trial. Horrifically, she relived the moment the gunman had appeared. Cal listened intently, only interrupting once for clarification.

'On the sixth shot, his gun jammed. The chemists were already dead, as was the guy who'd arranged the cabin cruiser for us to hold our meeting on. I didn't witness it at the time, but we later found out he'd had his throat slit, outside on the pontoon. He turned up as the victim of a domestic incident the next day. A fabrication, of course.'

She paused for breath, shifting in her chair.

'That left me and Sofie. I had been hit here,' she touched her shoulder, 'and Sofie was still in the toilet, where she'd gone in the middle of our meeting. Said she'd felt sick. The gunman was clearing the jam when she reappeared. Luckily for me, he went after her. Assumed I was incapacitated, I guess. In the chaos, I managed to drag myself out onto the deck and into the river.'

'Jesus,' Cal muttered.

'That's when I blacked out. They found me downriver hours later and took me to hospital in a coma. I had no ID on me. They thought I was a suicide attempt.'

Cal looked incredulous. 'What, with a gunshot wound?'

'Nobody noticed it, initially. It wasn't until I got to ReSus that they discovered it. Incredibly, although there had been a report of a shooting by the river, no one connected the dots. The hospital I was taken to was several miles away. They couldn't identify me.'

'So how did they figure it out?'

'A colleague found me. They'd been searching all over the city.'

'Another journalist?'

'Kate's not a journalist, Cal,' Hart cut in. 'She's one of ours.'

Kate looked at Cal meaningfully.

'I work for the Security Service,' she said.

Cal let out a low whistle. 'Did your friend know that?'

'Sofie? No.'

He sat back, his mind racing. What was an MI5 agent doing meeting those two whistleblowers? Who had tried to kill them? Why, when she surfaced, didn't they report it to the police?

'It *was* reported, Cal,' Hart said. 'But we took it out of their hands. We can't afford this to go public until we have a handle on what's going on. Besides, as far as they are concerned, Kate is dead, and we'd like to keep it that way.'

He got up and poured himself a drink, waving the bottle of Evian water in their direction, but they both declined.

'We need time to unravel who is behind this,' he continued, resuming his seat. 'What happened that night points to a rogue actor within the Service. Working with whom, or for whom, we don't yet know, but it's clear they are out to protect Crane. The fact that the bodies of the whistleblowers disappeared, and that someone planted a press story about Kate's death in Ukraine after she had gone missing - it all points to a massive conspiracy.'

He paused to straighten a pencil on his desktop.

'Now, as I said before, the reason we are here talking to

you, Cal, why we've asked you in, is that we want your help getting Sofie out.'

Cal looked from one to the other but said nothing, wondering what was coming next.

'What you and Frank Ryan found in her apartment earlier this week suggests she has information on the drug trial. It could help us uncover the truth.'

'Why do you suppose she was sent it?' Cal said.

'Because they think she's a journalist. They believe Kate is dead, so now they are trying to get the story out via Sofie.'

'I see.' None of this, he thought, explained why Sofie was with Kate that night in the first place.

'Remind me, Cal,' interrupted Kate. 'Why were *you* looking for her?'

Cal explained how Cambridge Bio had given him responsibility for the security of the two whistleblowers, based on intelligence received, that they were at risk of a kidnapping attempt.

'All bullshit, as it turns out,' he continued. 'They simply needed someone to keep tabs on them. When you all went ashore and boarded that cabin cruiser, I was right behind you and ready to intervene, but they pulled me off and ordered me back to the hotel. So naturally, when they didn't return, I became concerned. Until you told me just now, I had no idea what had happened. All I knew was that you were reported killed in Ukraine two days later, which clearly could not have been true, and that Sofie and the chemists were missing. I had no way of finding out what happened to the whistleblowers, but I did have a lead to Sofie - a telephone number left on her guest pass. That was the lead I was following.'

'Independently? Or on behalf of Cambridge?'

He shook his head. 'On my own. They made it very

clear they didn't want my help, but at the same time, it looked like they were trying to set me up as the fall guy.'

'You're talking about Laura Boyd?'

'And a guy called Charles Gebler.' He frowned. 'What really shook me was when the estate agent got killed. It was her phone number that I had found on the guest pass. Someone hijacked the meeting we had arranged. Got there first, pretending to be me.'

Kate's face paled. 'Yes, when I heard that, I was shocked. I feel responsible.'

'You knew her?'

'Very well. It was I who wrote her number on Sofie's pass.'

'It was *you*?'

'Pure coincidence. I was using my work phone that night and jotted it down because I'd said I'd call her later about a dinner we were organising. Nothing to do with the investigation at all. I meant to write it on my own pass, but ended up writing it on Sofie's by mistake.'

'It still doesn't explain why she was murdered,' said Cal.

'I think it does,' Hart countered. 'Alice Wickman probably became suspicious and had to be silenced. What it does prove, however, is that your life is in danger too. You know too much already.'

Cal laughed bitterly. 'I do now.'

Hart's expression softened. 'I'm sorry you've had to get mixed up in this.'

He doubted it.

'Who else knows about this?' he said.

Hart took a sip of water. 'Other than us? Nobody.'

'Which is why we have to remove Sofie somewhere safe,' continued Kate. 'I would never forgive myself if something happened to her as well.' She glanced at Hart, a pained look in her eyes. 'Unfortunately, there's little I can do to help her from this bloody wheelchair. I'm out of the game for now.' She regarded Cal. 'Which is where you come in.'

'So how can I help you?'

'We need your support in extracting her. She's in a lot of danger, running around on her own. We've had intelligence that whoever tried to kill us is closing in on her.'

'But why me? You think she'll trust me?' He turned to Hart. 'I think that's highly unlikely. I was working for Cambridge, remember.'

'True,' Hart said, 'but at least she's met you, and you can explain that they're after you too.' A beat. 'Besides, we're not sure who we can rely on, outside of this room.'

A better reason.

'We need you to find out how much she knows. For example, the document you found in her flat. Is there more? Has she been in touch with others at Cambridge Bio since the killings? And what about on the boat? Did she get a sight of the killer? Kate tells me he was wearing a motorcycle helmet. Perhaps Sofie got a better view of him.'

'And then?' Cal said.

'Once we have her in a safe place,' Kate replied, 'we'll arrange more permanent protection for her. To give us time to resolve this …' she searched for the right word '… situation.'

'So. There you have it,' Hart said, rising. 'Do you need time to consider? As I said, we don't have much time.'

Cal regarded them both in silence for a moment.

'OK,' he said. 'I'll do it on one condition.'

Hart stood by the edge of his desk..

'What's that?'

'I want Frank in the loop. I'll need his help.'

Hart hesitated, as if weighing it up.

'OK,' he said finally. 'Agreed.' He walked to the door and opened it. 'And now, I suggest I leave it to you and Kate to make a plan.'

46

Friday 4th November

'You can't be serious?'

Sofie stared at Cal like he'd just told her the Pope had been outed as a woman. They were seated around the kitchen table of Frank's farmhouse in Suffolk.

'It's true. She works for MI5.'

Sofie blinked. 'But I've known her since we were at Uni together! How is that possible?'

'Well, that's the point. Spies live double lives.'

'Surely I would have known?' she said. 'Besides, as far as I'm aware, she's still working as a journalist. When she got me involved in her investigation, she said it was for the Sunday Times.'

'Can't those two things both be true at the same time?' Frank interrupted. 'What better cover than to be working as a news reporter?'

'Hardly ethical, is it? You wouldn't last long once as a journalist once suspicions were raised. Or a spy, come to that.'

'Sofie, ethics don't enter into it,' said Cal. 'Her press credentials help her get to places others wouldn't be able to go. It's all about access.'

Sofie got up abruptly and went to the window, flicking her ponytail in short, sharp movements, like a horse about to bolt. Outside, a pile of autumn leaves was swirling about the yard, a north-westerly breeze beginning to pick up on the river from the direction of Woodbridge.

'But wasn't that the opportunity to tell me, that day in the cafe, what her real motive was?'

'If she had, would you still have got involved?'

Sofie didn't reply. Frank's wife, Emily, stuck her head around the door.

'Lunch will be ready in twenty minutes,' she mouthed.

Sofie shook her head in disbelief. 'I have to say, I feel betrayed.'

'She didn't say anything on the phone when you spoke to her this morning?'

'Nothing.'

'Maybe she feared it would be too much for you to process. The fact that she survived the shooting, more than you could handle. She left it to me to break it to you.'

Sofie swivelled back to him. 'OK, now you have, where does that leave us? Give me one good reason I should stay?'

Cal glanced at Frank. She was clearly in shock. The question was, how much should he tell her at this stage without frightening her off?

Frank took the hint and got up. 'You two obviously have a lot to talk about. See you for lunch in a while?'

'Thanks, but we'll skip. Sofie, let's do this in the pub. I do need to ask you some questions, I'm afraid. And if you're still not convinced, I'll drive you to the station.'

~

TEN MINUTES LATER, THEY WERE BUMPING DOWN A MUDDY track in Cal's car, toward Ramsholt. To the right, the River Deben glinted cold and wide beneath the cloud-thick sky. To the left, the earth rose in sandy bluffs still scarred by last week's storms. At the end of the lane, Cal pressed a fob, and a gate slid open. Sofie caught sight of the CCTV camera mounted on a pole beside it.

'What's with all this surveillance?' she remarked. 'It feels like we're in the middle of nowhere. Bit paranoid, isn't it?'

Cal grunted but said nothing. Beyond the gate was a church. The road forked, and he turned towards the village. The pub they were headed for, The Ramsholt Arms, was on the water's edge. A dozen sailing boats were pulled up onto a small quay.

Cal parked, and she took a seat outside while he went in to order drinks - Bloody Mary for her, Coke for him. When he returned, she was staring out across the marshes, deep in thought.

'Penny for them?' he said.

She didn't answer. He sat down beside her.

'OK, I get it. You feel blindsided. Who wouldn't?'

'That's an understatement,' she muttered, without shifting he gaze.

'You witness a murder, you almost get killed. And now you wake up in a farmhouse surrounded by strangers. It's a lot.'

Strands of her blond hair swirled in the wind. She was like a cornered animal. Again, she didn't respond.

'But if you run now, you'll be on your own. Whoever's hunting you won't stop.'

Finally, she turned to him. 'And I'm supposed to trust you?

He smiled thinly. 'You kind of have to, I'm afraid.

Remember, it's in our interest to protect you. You're a key witness to what happened that night.'

She gave a bitter laugh. 'Right. That's what I've been shouting into a void for days. The police didn't give a damn.' A beat. 'Anyway, I thought you worked for Cambridge Bio? It seems pretty obvious to me that they're the ones covering this up.'

'You're right, I did work for them.'

'Did?'

'My job was to protect those two chemists.'

She snorted. 'And how did that go?'

'Sofie, they prevented me. We need to find out why.'

She brushed her hair out of her eyes. She was prettier than he remembered.

'That still doesn't explain how you ended up rescuing me.'

'MI5 wanted someone you'd recognise. Someone who wouldn't freak you out, because we couldn't be sure we'd be able to drug you so quickly. In the event, you never saw me until you woke up this morning.'

He realised it sounded even less convincing coming from him than it had two days ago from the lips of Kate and Hart.

She looked astonished. 'Seriously?'

He could see that she was struggling to make sense of it, and wondered whether to relay what Hart had told him, that they feared the presence of a mole; that the attackers, whoever they were, couldn't be allowed to know that Kate had survived.

But for now, he decided against. Besides, he wasn't ready to explain how he had inadvertently caused Alice Wickman's murder. She would be even less inclined to trust him then. He had to calm her down.

'The bottom line, Sofie, is this: we need your help.'

She narrowed her eyes. 'How?'

'Well, first of all, why don't you tell me what happened that night, on the boat?'

Sofie sipped her drink. Her expression shifted.

'Surely you have all that from Kate.'

A hundred yards away, a small yacht was tying up at a buoy, sails flapping furiously in the breeze.

'Yes, but let's hear it from you. How did you get off? What happened next?'

Reluctantly, she told him. The first part of her story was a mirror image of the one Kate had related the day before in the MI5 safe house with Hart. No, she hadn't seen the face of the killer. Then she described what occurred after she'd escaped: her interviews with the police, and a brief outline of the attempts she'd made to find out about the Cambridge Bio drug trial.

He asked her what she'd discovered. Not much, was the answer, though he couldn't help feeling that she was holding something back.

But when it came to the attacker on her rooftop last night, she gave him something new.

'It was a woman,' Sofie said.

'Female?' he said. 'You're sure about that?'

'One hundred per cent. Short blonde hair, muscular, covered in tattoos. What was weird, was she seemed to be trying to make it look like rape.'

A classic ploy for covering tracks, Cal thought.

She stood. 'So. Got what you need? Can I go now?'

'Go where?'

'Anywhere. Away. Out of this nightmare.'

Before he could stop himself, he let slip a derisive snort.

'You don't still think the police will help you, do you?'

'Of course not,' she replied angrily. 'They're bloody useless. No, I mean, *away* away.'

Although Kate had insisted that Sofie's cooperation had to be voluntary, this wasn't part of the plan.

He softened his tone. 'You realise that whoever it was who attacked you last night will try again? You're still a witness, Sofie. You're a threat to them.'

'Not if I disappear. Not if no one believes me.' She sighed. 'Anyway, what option do I have?'

'The other one. You stay. We'll protect you.'

She stared into her glass and drained the dregs of the Bloody Mary.

'I wish I could believe that,' she said quietly.

47

'I THINK I MIGHT HAVE SOMETHING FOR YOU.'

Khan recognised the voice of DC John Tucker, a colleague from Stoke Newington.

'Sorry. Not with you.'

'Brooke Road, remember? You asked me to look out for a woman who lives there, a Sofie James?'

Khan sat up. When Sofie had first come into the station, she had spoken to Tucker to find out whether there was any previous on the girl, given that her home address, Brooke Road, was in Stoke Newington. At the time, he had come up blank.

'Ah. Yes. I remember now.'

'Well, we had a call last night. A guy named Martin Elliot reported a disturbance at her address. Said there was a party. Girl matching Sofie's description was seen running from the building, pursued by someone on a motorbike. Probably nothing, could be unconnected.' He paused. 'Thought I'd put you in the picture, that's all.'

Khan was already grabbing her jacket. 'I'm coming over.'

A minute later, she was in her superior's office.

'Sarg? Sorry to bother you.'

DS Bates carried on writing. She took a deep breath.

'I went to see Sofie James yesterday evening. In her flat.'

Bates paused.

'You what?'

'You weren't here, Sarg. She sounded distressed. I felt she might need help.'

He sighed and put down his pen. 'Listen, Khan, I told you to drop it, didn't I?'

'You did.'

'So a word of advice. Rule one - don't get emotionally involved. We've referred it to her doctor; that's all we can do. She's made us waste enough time as it is.'

'Well, I did, Sarge. I spoke to the doctor yesterday after I'd seen her, and he promised to call her. Thing is... I'm not so sure anymore.'

'Not so sure of what?'

'That she's not telling the truth.'

'Oh really? The girl comes in and reports the murder of a journalist and two whistleblowers on a riverboat. We find no evidence, no witnesses, zilch. Then it turns out that this woman - this journalist - was killed in Ukraine. She's obviously deluded, a fantasist. What more do you want?'

'But Sarge, there are too many coincidences. I've had Stoke Newington on the phone. They say there was a reported disturbance in her building last night, and a sighting of a woman fitting Miss James's description running from the house.'

Bates glared at her icily.

'So what are you asking me, precisely?'

'I want to go up there, check it out.'

He hesitated. Then waved her off like she was wasting

his afternoon.

'Fine. Then put it to bed. You're done after this. Understood?'

~

An hour later, DC Khan drew up outside Sofie's flat in her unmarked maroon Vauxhall Astra. A can was perched on a low wall, still half full of beer. She found Tucker waiting for her on the steps.

'I'm very grateful, John. Thanks for meeting me.'

'Sure,' he said. 'No problem.'

Khan pressed Sofie's buzzer. Nothing. She tried the one above.

A sash window scraped open.

'Hello?' said a female voice.

Khan stepped back onto the road and looked up.

'Can we come in a moment? We're looking for a Miss Sofie James.'

'Try the bell below.'

'We have. She's not answering. Was it your flat where the party was held last night?'

'What of it?'

'We'd like a word, if you don't mind. I'm DC Khan, and this is DC Tucker.'

The girl leant out of the window.

'Police? Shit, have there been complaints?'

'That's right, love,' yelled Tucker. 'You going to let us in or what?'

The window slammed. Seconds later, the door buzzed open.

Inside the hallway and all the way up the stairs, there was further detritus from the night before. Empty bottles, party streamers, a discarded hat, more cans. The door to the top-floor flat was off the latch, and they eased it open.

'Hi. Sorry about the mess,' said the girl, laughing nervously. She introduced herself as Vicky. She'd obviously dressed in a hurry, her hair still unbrushed. 'We had rather an epic night, as you can see.' She looked from one to the other. 'What's this all about?'

'We wanted to ask a few questions,' said Khan. 'There was a report of a disturbance. Do you know a Martin Elliot?'

'Martin? Yeah, he was here.'

'It was he who reported it. There was a fight on the roof. Says he was injured.'

Vicky looked shocked. 'Shit, for real? He didn't say anything to me!'

They followed her in. The place stank of alcohol. Someone had made a first attempt at clearing up, bottles and cans piled on a table.

Khan stepped gingerly over a discarded cushion. 'Do you know the woman who lives downstairs?'

'Sofie? Not well. Why?'

'What time did she leave?'

Vicky slumped onto a sofa, gesturing for the two officers to do the same.

'Why? Was she involved?'

'Just answer the question.'

She rubbed her hair. 'She wasn't here long, actually. I can't remember seeing her after about…what?... ten?'

'Was she distressed in any way?' said Tucker, flipping open his notebook.

'Not that I noticed. Mind you, we were all a bit wasted.' She frowned. 'Why, is something wrong?'

'She looked fine, normal, to you? You didn't notice

anything unusual?'

'No. I think she did go up to the roof with Martin, though. But I find it hard to imagine them having a fight.'

'Mind if we take a look?'

'Sure. Let me put some shoes on.'

While Vicky left to finish dressing, Tucker got up and wandered idly around the room.

'Not much to go on, I would say,' he said.

Khan frowned. 'Did this Martin bloke say he wanted to press charges?'

'No. But it wasn't Sofie he was on about. It was another woman who he claimed attacked them.'

Vicky returned and led them up a short flight of stairs.

As they emerged onto the roof, the pale winter sun was beginning to dip to the west behind Parliament Hill. They walked a few paces and looked around. There were no bottles or party debris up here, nothing but a few odd scraps of wood and an old plastic window box, the flowers long since gone.

Vicky rubbed her eyes and shivered, scanning the horizon. 'Blimey, never been up here in the day. What an amazing view.'

Khan didn't answer. She had noticed something in one corner, next to the low parapet that bounded the edge.

She walked over. A scrap of cloth, caught on a crack. She picked it up with a stick. The stain was unmistakable.

'Over here.'

Tucker joined her.

'Blood?'

She pulled out an evidence bag and sealed the fabric inside.

Tucker pointed to a steel rod nearby. 'And what about this?'

They both knelt. One end was rusted. The other bore the smeared shape of a handprint: dried, dark, and unmistakably red.

After they'd left, Vicky ran a bath. She felt unsettled. They had taken away what they called evidence. Evidence of what? Why hadn't Martin said anything?

Still trying to rack her brains in an effort to remember who had gone up there with them, she went into the kitchen to fill the kettle, badly in need of a shot of caffeine. She pressed the tit down to switch it on and as she did so, there was a loud bang. She jumped and smacked her head on the cupboard above.

'Shit, what was that?' she cried out loud.

It was uncanny, as if she'd unwittingly detonated it herself. Outside, there was the sound of a car reversing, then a screech of tyres. She hurried into the sitting room and leant out of the window.

'Oh my God,' she whispered.

A hundred yards away, a body was lying immobile in the middle of the road. She searched the street for the two police officers, thinking how lucky it was that they happened to be on the scene.

But there was no sign of them.

48

Cal pulled up fifty metres short of Woodbridge station, a sinking feeling in the pit of his stomach.

'You sure about this?' he said.

She opened the passenger door without replying. Three minutes later, she returned with a bottle of water and a sandwich.

'Train leaves in half an hour.'

'Where will you go?'

She stared out of the window. 'Why would I tell you? You'll only come after me.'

'I wish you'd speak to Kate.' No response. 'Because she'll say the same. That you're making a big mistake.'

That got a reaction. A dry laugh, bitter at the edges.

'Coming from the guy I met when this all kicked off? The guy who kidnapped me? What do you expect me to do?'

He didn't argue. What was the point? He regarded her for a moment, then reached into his jacket and handed her a card.

'Here's my number. You still have the phone we gave

you?'

She nodded.

'If anything happens - anything - you call me. We'll come for you. No questions. And don't go back to your flat. It's not safe.'

'I'm not stupid.'

Debatable, he thought. She reached into the back seat for her backpack and turned to him.

'And please don't try to follow me.'

He watched as she made her way across the road into the station forecourt. He had every intention of following her. He had to. Those were his instructions from Kate and Hart. Plan B, if she decided to bolt.

First, he needed to park out of sight and change. There was just enough time before her train was due. He composed a brief text to Kate and another to Frank and pressed send, then fired up the engine and executed a sharp U-turn, glancing in his mirror as he pulled away to check she had gone in.

But his view was blocked. A long line of schoolchildren was snaking down the hill, double abreast, on their way to the Viking ship museum. As the lead teacher ushered them over the crossing, a silver Ford Mondeo approached and stopped. Was it waiting for the children, or to turn into the forecourt? Two men in the front, both dressed in dark colours. Unremarkable.

But that was the problem.

Cal had seen the same car fifteen minutes earlier, back on the main road just outside Ramsholt. At the time, it hadn't registered. It was the kind of vehicle that he'd used himself, back in the day. But in this case, the two occupants looked out of place in the depths of the Suffolk countryside.

The procession passed. The Mondeo pulled slowly into

the station.

49

Sofie crossed the road without looking back. She half expected him to come after her.

She slipped through a pack of schoolkids who were crossing the forecourt and entered the station. Once inside, she stole a furtive backwards glance. He was gone.

The booking hall was busy with afternoon shoppers catching the once-an-hour train into Ipswich. She ducked into the waiting room and dropped her backpack on the bench. Buried beneath a sweatshirt was the burner phone Cal had given her.

She didn't hesitate. She chucked it straight in the bin. Who knew what tracking tech it harboured? Did he think she was an idiot?

But now, alone again, the weight of what lay ahead pressed down. Her plan, if you could call it that, was a desperate one - to make her way to Gibraltar. It was the one lead that remained to her, the contact the whistleblowers had given her that night on the boat. Although she no longer had the business card - it had been lost somewhere in the scramble to escape - she still remembered the PO box number. 758001. Her father's birthday, written backwards.

Looking up, she noticed two men enter and sit at the far end of the room. Both were dressed in tracksuit bottoms and trainers, oddly out of place amongst the middle-aged women waiting for the 2.15 to Ipswich. Above them, an old-fashioned wall clock marked the time. She stared at the minute hand as it ticked in slow, deliberate jerks - twelve minutes to go.

She touched the back of her neck, her hair damp with sweat, pulled out the tie and re-fastened her ponytail, trying to ground herself. Breathe, Sofie. Focus.

Once more, she went over the events of the last two weeks, and the previous twenty-four hours floated into sharper focus. So shocked had she been by her drugging, and waking that morning in a strange bed, that she'd blocked out what had happened on the roof. Now it all came flooding back.

How did that woman find her? Could she have been the same person who had attacked them on the boat? All she remembered when she'd slid open the door on that terrifying scene was a full visor helmet. The face of the assassin was hidden. Now, she dimly remembered that it was a motorbike that pursued her as she'd run from the building and jumped in that taxi. Were they one and the same?

And Martin? She had a memory of him yelling and the sounds of a scuffle. In her haste to get away, she hadn't stopped to check whether he was hurt. She prayed to God that he was OK.

She took a series of steady breaths to calm her nerves, wondering whether she was doing the right thing. If she was going to change her mind, she didn't have long.

Five minutes later, she walked out to the platform. A

sudden ringing echoed from down the track. Startled, she looked along the line and felt her heart skip a beat as the rail barriers came down. The image of her father on his bicycle filled her head. Feeling faint, she sat down on a bench. The train pulled in with a screech of brakes.

She was paralysed by indecision. A few metres away, out of the corner of her eye, she noticed the two men also hesitated. Something didn't feel right. Were they there for her? On impulse, she jumped up and leapt into the carriage, standing just inside the door. They entered the next one along. Lights started flashing, and a high-pitched whine sounded as the automatic doors prepared to close.

Just as they began to slide shut, she leapt off. Seconds later, one of them blocked the doors. Both stepped back onto the platform.

Her stomach dropped. There was no time to think. She bolted.

Fleeing to the waiting room, she reached into the bin for the phone she'd discarded, then ran out into the forecourt and made for the quay. Fifty yards ahead, the gaggle of schoolchildren she'd seen a few moments before were milling around the museum entrance. From behind her came the sound of running footsteps.

She barrelled past the crowd and disappeared inside.

A man was in the middle of giving a guided tour. Breathless and panting, she joined his group. Keeping one eye on the door, she dialled Cal's number.

'Changed your mind?' he said.

'There's someone after me,' she whispered. 'They tried to follow me onto the train.'

His tone sharpened. 'Where are you?'

'In some kind of museum. I think they're outside. Two guys.'

'Right, wait there. I'm coming to get you.'

'How?'

There was a moment of hesitation at the other end of the line.

'What can you see?'

She scanned the space. 'I'm next to a Viking rowboat.'

'OK, go towards the display cases at the back. Beyond them, there should be a pile of timbers.'

She stepped away and started walking. Several large oak beams were stacked up against the rear wall, next to a lathe.

'Got them.'

'Great. To the right, there's a blue door. It should be unlocked. It leads to a car park. Leave through there when I text you, but don't move before. I'll be there in five.'

He hung up.

She drifted back to the group, keeping her head down. Minutes passed. Then, her phone buzzed.

<GO.>

She glanced towards the museum entrance. One of the men was silhouetted outside, pacing the quay. There was no sign of his partner.

She moved fast, past the display cases and through the blue door.

Cal was waiting in the car. Oddly, he seemed to have changed since she'd seen him last and was now dressed in a black hoodie and a pair of jogging pants. A pile of clothes was stashed in the footwell. She said nothing as she jumped into the passenger seat.

Cal sped out of the car park onto the road at the rear of the museum and accelerated away.

'Thanks,' she said sheepishly.

'You're welcome,' he said.

'So what now?'

'Back to the farm,' he said. 'Back to plan A.'

50

'YOU'RE LATE,' SAID LAURA, IN RUSSIAN.

Tasha pulled off her helmet and rolled her shoulders like a boxer winding down from a bout. Her cold blue eyes scanned the riverbank.

'So what the hell happened?'

'You tell me,' snapped Tasha. 'I had her, but then she was spirited away. If you'd let me use my Glock, she'd already be dead. Why the fake rape?'

Not for the first time, Laura wondered whether she had done the right thing in asking for her on this operation. They'd trained together as GRU recruits, back in the day in St Petersburg, and Tasha Mazour had developed quite a reputation since then. She was meant to be one of the best. Which is why, against her better judgment, Laura had given her a second chance.

'You know as well as I do. We can't afford this to be linked. You had one task, and you fluffed it. Again. How did she escape?'

Tasha clenched her jaw. 'The girl had more fight than I expected. And that was no taxi she got into. That was a professional extraction. Was it Gebler?'

Laura gazed into the distance. 'I have no idea. They're no longer involving me.' A beat. 'It might be embarrassing, but let's hope so.'

'But why would they want her alive?'

'I agree. It doesn't sound like them.'

Tasha massaged her head and yanked a water bottle out of a pocket of her saddlebag. She was tall, six feet to Laura's five feet seven, with, like her, a square jaw and high cheekbones. Where they parted company, other than how they dressed, was in the way they wore their hair: where Laura's was straight, shoulder-length and precisely shaped, Tasha's crew cut gave her an elfin look. A few stray peroxide strands had been left to float down the base of her neck, framing a green tattoo of Osiris, the Egyptian God of the afterlife.

Tasha took a deep swig, watching a flock of birds skim low over the water, and wiped her mouth. They were in Barnes, on a stretch of river between the railway bridge and Chiswick Bridge, with wide views in either direction. She replaced the matt black bottle in her pack and turned to face Laura.

'Do you remember what they taught us back in the dacha in St Petersburg?'

Laura closed her eyes, rubbed them, then opened them again to refocus. She could do without this right now.

'We learnt a lot of things in the dacha.'

'You stay the course,' said Tasha.

Laura looked up sharply. 'Is that a dig?'

Tasha smiled thinly. 'We're not all cut out for wet work. But no, I meant that if you start a job, you finish a job.'

'And if you can't finish it, you cut your losses and change the plan.'

'That's easy for you to say.'

Laura sighed. 'You've had two shots at this now. We can't afford any more screw-ups. You are to stand down.' Tasha spat on the ground. Laura turned away. 'I mean it this time. Go home to Madrid. Or better still, go on holiday, disappear for a while. That's an order.'

'What if they know who I am?'

'No one knows who you are.'

'She might be able to identify me.'

'How could she? You were wearing a helmet, no?'

'Not on that roof.'

'Shit, Tasha, how close did you get?'

'Close enough.'

Laura hesitated. Her colleague was in danger of becoming a liability. If it ever became known that the Russians were involved, then it was game over for Crane.

'All the more reason then to leave the country.'

A beat.

'And your security guy? The one who's been giving you all the trouble?'

Laura's gaze shifted towards the bridge, where two rowing eights were battling against the tide. The thwup, thwup, thwup of their oars, turning in their riggers in unison, echoed across the river.

She had her there.

Because Cal had disappeared.

51

Saturday 5th November

The man Laura was worried about, the one who had disappeared, dropped into the chair at the dining room table and flicked a switch. A large monitor on the wall flickered into life just as Frank walked in.

'Any movement?' Cal asked, not looking up.

Frank shook his head.

'All quiet. None of the cameras has registered any movement. Either they know we have monitoring in place, or they're not bothered to come closer than the village, considering there's only one road out of here.' He nodded toward the empty chair. 'Where is she?'

'Down in a minute.'

Cal navigated to the remote video link and logged in. A face appeared on the screen.

'Morning, guys.'

Kate seemed to be floating in space. The scar along her cheek was still there, camouflaged under a layer of careful makeup. Palm trees and a brilliant blue sky swayed behind her, her virtual backdrop at odds with the tension in her eyes. The edge of her wheelchair peeked out at the bottom of the frame.

A moment later, Sofie bustled in with a steaming cup of coffee and slumped down awkwardly at the head of the table. Kate's expression didn't change: nervous. It was the first time the friends had been face to face since the night on the boat.

'Hi Doll, how are you feeling?'

Sofie gave her a clenched smile.

'As well as can be expected.'

'Right,' Cal began hastily, eager to keep it professional. 'Let's get started, shall we? Kate, you want to explain what happened yesterday?'

She seemed taken aback.

'You mean the two men you thought were following you?'

'Thought?' Sofie snapped. 'There was no doubt about it.'

Kate raised her hands. 'Not ours, if that's what you're implying.'

Frank leant forward. 'You sure about that?'

'So how did they find us?' said Cal. 'I thought no one outside this call, other than Hart, knows where Sofie is?

'That's correct.'

Cal sat back. 'Which means you must have been compromised.'

Kate hesitated. 'Have you briefed Sofie yet?'

'Nobody's told me a damn thing,' Sofie cut in.

'Good. Because there's been a change of plan.'

Cal raised an eyebrow.

'Hart wants Sofie in Paris. Tomorrow.'

Sofie started in surprise. 'Paris?'

'He'd like you to be debriefed at the embassy.'

'What on earth for?'

'Because we need to get you out of the country. We have a secure facility there, run by Vauxhaul.'

A look of confusion clouded Sofie's face.

'Vauxhall?'

'The Secret Intelligence Service. MI6.'

'But I still don't understand. Why can't that be done over here?'

Kate leaned forward into the camera. 'Listen, Sofie, trust me. There's stuff I cannot tell you, but this is how they want to do it. It's the safest way.'

Sofie's voice was low and tight. 'I trusted you before, remember? I'm sorry for what happened to you, but seriously…'

Kate winced. 'I get it. And I'm sorry. I really am. But once this is over, we'll sit down. I'll tell you everything. Just… not now. We've booked you on the early evening Eurostar.'

Cal exchanged a look with Frank. It was clear to him what was running through his friend's mind. It sounded as if someone had decided to remove the investigation from MI5 and hand it to its sister service. However, now that their whereabouts had been leaked, it was hard to know who to trust. Even Kate.

'We're not saying no,' said Cal. 'But after yesterday, we're going to do this our way. We can't take any more risks. You give us a time, a place, and we'll get her there.'

Kate hesitated. 'I'm not sure. My instructions… '

'Screw your instructions. Take it or leave it.'

Sofie looked at Cal in surprise. Then, back to Kate. There was a tense pause.

Finally, she said: 'It will require authorisation.'

'Sure. Do what you have to do.'

'I'll come back to you by midday.'

The screen went blank.

52

Sunday 6th November

SOFIE DIDN'T SLEEP THAT NIGHT.

It wasn't just the Bonfire Night fireworks from across the river in Woodbridge that kept her awake. Even after they were over, she carried on tossing and turning, running over in her head whether she'd made the right decision.

Yeah, she was grateful. But once the adrenaline wore off, the facts started lining up - and not in Kate's favour. The truth was clear now. Protecting Sofie wasn't the point. She was leverage. A pawn in unlocking the Cambridge Bio scandal. That had been Kate's play all along. Sure, maybe now she felt guilty. Maybe she even wanted to make it right. But what happened at the station in Woodbridge didn't fill Sofie with much confidence. And now they wanted to whisk her off to Paris?

Seriously, Paris? Surely there was somewhere closer they could keep her safe?

When they'd returned, Cal had told her not to leave the farmhouse, not even for fresh air. So all afternoon she'd hunkered down in Frank's TV room, watching an old Netflix series on a squashy sofa in front of a log fire, while the two of them worked on some complicated plan to get her out.

From time to time, Emily came in with tea and cake. But no sympathy. The woman was frosty, standoffish, without a shred of sisterly concern. To her, Sofie was an inconvenience. Or so it seemed.

All it did was make her feel alone. And more vulnerable than ever.

Eventually, exhaustion took over, and she drifted off. Only to be woken as dawn broke by the sound of someone moving about in the garden. Suddenly fearful, she jumped out of bed and peered out of the window. It was Frank, wheeling a handcart down towards the river. Twenty minutes later, she heard the chug chug chug of an engine. She leapt up again. A small boat was approaching the jetty at the end of the garden.

Now what?

Cal confirmed her suspicion when she came down for breakfast.

'Morning! You packed?'

'Is that boat for us?'

He nodded.

She laughed. 'What's your idea? That we cross the channel and sail down the Seine?'

He smiled. 'Glad to see you've got your spirit back. Not quite. We're heading for Harwich. We're booked on a ferry to Holland tonight.'

Sofie poured herself coffee.

'Clever. I suppose. You don't think they'll see us leave?'

'Well, that's the point. They'll be watching the road. So I'd say it's unlikely. No one will be covering the river.'

'Christabel', it turned out, was one of two boats Frank owned, an East Coast crabber which, he explained, he used

for fishing trips and motoring up the coast to Aldeburgh. Now they were going, Emily suddenly became solicitous, relieved to be rid of her unwanted guest, insisting that Sofie borrow a new set of clothes to supplement the little she'd had in her backpack when they brought her in.

Before boarding, Cal outlined the plan. Once across the Channel, they would take a train to Paris. Kate had sent details of a hotel she'd booked. The Meurice, near the Place de la Concorde.

Sofie googled it. 'Looks swanky.'

'Don't get your hopes up.'

She raised an eyebrow. 'No?'

'The less interaction we have with Kate and her lot, the better.'

While Frank stocked up on fuel, she and Cal clambered aboard. The boat was a single-cabin affair with a small galley kitchen and two bunk beds up front. She shuddered at the memory of the last one she'd been on.

Preparations complete, they set off in a light wind, motoring at a steady five knots towards the mouth of the Deben. Thankfully, the weather was clear. The tide was out, and Sofie could see glistening patches of fresh mud beginning to emerge along the banks, close to the riverside path, leaving boats marooned at alarming angles. Frank had his binoculars out most of the way. Occasionally, he would point out curlews, lapwings and widgeon. Sofie was amazed at his nonchalance. Birdwatching? And then she realised. He was scanning the shoreline. Her nerves cranked up a notch.

Watching Cal and Frank banter together, she wondered about the odd relationship between the pair. Private school-educated ex-army officer Frank, married to a posh girl and living a country life, and his former Sergeant and sidekick

Cal - or so it appeared to Sofie - who dossed in a caravan in his backyard. Of the two of them, Cal was the taller and better-looking, though Frank had a certain awkward charm. But he was a bit of an enigma. He certainly didn't act like a charity case.

When she'd asked them about the outfit they'd been in, both of them were cagey. She knew something about the army, having once dated a soldier, so it didn't take a genius to guess it was something to do with Special Forces. She ought to be reassured. But somehow she wasn't.

When they reached open water, they turned south, hugging the coast past Felixstowe until they arrived at the entrance to the River Orwell. The waters of the North Sea were smooth, a slate grey against an opaque winter haze on the horizon. Once in the estuary, it was a short distance to the quayside at Harwich. A large white sign announced *'Ha'penny Pier'*.

They docked. Frank didn't want to hang about. They waved him goodbye and set off on foot for the town centre. For the first time since everything had kicked off, she began to feel hopeful that this nightmare might soon be over. Someone was finally listening to her. Taking her seriously.

This had to be the beginning of the end, right?

53

Tuesday 8th November

'How is she?'

Cal wearily lifted himself onto one elbow, juggling the phone, and peered at his alarm clock. 6:00 am. It had taken over twenty-four hours to get to Paris, and he hadn't slept well.

'No issues,' he replied. 'Are we still on for today?'

'They're expecting you at nine-thirty,' said Kate. 'We've arranged a car for you. Call Avis in Rue de Lamartine, speak to Marie-Claire, she'll send it over. But Cal … where are you? You never checked into the hotel.'

'Sorry. Preferred to make our own arrangements.' He hesitated. 'Why can't we go by cab?'

'Take the car, please. You need to be identified before you're brought in.'

'You mean I should wait outside the embassy?'

'Exactly. In the vehicle. Someone will come out to get you. You'll find a security pass in the glove compartment for ID. Please show it to the embassy staff. You're coming from the north, am I right?'

This early in the morning, he had no idea.

'Then park on the opposite side of the street.'

'If you say so.' This all seemed unnecessarily convoluted. There was silence at the other end. 'Anything else?'

'No.' Her voice was crisp and businesslike. 'Thanks, Cal.'

'You're welcome, Kate,' he replied, but she'd already hung up.

~

TWO HOURS LATER, CAL WAS SITTING ON THE TERRACE OF A cheap Ibis he'd found for them last-minute, pouring coffee. Sofie was late.

As if on cue, she appeared at the top of the steps, blonde hair loose, a touch of makeup softening the edge in her expression.

'Morning,' he said.

'Hey.' She sat. 'Bit early, isn't it?'

'We're on parade at nine-thirty.'

'On parade?'

'Sorry, army expression. That's when they want us at the Embassy.'

'Good. The sooner we get this over with, the sooner I can get my life back.' She tore off a corner of a croissant. 'Any idea what's going to happen when we get there?"

'Debrief, most likely.'

'But I thought we already did that?'

Cal smiled faintly. 'You know what these people are like.'

'Surprisingly, I don't.'

'They'll want you to go through it all again, and in much more detail this time. These guys will be forensic.'

'Gee, can't wait.'

'They'll also arrange protection for you.'

She frowned. 'For how long?'

'No idea. But Crane's set to be elected party leader in four weeks. It's him this implicates, so my guess is that they'll want to get this sorted before then.'

'And after that?'

'If Crane falls, and this thing's in the open, there's no longer any incentive to silence you. Besides, once they realise Kate is still alive, you're no longer the only witness. You're off the hook.'

Sofie frowned. 'So why don't they just come out with it now?'

It was a good point, and he didn't have the answer.

For a moment, he wondered whether he should make more of these last moments with her. There was a lot he still wanted to ask. He had a nagging feeling she was holding something back. But he was out of time. He picked up his room card and stood up.

'Meet me in the lobby in thirty.'

~

By the time they were finally on the road, a few minutes after nine, the morning commuter traffic was in full flow. Marie-Claire from Avis had said they'd be sending a Mercedes, but what showed up at the hotel was a Peugeot. Before they left, Cal checked the glove compartment for the security pass that Kate had mentioned. *British Embassy Paris*, it said, with the word *Guest* and a six-digit number. He pocketed it, and they set off.

As they drove along the Avenue Hoche, Sofie remained silent. It suited him. He wasn't used to driving in Paris, and there was a complicated one-way system he had to navigate on the approach.

Turning south down the Rue de Saint-Honoré, their progress was slowed by clusters of tourist buses. A diversion was in place. Cal swore under his breath.

'What's the matter?'

'Paris traffic. It's a mess. I don't understand why we couldn't do this in a cab. Or on foot, come to that.'

The diversion forced them north, to approach the embassy head-on via the narrow Rue d'Aguesseau. Kate had said to park on the left of Faubourg St Honore, a few yards before the embassy entrance on the opposite side of the one-way street, but Cal realised they had overshot, and he'd have to go round the block again and come at it from further up. As they drove past the gates, a small van was backing out, and a gendarme waved for Cal to stop. He slowed, and it was at that point that he noticed an electric BMW parked on the right, a few yards up. Two men were sitting in the front seats, one talking into a mobile phone. Judging by the complex instructions he'd been given, he wouldn't be surprised if it was there for him.

The van pulled out, and the gendarme ahead of them motioned them through. He heard a sharp intake of breath beside him.

'What is it?'

Her face was creased with worry. 'That man in the car over there!'

'What are you talking about?'

'It's the guy from Cambridge Bio!'

He couldn't process what she said for a moment.

'Cambridge Bio? What the hell are you talking about?'

She'd gone very pale. 'I'm sure of it!'

'OK, Sofie, don't turn round. Look in the mirror and

tell me which man? Which car?' He brought the Peugeot to a halt beside the gendarme to give her a proper view. He wound down his window.

'Bonjour,' he said, leaning out.

The policeman didn't budge. '*Allez! Allez!*' he snapped, waving them on impatiently.

'*Definitely!* He's the guy from the party boat!'

Cal glanced in the driving mirror, but another car had now pulled out, obscuring the BMW. He closed the window and drew away. As it came into view again, he caught a brief glimpse of the man in the passenger seat. The tight black curls and boyish face were unmistakable. It was Charles Gebler.

It started to move. They'd been seen.

'I don't get it,' he said uneasily.

'What's going on? Is this a trap?'

He accelerated to the intersection, then swung hard right into the Place de la Concorde as the traffic lights were turning red. There was a cacophony of horns, and the BMW was forced to stop three cars back. As he drove away, Cal caught it in his wing mirror as it swerved into the oncoming traffic and shot between two buses, tyres squealing on the tarmac. A taxi skidded to a halt, the driver gesticulating out of his open window.

'What the hell are you doing?' Sofie cried in alarm.

They raced up the Champs-Élysées, the BMW a hundred yards behind, and then hard right into the Avenue de Marigny. They were now coming at the embassy from a new angle. The Union Jack fluttered ahead. He slowed.

Think, Harrison, think. Why was Gebler here? Had someone tipped him off?

He pulled over beside the traffic barriers, exactly where Kate had told him to wait. Checked the mirror again, but the BMW was now out of sight. He turned in his seat.

No, there it was, stopped two hundred metres back. Across the road, the gendarme was pacing up and down outside the embassy gates. Cal glanced at his watch. Two minutes to go. Whatever the contact, they'd make it at 9:30. Beside him, Sofie was twisting about like a trapped animal.

She looked terrified. '*We're not going into the embassy at all, are we?*'

He flexed his hands, trying to focus. At one minute thirty, she made a sudden movement.

'I'm sorry, I'm getting out of here...'

He clicked the door locks shut.

'Wait!' he snapped.

Straining to see past her, something flashed across his peripheral vision. They were parked outside an old apartment building, and on either side of the entrance were two long, faded mirrored panels. In one was reflected the profile of the car. Something was off about the line of the chassis.

He checked the time again. A minute to go. The BMW was still parked up and silent, its tinted windows now obscured by the sun breaking through the clouds.

He returned to the vehicle's profile. It was nagging him. Then he saw it, clearly this time. There was an object clamped underneath.

It suddenly hit him. They'd said to expect a Mercedes, but they'd delivered a Peugeot. Had Gebler switched it?

Forty-five seconds remained. Sofie's face was set rigid, her breathing slowed.

He remembered something else that Kate had said - to stay with her in the car until they were approached. Was it possible? Surely not?

Oh, for God's sake....

He gently clicked open his door.

'Don't move.'

She barely looked at him as he got out.

He was in full view of the BMW now. He dared not stoop down. Instead, he walked around to the pavement. Sofie watched him steadily through the windscreen, a look of alarm on her face. He stepped back into the street.

Waiting for a taxi to pass, he started to cross towards the embassy. The gendarme was beginning to regard him with interest. Halfway across, he stopped and turned around. He judged his moment finely. As a van approached from the west, obscuring the view from the BMW further down the street, he ducked down and got a clear view of the underside of the Peugeot.

Whatever it was that was clamped underneath, there was no time to figure it out. He was still crouched down when the van shot past, leaving him exposed.

The gendarme shouted something. The passenger door of the BMW opened.

Remain with the car, Kate had said.

He sprang to his feet and started sprinting towards the Peugeot.

'*Arrêt!*' yelled the policeman.

He flung open her door.

'*Get out, Sofie, now!*'

She blinked, startled. 'What … ?'

He dragged her out by the wrist and propelled her, stumbling, onto the pavement. There was a shout behind them. She began to run, catching his urgency. They reached the Rue d'Aguesseau.

'Turn left! *Left!*' he yelled at her.

He halted at the corner to glance back down the street they'd come from. Gebler was crouching on the far side of the Peugeot, staring at the gendarme crossing the road towards it. Cal had seen enough. He bolted after Sofie, against the one-way traffic.

'*Now fucking run!*' he yelled.

Then behind them - BOOM.

The Peugeot exploded.

54

They didn't stop running until they reached the Avenue Montaigne, halfway up the Champs-Élysées. Pressing into a doorway, Cal scanned the street for any sign of pursuit. His lungs were burning. He cursed his lack of fitness.

Thick traffic was crawling its way towards the Arc de Triomphe. He briefly caught a glimpse of the BMW racing north, lights flashing.

Sofie was crumpled at his feet, panting hard. He crouched down to her.

'You okay?'

No answer. Her cheeks were blotched, hair plastered to her forehead, sweat glistening at her temples.

Finally, she rasped, 'You betrayed me. You said I'd be safe.'

'Fuck off!' he retorted. 'That was meant for me, too. I got you out, didn't I?'

Inside, it wasn't fear he felt, but fury. Gebler had tried to kill him. The only way he could have been there at that precise location, at that precise hour, was if he'd been aware of the operation. Cal had been instructed to stay in the car until 9:30. The bomb had exploded at 9:30 on the nail.

He leant on a parking meter, breathing more easily now. Sofie stayed on the ground.

'I can't do this anymore,' she murmured.

His mind snapped back. 'We need to regroup.'

He pulled her up by the arm. She didn't resist.

'But not here. There's a place I used to know, up in Montmartre. It'll be full of tourists. No one will think to look for us there.'

~

Twenty minutes later, they were holed up in the warm fug of a brightly lit cafe on the hill by Sacré Coeur. Sofie had regained her composure in a numb sort of way. They ordered coffees and while he went to recce exit options, she settled at a table in the back, where they had a clear view of the entrance and anyone entering from the square.

When he returned, she looked up.

'I have to make a call,' he said.

'Won't they trace it?'

'Not with these,' he said, pulling a phone out of his backpack. 'In fact, you should have one,' he added, handing it to her. 'We need a way to communicate. Give me ten minutes.'

She hesitated. 'What if you don't come back?'

'I will.' He scrawled a number on a napkin. 'But here's Frank's number. In case I don't.'

He drained the last of his coffee and left, striding down the hill towards the church. On the way, he pulled out a new phone and ripped open the packaging with his teeth. He stopped by a crepe stand to slot in the SIM.

When he got to the terrace at the head of the Sacré Coeur steps, he looked up. As he suspected, a radio mast was attached to the outside of the balustrade of the north cupola. Fortunately, churches were always the greediest to take the telecoms companies' cash, and for the call he was about to make, he needed a rock-solid signal. Plus, worst case, he didn't want it triangulated to where he'd just come from.

He dialled the Cerberus encryption server, waited for the beep, then tapped out the four numbers that would re-route the call to Frank.

The tone cut out, as if there was a fault. Cal cursed and redialled, but this time, after the beep, he punched in the number that Kate had given him that morning to confirm Sofie's handover. The same thing happened again. Was there a problem with the server? Something had taken it offline. He realised he'd have to go direct. This time, it was answered immediately.

'Cal?' Kate sounded tight. 'Where are you?'

So it was a single-use number. That's why she knew it was him.

'Let's cut the bullshit, ok? Gebler just tried to kill us.'

'Tell me where you are. Are you with Sofie? We'll come and get you.'

She sounded as if she knew. No *'what the hell are you talking about?'*

'How did Gebler know? First, the men following us in Woodbridge. Now this. Your outfit is leaking like a sieve.'

A beat. Tense.

'We don't know what's going on. The important thing is to bring you and Sofie…'

'Are you kidding, Kate? The important thing is that if

I'd followed your instructions, we'd both be dead. What is Gebler doing here?'

'Is Sofie with you?'

'Answer my question, dammit.'

Hesitation at the other end.

'You could've been mistaken...'

'No. I saw him. I'd like to speak to Hart.'

'I'm afraid that's not possible at the moment. Tell me where you are and...'

He glanced at his watch. They'd be able to triangulate him any minute now.

'Kate, let me be crystal clear. No more dicking about. I'm dealing with no one but Hart on this. I won't be calling again. The next time you'll hear from me will be in person. Got it?'

'We'll do our best, Cal.'

He rang off, sprang the SIM, and tossed it with the phone over the edge of the terrace. There was a clatter as it hit a gravel path far below. In the distance, a beacon flashed from the top of the Eiffel Tower.

55

In the bar, Sofie was beginning to get anxious. He'd been gone twelve minutes.

In a corner, two teenage boys were playing pinball, lights flashing in rhythm with the electronic sing-song. The machine shuddered and shook as they slammed their bodies against it in an attempt to influence the run of the balls.

She tore her eyes away and gulped down water to smother a rising panic. The explosion had numbed her. There was only so much she could process. She search the street outside for any sign of him and caught sight of a girl. She was staring at her, ragged and wild. With a jolt, she realised it was her reflection in the window.

Then she spotted him cutting back across the square.

'I was starting to get worried,' she said as Cal reached her.

'Sorry. Took longer than I thought.'

'Who did you call?'

He ran his hand through his hair and drew his leather jacket more tightly around him, shivering.

'I'll tell you later. Come on, we have to leave.'

He turned towards the door.

'Where are we going?' she said nervously, hurrying after him.

'We need to keep moving.'

They walked quickly downhill toward the metro, blending into the tourist crowd. He said something about staying in populated areas. And about needing time to think. She reminded him - pointedly - that she was in this too. Because his presence was only semi-reassuring. The stakes were ratcheting up again.

They took the train to Bir Hakeim. From there, it was a short walk to the Eiffel Tower.

'Cal,' she said when they arrived, pulling on his arm, 'can we just… sit for a moment? Please?'

She was exhausted. He nodded and led her to a bench near the river, and eased off his backpack.

Eventually, she said, 'Honestly, what are we going to do?'

'I need to figure it out.'

'You don't say? Jesus, Cal, that's three times... *three times*… somebody's tried to kill me. I thought I was through this. You said I'd be safe. When is it going to end?'

She waited for him to say something, but he seemed to be watching the crowds of tourists clambering off the tour buses across the street.

'Cal,' she said sharply, 'are you even listening to me?'

His eyes met hers. Clear, but unreadable. The scar on his temple was a worrying reminder that this guy was not infallible.

'I mean, who are you, really?'

'You know who I am. I'm here to bring you in.'

'Well,' she said, with a bitter smile, 'you're crushing it so far.'

He looked away, jaw flexing.

'You're right. This isn't how it was supposed to go. I think it's time we came clean with each other.'

ALL THE WAY FROM MONTMARTRE, HE'D BEEN WEIGHING UP whether to take Sofie into his confidence.

Because if they were going to get out in one piece, they had to work together. Which meant trusting each other. Besides, he was beginning to feel responsible for the girl. It was not a comfortable sensation.

So he began. He explained about his own efforts to locate her, when he realised that the whistleblowers were missing; how Cambridge Bio had tried to get him out of the country, to start work on their conference in Oslo; about the MI5 agent he met up with - the Canadian in the pub - and finally about how he and Frank had gone to her flat and found the faxed document.

She looked shocked. 'You mean it was *you* who broke in?'

'I'm sure every other investigator's been up there since. We were just lucky enough to get there first.'

He went on to tell her about Alice.

'God, I wondered how that had happened. You must have led them to her, no?'

'Afraid so.'

'Shit, Cal.' She stared at the river, chewing her lip. 'But what I still don't understand is why you decided to look for me in the first place? Why didn't you fly to Oslo for their next event, as Cambridge asked you to? Why come after me?'

It was a good question, and one to which he had no

obvious answer. Call it professional pride, he told her, because he was angry at Laura and Gebler and the way they had used him. After Alice's murder, there was no turning back.

When he had finished, Sofie stooped to pick up a stray leaflet that was floating under their seat and screwed it up in a ball. She turned it over and over in her hands, as if she were trying to decide something. She gazed up at the curved grey steel that soared giddily over their heads.

'So,' she said, 'after everything that's happened, are you any closer to knowing what's going on?'

He watched a gendarme stroll past in the distance. When he had disappeared, he turned to her.

'I know three things.' He counted them out on his fingers. 'One: you're a witness, and someone wants you dead. Two: someone wants me dead, because I got too close. And three: whatever this is, it's big. Bigger than anything I've ever seen before. They erased evidence. Faked Kate's death in Ukraine. That takes power, and reach. Institutional reach. Which leads me on to something else.'

She looked at him now. Hard. He paused.

'Kate and Hart think there could be a mole in MI5. Potentially a secret conspiracy in the heart of the establishment to protect Crane. They suspected it even before we discovered those two men tailing you, which would only have confirmed their fears. It's why they asked me to step in, and why we took you to Suffolk, where we thought you would be safe. Only Kate and James Hart knew you were there.' A beat. 'Or so we believed.'

Her focus had shifted. She remained silent. Was she listening?

'Which brings us to today. How did Gebler know that we would be in that exact vehicle, at that exact time, in that exact location? The bomb was planted before that car was delivered to us.'

A truck had broken down on the embankment, and cars began hooting furiously. Sofie started as a mechanical toy bird came flapping down beside them. A little boy ran up to retrieve it.

'As I see it, we've got two options. We can go our separate ways, take our chances. Or we work together.' He touched her arm. 'But if we're going to do that, Sofie, you have to tell me everything. Like I've just done with you. Because…' he hesitated '…I'm getting the sense that there's something you're holding back.'

Still, she didn't answer.

'I mean, what precisely happened between the moment you escaped from the boat and the night we picked you up? That document we found in your fax machine. What was it, and why was it faxed to you? Who sent it? If you have that information, Sofie, you have to tell me. Kate and Hart need to know.'

Finally, she reacted.

'Are you out of your mind?' She sprang up angrily. 'You said it yourself! We can't rely on them! It was because of them that someone tried to kill us!'

He stepped back, unprepared for her outburst.

'Sofie, we can't be sure of that. Yes, the operation was compromised, but surely you can trust Kate? She took a bullet for you on that boat. Any information you have could be critical.'

She was wild-eyed now. 'And Hart? What do you know about him?'

'If we trust her, we have to trust him. Besides, what's the alternative? We try to disappear?' He snorted derisively. 'Wise up.'

She shook her head.

'Listen,' he went on, gentler now. 'I'm trained for this stuff, remember. But you? You'll be running, Sofie, constantly looking over your shoulder. How can you survive out there on your own?'

A gaggle of noisy children ran screaming across the road towards the river cruise docking in front of them, heading for the ticket booths.

'Aren't you forgetting something?' she countered. 'There's another option. We crack it ourselves. Together. Forget Kate.'

'Sofie, do you have any idea... *any idea*... of what we're up against?'

'Of course I do!' She flicked her hair back and laughed bitterly. 'But it's the only way I can go.'

'Which is why we need to work with Kate.'

'And you can trust them after today? After what happened in Suffolk? We're expendable. Surely you can see that? Kate might retain some vestige of loyalty for me as her friend, but do you think this guy Hart cares what happens to us? Sorry, Cal, no, we do this ourselves. Because you're right, I haven't told you the half of it. The reason I was there with Kate that night was because those two chemists said they would only deal with me. My father was a victim of that drug trial. He committed suicide.'

Cal's eyes narrowed. 'Sofie, why are you only telling me that now?'

'Because you never asked me.'

'Was Kate aware of it?'

'Of course she was! It's why she got me involved in the first place.'

She sat down again to retell the rest of her story. About the messages and her father's diaries. About the mystery doctor, a woman friend - or girlfriend, Sofie wasn't quite sure - called Alex, who had been prescribing the drug to him. When she got to the bit about visiting Harry Erskine, Cal did a double-take. Why did the name sound familiar? But he didn't interrupt her, and when she'd finished, she looked up at him beseechingly.

'So now do you see? You said it yourself - with the leadership election coming up, they want to shut this down. But if we can find my dad's doctor, we can break this wide open! That's the time to go back to Kate and MI5. When we have hard evidence. Then we'd be untouchable.'

He felt his blood run cold. She was insane.

'Besides,' she went on, passionate now. 'This is important. Do you realise what they're doing with this drug?'

He frowned. 'And how do you propose we find this doctor, if all you have is a first name?'

She looked at him triumphantly. 'Through a lawyer that the two chemists told me about in Gibraltar.'

'You have their details?'

'Sort of. I lost the business card they gave me, but I do remember the P.O. Box number. It was the same as my dad's birthday. Written out backwards.'

Cal stared at her.

'See, I remember things like that. Patterns in numbers. It's how I work.'

A child ran past them, chasing a ball. A small white dog was dancing about its heels, careful at every step not to knock the boy over. Eventually, he got hold of it and, with a swing, lobbed it a few yards, where it bounced off a litter bin and dribbled to a halt. The dog panted expectantly.

Cal sighed. 'Sofie, I'll be honest with you. I want to help you, I really do. I know how strongly you must feel...'

She shot him a look and was on the point of saying something, but Cal held up his hand to stop her.

'But I'd be responsible for what happened to you. I'm not sure I can handle that.'

He paused. Her face had turned to stone.

'Your *responsibility*?' she said, incredulous. 'Fuck you!'

'I mean, I have what's coming to me. It's at my own risk; it's what I'm paid for. But you? You shouldn't be here at all, for Christ's sake. Leave this stuff to other people. I'll take you back to see Kate, I'll explain...'

There was no humour in the dry little laugh that escaped from her now.

'And become the victim of one of their leaks again, is that it?'

'I'm trying to protect you, for fuck's sake.' He felt suddenly exasperated.

'No, you're not, you're trying to control me!'

'At least you'll have a chance. Or if you really want, go to your own people...'

She was trembling now. Her voice rising.

'My own people?' she cried. 'Your *responsibility? What the hell?* I don't have any people! I'm on my own. You're a misogynistic bastard, it's whatever suits you, right?'

She began to quiver, her eyes ablaze.

'Ever since I met you, my world has collapsed. You know what? You're bad news.'

She jumped up off the bench.

'Sofie...'

'Don't Sofie me!'

Before he had a chance to stop her, she turned and vanished into the crowd. All he could do was watch.

And wonder if he'd just let the only real lead he had… walk away.

56

Cal felt something he seldom had before: helpless. His instinct screamed at him to follow her. But it was now a matter of his own survival, and there was no space for the luxury of emotion. It angered him. He hadn't asked for this.

He kicked at the gravel, frustrated, trying to figure out what he could do to help her. The answer was very little, unless…

He delved into his jacket for his phone, but instead his fingers brushed the sharp edge of the small plastic security card from the hire car. He inspected it. It seemed proof enough that the operation to bring him in was legit. Should he try to return to the embassy?

He got up and headed toward the river, where the big sightseeing boats bobbed on their moorings. Still unable to make up his mind, he scanned the crowds for her, but she was nowhere to be seen. A paper boy was selling early editions of the evening news, *Paris Soir*. Next to him stood a gendarme. The boy was talking to him excitedly, holding out a copy of the newspaper and pointing at the boat. The policeman seemed to hesitate. Cal followed him with his eyes as he went to consult with a colleague. They made a radio call. Then the two of them began to stride rapidly towards the pontoon.

Cal walked casually over to the vendor, bought a paper, and moved on, flicking it open. On the front page was the news of a car bomb exploding: *'Une voiture piégée explose devant l'ambassade américaine. Un gendarme mort. Des bombardiers blessés mais s'échappent.'*

Car bomb explodes in front of the American embassy. One policeman killed. Bombers injured but escape.

Underneath was a large image of Sofie. Her colleague, the report went on, was a suspected terrorist.

Cal stopped dead in the middle of the quay. *Terrorist?* How could that be? Then it dawned on him. Sofie had been right. This was more than just a leak. It was a stitch-up. There was no photo of him yet, but it could only be a matter of time. The image of her had clearly been prepped, ready to roll out with the afternoon news bulletin.

He hurried back to the paper boy. Cal jabbed his finger at the photo.

'Hey, j'ai vu quelqu'un comme cette fille ici il ya quelques instants. Vous croyez que … c'etait elle?'

'Hey, I saw someone like this girl here a few moments ago. Do you think... it was her?'

The boy lit up. *'Je sais! Je l'ai vue aussi! J'ai dit au flic. Elle est montée à bord de ce bateau.'*

He'd seen her get on board, he said, nodding excitedly at the Bateaux Parisiens sightseeing boat moored alongside the floating dock. Engine still running, it was taking passengers for the two o'clock departure. The boy chuckled. There was no way out for the girl now, he continued, very soon they'd have the place cordoned off. He was already punching numbers into his mobile phone. He winked at Cal. '*Le TV!*'

But Cal was no longer listening. Pushing past a gaggle of schoolchildren snaking their way on board, he squeezed up the ramp. The two gendarmes stood hidden from the crowd in the office on the floating pontoon dock, scanning the passengers as they boarded.

Cal slipped through unnoticed and climbed to the upper deck. Kids milled around like flocks of starlings, scrambling over seats and playing tag along the aisles, as harassed chaperones tried in vain to corral them. Cal moved quickly, scanning the adults. No Sofie.

He doubled back, checked again, then descended to the lower covered deck. It was packed out with an American tour group in ponchos and windbreakers, sheltering from the kids and the Parisian breeze.

Cal cast a furtive glance towards the quayside through the window. The gendarmes were still at their look-out, but a furious argument seemed to have broken out between them and an official from the boat company. The last of the passengers had embarked, and the crew were waiting for the signal to cast off. A street vendor scurried past, eager to get back to shore. It gave Cal an idea. Shoving a twenty euro note into the man's hand, he snatched a blue baseball cap - '*Paris - Je t'adore*'.

And a plastic cowboy gun in a fake leather holster.

57

Sofie saw them too. She was leaning dejectedly against the bow rail, head down, watching the water lap against the sides. Thinking over what Cal had said.

A whistle went. She glanced behind her. Two crewmen threw the ropes and jumped aboard. A gendarme followed them. She turned back to the choppy water, beginning to churn now as the boat edged out into the Seine.

Her fingers toyed with a coin in her pocket. Next to it was the folded scrap of paper with Frank's number on it. Had Cal seen her get on? If he hadn't, she'd probably never find him again. Should she call Frank? Heads or tails? Stick or twist?

It didn't take long to have her answer.

'I've been looking for you,' a voice said at her elbow.

She stiffened, but her attention didn't waver from the water.

'What do you want now?'

'Seen the paper?'

The boat began to surge forward, frothing white in the water. He bent down to her.

'You're on the front page. The police are after us, Sofie, and they're calling us terrorists.'

She straightened up. 'What are you talking about?'

Cal handed her the paper. Her face drained.

'I don't understand. This is bullshit!'

'Of course it is.'

'But how can they say that?'

'They can say whatever they like. You were right all along. Sorry for doubting you. But more to the point,' his voice dropped to a whisper, 'someone saw you come aboard. They recognised you from the newspaper. That's what the gendarmes are here for.'

She looked aghast. 'You mean…'

'By the time this boat returns in an hour, the quayside will be cordoned off, there'll be marksmen in bulletproof jackets, jagged steel plates on the exit ramp, armour-plated vans. The whole shebang.'

Her voice trembled. 'So that's it, then? It's over?'

Cal shook his head. 'Not if we get off first.' He shoved a blue baseball cap into her hands. 'Put this on.'

She stared at him. 'And how do you propose we do that?'

He didn't answer. Just grabbed her wrist and propelled her along the deck.

58

Cal kept his head low, eyes scanning upriver toward Pont d'Alma, then back down toward the Trocadéro. Ahead of them, the first bridge they were due to pass under was a low, steel girder footbridge. Upstream of it were two piers. He inspected the riverbanks on either side.

'Mesdames et Messieurs, bienvenue abord Les Bateaux Parisiennes pour notre tour panoramique de Paris de la Seine.' began the commentary in four different languages. *'Ladies and gentlemen, welcome aboard..!'*

There was no sign of the gendarme.

He squeezed Sofie's arm. 'OK. Let's go.' She stiffened. He dug his fingers in harder. 'We doing this or not?'

Reluctantly, she gave way, and he hurried her toward the back of the boat, keeping her close to the rail.

'Meinen Damen und Herren...'

'Wait here.'

Cautiously, he climbed the steps to the top deck. The children were mostly quiet now, their heads bobbing around excitedly as they jostled for a view. Nearby, a small boy was leaning out over the rail.

A teacher was shouting at him. 'Attention, Pascal, *arrête*!' Beyond her, he spotted the gendarme slowly making his way forward along the aisle, his eyes sweeping left and right. The boat swung round in the river and began to churn steadily upstream towards the piers. Cal leapt back down the steps.

'Follow me.'

A couple approached, and she squeezed against the side to allow them to pass, her face averted.

They emerged on the upper deck. The gendarme was walking towards the bows.

Sofie gasped. 'Cal…'

'This way.' He pulled her aft, towards a little gangway that ran beside the wheelhouse. A small metal sign dangled on a chain - *'Entrée Interdite.'*

Cal had let go of her hand and was about to step over it when there was a terrifying, high-pitched scream. He looked back as Sofie turned in fright. Ten feet away, the little boy was dangling over the edge, his friend crying hysterically.

'Come on!' Cal hissed. But Sofie was frozen to the spot.

A teacher was running down the aisle. The screaming continued. She hesitated for a brief second and then lunged back towards the child.

'*Sofie!*'

She got to him just as the teacher did, and in one swift movement, they hauled him back up. People rounded in their seats in consternation, wondering what the commotion was.

'Behind you, you can see the massive Palais du Chaillot, built in the 1930s to house a number of museums…'

The gendarme had turned too. He was now staring at them.

'Pascal!' shouted the mother. *'Mon Dieu! Jamais, jamais fait ia, qu'est-ce que je t'ai dit?'* The boat was beginning to pick up

speed, and the piers were rapidly approaching. The footbridge loomed beyond.

'*Come on, for fuck's sake!*' yelled Cal again.

The policeman began walking back towards them.

Sofie broke away and ran back towards Cal. He spun round and raced towards the wheelhouse. She stumbled after him, panting.

'I couldn't leave him, Cal… ' she gasped.

Cal glanced toward the bridge. Sixty seconds, maybe less. The margin between success and failure was wafer-thin. He looked back. The gendarme was busy with the teacher. Apparently, he'd not clocked them. But for how long?

'Cal?'

He raised a finger to his lips, holding his breath. Ten seconds. Twenty. Thirty. She looked up at him questioningly. The first of the piers loomed, and then they were level.

He waited until they were midway between the two. The footbridge was less than three hundred feet away. He clutched the toy gun, edged around the side of the wheelhouse, and opened the door. The captain spun round, startled, a cigarette clamped between his teeth.

'Cut the engines!' shouted Cal over the din.

'Eh?'

'*Arret! Halt the bateau!*'

He lined the fake gun up at the man's head. It was realistic enough in the split second the captain had to assess the situation. The cigarette dropped from his mouth as he scrambled for the lever.

There was a thudding noise from below as the boat shuddered into reverse. They were passing the last of the piers now, and the bows would soon be under the bridge.

'You're crazy!' screamed Sofie.

Through the window, Cal could see the gendarme. He had finished with the teacher and was now making his way in their direction.

'On the floor,' growled Cal, motioning aggressively.

The petrified captain flattened himself.

'Head down!'

With the gun still trained on the captain's cowering body, Cal backed out to the deck, dragging Sofie with him. Outside, a metal ladder led up to the roof of the wheelhouse. With one hand, he pushed Sofie up. For the first time, it seemed to dawn on her what he had in mind.

'You surely don't…?'

'Up!' he commanded. He followed close behind her, and they grabbed a small, white radar dome for balance.

The boat glided underneath the footbridge, the reverse thrust of its engines slowing it to a crawl. He saw the gendarme stop and look up in surprise. They'd climbed up a fraction too early, and for a few precious seconds they were silhouetted against the skyline before being lost against the blackened steel of the bridge overhead. But it was too late to worry about that now.

The girders slid by. It was going to be close. The lowest was still almost four feet above them.

He rapidly reassessed.

'Follow me!' He scrambled onto the radar, pulling her with him. The gendarme started running.

'Now!' Before she had a chance to protest, he was hauling her up towards the girder.

She grabbed it.

'Got it?'

'Cal!' she screamed.

'*Now go!*' he yelled.

He shunted her up on his shoulders, staggering to steady himself against the movement of the boat, and she was away. They had come to a standstill, but the engines were churning, and slowly the boat started reversing. Sofie and the girder drifted away, and then all there was above him was a cavernous black space.

The gendarme shouted something, his voice echoing amongst the hollow steel. Cal saw him draw the gun and kneel, trying to get a line on where Cal was standing. It was dark, but in less than a minute, he knew he would be back where he was to start with, in brilliant silhouette, an easy target.

People began to scream. Cal hesitated, then waved the gun and yelled as hard as he could. The noise in the confined space was piercing. More screams erupted as people scrambled to the deck.

'Et maintenant, a votre gauche,' the pre-recorded commentary echoed metallically, now hopelessly out of sync, *'vous passez le Palais du Tokyo, aujourd'ui La Musee d'Art Moderne. And now, on your left, you are passing...'*

He looked up. The end girder was overhead again as the boat began its retreat. His last chance. He lunged towards it, slipped, and almost fell, but with one hand on the edge of the metal, he heaved himself up with a grunt, his feet dangling above the boat. The cabin roof dropped away, and then it was only open deck twenty feet down.

He flinched as his hand caught something sharp. He held on grimly. With an immense effort, he swung his feet up and swivelled round until he was horizontal. He collapsed onto the steel. It was damp and greasy.

He searched the gloom. Sofie was two girders along, rasping heavily. Water dripped from above.

'You OK?'

She didn't answer. Below them, the boat rapidly started pulling away, people crouched down in terror, the ones in front twisted in their seats, trying to see what was going on amongst the ones in the back. They slid past, their cries amplified, peering around with bewilderment in the shadow of the bridge.

Then it was gone, and was turning in midstream, the figure of the gendarme running like a frightened rabbit towards the stern.

'A destra. dopo la ponte di Alma, passiamo lungo il Quai d'Orsay,' boomed the receding commentary.

Cal brought up first one leg and then the other until he got his footing. He stood up and gingerly climbed across the criss-cross of girders until he got to her. Water reflections flitted around them. The sound of the boat receded until there was only the dull rumble of traffic above.

She was breathing heavily. 'Now what?'

He surveyed the length of the bridge, searching for a way out.

He grinned. 'Now comes the difficult bit.'

They made it out barely in time. As they climbed the steps from the concrete embankment up to the road, three police cars, lights flashing and sirens wailing, converged on the bridge. Gendarmes began to spill out.

Cal and Sofie mingled with a small knot of tourists craning to see what the commotion was about.

Then, heads down, they slipped quietly away.

59

Cal's first thought was to get them as far away from the centre of Paris as possible. But he dared not risk public transport for fear that someone would recognise Sofie from the press report.

'I need you to do exactly as I say,' he whispered, drawing her to him as they approached a taxi stand. Several drivers were standing in a huddle, smoking beside their cabs. 'We've got to make out we're together. Lean on my shoulder.'

She pulled away for a second to give him a look, but did as he ordered. Her ponytail had come loose during their escape from the boat, and she ruffled her hair to obscure her face.

'Taxi?' queried Cal hopefully.

'Vous allez où?' asked one of them, eyeing them with Parisian indifference.

Cal gave him the address he had memorised. The man nodded, and they bundled into the back of his cab.

On the way, they didn't say much. Sofie clung to Cal tightly, feigning sleep, while Cal stared blankly out of the window. Merely two more lovers in Paris on a windy afternoon. But his mind was in overdrive, reviewing their options, trying to find the best way forward. It felt unsettling having her snuggled up next to him. What had been a responsibility, he realised, had now become a liability.

On impulse, he reached inside his jacket and took out the British embassy pass. It was going to be of no use to him now. It was then he noticed, for the first time, a tiny gold chip inserted at one end, like in a credit card, but smaller. Surely not? A bug? Hard to tell, but it wasn't worth the risk. He stuffed it in the gap in the seat beside him.

When they arrived, the driver was more concerned with counting the notes Cal handed him than paying them much attention, so Sofie was able to slide out unobserved.

They found themselves in a suburb, and judging by the landmarks they'd passed, far to the south. As Cal had planned. He had taken the address off a poster advertising go-karting, correctly guessing that the venue would be on the edge of town. The gates to the site were closed, but to one side were a line of four towering apartment blocks, run down and covered in a web of graffiti. A group of children were playing tag up and down the stairwells.

'Well?' she said, standing apart from him.

He surveyed the scene. To the right of the gates was a ragged gap in a tall chain-link fence. It appeared to be a former industrial site, fringed with rubble, the centre of which had been converted into a makeshift track, with a couple of Portakabins at the far end. Two yellow bulldozers sat idle. There was no one about.

'We'll rest up in here for a while,' he said. 'It buys us some time. Out of sight.'

They crawled through the fence and made their way across the wasteland, flopping down on a grass verge in the shadow of one of the cabins.

'Do you have any water?' she said. 'I'm parched.'

He tossed her a bottle from his pack. She drank deeply and shook her head.

'I can't believe what just happened. Did we really just jump off a boat in the middle of the river?'

Cal grinned. 'You were good.'

'I was shitting myself. And why am I all over the papers?'

'It's a fit up. Just like you said.'

'So, it's back to my plan now, right?' she said, handing back the bottle. 'Gibraltar?'

He scanned the area for signs of movement. Syringes were strewn all around them, alongside discarded wraps of silver foil. A drug user's hangout.

'Easier said than done. We'll need new identities.'

'Why?'

'They'll have us on a watch list by now.' He paused. 'However, I might be able to fix that. I know someone in Amsterdam who's a wizard at producing new documents.'

She frowned. 'You mean - fake ones?'

'Precisely. However, before we head to Gibraltar, there's another lead I think we should follow up. Your friend Harry Erskine. When you mentioned the name, I thought I recognised it. I'm sure he was on the delegate list for the party that night.'

Her eyes widened.

'You're kidding me! Surely I would have seen him?'

'Perhaps, perhaps not. Did you get sight of everyone on the boat that night?'

'True. But if he was, chances are, he didn't see me either.'

'What if he did? What if he knew you were there, but

wanted to stay hidden from you? Could it have been him who set up that contact between Kate, you and the chemists?'

'You think Kate was in touch with him?'

'Who knows? Anyway, my point is, from what you told me about your meeting with him, and from what I suspect, he may well have been on that delegate list. If he were, there's bound to be more he can tell us. About the trial, for example. And about your father's doctor.'

She nodded. 'He was cagey. But yes.'

'So I'll do some digging. Find out if he was on the boat that night and if so, let's pay him another visit.'

'Are you sure that's safe to back? To the UK, I mean?'

'With new IDs, why not?'

She fell silent. She seemed to be weighing it up.

'You don't seem convinced,' he said.

'It feels like a big risk.'

There was the sound of movement by the gate. Three figures were climbing through the fencing.

'Shit,' he said. 'Looks like we've got company.'

The figures drew closer. Faces obscured by hoodies, they didn't look friendly. The tallest of the three approached and said something in French, gesturing.

Cal got up. 'Sorry mate, I don't speak French.'

The man jabbed his hand in his direction while his companions, who had held back, took a step forward. Cal realised he was pointing at the watch on his wrist. He raised his palms in a gesture of appeasement, while subtly shifting his balance to be ready for the opposite.

'Guys, we're just leaving.' He glanced at Sofie. 'Take the backpack. Let's go.'

She bent to grab it. The tall guy blocked her path.

'The watch,' he growled. 'Phones.'

Cal shook his head slowly. 'Really? You sure about this?'

The three laughed, and there was a sudden flash of steel. Cal tensed. As the taller man made to grab his arm, he went with the movement, absorbing his forward motion and simultaneously swivelling his body round and chopping into the solar plexus with the side of his hand.

His assailant doubled up, gasping for breath. His two companions raced forward. The first was met with Cal's fist, and as he staggered back, Cal side-stepped the second and shoved him hard, forcing a stumble. In one swift movement, he was above him and stamping the man's hand into the dirt. He released the knife with a yelp, and Cal kicked it away, then swung his leg with full force into the man's ribs. He yelled out in pain.

Behind him, Sofie screamed. Cal spun round. The one he'd punched was trying to wrestle his arm around her neck, blood streaming from his broken nose, as she swivelled and kicked against him. Cal dropped down and, scooping up a fistful of grit, flung it towards Sofie and her attacker, simultaneously shouting at her to shield her eyes. Caught off guard, the sharp flints hit him full in the face, forcing him to release his grip. She spun away, leaving Cal to finish the job: a knee in the groin and an upper cut to the jaw and the man was down, out cold.

Cal stepped back, wiping the blood from his hand. He'd hardly broken sweat. The two others were already hobbling away in the distance.

'Jesus, Cal, where did you learn that?' Sofie panted breathlessly.

'I did warn them.'

She laughed with relief.

'They obviously didn't understand your terrible French.'

'Let's not kid ourselves. They'll be back. We should

leave.' He inspected her. 'You OK?'

She wiped some dirt off her cheek to reveal a thin streak of blood.

'Fine.'

He picked up his backpack.

'Have more faith in me now?'

'Maybe.'

On impulse, she walked over and hugged him. He started in surprise. She peered at his face.

'You're a mess. Let me clean it up.' He flinched as she dabbed his face with her scarf, soaking it with water. The blood, it appeared, was not his, but there was the beginning of a livid bruise where one of the men had caught him on the chin. Her fingers were cool and gentle, and he saw himself reflected in the pools of her brown eyes as she worked her magic. Satisfied, she stepped back.

'Better,' she said. 'Shall we go?'

He hesitated.

'Listen, Sofie, I want to get one thing straight.' She arched an eyebrow at him. 'I don't want you thinking that I'm doing this to get justice for you. Or for your father, with all due respect. That's your affair.'

She smiled. 'God forbid.'

'I'm doing it because getting to the bottom of this is my best chance of getting out alive. *You* are my best chance. Better to be honest with one another. Right?'

From somewhere in the distance came the faint rise and fall of a siren. Police or ambulance, it was impossible to tell. A second joined it, and they both stood still, scanning the street beyond the fence. The sirens receded.

She turned to face him, a faint smile still playing about her lips.

'I seem to remember you saying something about me

not surviving this on my own.' When he didn't reply, she added, 'After which, I suppose you will dump me again, right?'

'That's harsh. I didn't dump you, you dumped me, remember? But no, Sofie, I can't promise you anything. If you want out, that's fine. I won't stop you.'

They stared at each other in silence. The sirens started up again, much closer this time. Finally, she stuck out her hand.

'I like honesty. Especially from a man. Deal.'

60

Frank was down at the water's edge when the call came. It was the second he'd received that day from a withheld number.

The vibration stopped. Could it be Cal? He'd already had a failed comms alert from Cerberus. The server was down. Still, surely he wouldn't be stupid enough to contact him direct?

Then came the ring from the house phone. He bolted across the lawn.

'Emily, hang up!'

He burst into the kitchen just as she was setting down the receiver. She glanced up from the note she'd been scribbling, brows raised.

'What's up with you?'

'You shouldn't have answered it.'

'Excuse me?' She sounded annoyed. 'What do you expect me to do - stop living in my own house? I'm not about to tiptoe around like some kind of fugitive.'

'I know. I'm sorry. I should've warned you. Cal is in a bit of trouble, and he might attempt calling the landline. I think it's been compromised. As soon as we pick up, they can trace him.'

'Oh, for God's sake!' she snapped, exasperated. 'I'm fed up with your little games! So why doesn't he call your mobile like a normal person?'

'Emily, this is no joke. His life is in danger. And so is the girl's.'

Her eyes narrowed. 'I thought we left all this behind. I've got spy gear tucked behind the bread bin, Frank. Surveillance drones in the attic. And now I can't even answer my own damn phone?'

She turned, tossing the pen down with a clatter.

'Oh, and by the way, there's a car parked up by the main road on the edge of the village. Been there for two days now.'

'You saw them?'

'I was tempted to bring them coffee. Yes, I saw them.'

Frank slumped into a chair. When Emily was like this, he knew from bitter experience it was best to stay out of her way.

'So who was it?'

She handed him the note.

'He left a number. Says it's urgent.'

He squinted at it.

'Hurt?'

'H.A.R.T. Hart.'

61

THERE WAS NO TIME FOR ELABORATE PRECAUTIONS. LAURA had only requested the contact a few hours before. The email had landed in her inbox by return. Because it was so last-minute, the *What3Words* meeting point was within walking distance.

She left her heels under the desk and changed into trainers.

Horse Guards Parade was wet with rain. By the time she reached Clive Steps and cut down into St James's Park, the sky had turned pewter. She shivered beneath her cashmere coat - good for appearances, useless in a downpour.

But what really had her on edge wasn't the weather.

APOLLO had promised a cleanup. No loose ends. Nothing that could tie back to them or destabilise the campaign. But apparently the girl was still out there.

The park was almost empty. Laura moved fast, winding around the south side of the lake with her app open until she reached the three-metre square map grid she'd been given. *Jumps.Panic.Party*. Oddly apt. She hoped to God they'd get to the party bit.

A small group of schoolchildren was sketching ducks in the fading light. She walked on a few yards until she reached a park bench.

Five minutes passed.

Then ten.

He was late. That wasn't like him.

Finally, a man approached. Thirties, maybe. He perched gingerly on the edge of the bench. Laura eyed him. He had short fair hair and wore thick, black-framed glasses, and she sensed a nervousness in his posture.

'Laura?' he said, without meeting her eyes.

She stared at him coldly.

'And you are?'

'APOLLO sends his apologies. He's not in town.' He forced an awkward smile. 'What can we do for you?'

For a moment, she considered aborting. They sat in silence for thirty seconds before she spoke.

'Tell me what happened in Paris. The girl is all over the news.'

'They got away, I'm sorry to say.'

'*They?*' Her eyes sharpened. 'Are you telling me that Harrison's with her?'

'That's our understanding.'

Laura exhaled through her nose. 'You realise what a disaster this is?'

She noticed a barely perceptible flinch.

'I need to speak to him.'

'Like I say, he's out of town…'

'No, not APOLLO,' she snapped. 'Harrison.'

The man looked alarmed.

'That would be a mistake. Cal Harrison is extremely dangerous.'

'You think I don't know his background? I recruited

him, for God's sake. He'll listen to me.'

'If you can find him.' The man shifted on the bench. 'It's unfortunate that he got caught up in this. However, I'm speaking for APOLLO when I say that your instructions haven't changed. We will handle it.'

Her instructions? It was infuriating. She didn't owe these people anything.

'What about Gebler?'

'What about him?'

'Is he still in play?'

'I'm afraid I can't divulge operational…'

She cut across him. 'So what's your plan?'

A pause. He fiddled with his coat, then said, 'We think we know where they're headed.'

'Where?'

'Gibraltar.'

Laura looked startled. 'Gibraltar? What's in Gibraltar?'

'We understand that the girl, James, has a contact there. She believes they have evidence.'

This was a fascinating piece of intelligence, thought Laura to herself. She might be able to do something with this.

'What sort of evidence?'

'Against Cambridge Bio.'

'And it implicates Crane?'

That gave him pause. He seemed unsure of how much to tell her.

'We don't know what it amounts to,' he replied eventually. He coughed lightly. 'However, it gives us an opportunity to find the source. We have assets on the ground there. More room for manoeuvre.'

He stood and looked out over the lake. Then back at her.

'But the plan remains the same. We have it covered. Please do not contact us again. We'll update you when it's done.'

Without waiting for an answer, he strode away.

As soon as she returned to the office, Laura messaged Tasha. She rang back almost immediately.

'What did you find out?'

'The girl's abroad. She's on the run with Harrison.'

'She's still not been dealt with?'

'No.'

'Fucking amateurs,' muttered Tasha.

'You can talk. You had your chance. Two chances.'

Laura could feel Tasha's anger hanging in the silence.

'And there's something else,' Laura went on casually. 'Apparently, they're on their way to Gibraltar.'

More silence.

'Tasha, you there?'

'Why Gibraltar?'

'I hope you're not going to get any ideas into your head,' Laura said, guessing that there was a more than evens chance that she'd just handed Tasha the girl's head on a plate.

'Like what?'

'Well, you're in Madrid, right? What's that, four hundred miles?'

'Let me know if you receive more news.'

'I certainly will.'

Tasha rang off.

Laura smiled at the phone. Knowing Tasha, she'd take the bait.

62

The moment Tasha ended the call, she went in search of her black canvas holdall. She hadn't unpacked it since getting back to Madrid, but somewhere at the bottom of it, she knew, was something that suddenly made sense after what Laura had told her.

She crouched by the bag in the hallway of her Lavapiés apartment, unzipped the side pocket, and felt the edges of the business card: small, stiff, and forgotten until five seconds ago.

She pulled it out. Cream stock, clean type. Typical law firm. One word jumped out: Gibraltar.

Philip Rast, it read. *Chambers, Rast & Associates. P.O. Box 758001.*

She'd found it that night on the cabin cruiser, in the thirty seconds she'd had to sweep the place before escaping.

She would get the bitch yet.

It was already past three. Google Maps showed a driving time of six hours to the border. On her BMW 1200GS, she could do it in four and a half. Maybe less if she pushed hard. It would give her plenty of time to make a plan to welcome the girl when she arrived.

She threw her jacket on, grabbed the holdall, and was halfway to the door before stopping mid-stride. She couldn't walk into a lawyer's office looking like she'd just stepped out of a black-ops training camp. She needed to look the part. She backtracked, rifled through the closet, and yanked out a sharp navy blazer and a pair of low heels. They went into her roll-top pack. With that, she locked up and headed for the metro.

The place she was headed was on the edge of a newly constructed industrial estate in Carabanchel in the south of the city, home to a printing company and a distributor of motor parts. It was anonymous enough to suit Tasha's purposes, with an entrance onto a side street at the back free of CCTV. As she exited the metro, the sun was already dipping towards the hills to the west, and the traffic on the streets was starting to build for what promised to be a busy night. There was a fiesta on, and people were dressing up. A five-minute walk brought her to a concrete wall capped with razor wire and, a hundred metres further on, a green metal door.

She punched four numbers into the analogue code box beside it and, once through, turned right down a wide alleyway that ran around the inside perimeter of the site and past the rear entrance of the printing company's warehouse. Steel shutters were down on its three loading bays. Next to it was a row of garages. Hers was the second of four.

She unlocked the heavy steel padlocks, slipped her key into the shutter lock, and pressed the button to release the electric roller doors. Before stepping over the threshold, she made one last check: that the nylon tripwire across the entrance was still intact. Satisfied, she stepped in and flicked on the light, closing the doors behind her.

Now the real work started.

First, the playlist. Billie Eilish's *"Everything I Wanted."* It was a ritual she followed. To get herself centred.

Next: the gear. She swivelled a combo lock, and a tall metal cabinet on the back wall clicked open. Inside was a range of firearms. Her go-to choice for operational teamwork, the Heck and Kochler MP5 sub-machinegun; the Walther P88 autopistol, a sexy little number that packed fifteen rounds and was fully ambidextrous, like her, and excellent for aiming in low light conditions; and two semi-automatic Glocks - the 17, and her personal favourite, the compact 19. That little baby would do perfectly for what she had in mind - something she could conceal at close quarters. It also came with a lightweight carbon fibre suppressor.

She packed the gun with three mags of fifteen rounds each, and a spare Dutch passport to match the Spanish one she normally carried. As backup, just in case. Finally, from a small safe set in the back wall of the garage, she pulled $4000 in cash.

Finally ready, she flung off a set of canvas covers to reveal a gleaming black and silver motorcycle. It was a beautiful piece of kit, ideally suited to the off-roading she liked to do at weekends in the Sierra Norte mountains north of Madrid. Weapons and cash went in one pannier. Her blazer and heels, holdall, and extra gear in the other. She reopened the garage door, rolled the bike out, reset the tripwire, and secured everything behind her.

She checked her watch. 17:15.

With a fair wind, she'd be in La Línea, within sight of the Rock, by ten.

63

The Saturday afternoon Paris to Amsterdam service was packed. As the coach ground its way through the city's rougher northern banlieues, Sofie leaned her forehead against the window, watching it all slide past: row upon row of anonymous tower blocks, graffiti-tagged walls, shuttered up shops. And pondered. What did the next stage of her journey hold in store? It surely couldn't get any more intense than the previous twenty-four hours. She was fried, physically and emotionally. Her thoughts a scrambled mess.

The coach slowed. She soon saw the reason: people were starting to spill out onto the pavements around the St Denis rugby stadium. A group of men in blue and white stripes were chanting, and as they passed, one of them caught her eye through the window and gave her the thumbs-up sign. She looked away, fingering her short black wig self-consciously. God, what a sight she must be.

She twisted it to try to ease the itch. When they'd picked it up in the party shop on the way to the bus station - Cal's idea - it had reeked of cheap perfume. She'd insisted on washing it in the public toilets before boarding. He'd got annoyed. They needed to conserve cash, he'd said, and the shampoo she'd bought was an extravagance. But she was glad of it now. She'd blow-dried it under the hand dryer while he had gone for a buzz cut at a barber in the station concourse.

She leant out into the aisle. What the hell was keeping him? He'd already been in the toilet for over five minutes. Rucksacks jutted out of overhead racks, scruffy parkas were stuffed against windows. From the front came the smell of fried food. And, from time to time, something else.

A minute later, she saw him climb up from the toilet well. His head was shaved to a fuzz. She gave him a wry smile as he slumped down beside her.

'What kept you so long?'

'Needed to make a call. Check that Redtop was expecting us, that Frank's message got through.'

'Redtop? I thought you said she was called Sam?'

'Her nickname was Redtop in the unit.'

'Let me guess. Red hair.'

'You're catching on.'

'And?'

'All good. She's going to see if she can track down the Gibraltar law firm you have a lead on.'

'Tell me about her. You served together?'

He nodded.

She hesitated, wondering if now was the moment to broach the subject.

'You still haven't told me what unit you were in,' she said.

'You wouldn't have heard of it.'

More deflection.

'Try me.'

He pulled off his leather jacket and bunched it up

behind his head. 'I suggest you get some shuteye. We've got seven hours to get through.'

Seven hours to get to know you, she thought, if you really wanted to open up. But she let it pass - it was obvious he didn't. She turned away. Whatever he'd done for a living, he'd clearly learnt some skills. But still, despite everything they'd already been through, she barely knew him. Yet here she was, entrusting her life to the guy.

The coach hit the A1 and picked up speed. Outside, the light was beginning to fade. They passed a large industrial park, where rows of Carrefour lorries were backed up in loading bays. The road blurred. Sofie exhaled, leaned her head against the cool glass, and shut her eyes.

Not for the first time, Cal had a sense of how precarious their situation was.

He tilted his head, glancing sideways. She was out cold, curled up like a kid, knees tucked in tight, the wig a little askew and pressing into his shoulder. It smelled faintly of almonds. She'd wasted ten euros shampooing the bloody thing. They'd have to conserve cash from now on. It was not even her hair, for God's sake.

His mind wandered to the person they were on their way to see. Sam. The last time he'd seen her was at one of their irregular unit reunions. It had been at Frank's farmhouse, she'd got well out of order, and ended up floating across the river in a rubber dinghy, paralytic.

Eventually, the rhythm of the road lulled him into a shallow sleep.

Two hours later, he woke with a jolt. The coach was stationary, and there was a sudden influx of cold air as the doors opened. A man and a woman got up to take their bags down from the rack. Had they arrived? It was dark. He glanced at his watch, but there were still several hours to go.

The two passengers got off. He heard the slamming of doors as suitcases and backpacks were retrieved from the luggage compartment below, and then three new people clambered aboard. Out of habit, he noted their age and appearance and what they carried with them, but there was nothing to indicate that they were anything other than fellow travellers. A couple in their mid to late twenties, the girl quite pretty, and the bearded man clutching what looked like a laptop case. Followed by a single woman, older, with a small carry-on, which the man lifted onto the rack for her. She muttered her thanks and squeezed in beside a sleeping child.

'Cold out there?' Cal asked the man.

He looked surprised to be spoken to.

'You could say that,' he replied. 'But thank God, it's warm in here.'

Dutch accent. It was a trick they taught in training. One of many ways to check if you're being followed. Engage them in conversation, and more often than not, they'll give off a tell. The flicker of the eyes, the intonation in the voice, the altered physical stance. This man seemed clean.

The baggage doors slammed shut. A few seconds later, the driver climbed back into his seat, the engine fired into life, the passenger door hissed shut, and the coach began reversing, the warning message shrill and insistent.

Cal peered into the darkness. A sign said *Lille Centre.* He glanced again at Sofie beside him. She hadn't stirred. How could she sleep so easily? There was an endearing innocence about her that he found uncomfortably attractive.

64

THEY ROLLED INTO AMSTERDAM A LITTLE AFTER NINE IN THE evening and were dropped off near Centraal Station. Although he hadn't planned it this way, it was the ideal time to cross the city, when the streets and canals would be crammed with night-time tourists. While Sofie had slept, he'd mapped out the route to Sam's place on a napkin. He felt uneasy walking with her. The Red Light district was riddled with security cameras. Despite her wig and his buzz cut, they were still not entirely safe. Especially if spotted together.

As soon as they arrived, they grabbed a quick snack in the station café. When they finished, he brought out the map.

'Here's the drill,' he said, laying it flat on the table. 'I'll go first, you follow me at a distance. If you lose me, you can find your way with this.'

She scanned the hand sketch dubiously. 'So where are we now?'

He tapped the flimsy paper. 'Here. And over here, just behind a place called Waterlooplein, is where we're headed.

Sam's apartment. Just keep me in view. If I stop, you stop. Got it?'

She nodded. He drained his coffee and stood.

'Good. Count to ten, then follow me out.'

As soon as he was in the street, he set off to cross the canal and onto the Amrak, a wide road running from the central square. Without looking back to check she was following, he struck left past a café called the Grasshopper and into the maze of alleys that led towards the Oude Kirk and the Red Light district. The tatty souvenir shops and kebab joints soon morphed into a string of street-level windows with drawn curtains, and as he entered the area around the church, he could see that a couple ahead were occupied with women sitting on stools. The foot traffic was light, and they looked bored, as indifferent as mannequins. A platinum blonde was painting her nails, and as he approached, she gave him a sly glance. Her neighbour, a black girl with a bright pink frilly bra and high-heeled shoes to match, beckoned him in silently from the other side of the glass, a coquettish smile playing on her lips.

He walked on, then crossed a bridge and branched right along the Achterburgwal canal. The crowd of gawping tourists was thicker here, the windows more concentrated, forcing him to slow his pace. The girls in this section were tall and skinny, with hard, pale faces. He heard a loud commotion and raised voices. A few paces behind him, a tourist was attempting to take a photograph of one of them. She came marching out of her doorway in fury.

Ignoring them, Cal's eyes flicked towards the bridge he'd just crossed. A tour boat glided below, its lights rippling on the water. No Sofie.

But something else instead. Two men in dark leather jackets, watching the scene from across the canal. For a moment, one of them caught his eye - and held it, just a fraction too long.

He kept moving. A hundred paces on, he stopped outside a bookstore, pretending to read the sign above the door. It gave him just enough time to look without looking. About fifty yards away, but continuing in his direction, were the two men. Beyond them, he glimpsed Sofie's dark wig. She raised her hand in acknowledgement, like a schoolgirl waving at her dad at the school gate. He ignored her. It was too much, he supposed, to expect her to know how to behave. He stepped into the shop, confident that she would have seen him go in.

'Can I help you?' said a man behind the counter in English.

'Just browsing,' Cal said. 'I noticed something in the window. Mind if I take a look?'

'Be my guest.' The man returned to his newspaper. The shop smelled musty, crammed with second-hand books in uneven stacks from floor to ceiling. He leafed through an early edition in a plastic dust jacket, keeping an eye on the canal outside. He did not have long to wait. A minute later, the two men strolled past, one scanning ahead, the other tracking the far bank of the canal. They disappeared from view. He waited a further thirty seconds, closed the book, thanked the man, and left, the little bell on the door tinkling softly behind him.

To his right, the two men had passed the cross street and were continuing along the line of the canal into the darkness. Neither broke stride, and appeared to have other fish to fry. They were almost certainly plainclothes police. Cal turned left.

She was closer now, standing beside a bike rack, pretending to study the map. He had to admit, it wasn't bad. Her posture was relaxed, and she looked like just another tourist lost in Amsterdam's labyrinth. Most people wouldn't give her a second glance.

He caught her eye. She saw him. No wave this time.

Good, she was learning.

65

'Hey, Sam.'

The woman standing in the doorway was wiry-thin, early thirties, hair dyed a violent shade of red and shaved close on the sides. She wore a green sweatshirt two sizes too big and a pair of scruffy black jeans worn white at the knees. She grinned and pulled Cal into a hug.

'Good to see you, boss,' she said, in a thick Glaswegian accent.

Cal smiled. 'You recovered from that hangover yet?'

She laughed at his reference to the last time they'd seen each other. Her eyes flickered to Sofie.

'Let me introduce Sofie. Sofie, Sam.'

'Nice to make your acquaintance.'

'You too.' Sofie peeled off her wig, revealing a mess of damp, flattened hair. She glanced at Cal. 'OK to ditch this vile thing?'

'Go ahead.'

'Thank God for that.'

The place where Sam lived was a narrow canal house on the New Gentleman's Canal, five stories high with a steel lifting beam protruding horizontally from the gable. It was squeezed into the gap between two larger properties and tilted slightly, like a crooked tooth. Music was pulsing out of a crowded bar next door.

Sam stepped aside and waved them in. The hallway was tight, dimly lit, and led to a narrow staircase. It was the sort of house that made Cal on edge, with just a single exit on the ground floor.

She led the way. Bright red strands of her hair had been threaded on the top of her head, and she had a fresh tattoo on her arm since the last time he'd seen her - something that looked like a skunk, or maybe a fox.

'Find the place alright? Weather's pure shite. Don't mind the mess.'

The stairs creaked underfoot. Small rooms radiated off at each level, and through the open doorways, Cal caught glimpses of piles of bric-à-brac and odd bits of mismatched furniture. As they climbed, they passed two windowless rooms on either side, revealing banks of computer screens and arrays of flashing coloured lights.

They emerged on the top floor into a studio space. A pair of old wooden double doors was set in one wall, opening onto a sheer drop of a hundred feet to the street below. Cal peered over the metal guardrail. Above was the rusted hijsbalk - the steel hoist - jutting out of the brickwork, with a short stretch of a frayed rope dangling down. An exit of sorts, if push came to shove.

'Anyone fancy a bevvy?' Sam cracked open a beer from a tiny fridge and held it out.

Sofie took it. 'Thanks.'

'Cal?'

'Got something soft?'

She reached inside and tossed him a Coke.

'So. Frank's telling me you're in the shite again.'

'Again?'

She laughed. Reaching into the drawer of a desk, she pulled out a thick brown envelope.

'Before you settle in, you ought to have these. Check they're OK.'

Cal raised an eyebrow. 'What is it?'

'Open it. I think you'll be pleased.'

Inside were two maroon passports with gold harps on the front.

'Irish?' he said, flipping one open. 'Seriously?'

'They're cheaper.'

'I don't sound Irish.'

Sam laughed. 'Better get practising then, big man.'

Cal flicked through the pages. It was good work. Stamps, seals, fake travel history. But -

'Where are the photos?'

'We're not some sort of magic fairies, you know!'

Cal smiled to himself - how often had he heard that phrase from Sam in the past?

'So what's the plan?'

'I've booked you both into a studio tomorrow morning. Oh, and before I forget, this came for you as well.'

Sam leant over the desk, touched a screen and tapped in a password. A new window appeared, and she entered a second. A secure messaging app opened. She stepped back.

Cal scanned the message on the screen.

'Cal. Welcome to Amsterdam. Hope the trip wasn't too rough. Passports arranged as agreed. Sam will fill you in. Be careful. The farm is still under surveillance, and Cerberus seems to be down. Everybody is looking for you. I will do what I can to help, but don't try to reach me via the usual channels. Telegram may not be secure. Repeat, NOT SECURE.'

'What does he say?' said Sofie, leaning over his shoulder.

'Advise you strongly to lie low for a while. Hart has been in touch. He is still going on about a leak, but not sure we should trust them any more. No word from Kate.'

'I hope she's OK,' she muttered.

'Suggest you don't return to London until I have found out more. I will be in touch via Sam. Good luck. I have covered most of the cost for you, but she will still need 1k in cash. Yours aye, F.'

'Yours aye?' said Sofie. 'What does that mean?'

Cal stepped back. 'Just some weird way he has of signing off. It's a Scottish thing,'

'But he's not Scottish.'

He shrugged. 'Comes from some regimental tradition, I believe.'

'No bother about the dough,' said Sam. 'Just give it to me when you can.'

Cal turned to her.

'Appreciate it. Did you get anywhere with that PO Box in Gibraltar? The lawyer?'

'Aye, nearly forgot to tell you. It's a law firm called Chambers, Rast & Associates.'

'Can you find out availability?'

'Sure. When do you plan to be there?'

'Four or five days? We need to go back to London first.'

'You sure that's wise, boss?' Sam gestured at the message. 'Frank says it's not safe.'

'We don't have a choice, Sam. There's one more loose end we need to tie up.'

Sam shrugged. 'Suit yourself.' She turned to Sofie. 'You must be tired? Shall I show you where you're sleeping?'

'Thanks,' said Sofie. 'You're right, it's been an intense day.'

Sam glanced at Cal.

He yawned. 'Sofie's right. Intense is not doing it justice.'

'You going to tell me about it?' Sam said.

'Sure. What about a smoke before we kip down?'

Cal cast a querying eye at Sofie.

'Nah, I'll turn in,' she said, 'I'm knackered.'

Sam showed her to a small room on the floor below and, after bidding them goodnight, she closed the door.

~

A WHITE DUVET LAY NEATLY FOLDED ON THE BED. BESIDE IT was a framed photograph of a group of soldiers in front of a landrover in desert camouflage. Sofie recognised him right away, next to Sam and five other figures. They were young and sunburned, Cal in a keffiyah, all posing for the camera like a band of brothers.

She climbed into the bed fully clothed, too tired to care, her bones aching. The sound of muted conversation seeped through the ceiling.

But it was impossible to still her churning mind. She turned over in her head everything that had happened over the past twenty-four hours. She hoped to God that Cal was right. Returning to London seemed a hell of a risk.

Outside the window, drinkers in the neighbouring bar were beginning to wind down and head for home. There was the sound of shutters being closed. At some point, she must have drifted off, because when she stirred again, her skin was damp, her sheets clinging with sweat, and the street had gone quiet.

But she could still hear the soft hum of voices from upstairs. Were they still at it? It amazed her that Cal still had the energy. Her own body felt like lead, as if she'd been drugged. She lay comatose, eyes half closed.

Before long, she relapsed into a deep sleep.

66

Wednesday 9th November

When she next woke, she was alert almost immediately.

The silence had changed. No longer the heavy stillness of the night, it had morphed into the thin quiet of early morning.

Her mouth was dry. She slid out of bed and padded into the hallway barefoot. Across the landing, a door stood slightly ajar. A low murmur came from inside.

She paused. Leaned closer. Cal was mumbling in his sleep. Half-formed words, fragmented and unintelligible, except for one: a girl's name.

She moved on down to the bathroom. Filling a glass, she drank deeply, the water cold and metallic. Her reflection stared back at her in the mirror - pillow-creased cheeks, smeared eyeliner, the brown of her eyes echoed in the Delft tiles behind her. She twisted her damp hair up and grimaced.

Did he, then, have someone else? She didn't know why it mattered.

Back in the hallway, she hesitated again at his door. The

mumbling had stopped. She pushed it open gently and stepped in. Cal lay on his side, face partly buried in the pillow. His bare back curved toward her, lean and solid, muscles bunched like a runner's. The sheet was tangled around his hips and ankles, one leg hanging loose off the edge. His breathing was soft and even.

Something about him in that moment - unguarded, utterly still - struck her. For once, he didn't look like the man who was always calculating; the wound-up soldier, three steps ahead. He looked… wounded, exhausted and vulnerable.

She stepped closer without thinking, until she could see the small scar near his temple. The one she'd noticed back in Paris. How had he got it, she wondered? For a moment, she felt a crazy, ridiculous urge to lean in and kiss it.

She held her breath, fighting the impulse. This wasn't that. They weren't that. And maybe that was the whole point - it was safer this way. Martin had wanted everything. Ownership, control, submission. Cal wanted none of that. He didn't even want her.

She stood there for a couple more seconds, then quietly slipped out, easing the door shut behind her.

~

Cal jerked awake at the sound of running water. He lay still, listening. The water stopped. There was a soft shuffle of footsteps.

He turned back to face the wall. And then, just barely, he heard a floorboard creak. Followed by the faintest squeak of a door hinge.

Suddenly, he realised she was in his room. He tensed. Closed his eyes, feigning sleep. What was she doing? He waited for the voice in the darkness, but none came. Instead, he caught the faintest trace of her - a warm, feminine scent. She was inches above him now, breathing softly. All it would take, he knew, would be for him to turn around.

He remained completely motionless, daring not to breathe, his eyelids so still that he struggled to keep them from fluttering.

After what seemed like an age, he felt the air stir again, and she pulled away. There was a creak of floorboards and the soft click of the door.

She was gone.

Only then did he open his eyes.

And stare at the wall.

67

CAL TOUCHED DOWN AT HEATHROW JUST AFTER FOUR. There was no way to tell if someone was watching. If they were smart, they wouldn't be obvious. But he scanned anyway. Police with carbines and sniffer dogs were patrolling the terminal as normal. Nothing jumped out.

The immigration guy barely looked at his Irish passport.

'Staying long, sir?'

'Just a week,' said Cal. 'Visiting relatives.'

Cal had no idea why he said that. It was a risk, given that he had no cover whatever for the persona he was travelling under. But the official didn't pursue it.

'Have a good trip.'

As soon as he was through, he powered up his burner and tapped out a message.

<Good to go.>

Sofie was still back at Schiphol. They had agreed to meet at a small hotel in Earl's Court. He glanced at his watch - she'd be at least three hours behind him, he calculated.

He travelled in on the Elizabeth line and then took the

tube from Paddington to Earl's Court.

'The Royal' was a small, rundown hotel behind the Exhibition Centre. Once he had checked in, he dumped his bag and headed right back out in the direction of Knightsbridge.

Sloane Street was busy at that hour. It was dark and damp, the puddles on the road and the wet roofs of parked cars all that remained of a recent downpour. Workers had begun their evening commute, while others were on their way into town for the evening. A few shoppers were finishing up purchases before the stores closed.

He checked his watch. 6:30 - too early. The Cambridge Bio office might still have people inside, people who could recognise him. On a whim, he took a detour down Pavilion Road. There was less foot traffic here. Most of the buildings led into the backs of offices or restaurants on the parallel streets, and large bins had been wheeled out into the street to await the evening rubbish collection.

After a few hundred yards, he found the familiar blue door.

The Special Forces Club.

On the wall beside it was a metal box. Even if he had his membership card with him, he would never risk swiping it on the electronic reader. Despite the unlikelihood of anyone looking for a trace of him here, the first thing they would ask for would be a record of entrances and exits. If the request came from somewhere other than Hereford itself, it would, of course, be denied. But even so….

He rang the bell and prayed for Jimbo. The door buzzed. He stepped inside.

'Hello, sir,' said Jimbo, looking up from his screen behind the cramped reception desk.

'Jimbo! Am I glad to see you!'

The man hadn't changed. Squat, verging on the rotund, he still had that flushed face and those soft eyes that flickered with mischief. How he ever made Selection, Cal would never know, but he remembered him as a fine soldier, strong and resilient back in the day. Time and booze had padded the edges.

'Long time no visit, sir,' Jimbo said, the 'sir' dripping with irony. 'Staying long?'

Cal was never quite sure whether he used the honorific in his capacity as a janitor of the secretive club or as a quiet screw-you from one of his old squaddies.

'Fraid not this time. I'm early for a meeting. Thought I'd drop by to say hello. Felt like seeing a familiar face.'

Jimbo regarded him with a wary eye.

'Why not. Quiet night. You'll have the bar to yourself, sir.'

Cal nodded. He started to go, then paused.

'Oh, and Jimbo?'

'Yeah?'

'You haven't seen me.'

'Mum's the word, sir.'

Cal took the stairs two at a time, past the bust of David Stirling and the painting of the Long Range Desert Patrol. Upstairs, the bar looked just the same: shabby. He sank into an armchair and grabbed a paper. No one would disturb him here. It was the most discreet club in London, as good a spot as any to while away half an hour. The bartender wasn't at his post, which suited him fine. He wasn't about to order anything.

The only sound was the ticking of a carriage clock on the mantlepiece, under the modern portrait of some former general. It was a place that always calmed him. Back in the day, it had been a decent crash pad, whether or not he had company. It even reminded him a little of his old boarding school in Scotland, with the smell of polish and the threadbare furniture. A bartender appeared, as if from nowhere, and Cal waved him away.

Twenty minutes passed. Then his phone buzzed.

'Landed x.'

He felt a little jolt inside. A couple of old geezers had wandered in and were chatting quietly in a corner over glasses of gin. Cal checked his watch and hauled himself out of the chair, nodding politely on the way out.

Outside, he cut back toward Sloane Street, replaying the plan in his head. While his Cambridge Bio systems access would likely have been scrubbed, he gambled that nobody would have thought to delete his guest credentials, which were issued for a set period and which had an expiry date two days in the future. On top of that, no one was likely to recognise him with his shaved head, especially out of office hours. And since the IT crew didn't work nights, they wouldn't spot his digital footprint until the following morning - even if they were looking for it. By which time it would be too late.

He swung through the revolving doors into the brightly lit foyer of CB's London headquarters. A lone uniformed doorman was watching a movie on a laptop. He looked overweight. It would be a simple matter to incapacitate him if necessary. But that was Plan B.

Cal strode confidently towards the gates and swiped his card. He held his breath. The glass barrier slid open with a hiss.

The doorman rose from his chair. 'Can I help you, sir?'

Cal was almost at the lift. He turned, flexing his arms and altering his stance to be ready to move.

'PR and Comms department, fourth floor,' he said,

producing the scuffed plastic pass. 'Left something here a few days ago which I need to collect.'

The guard squinted at the card. 'They've...er...they've all gone home, sir.'

Exactly what I want to hear, thought Cal. 'I know. Thank you. I won't be long.'

Cal pressed the button and instinctively looked up at the floor indicator. The lift arrived, and he stepped in unopposed. *That* was easy. They'd gone to all the trouble of offboarding him from their systems, and nobody thinks to remove his guest access before it expires? Muppets.

Upstairs, the cleaners were vacuuming, headphones in, and they didn't give him a second glance.

The desk he'd used during his brief stint had been reassigned. But it didn't take long to find what he was searching for. He punched in a four-digit code, and the filing cabinet sprang open with a gentle pop. And there they were, the convention files exactly as he had left them, with their printout of the daily itineraries and schedule of arrivals and departures. He thanked God that he'd printed all this out at the time, given that he was no longer able to log on to the company network. He was old school like that, preferring to have hard copies of everything important. Now it was paying off, big time.

He flipped through the pages quickly. Names. Titles. Itineraries. Then, there it was, on page two.

Professor Harold J. Erskine. Oxford University.

His hunch had proved correct.

~

An hour later, he exited the tube at Earl's Court, blinking against the low grey sky, his collar turned up against the wind. He moved slowly toward the hotel, scanning the street out of an abundance of caution. For some reason he couldn't put his finger on, after swanning through immigration and CB offices with barely a jitter, he now felt apprehensive, on edge.

She was already there when he entered the hotel bar, nursing a glass of wine. She looked like a different girl from the frazzled mess he'd left behind in Amsterdam. Her blonde hair was tied back in her familiar ponytail, and she had spruced herself up with fresh makeup.

'Any issues?' he said, sliding into the seat beside her.

Sofie smiled at him. 'No issues at all. Glad to see you, though. And you?'

'I've been back to CB's offices.' He leaned forward, lowering his voice. 'And guess what?'

Her eyes twinkled at him.

'My hunch was correct. Your professor friend *was* a guest that night.'

The sparkle turned to concern.

'Really? How did I miss him? Are you sure?'

'It doesn't mean that he actually showed up, but he was definitely on the guest list.'

She frowned. 'He didn't mention anything when I saw him.'

'Which proves my point. He must have had something to hide, no?'

She pulled out her phone. 'Why don't we find out?'

He laid a hand on her arm. 'Wait.'

She looked up. 'Why ever not?'

'We don't want to spook him.'

'But surely if I explain?'

'We're better off doing it face to face. Besides, what if he's under surveillance? What if his phone's being monitored?'

She bit her lip. 'You think they're on to him, too?'

'Considering everything else that has happened, I'd say it was a high likelihood, wouldn't you?'

She slowly set her phone back on the table and took another sip of wine, her expression clouding over.

'But wait. What if it was he who was faxing all those documents to me after the chemists were killed?"

'Documents plural? What are you talking about, Sofie? Frank and I only found one.'

'Yes, didn't I tell you? There was a whole bunch of stuff.'

A look of alarm crossed Cal's face. In Paris, he thought they'd been clear. If they were to get out of this alive, they had to share everything. What else was she holding back?

'They were newspaper clippings, mostly,' she went on. 'Stories about people who had taken their own lives after being medicated by doctors. All in East Africa as far as I could make out.' She brightened. 'Yeah, it's beginning to make sense now. Who else would know that Dad still had a fax machine?'

He groaned. 'Jesus, Sophie! Why didn't you mention this before?'

68

Cal was right. Why hadn't she told him about all the other faxes that she'd been sent? Something had held her back.

'I don't know,' she said. 'I suppose I didn't think it was important.'

'Christ.' He shook his head. She could see he was frustrated. 'It's like I'm trying to help you with one hand tied behind my back. I need to know everything. And I mean everything.' He stared at her. 'So what did you do with them?'

Good question. She tried to remember if she'd seen them when she'd revisited the flat with DC Khan.

'Probably still in my flat.'

He shook his head. 'Not anymore. Someone else will have found them. And if your friend Erskine really did send them, I don't fancy his chances.'

'How do you mean?'

'Because a fax has the sender's number written all over it.'

She put her head in her hands. 'God. Not him too.'

'We must warn him.'

'But I still don't get why he didn't say anything?'

'He was protecting himself. Think about it, Sofie. He'd already sent you the list that Frank and I found when we broke into your flat. That was all he needed to do.' Cal paused. 'And because you never actually received it, you never thought to mention it to him, did you? If you had, you would have wanted his expertise to help you decipher it.'

The logic hit her like a cold shower. It would explain the message: *'Your father would have been proud of you.'* It would have been easy enough for him to believe her in this new investigative role - what could be more natural than a journalist daughter looking into the suspicious circumstances of her father's death?

And now she thought about it, there was something else, too, something about his behaviour that day that didn't quite add up. Actions that, in retrospect, looked odd.

'There's more. That day we met, when I said I was a journalist, he didn't even blink. Last time we spoke, at the funeral, I'd mentioned I was done with journalism. The only person who could've told him that was Kate.'

'They knew each other?'

'I don't know. Maybe they did.' She scratched her head. 'Two other things were strange. First, he wouldn't let me record the conversation, even though what we ended up discussing was pretty harmless. And second, he insisted we meet at a pub in the village, not his place. Then he was an hour late. We had to walk across the fields to get to his house. I left the same way.'

Cal raised an eyebrow. 'So you never used his front door?'

She shook her head. 'We went in the back, through the

garden.'

'And did he say why he wanted to meet you in the pub?'

'Not exactly, though he hinted that it was something to do with his wife, Sarah. Which is why, when she decided to drive up to London at the last minute, he thought it was safe to take me back to the house. But then when we got there, he picked up two days' worth of mail from the mat. If Sarah had been there, why was there so much of it? It sounds like he hadn't been home at all.'

Cal scratched his chin. 'This is all very Sherlock Holmes. But why would he not want his wife to see you?'

'Because she gets jealous.'

'What, about you?' he exclaimed, surprised.

She shifted uncomfortably. 'Harry and I had a brief fling when I was at Uni.'

'But I thought you said he was a friend of your father's?'

'He was.'

'A lot older than you, then.'

She narrowed her eyes at him.

'So?'

Cal let out a low whistle. 'This is getting more interesting by the minute. Sounds to me that he didn't want to be seen meeting you.' He got up. 'Fancy another drink?'

'I'm fine,' she said through gritted teeth.

A few minutes later, he returned with a Coke.

'You're addicted to that stuff.'

'No, I'm not.'

'What are you addicted to, then? There must be something?'

'Not really, I'm boring as hell.'

She regarded him for a second. He had two days' worth of stubble and was beginning to look dishevelled. But still uncomfortably attractive. 'So you don't drink?'

'Occasionally. Mostly not.'

Her tone softened. 'Any particular reason? Did you abuse it, back in the day?'

He shrugged. 'I just don't like to drink when I'm working.'

She eyed him over the rim of her glass and gave him a wry smile; her anger at his previous remark dissipated.

'I wish I had your self-control.' Then: 'By the way. Something else has been bothering me.'

Cal gave a half-smile back. 'Only one thing?'

'I still don't know anything about you.'

He let out a low chuckle. 'You want to do a background check?'

She met his eyes. 'I'm serious.'

'So am I.'

'Okay, fine.' A beat. 'Answer me one question, though. Who's Lucy?'

'How do you know about Lucy?' His tone had sharpened.

'You were sleep-talking the other night. In Amsterdam. I went to the bathroom and heard you mumbling. That was the only word I could make out.'

He held her gaze. 'Lucy's my daughter. She's eight.'

'You're married?'

'Was. She lives with my ex.'

'I'm sorry.'

'No need. It didn't work out. Shit happens.'

'You see her much?'

'Once a month, if I'm lucky. Depends if I'm working. My life is not - how shall I put it? - conducive to stable relationships.'

She tilted her head at him.

'Worked out for your friend Frank, though, no?'

'Sort of. Emily's very tolerant.'

She laughed. 'I didn't get that impression.' She took another sip of her wine. 'How long ago was it? Your divorce?'

He looked away. 'What is this, the Spanish Inquisition? Technically, we're not divorced.' He stared into his glass, swirling the liquid around until the ice clinked. 'And that was half a dozen questions, by the way. Like I said, I try not to mix business and personal.'

'You didn't say.'

'Well I've said it now.'

They were silent for a moment. Then she said softly, 'That's a shame. You're not bad company. When you're not being an arsehole.'

69

Thursday 10th November

THEY DEPARTED AFTER BREAKFAST THE FOLLOWING MORNING. It was term time, and there was every reason to suppose they'd find Harry working at home in the afternoon, as was his habit.

En route, they decided to stock up on clothes. The weather had taken a turn for the worse, and an early snowfall was forecast. Sofie detoured to a charity shop she knew, and while Cal picked up a puffer jacket, she bought a vintage woollen coat, a couple of beanie hats and a thick scarf.

The coach to Oxford was late. When they finally arrived, the connection to Woodstock had already left, and the next one was in forty minutes, according to the timetable pinned behind a dusty scrap of perspex on the wall of the bus station. Sofie felt frustrated. She desperately wanted to get this over with. But when she began searching around for a cab, Cal pulled her back.

'What are you doing?' she said. 'What's the point in hanging about?'

'Sofie, don't be impatient. Mistakes happen that way. A

taxi is not a good idea.'

'Why? If we pay in cash…'

'People notice cabs, and cabbies remember faces. Who knows who's watching Harry's house? A random couple stepping off a local bus is less remarkable.'

She sighed. He was annoyingly right. Again. They were about to settle down in the bus station café to wait for the next departure when she had a brainwave. She grabbed his arm.

'I've got a better idea,' she said.

Cal raised an eyebrow.

She stood up. 'Really. Come on, it's my turn for a hunch. There's somewhere I want to take you. It's not far. We can be there and back in time for the next bus.'

'I need a coffee.'

'Screw coffee. We may as well make use of the time.'

She walked out into George Street, Cal following reluctantly behind. Eight minutes later, they arrived at the entrance of a college.

'What's this?' he grunted, eyeing the grand entranceway. 'Your old Alma Mater?'

'It's where Harry teaches. Pembroke College. He's a professor here.'

He sniffed.

'Trust me.'

Inside the lodge, it was fuggy, condensation streaming down the windows. The porter sat hunched up at the back over a radiator.

'Brr, it's cold out there,' said Sofie, flashing him a smile. He got up and ambled over.

'Can I help you?'

'Sorry to bother you,' she continued. 'I was wondering. Do you have such a thing as a college prospectus?'

'Indeed it is, young lady, and indeed we do,' said the man. 'Tom?' he shouted at someone in the back office. 'Fetch us a prospectus, will you?'

After a few moments, a younger man in a matching uniform appeared and handed over a glossy colour brochure. The porter slid it across the counter to Sofie, looking down at her through spectacles perched on the end of a bulbous nose. 'Are you applying to admissions, madam?'

'No, I was curious, that's all.'

'For the curious, there's a charge of £2.50.' He noticed her surprise. 'I'm afraid, Madam, in these times of austerity, we have to rely on more commercial sources of funding. T-shirts are a tenner if you're interested.'

Sofie laughed and handed over the money. In the quadrangle, Cal was no longer where she'd left him. She wandered towards the college chapel and opened the brochure. And there it was, in bold blue and red, on the first page. The Cambridge Bio logo, along with two others.

Bingo! Her suspicion had proved correct.

'Generous funding by Cambridge Bio Pharmaceuticals gratefully acknowledged.'

She quickened her pace. 'Cal?'

She'd almost reached the chapel when she felt a hand on her shoulder. She started with fright.

'Shit, Cal, don't do that!'

Cal released her. She waved the brochure at him.

'What is it?'

'My hunch.'

He riffled the pages. She stood behind him, brushing the hair out of her eyes and pointing at the page.

'See what it says there? Funded by Cambridge Bio.'

He read it. 'Interesting.'

She jumped back. ‘Interesting? Is that all you have to say? Don’t you see, it’s all beginning to make sense! No wonder Harry couldn’t talk.’

Cal nodded slowly, processing.

‘It certainly explains his connection to them.’ He paused. ‘He’s probably tied up in some research agreement. Maybe even under NDA.’

‘Exactly.’

‘Well, we’ll know soon enough. But even if it’s not, he’s bound to have found out about the drug programme through his connections with CB.’ Finally, he smiled at her. ‘Good work, Sherlock.’

‘You’re welcome.’

‘Sorry for doubting you.’

‘You mean you doubted me?’

He didn’t answer. They looked at each other awkwardly for a second, the winter wind curling around them.

‘Come on,’ she said eventually. ‘We’ll miss the bus.’

70

The S7 to Witney via Woodstock pulled out at 2:00 p.m., right on schedule. Neither of them spoke much. The countryside was wet, the sky grey, and in the villages they passed, people were going about their business without hanging about, wrapped up against the weather. Sofie shivered involuntarily as she watched the damp countryside sliding by through fogged-up windows, the outside world blurred into greys and browns. It was a parallel universe.

After forty minutes, they got off at the Hill Rise stop at the far end of the village, and she led him in the direction of Harry's house, half a mile back down the road. The sun was dying on the afternoon, the autumn air, now they were out in it, brisk and icy.

They hurried along in silence.

Only once did Cal halt, briefly, to peer through the gates of a large house, as if he were a curious tourist. There were only a handful of people about, mostly local shoppers, together with a couple of Tesco delivery vans running drop-offs.

They passed a church, the grey tombstones angled with

age. Against the low stone wall that marked its boundary was what looked like a recent shrine to a traffic accident, several forlorn and wilting bunches of flowers piled up in a little pyramid.

Without pausing, they pressed on. After another hundred yards, Sofie indicated a narrow turning.

'It's left here,' she said. 'The pub where I met him is up ahead. From there, it's a short walk across the field to the back of his house.'

The lane was narrow and overgrown, high hawthorn bushes on either side providing good cover. Sofie led the way. After a few minutes, they reached a small car park, where they crossed the road and climbed over a stile into the field beyond.

Mud clung to their shoes. They edged around the boundary, following the line of the hedgerow. In the distance, the outline of Harry's house appeared - red brick with a walled garden. Sofie reached the back gate first. She clicked it open, walked up the stone path, and rang the back doorbell. Nothing. She waited a beat, then rang again, longer this time. Still no answer. She cupped her hands to the window and peered in.

'His car's still here,' said Cal, nodding at a blue Mercedes parked at the front of the house. 'He can't have gone far.'

'What shall we do? Leave him a note?'

He pulled off his beanie and scratched the back of his head.

'We'll come back later.'

Dusk was rapidly approaching. The wind was more biting than ever as they retraced their steps towards the pub. Inside, a fire blazed, and several locals were already gathered about the bar. Sofie waited while Cal ran his customary checks - a routine she was getting used to - before settling on a corner table.

'The usual?' she said.

He nodded.

The barman was wiping the surfaces.

'What can I get you, love?'

'Vodka and tonic. And a Coke, no ice.'

As he was preparing the drinks, she asked him about Harry. When they met, he had told her he often stopped in for lunch on his way back from Oxford, after lecturing in the morning.

The man took his hand off the pump and looked her full in the eye.

'Has he been in today?' she pressed.

'Sorry, love, hadn't you heard?'

Her chest tightened. 'Heard what?'

He leaned in slightly, lowering his voice. 'He was killed in a hit-and-run accident five days ago. On the corner by the church.'

She felt herself go faint. *Five days ago?* That was the day after she'd seen him. Her vision suddenly began to blur. She clutched the bar top to stop herself falling, then, without a word, picked up the drinks with shaking hands and walked back to the table. Cal was fiddling with his phone.

'Damn,' he muttered. 'Cerberus is still down. I can't get hold of Frank.'

She dropped the drinks on the table and bolted.

He looked up, startled. 'Sofie?'

She didn't hear the rest. She was already out the door, her coat still on the back of the chair. For once, she didn't feel the cold. Only the stinging heat of her tears, strands of her hair clinging to her cheeks in the biting wind.

She ran, weaving across the road between a stream of

traffic. A small van had to brake suddenly as she careered in front of it, hooting furiously. In the distance was the church they'd passed less than an hour before. She slowed, panting and out of breath, bent double and shaking with sobs. Finally, with a last effort of will, she raised herself and stumbled the last few yards in a daze. She came to the little shrine beside the wall on the corner.

Only now, it looked completely different to her.

She stooped down to read the cards pinned to the cellophane-wrapped bunch of flowers.

Darling Harry, one said simply. *Died before your time.*

That was it. The dam broke. Her knees gave way, and the tears started cascading down her cheeks. A few early snowflakes floated down and landed on her hair, melting instantly. But she didn't feel them. All she felt was the guilt.

Because this, surely, was all her fault.

71

It was late in the day when Frank contacted Sam in Amsterdam for an update. She informed him that Cal and Sofie had returned to London and had booked into a hotel in Earl's Court. Frank cursed under his breath. He'd warned Cal not to come. He only hoped that they were not foolish enough to go to her flat.

Frank happened to be in the City for the day for a business meeting and had planned to travel back to Suffolk that evening. Making a snap decision, he jumped in a cab and made tracks for Earl's Court instead.

How and where to meet Cal, he wasn't yet sure. It was not simply a matter of turning up at their hotel. Because he was being tailed, he was sure of that now. He'd already noticed them on the Woodbridge road, waiting for him to leave the farm. The same people, presumably, who had spooked Sofie. They'd been with him ever since. So far, he hadn't tried to shake them. After all, he had nothing to hide.

But now things were different,

He ordered the driver to drop him off at a block of flats in Collingham Gardens, the address of a friend whom he happened to know, from her social media posts, was in Greece. It served as a plausible cover for his visit, even though, for once, his tail had managed to make themselves invisible. He didn't doubt that he, or she - or more likely a combination - were out there somewhere.

After a pretence of irritation, he retraced his steps and turned towards Earl's Court. His route took him right past Cal's hotel.

As he was about to turn the corner, he noticed a marked van parked on the curb, full of bored-looking policemen. Frank slowed, taking in the flak jackets. These weren't normal beat cops. They weren't here for crowd control. A few paces on, down a narrow mews, he spotted a second van - less obvious, but there all the same. Engine off, lights dimmed. Watching and waiting. But for what?

With a sense of foreboding, he took a right down Nevern Place.

At first, he didn't see it. The road seemed normal: women with prams, shoppers going about their business, cars parking unhindered. Until he looked up.

Silhouetted against the skyline was not one, nor two, but a string of dark shapes. Barely visible, but definitely there if you knew what to look for. He followed the line of the roof. Six or seven of them, bulkily dressed in black, directly opposite the hotel. These weren't workmen. Workmen move about; they don't try to hide themselves. And the nearest scaffolding was three hundred yards away.

He had to be certain. Which meant disregarding his tail. As he drew level with the hotel, he stopped and, as if on impulse, bounded up the steps like an antelope, two steps at a time. He caught a glimpse of several men with earpieces lounging around in the reception area before someone approached him as he came through the swing doors, blocking his path.

'Excuse me, sir, are you a guest?' The male voice was polite but insistent.

He halted. 'Not yet. I'm here to book a room.'

'I'm afraid this hotel is closed for the time being. If you'd like to try again tomorrow...'

His worst fears were confirmed. Those were police marksmen on the roof. And Cal and Sofie were walking right into them.

He had to warn them. He realised, with sickening clarity, that at that very minute they could be on their way back. He had no idea where they'd gone, but the police were expecting them.

Even though he had no way of contacting Cal, he decided to reboot his phone. It had been off for days to avoid tracking. But it was the only way to warn Cal if he called. The problem was that as soon as he did, he'd light up like a Christmas tree on a hundred surveillance systems.

Still, it was the only way. Cal might be using a burner, but maybe - just maybe - he'd try to reach out. Or had already, and had left a message.

Frank powered it up. No messages.

Gambling that they'd travel by tube, he took off at a jog towards Earl's Court station. Cal would know that it would be far harder to track him on the underground, and besides, unable to use plastic, they would need to be conserving what little cash remained to them.

At the entrance to the tube, Frank paused, scanning the crowd. Even if he did spot Cal or Sofie, it would be madness to approach them directly. No, he'd have to devise another method of warning them. But he didn't have much time. It was already eight, and they could walk out any minute.

Crossing the street, he went into a café to message Sam. Had Cal been in touch?

Negative, she replied.

All the time, his eyes were glued to the tube exit. There was still no sign of them. If they came by cab or walked from the next stop down the line - Barons Court or South Kensington - he'd miss them, and they'd be screwed.

Directly across the road was an empty advertising hoarding. Some kids were taking turns to vandalise it with graffiti. Nobody paid them the slightest attention.

Then one of them broke off and ran into a shop. It gave him an idea. A one-in-a-million, batshit crazy, off-the-wall idea.

But he had to try something.

He hurried out of the café and after the boy.

72

It took quite a while for Cal to find Sofie, and several minutes for him to revive her. She was incoherent, near-hysterical, and needed a shot of whisky back in the pub to calm her down.

He was nervous. He knew it was dangerous to attract attention. The bar staff were helpful, but curious. He got her out of there as soon as dared, and, ignoring his better judgement for once, found a cab to take them to Oxford in time to catch the coach to London.

She didn't say it, but Cal could guess what she was thinking. They'd been killed on account of her. First Alice, now Harry. Something was near to snapping in her, and Harry's death, coming on top of everything else, had stunned her. However much he pointed out that they may not be related. *'Hit and run,'* the man in the pub had said. She could not, would not, be reassured, and deep down, he knew she was right.

All the way back, he talked to her gently, his arm around her, her head cradled against his shoulder. She had stopped crying and was listening to him with a kind of dumb attention.

He walked her through, once again, why going to the police was no solution. The powers involved were too strong, the authorities too compromised. The investigation would be killed on its feet. And Sofie, even if she were eventually cleared of the trumped-up charges in Paris, would be perpetually in fear for her life. She was too dangerous to somebody to remain at large. Their only option, as they had already agreed, was to get to the truth before the truth got to them.

Because once it was out in the open, she would no longer be a threat. And it was no different for him. They couldn't afford to crack now.

Did she accept it? It was hard for Cal to tell. But she didn't push back, and that was a start. On the approaches to London, she appeared to fall asleep. By the time they arrived at Victoria, it was nearly eleven. He tried in vain to get them a black cab, but they came in streams from the direction of the railway station, and all had their lights dimmed. They began walking up Buckingham Palace Road.

'How are you feeling now?' he asked.

'Angry,' she said, her jaw set tight.

An empty taxi cruised past on the other side of the road, and Cal stepped into the street to hail it, but a couple at the bus stop opposite got there before him. He muttered a curse.

'We've got to nail those bastards,' she continued. 'Now more than ever, I owe it to my father. And to Harry. We have to keep going. I refuse to be broken.'

They'd almost reached the station. There was a queue of cabs curling into the forecourt, and a longer line of people waiting. They stood around for a few minutes, stamping their feet. It started to snow lightly, and though they were under cover, stray flakes were driven into their faces by sudden gusts of wind.

Sofie shivered. 'Come on,' she said, tugging at him. 'I'm going to freeze to death out here. Let's get the tube.' She led him down into the warm, damp throng of the underground.

There was a crush at Earl's Court station when they arrived. Crowds were spilling down onto the platforms from the road outside. They struggled against the human tide and eventually emerged at the gates. Here, they had another long wait to get through the ticket barrier. She felt Cal tense. Two policemen were standing to one side, watching people come through in both directions.

'They're probably for the concert,' whispered Sofie.

She was right. They went through unmolested and out onto the street.

Where Cal stopped dead.

'What's wrong?' she said.

He was staring up at a large illuminated billboard, the lower half of which was covered in paint-sprayed graffiti.

'What is it?'

He joined her on the kerb.

'Read that.' He nodded at the graffiti.

She squinted at it.

'Echo 9,' it said in a red scrawl. *'No return. For the birds. Yours aye.'*

'I don't understand.'

'It's my old army call sign. And that's his weird sign-off. Yours aye. The Scottish thing.'

'But…'

Cal looked around anxiously. 'Trust me. It's a message. A signal for us not to go back to the hotel. It can only have been Frank.'

'But how did he know we were here?' she said nervously.

His mind was racing. There was no time to debug this now. They had to move. He grabbed Sofie's arm.

'Follow me.'

He led her towards the mews. At the end was the entrance to their hotel. Halfway along, parked on the side of the road, was a police van.

'You see?' he muttered.

'Maybe it's a coincidence.'

'I don't believe in coincidences. You want to risk it?'

They began to retrace their steps. As soon as they turned back, they saw them: fifty yards away, and coming in their direction, were the two policemen they'd seen at the tube station.

'Shit,' he growled.

'Do you think...?'

'I don't think, Sofie, I know.'

He began to cross the road. Sofie followed. There was a crackle of radio behind them, a shout, and running footsteps. They broke into a sprint. In Child's Place was another police van, the occupants beginning to jump out. Cal raced back from where they'd come, dragging Sofie with him.

Then everything seemed to happen at once. Sirens started up; shouts for them to stop.

'Armed police!'

People froze in the street. There was a scream, and bodies began to scatter. They tore off the main road into a second mews and ran towards the end. Behind them, they heard a car turn in and begin to accelerate, bouncing off the cobbles.

'No!' screamed Sofie.

Cal yelled at her. 'We can make it! Come on, Sofie, run!'

They did, but barely in time. The car in pursuit screeched to a halt as a van suddenly appeared from a side entrance, blocking it, and as Cal and Sofie squeezed past and scrambled back out into the Earl's Court Road, they heard more shouted commands behind them.

But they were away - for now. People started to turn as they barrelled along the pavement and onto the street, weaving between the slow-moving traffic. A second police car was trying to force a way through fifty yards back, siren wailing, lights flashing.

They arrived at the junction with Old Brompton Road, panting heavily. From the South Kensington direction, they could see more blue lights approaching. Sofie veered to the right.

'*Over here!*' she yelled.

It was a cemetery. Cal didn't like the look of it. Even if they could make it, he realised, they risked being trapped inside. But there wasn't time to stop her. He followed, glancing over his shoulder. One of the patrol cars sped along a stretch of empty road, then ground to a halt at the snarled-up intersection. The gates to the cemetery loomed ahead.

'*Wait!*' he shouted. 'We'll be cornered!'

'Cal, *come on!*' She was screaming now.

He looked back again. Two police cars were converging and would be on them in seconds. They had only one small knot of traffic at the junction to negotiate. He turned towards Sofie. The gates were locked, and she was attempting to scale the wall.

'Cal, please!' She was beginning to cry.

'Sofie, it's no use.'

The sirens were on all sides now. By the time he reached

her, she'd given up and stood pressed against the gates, her hands raw, a look of desperation in her eyes. He prized her away.

'Come on, down here.'

They started running again, she stumbling behind him. Everything felt as if it had gone into slow motion. He could picture them drawing their guns. It would only be a matter of seconds before they'd be crouching down on the pavement, giving in to the inevitable.

There was a screech of tyres as a car pulled up alongside them.

'*Cal!*' It was a male voice, a different command. '*Get in!*'

Cal turned. He stared, not comprehending.

'Get the fuck in, won't you!'

Without thinking, he pulled Sofie through the open door, and before he had time to shut it, they were speeding away with a burning of rubber. Behind them, the police cars finally broke free of the tangle of traffic and began accelerating in pursuit.

Sofie began to hyperventilate.

'Dear me, Cal,' Frank began, grinning. 'What took you so long? I was all ready to pick you up on Earl's Court Road.'

Cal grunted, breathless. 'Where the hell have you come from?'

'You need looking after, clearly. Now hold on, you two. This is going to be brutal.'

Frank executed a screeching, sharp left over a small bridge and sped beside the railway line. They twisted and turned down the side streets, forcing Cal to brace against the seat in front.

Suddenly, he was back in the advanced driver's course they had taken together around Salisbury Plain. It was a case of extreme measures in pursuit, a procedure they had practised multiple times. Which meant collateral damage.

Up ahead was what looked like a line of market barrows, locked and battened down for the night. Two men watched in horror as they carried on accelerating into a T-junction, scattering as they passed. The wing of the car clipped one of the barrows, and it careered into a wall, spilling boxes. There were shouts. Frank took another sharp turn to the left onto a high street, forcing a lorry to brake violently, and a second turn, almost immediately, to the right, and once again they were off the main road and into the back streets. Behind, there was the crunch of vehicles colliding, and in the distance, sirens, but they were getting fainter now.

Cal glanced at Sofie, crouched down beside him. Her eyes were wide with shock.

'I'm going to be sick,' she moaned.

'One question.' Frank's eyes flickered to the rearview mirror. 'Have you got your passports with you?'

Cal nodded.

'And money?' He grinned. 'Or do you need me to stop at a cashpoint?'

73

Before Cal could reply, they suddenly swerved to the right again, and Sofie was smashed against the door frame.

'*Shit!*' he cried.

They began to gain speed down Munster Road towards Putney. She held tight to the headrests in front of her, eyes rigidly ahead. She knew this road. She had had a boyfriend who lived down here once, remembered the bollards, and sure enough, she now saw two of them rapidly approaching. They were especially narrow, to deter heavy goods vehicles, and you normally took them at no more than a crawl to be certain of not scraping. Frank was verging on sixty.

She shut her eyes, tight, but the crunch didn't come. When she opened them again, they were through.

'Oh my God,' she muttered, her stomach churning. 'Where did you learn to drive like that?'

'Nice to see you again,' said Frank, turning in his seat and smiling at her.

'*Watch the bloody road!*' she screamed.

A car had pulled out in front of them, and Frank had to yank hard on the wheel to avoid a collision. They careered onto the pavement, passed inches from a plate-glass window, bounced off the kerb and rejoined the tarmac with a sickening thud.

She clutched onto Cal.

'Mate, I appreciate what you're doing,' he began 'and I've no idea how you come to be here, but…' he leaned forward '... could you tell us where the hell we're going?'

Frank spun the wheel, and they veered into a residential street running north. Cars were parked on both sides, and there was only room for one car at a time in either direction. Two cyclists were approaching, and as they sped towards them, the riders scuttled into a parking space, mouthing obscenities.

'Southampton. I've organised for you both to fly out from there to Gib on Easy Easy Jet tomorrow morning.'

Did he mean EasyJet, thought Sofie? How was that going to work, with half the police force after them?

'A private plane,' he continued, as if reading her thoughts. 'Old mate of mine. Owes me a favour. You can kip at his place tonight. You should have stayed where you were, like I advised. There was no need to come back here. I was going to organise it from Amsterdam.'

'Thanks for telling me,' muttered Cal.

'Bugger me, Cal, what do you expect? I couldn't get hold of you! By the time I'd set it up, you'd left.'

He changed down, the gears racing in pain, and they were flung back in their seats again.

'And what about the lawyer?' said Cal. 'Has Sam traced him?'

'Sorted. We fixed you a meeting with a fellow called Philip Rast, the senior partner. Two PM tomorrow.'

'Did you tell him what we wanted to see him about?' asked Sofie.

'Not yet. Didn't want to risk scaring him off.'

Frank executed a sharp right, and they were into a clear stretch of the New Kings Road, heading for Putney Bridge.

'Can I give you some advice?' he added over his shoulder. 'You asked for my help, didn't you? So stop trying to do it all by yourselves.'

At the top of Putney High Street, they headed for the A3, but soon came off at the Kingston bypass, winding their way through the Kingston streets towards Esher and across the county line into the country lanes of Surrey. There was less chance of road cameras here, Frank explained, plus they weren't part of the highways agency ANPR network, whose roadside CCTV tracked vehicles leaving London on the motorways and main 'A' roads.

They began to relax. Marginally. 'Whose car is this?' said Cal.

Frank chuckled. 'Half-inched it.'

'And you reckon we'll get all the way to Southampton without being stopped?'

'Wait and see. I've got a plan for that.'

They lapsed into silence as Frank tore along the Surrey hedgerows, each in their own thoughts. After twenty minutes, they came to a straight stretch leading through woods. Juggling the map on his phone, Frank slowed, looking for a turning. Eventually, he found it, and they eased their way onto a rutted track leading into a forest.

Sofie peered out of the window. 'Now what?'

They rounded a bend. A hundred metres further on was a clearing and a parked car. A man was leaning on it, smoking a cigarette, watching them approach.

They screeched to a halt beside it in a cloud of dirt. It was a minicab. On its roof was the symbol of a top hat, and on the door was the legend 'Rob Lord Taxi Company'.

Sofie felt Cal tense beside her.

'Fuck me if it isn't Rob!' he said, laughing. He flung open the door and leapt out.

'Frank said you were in a bit of trouble,' the man said, giving him a bear hug. 'Least I could do, fella!'

Sofie clambered out after him. She felt severely shaken, and her hair was matted with sweat. She shook herself down, straightened up, and did a double take.

'Hang on. Don't I know you?'

The man eyed her, unsure.

'Do you?'

'Oh my God! You're the guy who drove me to Ringstead!'

A look of recognition flitted across his face. Cal looked from one to another, confused.

'You two know each other?'

'Yes!' Sofie cried. 'Well, sort of. He's driven me in his taxi in Dorset. When I was staying at my dad's house.'

'Bloody hell, what a coincidence,' Cal exclaimed.

She gave him a wry smile. 'That's rich coming from you. Didn't think you believed in coincidences?'

'Rob's an old army mate.'

Sofie stepped forward.

'Small world,' said Rob. He stubbed out his cigarette and shook her hand. 'These two fuckers been treating you OK?' She smiled grimly. 'Because they're trouble.'

He turned to Cal. 'Right, boyo, climb aboard. We haven't got time to hang about. They'll be looking for you. Next stop, Southampton.'

'Good luck, guys,' called Frank, starting to reverse. 'I need to return the car.' He winked at Sofie. 'And look after him for me, will you?'

74

CHARLES GEBLER WAS IMPATIENT. HE'D BEEN ON THE ROCK for thirty-six hours, but so far there had been no sign of the target. Now, a report had come in of a sighting in London. Did this mean they weren't coming?

He drained his beer in a bar overlooking Queensway Quay marina. The evening felt balmy for the time of year, and the lights of the harbour twinkling across the water made for a romantic setting. But he wasn't here for the scenery, and he wasn't the romantic type.

He checked his watch. 9:30. The last flight of the day, an Easyjet from Luton, would have disembarked by now. He pulled out his phone and, for the second time that afternoon, hit redial.

The voice on the other end sounded as tired as he felt.

'Borders and Coast Guard.'

'Gebler,' he said. 'Any movement?'

A beat. Then, 'I'm afraid not, Mr Gebler. Nothing so far.'

Gebler sighed. That meant no one fitting the description of Cal or Sofie, either singly or together, had arrived at the airport all day.

'Could they have come in by road from Spain?'

'Could have, yes, especially if they had help. If they got hold of a Gibraltarian residency card, for example, they'd walk through no problem.'

'Terrific,' Gebler muttered under his breath. He leaned back in his chair, watching a waitress wipe down an empty table, her earbuds glowing like fireflies. 'What about private flights?'

Another pause. Some tapping in the background.

'Nothing landed today. Three are due tomorrow. First one around noon.'

The man promised they would keep a lookout. Gebler ended the call and slipped the phone back into his jacket. That was it for tonight.

He left cash on the table and headed down the promenade, past the restaurants and moored yachts, into the darker streets beyond the marina. He'd been busy since he arrived: he'd already walked the loop twice, from Landport Tunnel to the Botanic Gardens, and from the Governor's residence down to the old dockyard road; rehearsed his routes, mentally mapped every option. If they showed up, *when* they showed up, he had planned for two scenarios.

Plan A was to let them lead him to whoever they were meeting. If he could stay invisible long enough, they'd peel it back for him. And for that, in support, he'd been promised two plainclothes officers from the Royal Gibraltar Police. Good enough for observation, he figured. Not so good if the shit hit the fan.

Which brought him to Plan B. To take them out if an opportunity presented itself.

He cast his mind back to the three IRA terrorists

gunned down in a petrol station forecourt by an SAS squad in 1988. Gibraltar had form when it came to that sort of thing. They played by different rules over here.

But first, he had to find them.

He adjusted his collar as a gust of warm sea air swept in. Although it was November, it felt like June.

There were only a handful of places they could stay. This wasn't the Costa del Sol. Once he got the passport names, it'd be a matter of cross-checking guest lists and waiting.

And, despite Harrison's reputation - he'd read the files - Gebler was reasonably confident he wouldn't notice a tail, because this was the last place he'd be expecting it.

Inshallah.

75

Friday 11th November

THEY BOARDED THE GULFSTREAM 280 JUST AFTER 8:00 a.m., the early sun casting sharp, clean lines on the tarmac at Southampton. The jet gleamed white. It had been arranged through a private charter company - a favour called in from a contact of Frank's. It was headed to Malta anyway, to pick up some oligarch's family from a yacht, so it was a small matter to add Cal and Sofie to the manifest and detour via Gib.

The interior was luxurious and muffled. The crew assumed they were going on holiday and offered them champagne and Michelin-quality snacks. Cal declined. Sofie hesitated.

As soon as they were airborne, he spread a map of the Rock out on the table between them. Two areas were circled - The Rock Hotel and the office of Chambers, Rast & Associates. They were about a mile apart.

'So, what's the plan?' Sofie asked, accepting a blini and half a glass. 'How do you think we should play this?'

'As far as they are aware, the meeting's been arranged to discuss a confidential property matter. But until we meet the guy, we can't be sure they're willing to talk.'

'Which is why I think we need to be straight with him. We mustn't hold anything back. We have to get them to trust us.'

Cal pursed his lips.

'Maybe. But think about it. They are likely to be scared after the killings. Don't forget that nobody knows that Kate survived. We have to tread carefully.'

Sofie cast her mind back to the boat. The chemists had told her that evening that her father's doctor, Alex, was nervous. Which was why any approach had to be channelled through the lawyer.

The problem, she realised, was that the conversation had been cut short. She remembered something about blood samples, but her memory was foggy, scrambled by stress and adrenaline and shock.

Would they even be expecting her?

'With any luck, Harry got a message through to them before he…' She trailed off.

'That's a stretch, Sofie.'

'And if the lawyer doesn't believe us?' she said quietly. 'What then? Or what if they've already destroyed the evidence?'

'If he's smart, he won't have touched a thing. Not until he knows where the danger's coming from. And that means we're still in with a chance.'

'And if they refuse to hand it over?'

Cal regarded her for a moment as she fingered another snack from the trolley. Best not to remind her that there were other ways to prise things out of people.

'Come on,' he said instead. 'Let's rehearse what we're going to say. We need to convince him that we're the safest option left.'

They spent the rest of the flight building the pitch. By the time the wheels touched down on the short strip that was Gibraltar International, the sky was already heating up. The Rock loomed over the tarmac like a sentinel, and the coast of Africa shimmered across the sea.

The crew bid them goodbye - *'have a nice holiday,'* they beamed - and they walked the short distance to the terminal, heading for the fast-track gate. The official inspected their Irish passports with more than usual thoroughness.

'Holiday or business?'

'Holiday,' said Cal, clutching Sofie's hand as if they were an item.

A beat.

'Wait here a moment, please, sir.'

He took them away into a side office, leaving Cal and Sofie waiting at the desk.

'What the hell's going on?' whispered Sofie nervously.

Cal said nothing, his face impassive. Two long minutes passed. Then the official came back, passports in hand.

'Apologies for the delay. Just a quick systems thing. Where are you staying?'

'The Rock Hotel,' Sofie replied, forcing a smile.

The official nodded and handed the passports back to Cal. 'Enjoy your stay.'

Outside, as they walked toward the cab rank, Sofie took his arm. 'That felt weird. You think it was routine?'

'Hopefully.' Cal tried to sound reassuring. 'They're unlikely to be looking for us here.'

He didn't mention the faint prickle at the back of his neck. The sixth sense he'd learned not to ignore.

76

After checking in, they headed straight back out. There was no time to waste. The meeting was booked for 2:00.

Gibraltar was dripping in Britishness: red phone boxes, fluttering Union Jacks, the usual high-street suspects: Waterstones, Boots, a random Greggs. Sofie ducked into a WH Smith, emerging with a small ring-bound notebook, plus a pen and pencil. May as well look the part.

The sun blazed overhead. It was hot. Africa hot. Down in the harbour, a Royal Navy frigate sat grey and hulking, a white ensign snapping in the wind. It all felt so familiar.

For the first time in days, she felt safe.

Their destination wasn't far, an anonymous office block on the edge of Ocean Village. A bored-looking security guard sat at reception, and behind him, a nameplate advertised *Chambers, Rast & Associates*. He waved them towards a bank of lifts and told them to take it to the third floor.

They emerged onto a small landing. To the right was a transport agency. To the left, a half-glass door with the firm's name engraved on it.

'Can I help you?' asked the girl behind the desk.

'We've come to see Mr Rast.'

'You have an appointment?'

'Two pm,' Cal said. 'John Davis from London, and this is my assistant Sofie. We're a little early.'

The receptionist eyed them. 'Ah, yes. I'm afraid Mr Rast travelled to Spain this morning and has been delayed. He sends his apologies; he'll be about twenty minutes late. Are you happy to wait?'

They sat down. The receptionist went back to her bank of phones and, keeping a wary eye on them, started varnishing her nails a glossy shade of red.

~

Cal carefully scanned the room. No CCTV in reception, he noticed, and he could see none here either.

Eventually, he said: 'Any chance of a coffee?'

She wrinkled her nose. 'Coffee?'

She didn't look too keen. He could see why. Her nail varnish was still drying.

'Milk, no sugar. Sofie?'

Sofie shook her head.

Grudgingly, the girl slid off her seat, her hands stretched out in front of her like someone playing a game of blind man's buff. After she'd gone, Cal rose and in two strides was at her desk.

'*What the hell are you doing?*' hissed Sofie.

Her monitor was showing some kind of booking system. It didn't take him long to find what he was looking for. He snapped an image of the URL with his phone and returned to his chair, and a moment later, the girl came back with a tray and dumped it ungraciously on the low side table beside him, followed by another woman.

'I'm going for a cigarette, won't be long,' the newcomer called as the girl sat down again. She disappeared along a corridor signed 'WC'.

Cal took a sip of the scalding hot coffee and got up.

'Mind if I use the toilet?'

The girl stared at him as if to say, *I see you, you're trouble.* After a moment's hesitation, she nodded. Cal made his way towards where the other woman had gone. The gents were at the end on the left. Straight ahead was a half-glazed door leading out to a small roof terrace. He just had time to clock the woman activate a round green button on the wall to release it. She slipped out, and the door clicked shut behind her. He waited a few moments before following and joined her outside as she was lighting up.

'Oh,' she said, a look of surprise on her face.

It was a narrow space, perhaps ten by fifteen feet, with a balustrade around the edge. The back of the building overlooked several similar office blocks. Evidently, renovation was going on because scaffolding had been erected along one side. He leant over and peered down at the street below.

'Can I help you?' he heard the woman say behind him, her tone halfway between curious and suspicious.

'I was looking for the toilet,' he replied, straightening up.

She laughed. 'Well, it's certainly not down there.' She pointed at the door they'd just come through. 'You passed it, on the right.'

'Oh, sorry,' he said, retracing his steps. He tried it, but as he knew it would, it had locked behind him.

He turned and gave her a helpless shrug. She sighed,

muttered something under her breath, then leaned past him and punched in four digits. 4-6-5-6. The lock clicked.

'Appreciate it.'

'You're welcome,' she muttered.

Cal ducked into the gents - just in case she was still watching - then returned to the waiting area, where he barely had time to burn his tongue again on the coffee before the office door swung open and in came a man with a battered briefcase.

The receptionist was on the phone. The man stopped just long enough to glance at her notepad, then vanished into his office.

The girl mouthed something to Cal that he couldn't interpret, and when her call was finished, she disappeared after him. A moment later, she reappeared.

'Mr. Davis? You can go straight in now.'

'Thank you.'

They entered his office. Cal advanced across the room, holding out his hand.

'John Davis from London, and this is my assistant Sofie.' Sofie smiled at him, straightening a short black skirt they'd picked up at Southampton airport. 'Thank you for seeing us at such short notice.'

Rast shook Cal's hand absent-mindedly. Off-guard. He was a tanned middle-aged man with a paunch, greying at the temples. He looked harassed.

'I hope this won't take long. I'm afraid I have another meeting in…' he glanced at his watch '… a quarter of an hour.'

'Five minutes, Mr Rast,' pressed Cal, 'that's all we need.'

He hesitated, looking from one to the other with pale blue eyes.

'Of course,' he said politely. He gestured for them to sit down and settled behind his desk. He opened his briefcase, got out a pad, a pen, and a small tablet device, arranged them in front of him, shuffled some papers, and swung back on his executive chair.

'So,' he said. 'What can I do for you?'

Cal glanced at Sofie. It was important now that she did exactly what they'd rehearsed. She looked away and bent her head over her ring-bound notebook, pencil poised. It all hinged on the lawyer's reaction.

He turned to Rast, voice steady. 'We're from the Sunday Times. We've come about two Cambridge Bio employees named Crome and Latimer.'

Rast seemed to freeze. Just for a beat. But Cal caught it. The man's eyes flickered to Sofie. He kept staring at her, as if mesmerised, avoiding Cal.

'The Sunday Times?' he said finally. 'In London?'

Cal said nothing. Let the silence do the work. Rast turned back to him. Was there a hint of fear?

'What did you say the name was?'

'John Davis.'

'And your colleague's?'

'My assistant? Sofie.'

'Sofie?'

It was then that Cal knew they'd come to the right place.

'James.'

Rast stood up abruptly.

'I'm sorry. I'm afraid I don't know what you're talking about.'

Cal made a show of protesting. But he didn't push it. Because he'd got what he'd come for.

'Mr Rast,' began Sofie desperately. 'If you'll let me

explain…'

'Do I need to call security?' said the lawyer, suddenly hostile.

'But I've met those research chemists. I was on the boat when they were…'

She felt a rough arm hauling her up.

'Come on, Sofie, we're done here.'

She shook Cal off. *'What are you doing?'*

Without waiting, he propelled her out of the office. The receptionist looked up in surprise as they passed through her office and out of the door.

Sofie said nothing, her face like thunder, until they got to the street. Then she let rip.

'What the hell was that about?' she yelled. 'I thought we decided…'

'I'll explain,' he snapped. 'But not here.'

They walked rapidly to the end of the block, where she followed him into a coffee shop. They sat down in a booth.

'OK,' she said, her voice low and still furious. 'I'm listening. This better be good.'

'First off, did you notice how he recognised your name?'

'Exactly. So why didn't we do what we'd agreed? Tell him what happened?'

'Because he immediately clammed up, don't you see that?'

'So? We hardly pressed him at all!'

'Listen, Sofie,' he said patiently. 'For some reason, he's suspicious. Maybe he won't talk to us in the office. He's probably scared. Wouldn't you be, given what's happened?'

'So what do you propose? It's too late now to try to talk him round.'

'We go back in when he's not there.'

She stared at him.

'Like, as in, break in?'

'We've established he's the right lawyer, and we can be pretty sure he recognised you. Chances are there'll be references to those research chemists and Alex in his office somewhere, perhaps even confidential client files.'

'Oh, lovely,' she snorted. 'Shall I go and buy a black balaclava?'

He grinned.

'That would be one method. However, I think I've found a better route to get us in.'

'Us?'

He smiled. 'You're right. Probably best you don't come, you'll only get in the way.'

'Fuck off!' she snapped.

They sat in silence for a while. Then she said, dejected, 'And there I was thinking we'd walk into his office and it would all be over.'

'Afraid we're not there yet, Sofie.' He paused. 'One thing I never asked you, though. What was your father's name?'

She blinked. 'Colin. Why? What's that got to do with anything?'

77

TASHA EASED OFF THE THROTTLE AS THE AIRPORT CAME INTO view at the end of Winston Churchill Avenue. The BMW's two-cylinder boxer engine popped and growled as she coasted into the Cepsa petrol station, drawing more than a few stares. The bike always did that - demanded attention. It was a chink in her armour, considering her line of work, but one she had come to terms with. The bike was just too much fun.

While she stood in line to pay for fuel, her mind turned to the lawyer. It was annoying to have to wait until the next morning for the meeting she'd come for. He had been cooperative, but he was not, it turned out, the person she needed to see. He was simply the gatekeeper.

Still, there was one good thing: she was ahead of them. They hadn't seen anyone else claiming to be Sofie James. Nor any sign of the man she was meant to be travelling with.

Because her plan had changed. It was no longer just about the girl. After talking to the lawyer, it was clear that there was some very significant evidence that the doctor wanted to hand over. When she'd mentioned it to Laura, she'd belatedly sanctioned the trip. It would cost her extra, Tasha said. Still, she could now kill two birds with one stone, as it were.

It was as she was walking back to her bike that she clocked a car pulling up in the next bay. It had Gibraltar license plates, and in the back seat sat a man on a mobile phone. She did a double-take. The face was somehow vaguely familiar.

She lowered her visor and walked around her bike to get a look at him from a better angle. There was no mistaking it now. He looked exactly like the guy who had run the clear-up team after the shootings on the boat in London two weeks earlier. The British agent who'd worked with Laura. Gebler.

Her first thought was, what the hell was he doing here? It lasted only a split second before a second drowned it out.

It was quite obvious why he was here.

She gunned her bike into life and indicated right towards town.

~

MINUTES LATER, THE CAR BEHIND HER LEFT THE FORECOURT in the opposite direction. At the far end of the avenue, past the airport and just short of the border, the driver drew into a parking lot. Gebler leapt out and hurried into a modern glass and steel building. The sign outside said 'Gibraltar Borders and Coastguard Agency.'

His contact was waiting on the third floor. They wasted no time. A man and a woman fitting the description of Cal Harrison and Sofie James had arrived on Irish passports by private jet from Southampton that morning and were staying at the Rock Hotel.

Gebler let out an oath. Why the hell hadn't he been informed earlier? An urgent call was made. Two plainclothes Gibraltarian policemen, who'd been on standby for the past twenty-four hours, were ushered in. A plan was put together.

Thirty minutes later, they exited the building alongside Gebler, jumped in his car, and sped off back towards the Rock, sirens blaring.

78

Leaving the café, Cal and Sofie headed back to the hotel via a hardware store, where Cal bought a box of latex gloves and a set of small steel Allen wrenches.

'For tonight,' he explained as they exited the shop. Then: 'Are we good?'

'For now,' she said grudgingly.

'Didn't mean to piss you off, but it really is best if I handle this alone.'

He set off again, and she fell into step beside him.

'If there's something stored on his computers or in his office, we need to find it. And if there isn't anything on Cambridge Bio, I want to have access to all his other data. If it comes to it, we might have to force him to talk.'

She gave him a sidelong glance. 'I don't want any violence.'

'A bit late to worry about that now, don't you think?'

They crested the hill and stepped into the forecourt of the hotel. Cal stiffened.

'What?' she said.

He nodded toward the ramp leading down to the

underground garage. 'The cherry picker. Was that there when we left?'

She followed his gaze. All the cars that had been parked across from the entrance were gone. In their place, a hydraulic cherry picker rested against a lamppost. A man in faded overalls reclined lazily on the raised platform, staring at nothing in particular.

'Not sure. What are you thinking?'

He shook his head. 'Probably nothing.'

Inside the hotel, they parted, agreeing to meet for a late dinner and a debrief after he returned.

'I hope to God you know what you're doing,' she said.

'Ah, shades of Paris. Do you know the SAS motto? *Who dares, wins.* But Frank and I adopted our own - *Don't Look Down.* Meaning, stay focused on the task at hand, not the fifty ways it could blow up in your face.' He laid a hand on her shoulder. 'I'll be back at nine.' He stepped into the lift. 'Order me a Coke.'

She was still shaking her head as the doors closed. When he reached his room, he messaged Sam.

<*Need your help again. Can you see what you can find here?*>

He attached the screenshot of the URL from the lawyer's office.

<*Looking for any references or files on Cambridge Bio. And two names: Crome and Latimer. Also, Colin James.*>

As an afterthought, he added: <*Or Sofie James.*>

The reply from Sam came swiftly. <*Roger, pal. How soon?*
>

<*ASAP. And if you find any alarms in the system, please kill them at 8 PM your time tonight.*>

When he had finished, he stretched out on the bed, boots still on.

It had been a long day.

And tonight would be longer.

79

When he awoke, it was dark. Streetlight streamed in the hotel window, casting long orange streaks across the carpet. He blinked, sat up slowly, and looked out.

The cherry picker was still there. But no workmen.

Instead, something small and boxy now clung to the platform's edge, angled toward the hotel entrance. He squinted. A camera? Or was he being paranoid? Paranoia had kept him alive more than once. He remembered his training. Always plan for the worst.

He threw off the covers and got moving. He packed his smaller, second backpack, locked the room and headed downstairs in search of a back entrance. As he reached the ground floor, his phone pinged. It was Sam.

<*Alarm deactivated. Text me when you're in.*>

It took him half an hour on foot to reach the rear of the lawyer's building. The surrounding streets were not well-lit, but squinting up at the scaffolding, he could see no sign of a builder's alarm, and the area seemed free of CCTV.

Scanning the area one final time to make sure no one was about, he donned a pair of latex gloves and began to climb.

The third-floor terrace came into view faster than he expected. He swung himself over the rail and crouched down, remaining completely still. He counted silently to ten. But all was quiet. Satisfied he was alone, he moved to the door, punched in the code he'd memorised - 4656 - and slipped inside.

The office was in darkness. A faint sodium light from the front of the building cast a sickly yellow glow at the far end of the corridor.

He padded silently to the receptionist's desk and set to work. The screen was still on. One nudge of the mouse brought up a login prompt. He messaged Sam.

<*I'm in. Found anything yet?*>

Sam replied almost instantly.

<*Negative. They have a high level of encryption. Stand by for a script.*>

A few seconds later, a long string of code pinged onto his screen. He followed Sam's instructions to the letter. Checked the system specs. Opened a command prompt. Started running the script line by line.

Ten minutes passed. Then a new message:

<Got it. I'm in. You can log off.>

He closed it down, wiped the keyboard with a gloved hand, and stood. Next, Rast's office.

He pulled the mini Allen wrenches from his bag. It took him less than two minutes to jiggle the pins of the lock and click it open. He started with the filing cabinets. Working quickly, he skimmed through to see if there was anything on Cambridge Bio, but, as he suspected, they were all hard copies of client files. Nothing useful here.

He rifled the desk, careful to replace papers where he found them. There was the usual detritus - a packet of

Aspirin, a stack of receipts, a crumpled drawing drawn by a child. Nothing significant.

Finally, he was done. On the way out, he relocked the office door, then retraced his steps to the roof terrace and climbed swiftly down the scaffolding. Once back on the ground, he peeled off his gloves, dumped them in a street bin, and disappeared into the night. The whole operation had taken less than twenty-five minutes.

The next message from Sam came as he was re-entering the tradesmen's entrance at the back of the hotel.

<*Downloaded a ton of client data. Nothing yet on three of the names you listed, but I found one entry for Sofie James. In a wee, remote contacts file. Added two days ago.*>

She listed a number. Cal stopped mid-step. Two days ago? It was a Gibraltar area code. That timing didn't make sense.

<*Good luck. Let me know what you need me to do with this shite.*>

He walked through the lobby and up to reception.

'Hi,' he said. 'Can you call this number for me, please?'

The receptionist dialled and handed him a house phone. It rang twice before answering.

'The Holiday Inn, how can I help you?'

So it was a hotel.

'Sofie James, please.'

'Do you have a room number?'

'No.'

'One moment, please.'

He waited apprehensively. After a minute, the voice returned.

'I am afraid there is no answer, sir. Would you like to leave a message?'

'Can you confirm which room she is staying in?'

'I am sorry, we are not able to give out room numbers.'

He hung up and headed upstairs. Sofie was waiting for him in the rooftop bar as arranged. It was 9:10. He didn't like being late.

'Thank God,' she said when she saw him. 'I was beginning to be worried. I don't like you leaving me like that.' She pushed a glass toward him. 'Your usual. Probably flat by now.'

He sat down and drained it in one go.

'Well?' she asked. 'How did you get on?'

'Like clockwork. We've now got access to their files.'

'That's great. Have you had a chance to look at them?'

'Not yet. But we did find something else.' He leaned in. 'Get this. There's someone else in town, pretending to be you.'

She started.

'Wait. What?'

'Sam found a contact file. For you. Entered into the system two days ago, staying at the Holiday Inn. I called them. Whoever it is, she's still there.'

Her eyes narrowed. 'No wonder Rast didn't want to talk to us.'

'He probably thought you were an impostor.'

'But how…'

'She must have got to him first. Warned him.' He crunched on a cube of ice. 'We're going to have to move fast. She may already have what she came for.'

Sofie shot to her feet. 'Then what are we doing sitting here? Let's go find her.'

Cal put out an arm to hold her back. 'Not tonight. Too risky.'

'But what if she checks out?'

'If she's there now, she'll be there in the morning.' He

picked up a menu. 'Now, let's order dinner, I'm famished.'

80

Saturday 12th November

Tasha was up before the sun, impatient to get on. After a quick shower, she began preparing for the day.

First, she emptied her backpack, laying the magazines out onto the bed. She counted the rounds, slipping a round out of each to check the spring. Then came the Glock 19. She racked the slide, slow and deliberate, making sure the breach was smooth. She locked in a mag, flipped the safety on and off, then raised the pistol, sighting down through the three red dots in the direction of the airport terminal building a mile away. *Boom*, she mouthed silently to herself.

Satisfied, she slotted it into her underarm holster and laid everything down beside the rest of her equipment.

There was a knock on the door.

Throwing a white towelling robe over the gear, she let the maid in with her breakfast, watching as she prepared the table: bacon, eggs, a glass of juice, a pot of black coffee and a yoghurt with a side of fresh fruit. When she had done, she sent the girl on her way with ten euros and settled down to eat and check her messages.

There were only two. The first was from her partner,

Julia, in Madrid, asking if she'd be back in time for a performance of Rigoletto that night. She tapped a quick reply: *Keep you posted.*

The second was a voice note from Laura, checking in, with details of where and when she was to meet to hand over the material the lawyer had organised for her to collect from the doctor. She grabbed a hotel notepad and jotted down the time and date, along with a three-word code: Laura's new favourite way to arrange meetings and dead drops.

She finished her eggs and slipped on the holster. With a final check, she pulled on her leathers, stuffed the last few bits into her motorcycle panniers and left the room.

81

'Sofie James, please,' Sofie said, keeping her voice level.

The receptionist, head down over a stack of invoices, barely looked up. The Holiday Inn Express was a smart business hotel squeezed between the Rock and the airport runway. It felt a bit weird to be asking for herself.

'Room number?'

'I'm not sure.'

She watched the man punch the buttons on his terminal: 1123. It was that easy. Her heart was thudding as she waited for the pickup. She'd rehearsed this with Cal. Even so, she mouthed a silent prayer.

The phone rang four times.

'I'm afraid there's no answer.' She breathed a sigh of relief. 'Miss James might be in the Harbour View restaurant having breakfast. Would you care to leave a message?'

'No thanks.'

She joined Cal in the hotel coffee shop.

'Room 1123. She's not answering.'

'Good work.' He checked his watch. 'Now let's go see

who she is.'

They paid the bill and took the elevator up to the first floor. The room was at the far end of the corridor, which, as far as Cal was concerned, was a bonus, because they could only be disturbed from one direction. However, getting in was another matter. The door was locked behind a keycard, so there was nothing mechanical to work his magic on.

'You'll have to bribe one of the staff,' he said to Sofie. 'Text me when you're in.'

So while Cal returned to the coffee shop, Sofie went in search of a maid. It didn't take her long to find one. A young girl was collecting a breakfast tray from a room in an adjoining corridor. Sofie explained - *so sorry to disturb you, I've locked myself out of my room, could you come and help?* The girl looked hesitant at first, but a twenty-euro note was all the motivation she needed, and a couple of minutes later, Sofie was inside 1123. She texted Cal, and within another thirty seconds, there was a tap on the door, and Sofie let him in.

The room was spacious, corporate and anonymous, with a 180-degree view over the runway towards the mainland. A crumpled backpack stood beside the wardrobe, and a couple of items of female clothing were piled on a chair. Whoever this woman was, she packed light. Sofie walked into the bathroom and flicked on the light. Everything was obsessively neat: toiletries aligned, towels folded.

'Who the hell can she be?'

'Whoever she is,' said Cal, joining her, 'she likes a drink.' He picked up a half-empty bottle of champagne from beside the bath.

They returned to the bedroom. Sofie checked the wardrobe drawers - each of them empty - while Cal ran his hands along the seams of the backpack. There was nothing there except a few scraps of paper and two pairs of new tights in a side compartment. And a smell. He sniffed it. Oily, sulphurous and faintly metallic, one he was all too familiar with: firearms residue.

Careful not to betray his concern, he zipped it up. Next to it was a low coffee table, on which lay a pad of paper and a hotel pencil. Sofie picked up the pad and held it to the light.

'Hey, take a look at this,' she said. There was a faint indentation across the top page, as if a note had been taken and the sheet ripped away.

They twisted it for a better viewing angle. Cal took the pencil and gently shaded over the marks, side to side, until the ghost of the message appeared.

12:30. 17 Nov.

Three words had been written underneath: *Town, Tooth, Town.*

Sofie frowned. 'What is it? Some kind of code?'

'The date and time would suggest a meeting. The words - no idea.'

'A bit weird, no?'

He pondered for a second. 'Agree. But whatever it is, let's keep it.' He ripped the page from the pad and slipped it into his pocket.

There was a sudden knock on the door. They stiffened, and within an instant, were scrambling towards the bathroom.

The knock came again. Three raps. Room service? Laundry? Or someone who knew the woman who was renting the room? They couldn't risk Sofie answering.

At any moment, they expected the slide of a card in the lock. But it didn't come. Instead, there was a rustle and a soft whoosh as something slid under the door, followed by the sound of receding footsteps.

Sofie was the first into the passageway. After a moment's silence, she let out a little cry.

'Yes!' she whooped, waving a sheet of paper. 'We've got her! It's a message from someone called Dr Alex Shelton.'

Cal peered at it.

'Dr Alex Shelton phoned. Please call before you leave.'

The note was timed at 09:35.

'Don't you see?' she said excitedly. 'It's the same Alex. Has to be. It's too much of a coincidence, and we don't believe in those, right?' She clenched her fist. 'Cal, we're getting there!'

Cal crossed to the window. 'We may be too late.' In the distance, an aeroplane was making its final descent. 'Let's just think about this for a moment.'

'Well, don't think too long! We've got to go find her, before this woman does.'

He swivelled round.

'But what do we have? Someone impersonating you, someone who has already met with a lawyer acting for this doctor, Alex. Next, we have a message from the doctor herself, suggesting that a meeting is about to happen.' A thought struck him. 'Am I right in saying that you never met this Alex?'

'Yeah. The first I heard of her was in my Dad's diaries.'

'So even if she knows *of* you, which is highly likely, she won't necessarily recognise you. Which means that whoever this impostor is, they will probably get away with it.'

'She won't if we find Alex first. It should be easy enough to track her down, now we've got the name.'

Cal looked sceptical.

'Plus, I can prove who I am,' she went on. 'This woman can't.' She grabbed Cal's wrist to check the time. 'OK, it's

9:40. This message says she rang five minutes ago. Which means their meeting can't have happened yet. We still have time.'

A room service card was discarded beside the bed.

'And look. She pre-ordered breakfast. 6:30 AM. She must already have left.'

Sofie was moving fast now, grabbing her bag, heading for the door. But Cal was still rooted to the spot.

'You coming, or not?'

Her feet were planted squarely apart, tensed to spring into action. After a moment's hesitation, he nodded.

'Let's hope you're right.'

82

'Are you sure it's up here?'

Sofie leaned forward as the taxi bumped along the uneven country road. They'd been in the cab for nearly an hour and had turned off the main road ten miles after Tarifa. Behind them, Gibraltar was wreathed in a low-hanging fog, but the Rock still managed to look majestic, its peak rising into a cobalt blue sky.

'This is the road to Sanctuary Farm,' said the Spanish driver.

It hadn't taken them long to find Dr Alex Shelton from a Gibraltar online directory. What they hadn't expected was an address across the border in Spain, buried in the countryside.

Without warning, a pick-up barreled around the bend ahead. The driver jerked the wheel. Gravel crunched as the taxi swerved hard onto the shoulder.

'Hey, take it easy, won't you!' yelled Sofie.

But Cal's concentration was elsewhere - on a mailbox at the entrance to a track that led off to the right. At the end of it, beyond a line of trees, he caught the glint of something industrial - long glass structures shimmering in the sun.

'What are those?' he said, pointing.

'Flowers, my friend.' The driver scratched his ear. 'And cannabis.'

They drove on. Ten minutes later, they came to a wooden sign on the left: *Sanctuary Farm*. The driver slowed to negotiate a cattle grid. A cloud of dust billowed behind them.

Ahead was a gatehouse. The barrier was raised. The driver wound down his window, but no one was around.

He shrugged, easing the taxi onto a gravel track.

'Do you see that?' said Sofie.

Cal followed her gaze. In the distance, a motorcycle was approaching. It seemed to be travelling very fast, bouncing up and down like a dancer. It turned onto the main track towards the gate and suddenly appeared dead ahead.

'Who would be biking out here?'

For the first time, the driver looked uneasy.

'Looks like a crazy man.'

The bike drew closer, a blurred shimmer of heat and dust. It was hard to estimate how far away it was. The track was barely the width of a car. The driver flashed his lights. But the bike kept coming, sun flashing off its chrome engine.

'Someone's in a hurry,' muttered Cal.

The driver checked his rearview mirror. Either side of them was an embankment, with no turning in sight. Unless the rider slowed, the bike would smash right into them.

'What the hell…?' Cal said under his breath.

It had now closed to fifty yards, powering towards them, a vortex of dust trailing behind it.

Sofie's voice cracked. 'He's not stopping!'

The driver spun into the embankment as the motorcycle flashed past in a swirl of grit. There was a loud clatter as it sprayed onto the car.

They held their breath. The stalled engine steamed in protest.

'*Mierda!*'

The driver muttered rapid-fire curses as steam hissed from under the hood. The front right wheel was sunk deep in the ditch. Cal heaved open the door, and they clambered out.

'Can you wait for us?' he asked, pulling a folded hundred-euro note from his pocket. 'We should be back in an hour. We'll help haul you out.'

The driver eyed the note dubiously. Before he could answer, they turned away and left him protesting behind them as they cut across a narrow path toward a row of low farm buildings ahead.

Fifteen minutes later, they reached the edge of the property. A low, single-story house sprawled before them, built from pale stone with a weathered tin roof - half colonial, half farmhouse. A veranda wrapped around the front, its posts lined with chipped white paint. A swing hung motionless from a tree in the centre of a perfectly manicured lawn.

From somewhere came the gentle swish, swish, swish of a sprinkler. Otherwise, all was quiet.

'Well?' whispered Sofie.

Cal didn't answer. He just stared at the place. Something didn't sit right. He didn't know what.

'I'm not sure,' he said finally.

'I think we should go in.'

He hesitated. 'Let me go first.'

Sofie blinked. 'Why?'

'Just a feeling.' He paused. 'You keep watch. I'll come and get you when it's clear.'

She peered ahead. 'Sorry, no.'

'Sofie…'

'This is my responsibility,' she snapped. 'Enough sidelining me, OK?'

Cal exhaled slowly and ran a hand through his dust-caked hair. He knew it was a bad idea. But she was already walking up the gravel drive.

83

Sofie set out with the kind of confidence she didn't entirely feel. The house looked still - too still. As she neared the front porch, she noticed the fly-screen door was ajar, nudged open just enough to suggest someone had either just left… or hadn't bothered to close it.

A gentle breeze rustled the trees, carrying with it a rhythmic knocking sound: wood against wood, soft but persistent. A swing, maybe? A shutter?

'*Hello?*' she called. 'Anyone home?'

There was no doorbell, so she rapped on the wood. No sign of life. A glance over her shoulder told her Cal hadn't followed.

Gingerly, she pushed on the door and peered in. A yellow light burned somewhere in the depths of the hallway, while just inside, a pile of unopened mail lay scattered on a table.

'Hello?' she ventured again.

Still nothing. She stepped back onto the porch, scanning the windows to either side. The shutters were pegged open, bright paint flaking in the sun. She peered through one of them. Empty.

Hesitating briefly on the threshold to cast one last look over her shoulder, she stepped inside.

It was a bare hallway, sparsely furnished. A faded gilt mirror hung on a wall, reflecting a second doorway and a room beyond. The door opposite was closed. She pressed her ear to the wood. There was the faintest tick of a clock.

Stepping across the passageway, she entered the kitchen. Here, there were signs of life. Someone had recently made coffee, the aroma still hanging in the air. But the silence made her uneasy. Straight ahead, a door with a glass panel gave onto a raised deck at the back, with what appeared to be a boot rack, and a garden beyond. To the left, a third door stood ajar. She pushed it open.

It was a study. Hundreds of books were displayed on floor-to-ceiling shelves, with more piled on the floor by a desk in the corner. In the middle of the room was a circular table with scattered papers and a jar full of pencils. She lifted one. It was sharpened to a clean point, with gold-stamped lettering on the side: *Cambridge Bio.*

Her pulse kicked. She was close. Closer than she'd ever been.

But something felt wrong. She couldn't quite work it out. And then it struck her: the silence. It had a different quality here, as if a door was open onto a garden, with the faint trace of noises carried away on the wind. Her sixth sense was also picking up a subtle change in atmosphere. She stood very still. Was she imagining it?

She crept towards the French doors at the end of the room and stepped out onto a deck.

The first thing she noticed was a steel cabinet and a rack of hunting rifles and shotguns. One had fallen out and lay on the ground. She was about to pick it up when her attention was snagged by something else.

She gasped.

A body lay slumped against the edge of the boot rack, its head wrenched back, a shattered bottle at its feet, red liquid seeping across the deck. For one breathless moment, she thought it was blood. Then the smell hit her. Wine.

She took a step closer. It was a man. Had he tried to defend himself with the bottle? He looked dead. Her throat clenched. She turned on her heel and bolted back along the veranda.

'Cal!' she shouted. '*Cal?*'

A snap behind her.

'Don't move.'

Momentarily, she froze. Then she began to run again, but before she could make it to the steps, something slammed into her shoulder, and she spun into the wall. She began to let out a scream, but a hand clamped over her mouth, and it died. She struggled to twist free, but his grip was too strong for her. She stumbled backwards, her heels skidding against the deck.

'If you make a sound, Sofie,' the voice hissed in her ear, 'you're dead.'

84

THE MOMENT SOFIE DISAPPEARED INSIDE, CAL STARTED TO move.

Walking around the edge of the lawn, avoiding the gravel path, his shoes sank silently into the soft earth. Every few yards, he paused to listen. Nothing. No voices, no movement. Only the whisper of wind through trees and the distant drone of insects.

He took the verandah steps slowly, one at a time. He needn't have worried. They were concrete and soundless. He reached the top, eased open the door, and slipped in, pulling it shut behind him with a soft click.

The hallway was empty. Antique engravings of mountain scenes were arranged on one wall, whilst opposite, beside a faded gilt mirror, was a battered hat stand. It held a floppy hat, a green felt jacket, and three gnarled walking sticks. In two strides, he was at the second door.

It was locked, a key still in the handle. Pressing his ear to the wood, all was ominously quiet. Where was she?

He stepped across the passageway and ducked his head

into a kitchen. Empty. Slipping in, he noticed a pair of clean cups on a tray beside a bowl, awaiting a still-warm pot of coffee. It smelled fresh, recently made. A jug lay on its side: a dribble of milk had splashed to the floor. Someone had been disturbed. Enough not to have picked it up.

At the far end was a pantry and a short flight of stairs leading down to a yard. Cal retraced his steps.

Step, stop, listen. He crept along a passage. To the right, a tap dripped behind a closed door, and there was a faint whiff of sanitary detergent.

Straight ahead, he entered what looked like a study, the walls lined with books. A cursory glance revealed they were almost exclusively medical titles. Again, he thought: where had Sofie gone? She seemed to have vanished into thin air.

He was on the point of calling out for her when he heard a soft, familiar click. Instinctively, he dived for the floor.

To his surprise, he reached it intact. He held his breath, but no shot rang out. He scanned his surroundings, his torso rammed up against the edge of the sofa. Was the shooter at floor level, beside the desk, or not even in the room at all? The door into the passage stood half open. There was a gap of almost an inch between it and the worn wooden floorboards, but no sign of anyone behind it.

Confident there was nobody in his immediate sightline, he twisted to get a view of the far end of the room. Daring not to divert his concentration for more than an instant, and still not satisfied he was alone, he leapt backwards and sideways until he was spreadeagled along the back wall. He braced himself once more, focusing all his senses on what might be about to happen. Again, nothing. No reaction, no movement, no sound whatsoever.

Could he have been mistaken?

He got up. The room was empty. Then he saw it. A small voice recorder on the floor beneath a round circular table, small enough to hold in the palm of your hand. Of a type used by reporters, with an audio mini-cassette. The click had been the sound of it coming to the end of its tape. He picked it up and slipped it into his pocket.

Suddenly, the silence was shattered.

'Cal?' She sounded desperate. '*Cal?*'

He bolted back towards where her voice had come from. And stopped dead. Through the window, half-lit by the sun, was the silhouette of a man.

It was Gebler.

85

Sofie felt cold steel on her neck. The man's hand slipped away from her mouth. She started to shake.

'That's better,' he said smoothly, spinning her to face him.

She recognised him instantly. She paled.

'Glad we've found you at last. You've been causing us a lot of trouble.'

Her voice cracked. '*You…!*'

'We met at the party on the Thames, remember?' He grinned, eyes flat.

'*What do you want from me?*'

'Where's your friend?'

'What friend?'

He jerked his chin toward the slumped figure on the verandah.

'Did he kill him?'

'What? What are you talking about?'

'Don't play cute with me!' he snapped. 'Harrison, where is he?'

'I don't know,' she said quickly. 'I swear.'

Without warning, he grabbed the base of her ponytail and yanked hard. Her head snapped back, and the butt of the pistol cracked across her jaw. She screamed.

'Don't screw with me, Sofie!' he hissed. 'We know he came out here with you.'

He glanced down the verandah, then out across the lawn.

'Cal!' he yelled. 'I've got your girl! Come out or I'll shoot her!'

Sofie cried out again as he twisted her arm behind her back, pain lighting up her shoulder.

'OK, Cal, we'll play it your way!'

She felt his hand shift near her ear, then -

BANG.

The gunshot exploded beside her head. It was deafening. Her vision blurred. A flock of birds rose like a black cloud from a nearby tree, screeching. When the reverberations had died away, Gebler jammed the muzzle into her temple.

'Next one, she gets it in the head!' he yelled. 'You better be out there! I'm counting to ten!'

Her legs started to tremble uncontrollably.

'One!' he barked.

'He's not here!' she pleaded desperately. 'He's gone back to Gibraltar!'

'Two!'

'*What do you want?* I can help…'

'Three!'

'Oh God, please! I had nothing to do with killing that guy. I don't even know who he is…'

'Four!'

'*I'm no use to you dead!*'

Gebler smirked.

'Imaginative. Five!'

'Please! I'll do anything you need! Tell me what you…'

'Anything? Six!'

Then came the sound of crunching gravel. Cal stepped into view, hands raised. Calm and defiant.

'Okay, Charles. Let her go.'

'*Cal!*' Sofie lunged, but Gebler yanked her back hard.

'Stop right there!' he said. 'Gun on the ground!'

'I'm unarmed.'

'We'll see. Down. Slowly.'

Cal lowered himself.

'Evans!' Gebler shouted.

A man Sofie had not noticed before appeared from behind them and bent down to frisk Cal. He was young, with short-cropped hair and a black baseball cap, in a tracksuit top and jeans.

'He's clean,' he said gruffly.

'Take her,' Gebler said, shoving Sofie toward the stranger. 'Tie her up.'

Evans caught her, twisted her arms, and yanked a cable tie tight around her wrists. She winced as the plastic bit into her skin. He motioned for her to kneel.

'Well, well,' said Gebler, approaching Cal and towering over his prone figure. 'Look what we got here? The meddler himself.' His eyes narrowed. 'We were all wondering what had happened to you.'

'I don't know what you think you are doing, Charles,' said Cal evenly. 'How do you suppose you are going to get away with this?'

Gebler laughed. 'With what? Get up!'

Cal raised himself from the ground. Before he was fully upright, Gebler slammed the butt of the revolver into the side of his head. Cal reeled. Ten feet away, Sofie gasped.

'That's for giving us all this trouble, you little shit.'

Cal steadied himself, blood streaming down his chin, one hand braced on the wall.

'Now,' Gebler said, 'tell me why you killed him. And what the hell you are doing here.'

Cal followed Gebler's eyeline and, for the first time, noticed the body.

'Who is that? The doctor?'

'So you do know who he is.'

'*That's Alex Shelton?*' Sofie croaked, unable to hide her disbelief.

'Why the hell would I kill him?' snapped Cal.

Another blow smacked into his jaw. He staggered against the wall and dropped to his knees.

'You think we're buying this crap?'

Cal spat blood. '*You...can...believe...what... you...fucking...well...like.*'

The sudden numbness began to recede, to be replaced by a sharp, excruciating pain.

'*Wait!*' he heard Sofie cry. 'Leave him! We just arrived. I found him like that! That's the truth!'

Cal was rasping for breath. Gingerly, he fingered his face. Gebler hauled him up roughly, slamming him against the doorframe.

'Last chance. Why are you here?'

Cal eyed him warily. He had to act. As far as he could tell, his companion was not armed, and, curiously, he was exhibiting signs of stress.

'I'm getting impatient here,' Gebler snapped acidly.

Cal lifted his head.

'We had a meeting with a lawyer called Rast yesterday,' he said.

Gebler frowned.

'He arranged for us to meet Dr Shelton this morning.' It wasn't quite the truth. 'Actually,' he added, glancing at Sofie. 'We were expecting a woman. Are you sure this is Dr Shelton?'

Gebler picked up a laminated ID card and jabbed it in Cal's face.

'That's what it says here. Dr Alex Shelton.'

Cal wiped blood from his lip. 'Well, it looks like someone got here first, doesn't it?'

That hit a nerve. Cal saw it: the hesitation. The flicker of something not quite sure. Was Gebler in the dark about the impostor? About what Shelton had planned? Something didn't add up. If Gebler was here to stop them from exposing Cambridge Bio and damaging Crane… why would he not also have killed the doctor who was about to release the evidence? He looked genuinely caught off guard.

But there was no time for conjecture. He readied himself for the next blow.

'Which means you're fucked,' he said, inviting it.

Gebler fell into the trap. As his fist swung in towards him, Cal swerved his body to the left and, grabbing Gebler's arm, twisted it with all his strength. But Gebler was well trained. Instead of resisting, he went with Cal's movement, and they both tumbled to the floor. Crucially, however, the gun remained in his hand, and, as the angle narrowed, he pulled the trigger and a shot smashed into the side of Cal's boot.

Sofie screamed as Cal doubled up, pain ripping through him. His grip momentarily slackened. Gebler tore free and jumped to his feet, panting, gun trained on Cal.

'So that's the way you want it,' he snarled.

Cal heard Sofie call his name, and the man who was guarding her starting to remonstrate with Gebler. A burning sensation flooded his body.

'We need to get them back to Gibraltar,' the man was pleading. 'The Policia will be here any minute. We shouldn't be in Spain at all.'

'You're right,' Gebler said. He eyed Cal warily. 'But first, I'll deal with this one. He belongs to me.'

He hauled Cal upright and shoved him roughly down the steps.

86

Gebler propelled Cal through a break in the fence, down a narrow slope to a large, open yard. Twin barns loomed on either side. Cal winced as pressure flared in his foot - walking was agony now.

'Where are we going?' he asked, not expecting an answer.

He didn't get one. Gebler just gave him another shove. Cal lost his balance and stumbled, and was hauled back up.

'Perfect,' Gebler said. Cal looked up. The man's attention was fixed on a metal shipping container resting on warped wooden blocks.

'This will do. You can go in there until I've decided what to do with you.'

He dragged Cal towards it, yanked open the heavy metal door, and hurled him inside. Cal hit the floor hard and skidded, the breath knocked out of him. A second later, the door slammed shut with a reverberating clang. He just had time to register a line of metal hooks hanging on rails before everything was plunged into darkness. He collapsed onto his back.

For what seemed like ages, nothing happened. The stink was unbearable. Whatever they stored in here was rotting. He prayed Sofie would be spared. The one glimmer of hope was Gebler's colleague. He didn't look comfortable. Would he protect her? Unlikely. But he was the weak link. If he took his eye off her, she might have a chance to get away.

He heard footsteps returning.

Then Gebler's voice - higher now, and manic. 'Tough shit, pal. I've been told you're expendable. You ready for some fun?'

A metallic click echoed - a magazine sliding into place. Despite the pain, Cal stumbled to his feet, heart beating furiously. So was this it? Would he be dragged out and shot?

He groped around for one of the hooks he knew was somewhere above him. Latching onto one, he felt for the door and flattened himself against the ribbed metal side of the container. He wasn't going easy. Gebler would have to drag him out.

But it wasn't dark for long. A sudden shaft of light shot diagonally across to the opposite wall as the first bullet sliced through the thin metal skin. There was a high-pitched zing as it ricocheted away.

'Jesus Christ!'

He ducked, stumbled sideways, and crashed into something sharp.

A second beam whipped inches from Cal's face. This time, the shot exited on the far side, a third point of light twinkling in at him from the sky. The pitch black was punctured now, his eyes adjusted, and he could begin to make out details of what was around him.

He was in what had once been a refrigerated meat locker. Patches of dried blood stained the walls, and the corners were littered with the fly-blown, rancid remains of carcasses. Outside, Gebler appeared to have paused momentarily. Cal lifted himself cautiously and put his eye to one of the ragged holes that had been shot away, gingerly avoiding torn splinters of metal. Gebler was cackling.

'You idiot, Harrison. You're like a rat in a cage, man. I'm going to enjoy this. Makes killing that much more fun, don't ya think?'

Cal couldn't believe what was happening. The guy was a psycho. As he ducked and frantically slithered across the floor, he felt something hard jab against his thigh. He suddenly remembered the tape in his pocket. It gave him an idea.

'I'll trade you!' he shouted, rolling quickly to his left. Three shots in quick succession punctured the spot where he'd been lying. Gebler must be beneath him now, on the ground, firing up.

'Foolish, Harrison, foolish.'

With an effort, Cal raised himself again, but he could no longer see Gebler.

'For God's sake, be sensible, Charles. Let's negotiate.'

'Ah, you wanna negotiate now, is it?' The voice was behind him. 'With what, may I ask? This is it, pal.' Two more shots skimmed through the wall. Cal yelled.

'Oh, have I hit someone?' Gebler roared. Another shot, more daylight, and a soft click. 'Whoops. Need another magazine. Hold on there, don't go away.'

Cal could hear him fumbling with the gun. He crawled to the far side.

'I have a tape, Charles,' he called, panting. His voice came in short, sharp rasps. 'I lied. We did meet the doctor. We recorded the meeting. It's all on there. The explanation of how the drug trial was run. Names. Dates. All the evidence needed to destroy Crane.'

There was the click of a breech being pulled back.

'Whatever,' answered Gebler. 'I'll get it off you anyway, right? Dead or alive.' The voice was coming from the left. From beyond a wall that was dark and still intact.

'But that's the thing, Charles. I don't have the tape on me. But I can tell you where it is.'

'Mmm. Good try. But I don't believe you.'

'It's a risk, though, isn't it, Charles? If it gets in the wrong hands…'

'Listen, all I need is you, Harrison. Dead. It was good of you to kill the guy. You've provided us with the perfect suspect. But you see the problem, don't you?'

Cal frantically tried to work out where the next shot would come from.

'We can't afford a cross-examination.'

He dragged himself along the wall, expecting a bullet, but instead, Gebler said, 'You've also been kind of a danger to me personally, Harrison. It was I who killed that pretty Alice girl back in London, but everyone thinks it was you. Now they won't be able to disprove it. You understand?'

Cal understood only too well.

'But if you kill me,' he cried. 'I'll blow everything! The tape will be released to the press.'

He rolled sideways in anticipation.

'Forgive me, Harrison, but if you're dead, how will you be in a position to blow anything?'

'Because it was recorded on the cloud.'

Another roll.

Gebler let out a low, hollow laugh. 'Was it now? Gotta do better than that. Besides, it doesn't mean shit without witnesses, does it? AI is pretty good these days.' He sniffed. 'You're dead. The chemists are dead. The doctor's dead. I think the girl's gonna have to die too.'

'And your accomplice up there?' croaked Cal. 'He doesn't seem too happy with the situation. I wouldn't be surprised if he's taken off with her already.'

For a second, Cal wondered whether to tell him about Kate. About the fact that they were on to him, and whoever else he was working with in the Security Service. But he dismissed it almost immediately. If he did that, she would be compromised, and Gebler would never be caught.

'Ready?'

Cal braced himself. A bullet came through the far wall at chest height. Silence. Another shot.

'What's the matter, cat got your tongue?'

The voice seemed nearer now, and nasty. Gebler had moved. The crisscross of beams was like some crazy fairground laser show. Cal shuffled along one wall and stepped on something sharp. Too late. In an effort to maintain his balance, he staggered and fell. There was an explosion, and all at once he was being sprayed with hundreds of tiny metal fragments. He sprang up as shrapnel peppered the inside of the container like needles, spinning him around. He collapsed.

The silence seemed to last a long time. He became dimly aware of the heavy door clanging open and someone stepping in. In agonising pain, but with an immense effort of will, he stayed down, playing dead. His whole body was on fire. It was all he could do.

A figure approached. At any moment, he expected the final shot in the head. A muffled voice said something he couldn't understand, as if from the end of a long tunnel. He could hold on no longer. A feeling of crushing tiredness washed over him.

He blacked out.

87

THE SECOND CAL DISAPPEARED DOWN THE PATH WITH Gebler, Sofie turned her eyes on the guy who'd stayed behind. He was young, barely older than her, and if his stiff posture and darting eyes were any clue, he was way out of his depth. And nervous. She guessed he was Gebler's subordinate, but the shock he was exhibiting suggested he was not used to his methods.

'What's going to happen to him?' she asked, keeping her tone calm.

He didn't answer. Just stepped away and pulled a phone from his pocket.

'Who are you, anyway?' she called after him. 'Do you work for Cambridge Bio?'

The man dialled a number. Someone picked up. His voice was low and rapid, and although she couldn't hear what he was saying, his stress was obvious. She caught a few words and phrases: *'Body in the house - Policia - armed - out of control.'*

When the call ended, he started pacing, agitated.

'You're from Gibraltar, right?'

'Shut it!' he snapped.

'Are you police?'

He turned sharply. 'Listen, if you don't resist, you'll be fine.'

'I'm not resisting,' she said, holding up her bound wrists. 'You tied me up, remember?'

He paced again, eyes flicking in the direction of the path that Gebler and Cal had taken.

'You think they're coming back?' she pressed.

He shifted his weight nervously from one foot to another.

'I don't get it,' she continued. 'Why are you here? All we did was come to meet the doctor. We found him dead when we got here. If you really believe we killed him, why not arrest us? Take us back to Gibraltar.'

'That's the plan,' he muttered, eyes still on the path.

'Doesn't look like it. Your colleague just shot my friend in the foot.'

'That was an accident.'

'Are you kidding me?'

She fumbled behind her for the cable tie. He'd not secured it very well. It felt loose and, given time, she was sure she could break free. There were shouts, followed by a loud gunshot.

Sofie flinched. 'For God's sake! He's a psycho! What's he doing down there?'

Another shot, accompanied by the high-pitched whine of a ricochet.

'*Do something!*' she screamed. 'He's going to kill him!'

The man hesitated, panic written all over his face.

'Sit down!' he ordered. When she didn't react, he forced her to the ground, her back against the verandah wall. Then: 'Don't move!'

He began walking rapidly towards the sound of the gunfire.

88

As soon as he had gone, Sofie rolled on her side and struggled onto her knees. With an immense effort, her shoulders screaming, she raised herself to a standing position. For a moment, she considered running after him. But then what? Her hands were still zip-tied behind her back, and if Gebler had a gun on Cal… no. She'd be useless.

Shots cracked in the distance. Quick bursts, in rapid succession. She could hear the echo of voices, including Cal's, which gave her hope. Had he escaped? It sounded like he was dodging Gebler around the yard. In which case, there was still a chance. But she didn't have much time.

In the far corner of the verandah, she spotted the shotgun she'd found earlier, lying on its side. She stumbled towards it. It looked similar to one her father had owned, an over-under double-barrelled Beretta with an engraved crest on the block. On a shelf above it was a box of cartridges. If only…

Two more shots rang out, along with a high-pitched, metallic splintering sound. Desperately, she searched for a means to set herself free.

Her eyes came to rest on a metal boot scraper next to the verandah door. Could she? She tumbled back down to the ground, oblivious to a splinter of wood snagging her leg, and began to shuffle sideways until she was able to align her hands with the blade. Frantically, she began to saw the plastic cable tie back and forth, pressing down hard with all her strength. She felt it beginning to fray.

Suddenly, with a snap, her wrists sprang free. She leapt up and grabbed the shotgun. It was heavier than the model her father had used when they'd gone shooting rabbits together as a child, on the farmland above the cottage at Ringstead. She snatched two cartridges, held the gun across one knee and broke open the barrel, then slotted them in and snapped it shut. Stuffing a couple more in her pocket, she clambered off the verandah and sprinted down the slope.

After fifty yards, she came to a gate leading to a yard. She skidded to a halt. The sight that greeted her would forever be etched in her memory. Ahead was a large metal container, beside which Gebler was reloading his revolver and laughing. At what, and why, she couldn't tell.

She rapidly scanned the buildings to either side, but his accomplice was nowhere to be seen. Satisfied she was hidden from view, she silently crept through the gate and positioned herself behind a small shed. Gebler was only ten yards away now, oblivious to her presence. Her heart thudded against her chest.

He raised his weapon and approached the container. Holding it with both hands, he yelled, *'Ready?'*

Taking steady, shallow breaths to centre herself, Sofie closed one eye and lined up the bead. Barrel steady. Stock pressed tight against her shoulder, the way her father had taught her - *it kicks harder than you think, Sof, lean into it.*

Then stepped out from behind the shed, took two paces, aimed, and pulled the trigger.

The first shot hit him square in the side, spinning his body around. As he fell, she pressed again. The second blast flung him backwards, lead shot slamming into the walls of the metal box. He staggered and fell, the gun's report echoing across the yard.

She stood stock still, blind with fury. He was down. But was it enough? From inside the container came a groan.

'*Cal!*' she screamed. She started to run. 'Oh my God, Cal, where are you?!'

She barely registered Gebler's crumpled, bleeding body, now motionless in the dirt, as she surged forward and yanked at the lever. The heavy door swung open.

In the distance, a police siren began to wail.

89

It took Tasha longer than she expected to return to the hotel. For some reason, the queue to get across the border at La Linea was bigger than usual. Every car was being checked thoroughly, the traffic - which normally flowed through in two lines - bottlenecked into a single lane.

She reentered Gibraltar on her Dutch passport, just to be safe. Four hours earlier, she had crossed into Spain on her Spanish one. She knew that the chances of anyone looking for her were remote. But you could never be too careful.

By the time she made it to her room, it was already past twelve. She didn't waste time. She packed up her things and checked out.

'We hope you enjoyed your stay with us, Miss James?' said the receptionist as she settled the bill.

For check-in, she'd used a fake Gibraltar ID card she had picked up in a backstreet dive in La Linea, a simple cut-and-paste job. It wouldn't have passed inspection at the border, but it worked fine for hotel registration. By the time the authorities entered the data into their systems - and she doubted they ever did - and discovered that there was no such resident as Sofie James, well, she would be long gone.

'Did your friend get hold of you?'

Tasha looked up sharply.

'What friend?'

'A woman was asking for you this morning.'

This morning? Did that mean she was finally here? But how had she traced her?

'Did she leave a name?'

'No.'

'What did she look like?'

'Fair hair, ponytail, English.'

So it was her. She hesitated. 'I missed her, unfortunately.' She followed it with a smile. 'But if she returns, could you give her a message? Tell her to stay safe.'

Outside, she mounted the bike, settled her helmet, and coasted down the hill toward the border. She had time to think. Not much, but enough to debate what came next.

Letting the girl walk might be a mistake.

She'd planned to deal with her if she resurfaced. Close the loop. But things had shifted. Laura had been clear: the evidence came first. The handover was arranged, and what she carried took priority - blood samples, lab records, photos of the Cambridge Bio trial victims. All of it packed tight in the left pannier.

There was a small chance that the girl could identify her from the time they spent together on the London rooftop. A small one, but a risk nevertheless, and she hated risks. Not to mention unfinished business. But she could live with it. She would have to.

For now.

And if she gunned it, she'd be back in Madrid by dusk and make Julia's opera after all.

Part Four

90

Saturday 19th November

'*EXCITEMENT IS MOUNTING AT PARTY HEADQUARTERS,*' announced the news presenter, '*as the candidates arrive for the final rehearsal.*'

The screen cut to a close-up of Walter Crane MP arriving in a black Mercedes and waving to a small crowd as he walked up the steps, flanked by aides. The debate was now less than forty-eight hours away.

Frank switched off the TV and chuckled.

'He doesn't know what's about to hit him. He'll be toast by next week.'

Cal didn't answer. He stared blankly at the dead screen for a few moments, then tried to get up, clutching the arm of the chair for support.

'Easy, old man,' Frank said, coming over to help him. He caught Cal's elbow to steady him. Cal shook him off and hobbled toward the sideboard, pouring water with a shaky hand.

'I could have done that, you know.'

Cal ignored him. Frank crossed to the window. Far below, the lights of London twinkled silently from a million windows, above a stream of red and white tail lights marking the Embankment. A siren rose and fell in the distance. They were in a suite on the top floor of the Park Plaza Riverbank, courtesy of the Security Service, from where there was a fine view of Lambeth Bridge and, beyond it, the Houses of Parliament.

'I hear that the Spanish are looking into what happened,' Frank said, still watching the city. 'Will the Met police want to interview you again?'

'Up to MI5, I guess.' Cal said, limping back to his chair. One arm was in bandages, and his leg was in a bionic-looking black metal brace. 'As you know, they leaned on them not to pursue it previously. However, considering where we are now, I imagine it's a given.'

'Presumably they haven't listened to the recording yet?'

He shook his head. 'No one has. Kate's taking it to Hart tomorrow, once she's heard it.'

There was a knock on the door. Frank went to open it.

'Hello boys,' said Sofie, pushing Kate in a wheelchair. 'How's the patient?'

'Speak of the devil,' Frank said.

'Patient's fine,' grunted Cal, struggling to get up.

'Sit down before you break something.' She planted a kiss on his cheek. 'You look like hell.'

'So this is the famous Kate,' smiled Frank. 'We've not met in person before.'

They shook hands. Sofie wheeled Kate into the room, while Frank went to the minibar to pour drinks.

'So,' Cal said. 'How's the investigation going?'

Kate locked her wheels into place. 'Slowly. You know what Thames is like.'

'I thought I did. Until a week ago.'

'Yes, well, we're very embarrassed about what

happened. What we put you through.'

'Embarrassed? Not sure that covers it.' A beat. 'Did you ever work out who Gebler was working for?'

'We're still looking into it. I'm not really supposed to talk about it.' She hesitated. 'Can I rely on your discretion?'

'Discretion's my second name.'

'We think he was in the pay of the Russians.'

Cal's jaw dropped.

'Really? But how was he able to co-opt the Gibraltar police?'

'You mean the plainclothes guy who was with him? Evans?'

'Exactly.'

Kate looked at him.

'Well, he was still, officially, an MI5 agent, remember?'

'But he must have had clearance for something like that from above?'

She shifted uncomfortably. 'As I say, I can't give you any more details at the moment. One thing we do know, however.'

Cal raised an eyebrow. Kate turned to her friend.

'The woman who was impersonating you in Gibraltar, Sofie, was likely the same person who attacked us on the boat and subsequently tried to kill you on the roof of your flat. A GRU operative called Tasha Mazour. Or at least that's her birth name, the name listed by the GRU. She uses several aliases, we understand.'

'So did you figure out what that note meant?' said Cal. 'The one we found in her hotel room? The date referenced was tomorrow, wasn't it?'

Kate looked blank. 'I've no idea. I passed it up the chain. Hart will have had it analysed.'

Sophie whistled. 'So she and Gebler were working

together. Wow.'

'Looks that way.'

'Odd Gebler didn't mention her,' Cal said. 'He genuinely seemed to think that it was me who had killed the doctor.'

Kate shrugged.

Sofie cut them off. 'Enough talk. Shall we put it on? That's what Kate's come for, right?'

Frank glanced at Cal.

'Sure,' he said.

Frank walked over to the desk and flicked open a laptop, while Sofie sat down on the floor against the wall next to Kate's wheelchair, flinging her shoes off with a flick of her feet.

'Ready?'

They nodded. The audio began to roll.

To begin with, there was a hiss of static, followed by silence. It was broken by a knocking sound and a muffled man's voice in the background:

'Are we on?'

'Sure.'

'So where do you want me to start?'

'That's the doctor,' Cal cut in. 'Alex Shelton.'

'Who turned out to be my father's boyfriend,' Sofie added softly.

Kate flinched. 'Shit, Sofie!'

'Sssh!' hissed Cal.

'OK, Doctor Shelton, this is what I want you to do. It won't take long. First of all, please explain how you got involved in this drug programme.'

'Call me Alex, please. But before we start, I'm curious. Your accent - I can't place it - is it American? Were you educated there?'

The woman's reply was unintelligible. However, Alex

must have been satisfied with the answer, because when he next spoke, nothing further was mentioned. Cal and Sofie had already run through this initial section. They listened in silence as the doctor explained the history of his involvement with what he called Cambridge Bio's 'Imagine Programme.' When he had finished, there was the sound of shuffling papers.

'Now,' came the female voice. *'This list. Can you explain to me the significance of the codes?'*

'Sure. There...'

'Hey, pause it a minute,' said Cal. He pulled a document from his jacket pocket and handed it to Kate. 'This is the one she's talking about. It's the same list we found in Sofie's flat. The one we took to your boss.'

She examined it. 'What does it mean?'

'You'll see. Just listen.'

Frank rewound a short way and restarted the recording.

The woman began again: *'This list. Can you explain to me the significance of the codes?'*

'Sure. There are three letters there, as you can see. Always in the same order, but some in upper case, some in lower case, some with a plus after them, some with a minus, some with an X. It's pretty logical, really. The three letters, N, S and D, each stand for one of the three chemicals in the brain which we know to affect mood. N for norepinephrine, S for serotonin, and D for dopamine. There's also an ID key, which references the specific chemical cocktail that each patient receives.'

There was a short pause. It sounded as if the doctor was pouring a drink.

'Now. This column on the left. This, very crudely, is a form of short-code analysis of where the subject starts from. A capital means their brain levels of that particular chemical are normal, a small letter means they are deficient in some way. The more detailed analysis can

be referenced from the ID key. These chemicals are very volatile. Most of us show an imbalance or excess of one or another. That is what makes us moody, or irritable, or hyped up, or optimistic. Being in love floods the brain with a mass of them. These levels will have been monitored over a very long period, and only suggest susceptibility, rather than static state, for they are obviously changing constantly. They are, if you like, very simplistic personality profiles.'

'The column of names on the left is the subjects themselves, while the column to the far right is a list of their prescribing doctors. The subjects are all HIV sufferers, and supposedly taking a new AIDS maintenance drug that Cambridge Bio has developed. They are also prescribed Cambridge Bio's main antidepressant, Imagine, as a way to even out mood swings. What they don't realise, what even the doctors, in most cases, don't know, is that in place of Imagine, they are being given a placebo, and in place of the AIDS maintenance drug, they are being fed an untested compound whose working title is Imagine 2. It is, in fact, a highly refined successor to Imagine, still being trialled. In short, they are being unwittingly used as guinea pigs, while all the time thinking they are taking an AIDS drug.'

'You see, Sofie, when you are suffering from AIDS, you will latch onto any new medicine that comes along, and the monitoring they receive only helps reinforce the belief that they are at the cutting edge of AIDS research. They are only too keen to be involved, especially in Africa, where most of this research is going on.'

He paused, and there was the rustle of papers again, and the sound of something being slid across the desk.

'But that's just background. These are what I'd like you to have.'

'What are they?'

'Blood samples. It's the hard proof you need.'

Frank pressed pause for a second time and turned to Sofie and Kate.

'So was that the proof those two chemists were meeting you about? The blood samples that they were keen to get to you?'

'Exactly.'

'But there was no sign of them at the farm?'

'No,' said Sofie. 'The Russian woman must have taken them. We found nothing on Gebler.'

Frank restarted the recording. Alex Shelton was speaking again.

'This compound, which is effectively a next-generation Monoamine Oxidase Inhibitor, was being given to them in varying strengths, each made up specifically for that subject, and that is what the second column, after the names, refers to. You see here? The minus sign signifies a chemical inhibitor, the plus sign a chemical stimulant. N-S+D+ means that the subject's norepinephrine level will be inhibited, their serotonin and dopamine levels stimulated. Each, as I say, is individually mixed for that subject, like a cocktail, using the brain as a test bed to see what happens, and these blood samples will back that up.

For example, if you follow the line across...here...let's take this name. He starts at NsD. The next column tells us what they are giving him: N-S+D-; and, theoretically at least, he ends up nSd, which is exactly what the third column signifies. Where you get an X in the 'cocktail' column, this means they left that chemical alone. See? This woman started as NSD - most well-balanced, it looks like. They give her N-XD- and she becomes nSd -1 can't say for certain, but something like depressed, angry and negative.'

There was a sharp intake of breath from across the room.

'Christ,' Frank whispered. 'It's like a graphic equaliser for the human brain.'

'And where is this leading, Doctor Shelton? Alex?'

There was a long pause, as if the doctor was pondering something. Eventually, he spoke.

'It's leading to the ultimate happy drug, Sofie. When they get it right. The perfect cosmetic. It will change our personalities to order,

rectify, if you will, our deficiencies, and, as here, it will be tailor-made for each patient. It will be like a neurological MSG, making life taste better. Of course, it will be expensive.' He paused. *'That's the theory, at least. But there are ethical problems. At least twelve have died because of it already. Maybe more. Some of these subjects simply... go over the edge. It is not only that these are tests, but to get the very best results, it seems the scientists conducting these trials will push their subjects to the very limit. To find out where the boundaries are, as it were.'*

'But they're all dying anyway in that part of the world.'

'Well, that's where you are wrong, Sofie.'

Frank glanced at Sofie, but she didn't flinch.

'With the drugs they've got today, these people can live as full a life as any AIDS patient in Europe. But no one will fund it. They're expendable. I mean, if an AIDS patient in Kenya dies in mysterious circumstances, goes berserk, kills himself - so what? No one bothers to do much investigating; everybody knows how much strain these people are under. And we have all heard Crane's views, haven't we? It's scary, he could become our next prime minister.'

'But even if we were to accept this, which of course we can't, there are others who suffer as well. Other victims of their psychotic behaviour. And as I say, they could easily live a long life while managing Aids. But they are being condemned, in many cases, to suffer, and some to die, because someone says their lives are worthless, and it is all done under the cover of a fiction, exploiting their desperation to find some hope of curing themselves, to live. Even the doctors are not aware of what is going on. I am a doctor, and I was prescribing this stuff for a while, and I didn't know.'

There was a brief silence. When the doctor spoke again, it was with an altogether different tone.

'As I think you understand, am I right?'

'What do you mean?'

'Your father.'

'What about my father?'

'I assume you were aware that we were friends?'

There was another pause. Cal glanced at Sofie. Her face was a mask.

'No.'

'Oh, I...er...we, Harry and I, assumed that was what spurred you to investigate.'

'Really? My father was involved?'

'He was one of the first victims, Sofie. I'm ashamed to say that it was I who initially gave the drug to him. Surely those poor chemists pointed that out to you when you met up with them?'

'I…er…don't think they did.'

The sound of Sofie's impersonator floundering was electrifying. She had made a crucial error.

There was a new suspicion in the doctor's voice when he next spoke. The first dawning of the awful possibility that the impostor his lawyer must have alerted him to, after Cal and Sofie had been to see him, might not be an impostor at all, but in fact the real Sofie James, and that here, before him, was ... who?

'It was part of the post-mortem. Suicide, I think they called it. Held two weeks after he died on Christmas Day.'

It was a simple trick, and she fell for it. How could she not?

'I see.'

There was an abrupt silence.

'You're not Sofie James at all, are you?'

There was an edge to the doctor's tone.

'Sofie's father died in February.'

A chair was scraped back.

'I think we're done with this interview,' said the woman.

'So... who are you?'

A door opened and shut. Silence. This was followed by

some indistinguishable sounds in the background and sudden footsteps. Alex shouted something.

More footsteps, running this time. The banging of the door, a loud cry. Followed, unexpectedly, by a muffled, silenced shot, and the sound of a glass smashing. And something nearer at hand - a frantic scrape of the table and the clatter of the recording device tumbling to the floor.

A woman's voice followed it, then a second shot, a yell, and the thud of a body falling.

Frank reached for the laptop.

Cal held out a hand. '*Wait.*'

The silence continued for over a minute, background noises barely distinguishable. Finally, there was the click of a door opening, and someone came into the room.

Cal motioned to Frank to switch it off.

'That's the sound of Sofie coming in.'

'Jesus, that was heavy,' said Frank, almost under his breath. They remained silent for a long while. It was only gradually that they became aware of Sofie curled up on the floor. She was quietly sobbing.

Kate leant over from her chair and touched her shoulder.

'Are you OK?'

Sofie nodded.

'Are you sure you're up for this?'

She wiped her eyes with her sleeve.

'I'm sorry. Yes, I'll be ready.'

'Have you prepared what you're going to say?'

'Pretty much.'

'Remember, you need to pick up the Sunday Times press pass from the Queen Elizabeth Centre at least an hour before it kicks off.'

Sofie smiled weakly.

'I'm bloody nervous. This time it's me who's the impostor.'

Kate shook her head. 'You'll smash it, I know you will! This is the start of a glittering new journalism career.'

They lapsed into silence.

'Do you realise,' Sofie said, 'that it's exactly one month since we met in that coffee shop in Islington?'

Kate shifted in her chair, grimacing with the effort. 'A lot has happened since then. I'm not sure I'll ever forgive myself for what I put you through.'

Sofie sighed. Not quite ready yet to absolve her friend, perhaps, but despite everything, grateful that she got the result she wanted.

'One thing I wondered, though,' she said. 'Did you never regret letting go of your own career?'

'You mean my journalism?'

Sofie nodded. 'Yes. Giving it up for MI5.'

Kate thought for a moment. 'Sometimes. But listen, this isn't about me anymore. This is your story to tell now.'

She smiled, softer now. 'Doll, you deserve it.'

91

Sunday 20th November

Tasha's early morning flight from Madrid landed at Heathrow a few minutes before nine.

In the arrivals hall, a driver held up a sign with a name she hadn't used in years. It was a shame, she thought as they headed for Oxford, that she no longer had her Kawasaki to get about on. She'd been forced to get rid of it after what happened at the girl's flat. Too many people had seen her ride off from the scene of the crime.

Besides, she was only staying for the day. Her return flight to Madrid was booked for that evening. She travelled light: no laptop, no change of clothes. Just a slim black backpack containing the blood samples and a couple of documents she'd taken from the doctor's house.

The driver dropped her outside the Ashmolean Museum just after ten. Her rendez-vous with Laura was not until two. She was early on purpose. There was something very special she'd come to see - something she'd meant to visit for years but never made time for. Until now.

She climbed the steps of the grand facade, passed underneath the museum's massive columns, and went up to the desk to buy her ticket.

'You'll need to check your backpack in the cloakroom over there,' said the official, pointing.

Laura had told her not to let the blood samples out of her sight. Tasha hesitated. But only for a second. This was the Ashmolean, after all. She smiled at the irony. The place was full of dried blood, most of it over three thousand years old. She handed over her backpack and pocketed the receipt.

She entered the first of the galleries with a growing sense of anticipation. She had no interest in marble busts or crumbling amphorae. The statues of half-naked Roman generals and anatomically detailed slave boys held zero appeal. She walked past them without pause, her boots quiet on the polished floor.

She was headed for the gallery at the back. The one titled *Life and Death in Ancient Egypt*. The light dimmed as she entered. The room was empty save for a bored museum guard who barely glanced up.

Tasha stepped toward the long glass case in the centre of the room. And there she was.

Djed-djehuty-iuef-ankh.

The name was a mouthful, but the woman herself - if that's what you could call her mummified corpse - was stunning. Three nested coffins, perfectly preserved, a cascade of linen wrappings and delicate shawls laid over her like the veil of a long-dead bride. Beside her, the Canopic jars stood sentinel: alabaster vessels shaped like jackals, falcons, and human heads. Inside were the shrivelled remains of lungs, liver, stomach, intestines, all neatly plucked and stored for the journey to the afterlife.

Tasha stood still in front of the glass case for several minutes before retreating to a bench, legs crossed and silent.

She let her mind drift. What would it take to mummify someone today? Realistically. The embalming fluid could be sourced. The process - washing, draining, and injecting into the carotid artery - was a matter of precision and patience. Messy, sure. But not beyond her, given the right setting. And the right subject. One with elegant bone structure, smooth skin, and a beauty that remained after death. Especially in death. Not as easy to come by as you would think in her line of work. But occasionally, you found someone perfect.

She smiled faintly before, finally, tearing herself away. She had an appointment to keep, and judging by her What3Words app, it would take her at least thirty minutes to walk there.

She collected her backpack from the cloakroom attendent, exited the museum and headed north.

92

James Hart didn't go to church that morning.

Instead, he told his wife he had a work thing - an urgent matter that couldn't wait. He kissed her cheek, promised to be back in time for dinner, and stepped out of their Holland Park townhouse wearing a sleek cashmere coat and trainers, and carrying a large holdall. Inside, he had packed a selection of sandwiches, a miniature Wi-Fi microphone, a recording device, a set of headphones, a bright yellow taser gun, and a change of clothes, including a brand new pair of brogues still wrapped in their cellophane.

He caught a black cab to Paddington Station and took the next train west to Oxford. He arrived just before ten. From there, a local bus took him north, out of the city proper. He got off at a stop on Banbury Road and walked the rest of the way along a narrow lane edged with mud and frost-tipped grass. His shoes weren't built for it, but he managed.

He reached the place well before Laura was due, which gave him plenty of time to prepare.

The place she had picked for the meeting, according to

the note that Cal had found in the Russian's hotel room in Gibraltar, suited him perfectly. A boarded-up restaurant on the banks of a small river, it was surrounded by builders' material, in the middle of restoration, and at least half a mile from the main road. And being a Sunday, there was no one about.

The day was crisp but dry, with shafts of sunlight from a pale winter sun filtering through the willows. A few punts bobbed around on the water, trussed up in canvas covers. Otherwise, he only had ducks for company.

The clue that Cal Harrison had sent to Kate - *town, tooth, town* - led to some riverside tables with benches on the outdoor terrace of the restaurant. It was Laura's fatal mistake to use Hart's own method of sharing meeting coordinates, one she'd obviously learned from him. The difference being, he would never communicate them unencrypted. She'd played right into his hands.

Fixing a Wi-Fi microphone under one of the four tables was easy. The problem was that Laura and her guest might settle down at any one of them, and he couldn't be sure that the sensitive microphone he'd brought with him would pick up their voices cleanly enough if they chose the furthest away, given the light breeze and the sporadic noise of the local wildlife. For the best results, he realised, it would be an advantage to have them pick the table he'd wired.

He walked the perimeter, thinking. Then his eyes landed on a workman's shed tucked behind the building. Beside it was a pile of old scaffolding - tubes and clamps streaked with rust, half-buried in gravel. It gave him his answer. Piece by piece, he ferried them over, annoyed at himself for not having dressed for the operation, carefully piling them up on three of the four tables, as if the workmen were preparing to erect a structure around the building. That left one table clear. So, unless Laura and the woman she was meeting decided to stand or walk away to conduct their business somewhere else entirely, the chances were that they would settle down at that one. The table he had rigged.

Satisfied, he turned his attention to where he should base himself. The shed seemed the obvious candidate. It was unlocked, but inside the door was a key on a hook, and he found he was able to secure it from the inside. So even if Laura made a pass of her surroundings, to check she was alone, she wouldn't be able to gain access, and would assume that it was no more than it appeared: a place the contractor stored his tools.

There was the added bonus of a chair to sit on and a chink of light where the door met the doorframe, so he had a clear view of the area outside.

He spent the next half hour testing the mic and positioning it correctly, until his voice came through clearly, even with the occasional rustle of breeze or birdcall. It would do. He wiped the chair clean with a tissue, locked himself in, sat down, pulled out a Tupperware box from his holdall, and unsnapped the lid.

Egg mayo. He settled down to eat. And wait.

93

He didn't have to wait long.

A few minutes past half one, Hart heard the soft crunch of gravel. Getting up from the chair, he glued his eye to the crack in the doorframe. Laura Boyd stepped into view. She was alone.

She stopped and scanned the area. He watched her cross to the restaurant and rattle the door. She was cautious. She peered through the window. Apparently satisfied, she walked down to the river's edge and glanced upstream before returning to the terrace. After a moment's hesitation, she sat down at the table that Hart had prepped and pulled out her phone.

He slipped on his headphones. Through the faint static, he heard the tap-tap-tap of her fingers. She was sending a message. Then, nothing. Just the lapping of the river and the breeze.

They both waited, Laura oblivious to his presence, barely twenty yards away.

Fifteen minutes later, another crunch. A second figure appeared on the lane. Female, late twenties, tall, lean, cropped hair, black leather jacket. More Nordic in appearance than Russian. One strap of a backpack was slung over her shoulder.

Hart had never seen Tasha Mazour before, but the posture, the eyes, the tension in her jaw - she matched every description he'd ever heard of the ghost from the GRU's unit 29155. She surveyed the scene like a soldier entering enemy terrain, then gave Laura a stiff nod.

'Random place to meet,' she said in Russian.

'I had a meeting in Oxford,' Laura replied. 'It was convenient.'

Tasha glanced along the empty terrace. 'Restaurant not open?'

'Afraid not.'

'So no coffee then.' She sniffed. 'Well, I've got what you asked for.'

She slung the backpack onto the table and pulled out a thick folder. Laura watched her every move.

'Did you see the girl? Or Harrison?'

Tasha shook her head. 'No. But I dealt with the doctor, so you won't have any more trouble from that direction.'

She removed a small plastic pouch.

'Blood samples,' explained Tasha. 'Without those, no one can prove the drug trial even happened.'

Laura turned it over, nodding slowly.

'Excellent work.'

'What are you going to do with them?'

'Moscow will decide.'

Tasha raised an eyebrow. 'So your man's in the clear now?'

'Hopefully.'

'I read this morning the leadership debate's tomorrow.'

'That's right.'

‘Then I wish you good luck.’

‘There is no luck,’ Laura said with a faint smile. ‘Only preparation. You remember what they taught us at the dacha?’

Tasha’s expression flickered, something bitter behind her eyes.

‘What about the girl?’

Laura didn’t answer right away.

‘I could have stayed, you know,’ Tasha added. ‘I could have dealt with her myself. If it wasn’t for this…’ She gestured at the folder on the table.

‘Third time lucky?’

Tasha ignored the barb. ‘Well?’

‘Listen, she’s been dealt with. Gebler was out there.’

Tasha’s eyes hardened. ‘Are you sure?’

Laura shrugged. ‘I’ve heard nothing to the contrary. My orders were to leave it to them. As for us, we have what we need now. For which I thank you. Sincerely.’

‘So that’s it? We’re done?’

Laura stood and held out her hand. ‘Keep safe. Until the next time.’

Tasha re-shouldered her now-empty backpack.

‘In that case, I’ll fuck off back to Madrid.’ He hesitated. ‘I assume the money will be in my account by the end of today?’

Laura smiled. ‘You have my word.’ A beat. ‘And by the way, it’s been a pleasure. After all these years.’

Tasha gave a curt nod and walked away.

From his hiding place, Hart watched her disappear up the lane. With his official hat on, he knew it was a missed opportunity. Taking out Tasha Mazour would earn him medals in several Western capitals. But that wasn’t why he was here - and doing it now would set off alarms that even he couldn't silence. Still, he'd got something no one else in Western intelligence had: a close visual. That alone would buy him credit.

He switched his attention back to Laura. How long would she wait before following? He had rehearsed several scenarios in his mind. She didn't appear ready to move and had sat down again, poring over the documents. Finally, she tidied them away into the plastic sleeve and placed them carefully in her bag. He heard her tap out another message. She stood to leave.

Hart waited until she passed the shed. Then he grabbed the taser, turned the key, and stepped into the sunlight.

'Hello, Laura.'

She stopped dead on the track.

He aimed at her back. 'I'll be having that, thank you very much.'

She swung round, a look of astonishment on her face.

'Apollo!' she gasped. 'What the hell are *you* doing here?'

Hart reached out with his free hand and yanked the bag away.

'I could ask you the same.'

She stared. 'How did you find…?'

'Let's not get into that.' He tossed the bag behind him. 'I'm afraid this is the end of the road.'

Her eyes narrowed. 'What does that mean?'

'If your colleague there hadn't screwed up on the boat, things might be different. But Crane's finished now. By tomorrow evening, he will have withdrawn from the race.'

She looked confused.

'That's absurd! We have all the evidence.' She nodded at the bag. 'It's all in there. Take a look. The two chemists are dead. The doctor who was leaking this is dead. Crane's clear.'

'That's as may be. But you forget one thing. The girl. Sofie James.'

Laura's expression shifted.

'Don't tell me that you haven't eliminated her? You assured me…'

'Sadly not. She and that security consultant of yours, Harrison, not only did they evade us in Paris, but when we tracked them down to Spain, something happened. I don't have the full details, but Gebler was killed.'

She reeled. 'They killed Gebler?'

'I'm sorry, Laura, it's over. This evidence is too late. Spanish police are investigating. It won't take long before they figure out who he was.'

'Exactly,' said Laura. 'One of your agents. That doesn't look good for you either, does it?'

He smiled. 'Ah, well, that's where you are wrong. Who else, other than you and Gebler, knows about our collaboration?'

'Tasha. Moscow. Plenty of people.'

'Have they seen me?'

'No, but…'

'Do they know who I am?'

'They know your code name. APOLLO.'

He smirked. 'My code name. Ah yes. Well, I'd better change it, no?'

She stared at him. Hart could see an awful realisation beginning to dawn in her eyes.

'So what do you intend to do?' she said softly.

'I'm going to kill you.'

'What, with that thing?' she scoffed, gesturing at the taser that was trained on her head.

'Let's make this painless, shall we?' he said, ignoring her. He flicked his head towards the river. 'I can drug you and drown you. Or I can simply drown you. Which do you prefer?'

He raised an eyebrow. His pale eyes were cold and dead, with not a flicker of the humour his voice suggested. She stood frozen to the spot.

When she didn't reply, he said:

'Tomorrow, perhaps the next day, or maybe next week, your body will be found downriver. Another unfortunate suicide, another person with a mental illness who has walked into the river and drowned themselves. The pressures of the campaign were too much for Laura Boyd. Or we can invent some embezzling you were caught up in, discovered after your death.'

He took a menacing step forward.

'So. Which is it going to be?'

Suddenly, she made a lunge for him, but he sidestepped and fired the Taser. Twin barbs arrowed into her neck. As soon as they found their mark, she twisted in pain, her face contorted, muscles paralysed. She staggered and fell, and he caught her as she hit the ground.

He kept the current flowing, one hand on the Taser, the other pulling a cloth from his pocket. He pressed it to her mouth and nose. In seconds, the chloroform had knocked her out cold.

He knelt beside her, switched off the Taser and pulled out the barbs. He inspected the puncture wounds. A sharp-eyed pathologist might ask some awkward questions, but he doubted they would link them to a Taser. More likely, cuts from rocks in the river. Certainly better than shooting her, he thought. A drowned corpse was one thing. A body with a gunshot wound was quite another.

Quickly, he dragged her to the riverbank and slid her into the water until her head was fully submerged. He held her there for a full three minutes, her blond hair floating free on the surface of the river, timing it on his Rolex, until he was sure she was dead. Then he hauled her out and frisked her for her phone. He slid it into his pocket and eased her body back into the current, wading in after her. It was shallow and muddy, and he had to tread carefully to avoid slipping. He floated her towards a small eddy under an overhanging willow tree, far enough from the path to be hidden from view, and wedged her beneath two rocks, so that from a distance, if someone did happen to glance in that direction, the shapeless form resembled a washed-up sack.

Finally, satisfied that she wasn't about to go anywhere unless there was a storm, he clambered out and returned to the shed to change into dry trousers. He unwrapped his new pair of brogues, removed his sodden trainers, wrapped them in the discarded cellophane, and stuffed them in his hold-all. Then he tied the laces of his new shoes. It was a moment of pure bliss that he would never stop getting off on: a brand new pair of shoes.

He retrieved the microphone from under the table. After a last look around to make sure he'd left nothing behind, he departed, his new brogues squeaking as he went. It was 3:00 pm.

He'd be home in time for dinner.

94

Monday 21st November

Sofie arrived at the Queen Elizabeth Centre a full two hours before the televised debate was due to begin. Parliament Square was already buzzing - camera crews unloading kit, aides rushing between cars and side entrances, security everywhere.

As soon as she'd picked up her Sunday Times credentials from the press office, she made her way to the auditorium on the ground floor.

The space was vast. Three-point key lights had been rigged up to focus on six separate podiums on the stage: five for the candidates, three men and two women, and a sixth for the chair of the debate, a moderator from the BBC.

A few journalists were already clustered toward the front, deep in conversation. She clocked them: familiar faces from Westminster briefings and media panels. She wasn't one of them. Not yet. She slid into a seat just behind, opened her notes, and pretended to read.

But it was hard to focus. Not least, because she couldn't help overhearing that, according to rumour, Walter Crane's Chief of Staff, Laura Boyd, had gone missing. Sofie remembered Cal talking about her. Did it have something to do with what was about to unfold? If Cal had been with her, she knew exactly what he'd say: he didn't believe in coincidences.

She settled down in her seat to steady her nerves and study the programme for the evening. The format was familiar. The show would kick off with a rehearsed opening statement from each of the candidates. These would be followed by a set of pre-scripted questions from the Chair, put to each of them in turn. That would take up the first hour.

After a short intermission, the next forty-five minutes would cover questions from the audience, a carefully chosen mix of ages, socio-economic groups, and professions. Time would be allowed to each candidate in between these questions for free debate on any subject raised, and for rebuttals to challenges by their peers.

Finally, five questions would be asked by pre-selected members of the Press, each of whom was allowed one question, with a supplementary if necessary, to pose to a single candidate. Crane had been assigned to the Sunday Times. In return for giving them an exclusive to break the story the following morning, under Sofie's byline, she and Kate had managed to secure her the privilege of asking it.

She looked back down at her notes. Tried to breathe. She couldn't remember being this nervous since her Royal College of Music grade six piano exams. That day, at least, she'd only had the examiner to worry about. This time, ten million people would be watching. Live. And across London, Kate, Cal, and Frank were waiting, drinks in hand, ready to watch from Kate's flat before taking her out for a celebration dinner.

Assuming there was something to celebrate.

Slowly, the hall began to fill up. Technicians scuttled about making last-minute adjustments to the lights, and the BBC moderator chatted amiably with the stage manager and a few members of the public. The candidates were in makeup.

A woman appeared beside her, clipboard in hand.

'Sofie James? Sunday Times?'

'That's me,' Sofie said, smiling. For the first time, the three journalists in front of her became aware of her presence. They swivelled round, evidently intrigued to see who this newbie was.

'We'll be starting in fifteen. Let me take you to your seat.'

She followed her down the aisle. The five selected press had been allocated the first row on the right. The others were already there, wearing lanyards with heavyweight names: Mail, Guardian, Sun, Herald. They looked up as she arrived.

'You must be new,' said the man next to her, glancing at her badge. 'John Crace. Daily Mail.'

'Sofie James.'

'You steal this from Roger?' He laughed. 'Thought he had the slot.'

She smiled tightly. 'Nope. They assigned me.'

He raised an eyebrow but didn't press. The unspoken question hung in the air: *Why? We've never seen her before.*

The lights dimmed. A hush fell. The moderator stepped forward.

A short housekeeping pep-talk followed for the public audience. No heckling, no jeering, respect at all times. Clapping should only come at the beginning and the end of the show. Finally, the music started, and the five candidates filed on stage. The audience clapped. The moderator introduced them, and the opening statements began.

It was the usual back and forth. Sofie listened to them intently, every nerve jangling. As the debate wore on, there was much questioning around some of Crane's more extreme views, with a string of personal attacks from his colleagues. He, too, seemed on edge. The hot stage lights made his skin glisten, and from time to time, she saw him wipe away a bead of sweat with a handkerchief.

They got through the moderator's questions without any major howlers. Crane, it appeared, was popular with the audience but unpopular with his colleagues. But he was clearly out of sorts. Sofie wondered whether it was the business about his chief of staff that had unsettled him. Eventually, the fifteen-minute break arrived, and despite being warned to stay in their seats, she bolted for the toilets.

Inside, she leaned over the sink, gulped water into her cupped hand, and splashed her face. Breathe, Sofie, breathe. In the mirror, she studied herself. She'd had a new haircut. Gone was the ponytail: she sported a fringe now, more polished. Kate's friend had done her makeup, and for the first time in weeks, she didn't look like someone who'd been running for her life.

She reapplied her lipstick, exhaled, and returned to her seat. The Mail guy gave her a look.

The audience segment began. Pre-approved questions on the cost of living, the NHS, immigration. Then something sharper - a question from an LGBT campaigner about a rollback of gay marriage rights in another country. The candidates condemned it. Everyone but Crane, who hedged.

Then came a question about prisons from a retired prison officer. Crane came alive.

'Prison reform,' he said, 'is essential. We spend way too

much on keeping offenders locked up. Reoffending is rampant. We need accountability.'

He leaned into it.

'New systems will be put in place - AI-driven tools to identify individuals most likely to commit violent crime before it happens. Prevention is better than cure.'

A ripple of unease moved through the crowd. Another candidate pounced, accusing him of supporting a surveillance state. Jeers broke out. The moderator struggled to regain control.

A moment later, things shifted. A final softball from a teacher: Which country would you most like to visit, and why?

Crane: 'Argentina. Always wanted to learn the tango.'

The crowd laughed. The heat dialled down. The candidates relaxed. They were on the home straight.

Except Sofie knew that one of them wasn't, not by a long stretch. For him, it had not even begun.

Finally came the press questions. There was no script, no preview. The moderator didn't even know what was coming. The man from the Sun went first - something about immigration policy inconsistencies.

Then, the Glasgow Herald and the Guardian.

Her stomach dropped. She was going to be last. Of course she was. Crane was the lightning rod. They'd want to finish on him.

The Daily Mail guy was next. A question on one candidate's voting record - safe stuff.

And then -

'And now, our final question,' the moderator said, 'from Sofie James of the Sunday Times, for Walter Crane.'

Her heart kicked in. The cameras swung to her. Twin red lights blinking like sniper dots.

She swallowed. Shit, she thought to herself, here goes. The events of the past month suddenly flashed across her consciousness. She'd been shot at on the River Thames; she'd been attacked on the roof of her flat; she'd fled from a booby-trapped car and a moving sightseeing boat in Paris, and been chased by the police in West London; and, as if that wasn't bad enough, she'd killed a man in Spain. It was already starting to feel like a terrible, ghastly dream. And now this. Perhaps she'd wake up.

'Walter Crane,' she began, 'I'd like to ask you about AIDS in Africa.'

A pause.

What? A ripple passed through the room. Puzzled glances. What was this? Was *that* her question?

Crane smiled, clearly caught off guard.

'I'd like to know whether you intend to maintain the UK's foreign aid commitments - specifically, the millions we spend fighting the AIDS epidemic in East Africa. You've previously suggested you'd cut those funds.'

He hesitated. Just for a moment.

'Yes, well,' he began, smoothing his voice, 'it is a tragedy. No question. There are many who've suffered, through no fault of their own. Particularly in places like Russia, who now have the highest rates in the world. Babies, drug victims, people born with haemophilia who've received transfusions contaminated by sexual deviants. We must support those innocent victims. And yes, I'd review aid packages to ensure help reaches those who deserve it.'

Sexual deviants. It landed like a bomb. Time for her sucker-punch supplementary. She struck.

'In that case,' she said, her voice icy calm, 'as the founder and Chairman of Cambridge Bio, can you tell us why you authorised secret clinical trials of an experimental psychiatric drug - trials conducted on AIDS patients in East Africa without their consent - trials that led to multiple deaths, including suicides?'

The silence hit like a gunshot.

For a full second, the room held its breath.

Then all hell broke loose.

Epilogue

A year later

IN FRANK AND EMILY'S GARDEN IN SUFFOLK, AUTUMN colours abounded. A riot of anemones and snapdragons jostled for space with clumps of dahlias along the boundary wall, and beyond, across the river, Cal could glimpse a line of sailing boats taking advantage of the fine October weather.

Emily had roasted a chicken - her passive-aggressive version of diplomacy - and now she, Frank, and Cal were slouched in front of the fire, half-talking, half-reading the papers. Mostly avoiding what had remained unsaid for far too long.

She brought it up anyway.

'So, Cal,' she said, curling her legs under her like a cat preparing to pounce, 'remind me how long 'six months' lasts these days?'

He looked up.

'Because, correct me if I'm wrong, you've been in the caravan now for eighteen.'

He smiled politely. 'It's rent-controlled,' he joked.

Emily gave him a look like she was trying to peel him

with her eyes.

Who could blame her? He hadn't exactly been proactive about finding alternative accommodation, and had had to cancel more than one viewing and lost numerous deals as a result of being suddenly called away. He made a mental note to get it sorted before the year was out. Besides, he didn't fancy another damp, dark winter with only a leaky wood-burning stove to keep him warm. Last winter, he'd gone from November to March smelling of wood smoke.

He returned to the newspaper. The lead article was about how the mapping app What3Words was helping aid workers in Africa. Which reminded him. He put the paper down and glanced across at Frank.

'You know that mystery message Sofie and I discovered in the Russian's hotel bedroom?'

Frank looked up. 'Vaguely. You mean the one about teeth?'

'Yeah, town, tooth, town. It didn't make sense at the time. We passed it on to Hart at MI5 and then forgot all about it.'

'So? What of it?'

'Well, I think it was a map coordinate. I was playing around with What3Words the other day, and I put it into the app just out of curiosity, and I got a hit. It turns out to be a location in Oxford. Just one hundred metres away from where Laura Boyd's body was discovered.'

Frank exhaled. 'Blimey.'

Cal pursed his lips. 'Think I should pass it on to Hart?'

'Nah, what's the point? It's old news now. Besides, if it was that easy for you to crack it, MI5 are bound to have figured it out at the time. You're probably telling them nothing they don't know already.'

They fell silent.

'Mmm,' said Cal eventually. 'You're probably right.'

He was about to float the idea of a riverside walk, knowing Emily wouldn't budge from the sofa, when Frank's office phone started to ring.

He struggled to swallow a smirk. How long would it take her to get involved? Sure enough, there was an imperceptible flicker of her eyes and the beginnings of a scowl. Finally, she could hold it in no longer. She flung down her magazine angrily.

'Oh, for goodness' sake, I wish you'd take your office somewhere else! Don't they know it's Sunday?'

Frank got up to take the call. Emily glared at Cal.

'Probably that dodgy Bulgarian, saying he needs a shipment of SAM missiles by yesterday.'

Cal laughed. 'Em, come on, you know he only deals in comms gear. He's not an arms trader.'

'That's what he says.'

He shrugged. 'He's your husband, Emily.'

'And he's your friend.'

Touché.

Secretly, he loved to wind her up. It was tempting to squat in the caravan for another year just to piss her off. He got up to go and make coffee. He was halfway to the kitchen when Frank returned.

His wife looked up. 'Well, was it him?'

'Who?'

'The dodgy Bulgarian.'

But Frank wasn't laughing.

'It was the MOD.'

Cal stopped mid-step. *The Ministry of Defence?* What did they want?

'They've called us up.'

'*They've what?*'

'Oh, for God's sake!' Emily exclaimed.

'Apparently, the spooks have picked up chatter that a terrorist cell is planning something big in London. They're calling in the cavalry.'

Emily had heard enough. She scooped up a couple of dirty plates from the dining table and stormed past him into the kitchen. The friends exchanged a conspiratorial glance. When she was gone, Frank pulled Cal into his study.

According to the MOD staff officer who had called him, he said, the Security Service had a number of 'persons of interest' in play, but their assets were stretched due to the G7 summit that was due to take place in London shortly. They needed a backup team spun up, and quickly. Since Cal, Frank, and the rest of their old SRR squad were in the Reserves, they were on standby for this sort of thing.

A Middle East outfit called *Al-Abnah Thalab* had been mentioned. The leader of the group had landed in the country five days ago. Frank had never heard of them. Cal had to look it up on his phone. The Wikipedia entry was sparse.

'Here we go,' Cal read. '*Formed in 2017 in response to the continued Israeli occupation of the West Bank, Al-Abnah Thalab (meaning 'Sons of the Fox', and more commonly referred to as the Al-Abnah Brigade) is a Sunni terrorist group based in Lebanon and Syria. It has been involved in a number of anti-US terrorist attacks in Syria, including a drone attack on al-Tanf base, in a remote area where the borders of Syria, Jordan and Iraq meet. The group is believed to be funded by wealthy backers in Lebanon and is led by Hassan Mansour, an Egyptian national who grew up in Afghanistan. He is the son of the former warlord, The Red Fox…*" Cal broke off. '*Fuck!*'

Frank met his eyes.

'What is it?'

'Don't you recognise the name? Says here he's the son

of the Red Fox, killed by British forces in 2009.'

Frank's face clouded over with a dawning realisation. 'Our last operation. So he must be…'

'Exactly!' Cal exclaimed. 'The boy we found on that roof.'

They stared at each other for a long moment.

'Are you sure?'

'Has to be. The rest of his family were killed, don't you remember?'

He passed the phone over to Frank and pointed at the image on the screen. It was of a man in his late 20s with a goatee beard wearing a keffiyah. He had his own brief Wikipedia entry, which gave his date of birth as 1997.

'The age fits, too.'

Frank let out a low whistle. 'Blimey, you're right.' A beat. 'So he's grown up, then.'

'Damn right, he has. They say he goes by the name of the Little Fox.'

'Of course he does,' Frank remarked grimly. 'Good times.'

Cal ignored his friend's irony and got up and went to the window. The sailing boats had disappeared. His equilibrium felt shattered. A flock of geese flew low over the jetty at the end of the garden, honking loudly.

'I think we should declare an interest,' he muttered.

'Why on earth would we do that?' said Frank. 'They'd pull us.'

Cal swallowed hard. The truth was, he hadn't told anyone, not even his ex, Amanda, about his nightmares. That boy had haunted him for years. Now he was over here, in this country. It didn't bear thinking about.

'I've promised to go to Lucy's ballet show next Friday. She and Amanda will kill me if I miss another.'

As soon as he'd said it, he knew how lame it sounded.

'I'm sure we can get you off for a few hours,' said Frank. 'Tell 'em it's for a family funeral.'

'Yeah, right! Apart from Amanda or Lucy, there's no family funeral I'd want to go to.' He snorted. 'Or would be invited to, come to that. When do they want us to start, anyway?'

'Can you believe it? Monday.'

The End

Sample chapter from 'Hunted', book 2 in the series

The drive out of Beirut took longer than Hassan expected. As they climbed the hill along the coast towards Byblos, cars and trucks inched forward nose to tail, the trucks grinding through the gears and spewing thick clouds of acrid smoke. On either side, half-built apartment blocks vied for space with roadside retail units selling kitchen units and imported furniture.

He soon saw the reason for the bottleneck. A double line of concrete blocks had been thrown across the cracked tarmac at the top of the hill. They were flanked by two guard houses, each covered in a tangle of barbed wire and painted in red, white and green. A crooked cedar tree was badly stencilled onto the whitewash. They slowed to a halt. A militiaman leant down to the driver's open window.

'Papers.'

The taxi driver pulled out a card and handed it over along with Hassan's Egyptian passport. He smiled, trying to make small talk, complaining about the traffic. The soldier grunted and switched his attention to Hassan in the passenger seat. He held up the open passport and squinted at the photograph. Satisfied, he handed it back.

'Have a safe journey.'

'Inshallah.'

They drove on for an hour. Progress was painful. From time to time they were forced to a crawl to navigate jagged potholes, each marked by a garishly painted oil drum, the cars squeezing into single channels to either side. The road plateaued, and they entered a bustling township, slowing to make way for pickups and vans jostling to unload their wares. Then they were through, picking up speed on the open road. After another twenty minutes, they reached a sign for a place called Wata El Ban. Hassan leant forward.

'Here.'

The driver turned right onto a small winding lane. They climbed into a forest of pines. Hassan caught a glimpse of the Mediterranean far below in a gap in the hills, then it was gone, and they emerged into a valley. Here the traffic was lighter. The houses and villages appeared more prosperous, a mix of recently constructed country villas funded by the Lebanese diaspora and older properties built in the French colonial era. Strings of low vines stretched up the rocky hillside, interspersed every few hundred metres with irrigation standpipes. After five kilometres the road narrowed into a series of hairpin bends. Halfway up they came to a large metal sign. 'Welcome to Chateau Liban.'

The driver turned in his seat, the worn leather squeaking.

Hassan peered through the windscreen and nodded. They drove up a steep slope past an old white manor house and parked in a gravel yard at the rear of the building.

Hassan paid the driver and hauled his battered canvas bag from the back seat. The taxi departed, the growl of the diesel engine growing fainter as it disappeared from view, and he was left with pure silence. A fly buzzed somewhere in the distance. He felt a trickle of sweat run down his armpit, and for a moment he stood immobile, taking in his surroundings. It was the first time he'd visited a winery. It belonged to his uncle's wife's family, Christian maronites from Beirut. Even so, it was an uncomfortable feeling. What was his uncle doing? Surely it was haram?

Two large metal cylinders, brand new and recently delivered, lay on pallets to one side of the yard, while a gleaming black Mercedes was parked under cover beside the house. In the middle of the building, a double set of steps led up to a main entrance on the first floor, above two large wooden doors at ground level that served as loading bays. A door opened, and a figure emerged at the top.

'My boy!' The man spread his arms out wide in a gesture of welcome. Large-framed and overweight, he was clean-shaven with the smooth-skinned face of a man used to good living. 'Praise be to God that you've arrived.'

Hassan climbed the steps to meet him.

'Uncle,' Hassan said, embracing his father's old friend. While no relation, the term was used for close friends of the clan. He hadn't seen Nuri Esfahani since he'd been a child, and he didn't look at all like he remembered him. Back then, the Iranian had been selling imported cars in Cairo. Today… well, he'd soon find out.

~

They didn't broach the reason for his visit until well after dinner. Nuri had insisted on giving Hassan an exhaustive tour of his in-law's winery, proudly showing off the cavernous rooms beneath a modern building up the hill which housed the state-of-the-art wine-making equipment.Gleaming steel vats containing red, white and rosé Chateau Liban reached almost to the roof, while beside them a bottling and labelling machine supplied pallets which were fork-lifted out into the yard. Even this late in the day, the place was a hive of activity, workers standing back deferentially to make way for Nuri and his important visitor. They ended the tour, as every visitor did, in the tasting room on the top floor, a bare, white space with large picture windows overlooking the valley below. From this side of the building, there was a clear view of the sea. On a hill to the left, a tangle of twisted steel reared up into the sky, like some avant-garde sculpture erected to showcase the culture of the region. In a sense it did. It had been a Hezbollah anti-aircraft defence post. Three militiamen had been killed up there the year before, in an Israeli airstrike.

A long table had been laid out, the windows flung open to catch the dying embers of the afternoon sun. They were soon joined by Nuri's extended family, fifteen of them in all. Someone put on some Western music. Food was brought in, though not wine, out of respect for their guest: plates of baba ghanoush, hummus, tabbouleh and sfeeha, minced meat wrapped in small parcels of pizza dough, a delicacy of Baalbek to the east. Dishes of fattoush salad followed, with its bright red pomegranate seeds, bowls of creamy lentil soup, and platters of falafel and shawarma. Throughout the meal, Hassan was regaled with tales of skiing expeditions in the mountains and shopping trips to Paris, along with laments about the state of the Lebanese economy. Ever since the port explosion - the result of another Israeli airstrike, according to Nuri - the economy had collapsed. Doctors were working as taxi drivers to earn foreign currency to supplement their meagre incomes. Schools had been closed for months, unable to pay their teachers. Banks had been refusing depositors their cash. But Nuri's family were the lucky ones. Nuri had done well for himself. He had dollars stashed away, and not in the banks.

And it showed. The furniture was new, and the women, none of whom were covered, wore expensive jewellery. Meanwhile, Nuri's six-year-old daughter spent the time dancing in front of a camera and making a video. No one seemed to pay her any attention.

Hassan joined in politely. But it felt decadent. Frivolous. Unseemly, even, considering what he had come here for. They finished the meal with fat slices of watermelon. Coffee and Turkish Delight were laid before them. When the sun had set, Nuri made his move.

'There's something I want to show you.'

Hassan got up and followed the older man out of the room. They descended a steep flight of stairs into a windowless cellar. It smelt of damp. The temperature dropped several degrees, and as they emerged into the darkness, a bank of bright strip lights came on, revealing another row of stainless steel vats stacked horizontally on racks. They were smaller than the ones he had been shown in the bottling room, and barrel-shaped, about a metre in height. Nuri gestured to a pair standing upright on the floor.

'This is what you will need.'

Hassan inspected them.

'What is this?'

Nuri pulled a tool off a shelf and unscrewed a metal plate from the top of one of the barrels.

'Some of the overseas customers do their own bottling,' Nuri explained. 'And to them, the product is exported in bulk to be re-marketed under their brands, as house wines. Western supermarkets, for example. Sometimes even blended, God defend us.'

He lifted the top off the barrel to reveal the interior. Inside, dark ruby-red liquid surrounded a double-skinned cylindrical tube. He unscrewed the top of the second barrel. This one was empty, allowing him to slide the tube out. He laid it on a table.

'Look closely,' he said.

Hassan bent down. He tapped it. What had looked like a double skin was, in fact, a second tube slotted neatly within the first.

'Go ahead, pull it out.'

The inner tube slid out smoothly and, on closer inspection, it was clear why. It was held in place and guided by a set of tiny fins on either side, each running within two grooves etched inside the outer tube. As it emerged, three larger fins popped out at the base end.

'Impressive,' Hassan remarked.

'You see what it is?'

'The casing for a rocket?'

Nuri beamed. 'Not any rocket, dear boy, but part of a completely new portable firing system we have developed. Precision engineered and modular.'

Hassan lifted it to eye level and squinted down the gleaming steel barrel.

'How is it modular?' he said.

Nuri gestured to the larger tubes.

'Bolt two of these outer ones together and you have the launcher. So for every two barrels, we can supply one launcher and two rocket casings. Each launcher is designed to be bolted onto another, in a honeycomb system. In theory, you could bolt an infinite number together, but for ease of transportation, and stability, we suggest a maximum of two rows of three, making six launchers, and twelve rockets.'

'That's a lot of wine, Nuri.'

Hassan couldn't but fail to see the delicious irony. Delivering death to the infidel in vats of their own alcohol.

Nuri laughed. 'Indeed! Nearly a thousand gallons.'

'So how are they fuelled?'

'Candy.'

Hassan looked surprised.

'Yes, old school I'm afraid. Sugar and fertiliser. But it means you can get everything you need on site. Besides, accuracy won't be so critical at the range I'm proposing. The only other engineering you will need are the nozzles at the base.'

He walked over to the far side of the room.

'Which brings me to these.' He picked up what looked like a tea-light holder from a box. 'Can I introduce one of our most popular exports.' He chuckled as he handed it with a flourish to Hassan. 'Especially at Christmas time. It's my wife's little business. Holds seven tea-lights. Also happens to fit neatly on the bottom of one of these tubes. All you need to do is knock out the metal at the base of the individual holders and weld it in place. And there it is. Voila! Your nozzle.'

Hassan turned it over in his hands, tapping the base. He had been sceptical to begin with. But this seemed doable.

'Who made all this?'

'We have clever engineers.' He paused to gauge the younger man's reaction, but he remained silent. Nuri spread his hands. 'You say you want to globalise the intifada? So this is how we'll do it. The show will be spectacular. And all on live TV.'

Hassan looked at the older man with expressionless eyes. 'Can you guarantee that?'

'I am working on someone to help livestream the protest march that our friends are organising to coincide with the operation. All eyes will be on London. I am hoping she will be there to cover it.'

'She?'

'Don't worry, my boy. She's one of us.'

For now, Hassan let it go. 'Have they ever been used?' he said.

'Tested, yes. Operationally, no. But for a short-range operation, they will be accurate enough.'

Hassan nodded.

'All you are missing are the shell cones. We are working on those.'

Hassan stepped away.

'It's impressive. I was not sure what to expect.'

Nuri watched him carefully. Eventually, he said: 'So, are we on?

Hassan stared at the barrels, fingering the steel rims like a collector stroking a precious antique.

'Timeframe for delivery?'

'There are monthly shipments to Piraeus. From there by truck. Ten days, door to door.'

'And border formalities? Surely they inspect the goods?'

'Yes, and let them. They always like to sample the wines, the stupid kafir.' He twisted a small metal tap in the side of one of the barrels on the rack, and a dribble of red wine splashed onto his patent leather shoes. He stooped down to brush it off, rubbing his thumb against his fingers.

'But if they do decide to take a barrel apart, all they will find is an interior tube, inserted for internal stability and to bring the volume of the shipped alcohol down from 75 gallons to 60. That's a more saleable unit, I'm informed. So rather than replace all the barrels, that's how Chateau

Liban prefers to deliver it. If anyone ever asks.' He spat. 'Which they won't.'

'Clever. What's the target date?'

'Early November. I have already planned to be in London for a hip operation. The date of the event is fixed.'

'And what about a team? I will need good people on the ground.'

'Don't worry about that. I have brothers ready to activate. Supporters of the cause.'

A beat.

'Ok,' Hassan said.

Nuri clapped his hands and threw a fatherly arm around Hassan's shoulders.

'I knew you'd be impressed,' he beamed.

'However, I have one condition,' Hassan added.

Nuri hesitated in the doorway. 'Oh?'

Hassan drew something out of his back pocket. He straightened it out on the table under a lamp. His fingers were unusually delicate for a man more familiar with an AK-47 than a violin. It was an image, printed on yellowing paper, and appeared to be a cutting from a newspaper. It showed four soldiers dressed in battle fatigues gathered around a jeep. Underneath was a caption. 'Helmand, 2009.' On the side of the passenger door was the crudely stencilled outline of a fox's head, in red paint.

Hassan lifted his head.

'These are the men who killed my father. I want you to help me find them.'

Order 'Hunted'

BUY NOW

The orphaned boy who Cal and his Special Forces team found on the Afghan rooftop fifteen years earlier, Hassan Mansour, has grown up. Intent on seeking revenge for the murder of his family, he has arrived in Britain with plans for a terrifying strike to the heart of the British state. Cal and Frank have been tasked with finding out what it is, and stopping him.

Codenamed Foxtrot, Mansour has assembled a team of sympathisers, including an embittered Iraqi refugee called Mo and the beautiful Samira, a Syrian exile studying journalism at the LSE. Her role is to seduce a government advisor and gather intelligence on the imminent State Opening of Parliament. However, despite her support for the cause, Samira becomes increasingly fearful about what Mansour is planning, as a seemingly random series of murders of veterans takes place across the country. Random, that is, until Cal joins the dots, and unwittingly puts his own family in danger…

In a shocking climax, Samira and Cal confront their demons in a bid to save the people they love.

Book 3 in the series

A NEW POPE. A MURDER IN THE VATICAN.

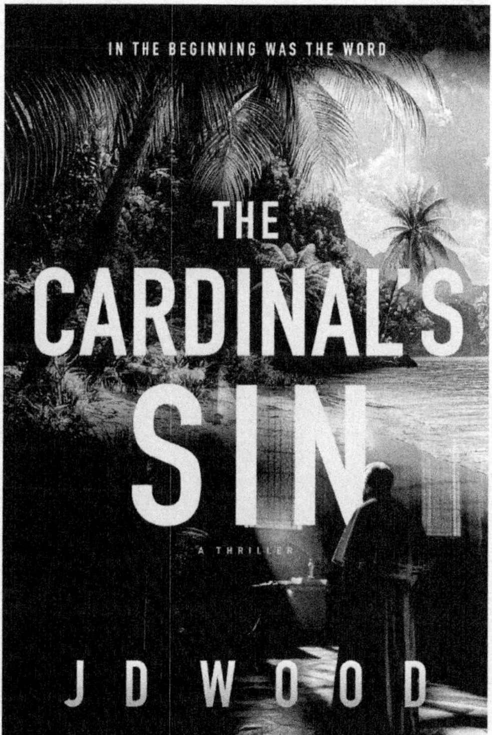

BUY NOW

A new pope is elected, and newbie journalist Sofie James is tipped off about a scandal in the Vatican; something so explosive that it reaches the very heart of the Catholic church.

But before she can get to the truth, a whistleblower is murdered, and Sofie is left with just one half of a tantalising puzzle. Calling on the help of her former collaborator, ex-Special Forces Cal Harrison, her investigation takes her on a roller-coaster ride from London to Rome to Portugal and finally, to the sun-kissed shores of the Caribbean, where a mysterious Catholic order 'saves souls' on a private tropical island. Shockingly, Cal finds out that, many years earlier and unbeknownst to him, this secretive paradise helped shape his own life. Overseen by one of the most senior Cardinals in the Vatican - the 'Sostituto', the Pope's Chief of Staff - and financed by the Chinese, Opus Christi shelters a dark secret.

Can Sofie and Cal expose it before they, like those before them, are silenced by the brutal forces ranged against them?

Sign up to my newsletter and receive my Tasha Mazour bonus chapter

Tasha Mazour Bonus Chapter

As a writer, you sometimes create a character who takes on a life of their own. That happened with me and the character of Tasha Mazour in 'Girl on the Boat'.

She trained as a GRU operative in the mysterious Unit 29155, a real outfit that exists today and is thought to be behind much of the asymmetric warfare and sabotage waged by Russia in Western Europe.

I want to write more on Tasha in the future, so watch this space. For now, here's a short bonus chapter on how she trained as a recruit in the birch forests just south of St Petersburg, as a thank you for signing up for my newsletter.

About the Author

This is JD Wood's first thriller in the Cal Harrison series. He lives and writes in London.

To learn more and for details of forthcoming releases, you can sign up to his newsletter 'Where To Write a Novel' at jdwoodbooks.com.

Printed in Dunstable, United Kingdom

66770305R00278